TRISHA LYNN

CITY OF STARLIGHT

 KEEPER OF THE KEYS BOOK 1

CITY OF STARLIGHT

For anyone who was picked last for anything, for anyone that was bullied, for anyone that has felt like they weren't enough, for anyone with birth defects and disabilities—
This one is for *you*.
I see you.
You are loved. You are enough. You are amazing.

We need to lift each other not tear each other down.
We need to spread love, not hate.
Life is so fleeting, embrace it. Let others embrace their life. Let them be weird, let them be beautiful, let them be. Embrace your weirdness, your beauty, your uniqueness.

PS: For anyone that has bullied another, I hope a Fire Drake eats you.

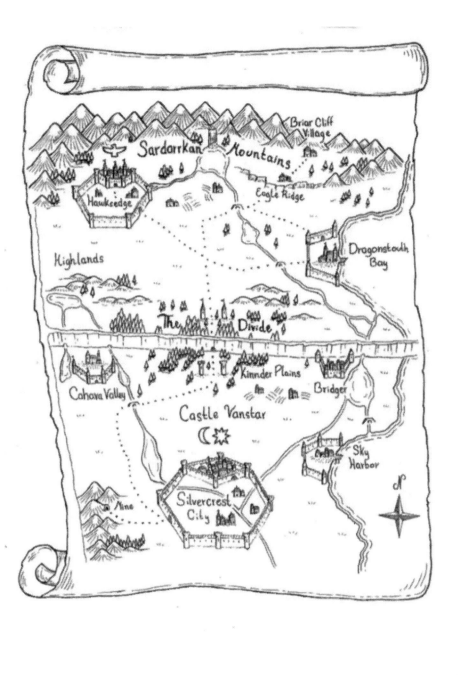

CHAPTER 1

Hope you like cat hair

My great-aunt Millie had been quiet, reclusive, and a bit strange. Honestly, she and I had been more alike than I wanted to admit.

After setting the saucer of milk down, I lay on my stomach and rested my chin on my arm. I let the loss of Aunt Millie settle into that quiet place in my soul where she and I shared space.

Aunt Millie had passed two weeks ago. With all of her belongings left to my mom, we had to go through and sell the house. I'm sure that sounds insensitive, but it's reality. It sucked. A lot.

Finally, I heard rustling and saw a set of luminescent eyes as the cat moved into the light.

After staring me down another second, he came to the plate. "I'm sure you're hungry."

Aunt Millie had eight cats. This one was my last to wrangle. My parents gave me the task to secure the cats because they thought I had a "gift" with animals. Which wasn't true. I was simply a quiet, patient individual.

The other cats had been older and not as frightened. We needed the vet to check them over then I had to find them new homes.

The lapping of the cat's tongue was all I heard in the spare room. It was rarely quiet at my house, so this was nice. I could imagine I was just visiting

Aunt Millie. This room was sparse and smelled like old books, sunlight, and cat fur. I loved it. I had loved everything about serene Aunt Millie and her quaint home. It seemed surreal she was gone. In five days, we would be back to our lives like nothing was gone.

I felt silky fur as the cat brushed against my hand.

"See, you're okay, " I crooned and scratched his neck.

He rubbed against me, and a moment later I was able to dip my right hand beneath him and pull him out from under the bed.

I sat up on my knees cuddling the cat to my chest before leaning back to look at him. He was a dusky silver with light stripes and white on his chest. His large eyes were stunning green-blue. He was lean, barely out of kittenhood, and beautiful.

"Let's go get you some food."

I pulled him back to my chest and headed out of the room. Once in the hall, I looked up and realized there was a pull-down ladder for an attic. My parent's voices drifted up the stairs. I didn't even realize there was an attic. I should have, considering the age of the house.

Curiosity won out.

The cat looked at me, then the staircase like he was interested, too.

Curiosity killed the cat. *Not funny, Kaidyn!*

I shifted the cat in my arms and pulled the string. The stairs came down noiselessly. I couldn't see Aunt Millie being able to make it up this narrow, flimsy ladder, so it was strange they came down so easily.

I set the cat on the ladder. I was adept at doing things with one hand but holding a cat and going up ladders might be stretching it for me. I hoped he wouldn't run off and ruin my work of wrangling him.

On the stairs he was at eye level with me, those uncanny eyes bright and a tingle of sensation swept through me as if I should understand something he was telling me. He flicked his tail and jumped up the stairs into the attic to be lost in the darkness.

"Wait for me," I mumbled as I gripped the slim rail and hauled myself up. Where the ladder was in the middle of the room was dark, but the rest of the attic was bright. Sunlight filtered in through three small windows.

My eyes landed on the cat, who was sitting in front of a chest. Trunk? I wasn't sure about the terminology, but it looked like something straight out of a pirate ship. It had a curved top, the brackets were a dull silver, and there was a lock on the top and one on the front, which I had never seen before. Otherwise, the attic was sparse, like the rest of the house.

"Alright, kitty, let's get out of here. Mom will be thrilled it's so bare up here."

I went to grab the cat, but he skirted around the trunk and hopped up on a chair that was directly behind it.

With my hands on my hips, I sighed. "Well, you look comfy."

I scratched the cat between the ears. He gave a soft purr in pleasure. Revisiting the urge to touch the treasure chest, my fingers hovered over the top lock. Weird tingling erupted on my fingertips, as an audible click of locks echoed. I jerked my hand back. The tingling stopped. I put my hand back and my fingers tingled again. *What the heck?*

Swallowing, I flipped the latch, and the trunk lid swung open with ease. I shifted my eyes to the cat, who dipped his head to look inside. Shrugging, I did the same.

A burgundy swath of fabric covered the contents. It looked silken, and I reached out tentatively. It was coarser and thicker than it looked. I noticed a symbol was stitched in gold thread—a dagger, point down, with two keys crossed over it. Interesting.

I lifted it despite my better judgment and was surprised to find it had a hood. It was some sort of robe or cloak. It was beautiful, like something a priestess would wear.

Beyond intrigued, I sat back. Had Millie been into cosplay in her younger years? Or was this something...else? I dropped it next to the trunk. I shouldn't be going through these things, they weren't mine. Another swath of fabric inside the trunk caught my attention. Slowly, I unfolded it. *What the heck?*

It was a sword. No, it was too small... A dagger? A unique, old-looking dagger with a silver blade, gleaming and deadly. The handle was braided. The cross guard, if that's even what it's called in daggers, came to a swirling golden flourish and I noted the blade had a key engraving on it.

A cloak and a dagger. What unusual things for my aunt to possess! Aunt Millie had just gotten a *lot* more interesting. But really what the heck did an old lady need with a dagger?

I inched closer and reached for the hilt. It seemed to hum in anticipation and my fingers tingled.

What. The. Heck. Was. Up. With. The. Tingling!

The sensation grew as my fingers hovered over the blade. My fingers touched the key engraving and a burning sensation zipped across my left hand. My deformed hand since birth. My parents had known it wasn't fully formed in ultrasounds, but I was whole and healthy otherwise. It was unclear why I had the abnormality—why my three other fingers never formed, but it didn't hinder me much. I have my thumb and pointer finger, but the rest is a stump of mottled flesh.

The back of my neck burned as if ten hornets stung me at once. I jerked back with a yelp. It ebbed from pain to an energized zing, but it was still terrifying.

I looked around for any culprit to the attack, as I rubbed the back of my neck. There was no welt yet. Slowly the sensation calmed. The cat was watching me with interest.

"Did you see bees?" I looked around again but saw and heard nothing. "Did we disturb a nest or something?"

The cat flicked his ear. I felt like that was feline for a shrug. I sighed. The attic looked unscathed by my drama. Dust particles danced through the air. I turned back to the dagger. It still looked deadly and mysteriously beautiful. As I drew closer, it hummed again.

I quickly tossed the fabric back over it and haphazardly tied the cord, avoiding touching the thing again. It had slid to the side from my jostling, and underneath peaked out a paper. I twisted my head to inspect it, nervous to touch anything at this point. This whole trunk was freaking me out.

The paper was thick, like... parchment. Something from a time long ago. To replicate such a thing would take a lot of effort. Curious, I pulled. It was a... map. A treasure map? Was this some sort of pirate ship treasure chest prop in a play? Had Aunt Millie been into that stuff? I knew so little about her. She'd been so distant. I couldn't imagine her in a play. She could have been a Broadway singer, for all I knew of her, but it just seemed unlikely. Since the paper didn't seem to hum or tingle, I dislodged it from the fabric that held the dagger and laid it atop the weapon.

I didn't recognize the map's landmass. Unsurprising, since geography wasn't my strong suit. The name *Evirness* was written across the top. I noticed in the corner was a symbol, the same one I'd seen on the cloak. A dagger pointing down, with two keys crossing over it in an x shape. It had to be connected to the cloak. My eyes swept down the page snagging on a few names. Silvercrest. Hawksedge. Sky harbor. Intriguing. Each place was lovingly written in a beautiful script and things were drawn next to the names—bridges, rivers, farmland, forests. A drawing even depicted castle parapets with the name Castle Vanstarr.

I ran a finger over the word Evirness, and my finger tingled and erupted in sensation. The back of my neck burned, along with the back of my left hand, just like with the dagger. I jerked away with a colorful curse, but the pain already ebbed. My fingers scratched at my neck, but I still felt nothing.

Was there some kind of chemical on this stuff?

Oh, no! Something to make it look aged. I'd never even considered that. I stood up abruptly and looked down at my fingers.

Suddenly, the map flashed bright, and the lines erupted in a golden light. The light flashed across the lines and my eyes could barely track the movement. My mouth hung open, my hand was at my chest, and my heart thundered.

What the—

"Kaidyn? Kaid, are you up there?"

My heart leaped, and my head snapped around as my mother yelled from the base of the attic ladder.

"Ah, yeah... Uh." I had to catch my breath, or she'd know something was wrong. Steadier, I said, "Be down in a sec."

"You got the cat?"

I scanned the cat, who looked unfazed by what had just happened. Maybe this was a common occurrence in this household. Had my aunt been a witch or something? I tried to dismiss that crazy idea, but I honestly couldn't. It was possible.

The cat. Mom. Right. "Uh, yes. Yup. Got him."

"Great, hon. Try to hurry. We're all hungry and the vet closes in an hour."

"Okay," I yelled, as my eyes still tracked the golden light as it traced the lines of the map over and over. I stared another moment—caught in the beauty of the gilded lines. I snapped out of my trance and shut the lid, trying to make as little contact as possible. I swooped up the cat, who made a distressed mew but settled in my arms. The trunk made an ominous click of locks and I hightailed it down the stairs.

"Oh wow, she's a pretty one."

"*He*," I said, without thinking.

"Oh," my mom said with a smile. "It won't take long to find *him* a home."

The thought hurt my heart. I'd bonded with the silver tabby over the last few hours. I didn't want our friendship to end, but I knew better than to ask to take a cat on the eight-hour road trip home. Plus, we had Zena, our shepherd mix. Her foster home had said she was good with cats, but we'd had her for five years and had never tested that theory.

My mom gestured to a crate set up with a blanket. "In you go, little guy."

I rubbed the cat's chin, then cradled him to my chest another moment. Finally, I whispered, "It'll be okay, I promise. The vet is just going to make sure you're healthy. We'll get you tomorrow."

I slowly put him in the cage. Those stunning eyes tracked me. He didn't seem upset, or even confused, as if he knew it was all going to be fine. I wish I shared his confidence.

"Pizza?" My mom asked, not sensing my distress.

"Did someone say pizza?"

My brother walked in. Kial was my best friend—or had been when we were younger. He was everything I wasn't. We were still friends, but like all things, our relationship changed as we got older.

"You find it, honey?" My dad asked as he walked in.

My mom shook her head as I nodded. Mom and I were both *honey* to him, and we often got confused.

He let out a chuckle and gestured to me. "The cat?"

"Yeah."

He looked at my mom, and she sighed. "No."

"Ah, well, Millie was an odd soul. I bet she hid it somewhere crazy."

He put his arm around her and kissed the top of her head. Their intense love for each other gave me promise for what I could someday have.

I caught Kial looking at me. I gave him a small smile. He was an intuitive and kind brother. He'd been my friend when few others would play with me because of my abnormal hand.

I snapped out of my reverie when mom gestured to the door. Oh right, I was going with her to get the pizza, and my dad and brother were taking the silver cat to the vet. I glanced at the cat carrier. The little silver cat felt like a part of me now, and I didn't want to say goodbye. I bonded easily with animals. They weren't judgmental like people, but this seemed...deeper.

Mom called dibs on the sleek red Camaro we'd rented, and I gave Kial a smirk as he walked with our dad to the Jeep. He stuck his tongue out at me, and I laughed as I slithered into the seat. I tried not to think about the cat as I admired the rental car.

I struggled to tune into my mom. *Where'd that chest come from? Why was my reaction to it so crazy?*

I had never experienced anything so peculiar.

I let out a sigh. Mom glanced at me with a smile. "Was wrangling cats tiring?"

I laughed. "A bit."

"How was the attic? Filled with crap? "

"Surprisingly, no. Not at all. There is this trunk up the—"

"Well, thank goodness for that. Aunt Millie didn't have a lot of stuff. Books and oddities, but not much else. Her garage was bare, except that old car your brother is obsessing about."

I hadn't seen the old car. I hadn't even looked in the garage. I'd have to ask my brother about it later.

CHAPTER 2

Silas

The smell of pizza hit me when I left the bathroom. I'd checked my neck in the mirror, but I was unmarked from whatever had happened in the attic. I stepped into our room. Girls were sharing one room and boys another. It was a silly thing we did in hotels. I didn't mind sleeping with my mom. She was a noiseless sleeper. Shockingly, since she was a loud, excitable individual.

"Mom, so that trunk in the—"

"Aha!"

The exclamation startled me. My mom was sitting cross-legged on the bed, papers were strewn around her.

"Her recipes." I just stared and she looked up. "Oh hey, sweetheart. I found Aunt Millie's will."

"I thought—"

She laughed at my blank expression. "Millie left me the house but had said months ago that she was leaving a few things to particular people in her own will—not a notified one. But she never told me where she'd left it. Before I tossed anything, I wanted to find it." She waved the paper.

I faked a smile as I picked up a brush to finish brushing my hair. I watched my mom as she read. Her eyes were very expressive; narrowed, widened, and rolled. I honestly didn't care if I'd been left anything, but it amused me to see my mom looking like that.

After she was finished reading, she let out an exaggerated sigh. "Well, Aunt Millie didn't disappoint. I'm not sure why I thought this would be a simple pack up a house and sell sort of thing. Ha!" Her eyes met mine. "Want to hear what she left you?"

My heart thumped. I had a bad feeling about this. "Sure."

"To my quiet little great-niece, Kaidy." Millie had always called me Kaidy, like my dad. "I leave all my books. Do with them as you wish, but just remember that a girl who reads lives a thousand lives. She can be anything and is as brave as she dares to be. Just make sure you open each book because never judge one by its cover."

The message was a lovely sentiment and didn't surprise me. It was an echo of something she'd said to me before. Books had always been an outlet for me, a way to live as a brave heroine, a princess, a dragon slayer, or a dragon rider— depending on the tale. When I slumped into a depressive state, a happy story helped me through. Something even counseling had never done.

My love of books came from Aunt Millie. She and I would sit together and read for hours. Only once, I had been foolish enough to ask her a private question. Why she'd never had children. I'll never forget how Millie's soft voice said, "*I loved deeply once, but that man was off-limits to me. I never loved again.*"

After that, she and I had come to an understanding. I could read her books and ask her any questions I wished about the tales, but no personal questions.

My mom smiled at me and pulled me back to the will. "Those are going to need to be shipped home, Kaid." Her voice turned serious. "So, please only keep the ones you want."

"Yes, Mom." I hid my excitement.

Mom turned back to the will. "I also leave the trunk in the attic and all its contents."

My stomach dropped. *What? No.* No. I didn't want it. It felt...cursed. I had been wrong about it being someone else's—it *was* Aunt Millie's and now...mine. It was terrifying, yet exhilarating, to think of the treasure chest. Did I want to see if the map still glowed? Yes. Was I dying to understand why the dagger hummed at my touch? Yup. Was I intrigued with my body's reaction to the items? I mean, no, but yes. I wanted to know why, but I was also not entirely convinced it wasn't some chemical or something. There was no way of knowing unless I did research and saw what else was in that chest. I wasn't overly happy that the cursed thing was now mine.

"And Silas," Mom finished.

My eyes scanned hers. *What?*

"What is a Silas? Like a Kindle, or e-reader?"

I giggled. Something shivered against my skin at the name. *Silas.* I knew. "I don't believe it's a *what*, but a w—"

We heard the main door open and then my dad's voice. "Guess what, babe?"

Before I could finish, she was already off the bed and striding out the door. I had little choice but to follow.

Silas. The trunk. What was I going to do with a *dagger*?

"So, the vet had info on the cats since that's where Millie took them. They're microchipped too. The vet gave me printouts." He turned to me, his arms around my mom. "It has their name, age, weight, and health info. Should help in getting them new homes. The vet said she'd ask around about homes. She also said the shelter is a no-kill."

I grimaced, but I took the extended papers. There was something I needed to check, something I had to know. I shuffled through the papers as my mom filled him in on the handwritten will situation.

"Dad, the last cat... did they have..."

"Yup, he'd only been in for his neuter, but his info is—"

I stopped listening because I had found it.

Breed: *tiger short-haired*

Color: *gray*

Age: *1 year*

Sex: *neutered male*

Name: *Silas*

The other information was unnecessary. The silver cat was Silas. He was mine. Aunt Millie had given him to me. But why? Had she left the others a cat? Had she known I would bond with him? I didn't know what to think.

"So, Mom. Um..."

She turned and saw the paper, and my sheepish expression. Her eyes narrowed. "Silas is a damn cat, isn't it?"

I couldn't help my spreading grin. It *was* funny. "Yup."

She groaned. "Your brother gets a car. You get a cat."

"*What?*" My brother and father exclaimed at once.

My mom threw up her hands. "Let's read the will together."

We did.

Millie left Kial the 1957 Chevy Bel-Air in the garage. My mom was given instructions on cash hidden in the house. She left my dad a few trinkets and some old camera equipment. A few things were going to the neighbors. I was given a cat. I was a little jealous that my brother got a car, but also ecstatic to be taking Silas home.

On our second helping of pizza, my brother grinned. "Let's hope Zena doesn't eat your cat."

Dad nearly choked on pizza. "That's a good point, Kaidy girl. We'll need to introduce them slowly."

Mom looked exasperated and frazzled.

I stuck my tongue out at my brother. "Zena will be fine. How do you plan on getting the money to have your rust bucket shipped home?"

He quickly glanced at our parents. Mom groaned, and I giggled. I asked to be excused shortly thereafter, to ie down. My hand and head throbbed. I needed a good night's sleep. I had slipped one of Aunt Millie's books back with me—one of my books now.

After changing to pajamas, I read until my eyes blurred.

The vet called the next day with great news; she had found a home for three of the cats.

"You're mine now, Silas. You'll be coming home with me," I told the cat when we returned to Aunt Millie's house.

He butted his head against my chin.

"It's a long ride home, though."

He never left my side after that. I think he understood that he was mine, and I was his.

I fought with my mom about bringing Silas back to the hotel. And lost. It was sad leaving him and the other two cats in the house alone, but they'd been alone for two weeks before we'd come, so one night wasn't too much to ask, but now Silas was mine. It pained me to leave him, but after the fiasco in the attic, I was too scared to stay in the house alone. The trunk truly felt cursed to me, and now it was mine. I tried not to think about that.

The next day, though, my dad asked, "Hey, honey, isn't there something in the attic for you? Want me to bring it down?"

It needed to come down. Eventually. Was I less likely to want to go in it if it was down here? Should I show my parents the dagger and explain to them what happened when I touched it? They would think I was crazy.

I was torn, but my father looked at me expectantly.

"A trunk?" He asked, a brow raised.

"Yeah. About that trunk, Dad... There's this dagger in there—"

"Honey, a trunk, right?"

Did he not just hear me? "Yes, Dad, but about the tr—"

"I can grab it now if you want."

"I know I'm just telling you—"

He shifted, staring at me.

What the hell? Did he not hear anything I was saying?

"Where's Mom?"

"She's in the kitchen."

"The trunk has a deadly looking dagger in it—"

"If it's in the attic, Kaid, I want it down now. Okay?" He looked annoyed with me.

"But..." *What the hell, Dad?* "Yeah, it's in the attic."

"Okay, I'll look."

I swallowed and nodded as he trod up the stairs.

What the heck just happened? Did he not hear me?

This was getting crazy weird. I should go up and help. I should make sure nothing bad happens.

"Kial! Come help me."

My brother threw me a look as he walked past. I bit my lip. It's not like the trunk was the problem... just the stuff inside and they wouldn't open it.

I can't believe Dad wouldn't listen to me... It made me uncomfortable—all of it.

When they came back down, they didn't look disturbed. So, the trunk just acted like that with me, but why?

"Hope you found a key, sis. This thing is locked tight."

"It..." *Hadn't been the other day.* Then I recalled hearing the locks snap into place when I'd hastily shut the lid. Crap. I shouldn't have closed the lid. Well, if Aunt Millie had left it to me, she had a key somewhere, right?

I groaned. Now I had to find a key. I'd ask my mom if she'd come across one in her cleaning. It wasn't like I was going to open the trunk anytime soon. No, thank you.

"I'll have to find a key," I said as much to myself as him.

He snickered and my dad asked, "You want to go through it before we put it with the stuff in the garage?"

"Uh, no," I blurted. I didn't want to go through it again, at all—yet I did. "The garage is fine. Thanks."

I tried not to think about the trunk as a gentleman came that afternoon to meet the last cat that needed a home. The oldest one. Amara was beautiful—snow-white with striking blue eyes and a long, luxurious coat. She'd been Aunt Millie's favorite and always laid across her lap. Amara had been moping on my aunt's chair, and I felt bad for her. I wanted to find her a loving home so I wasn't forced to take her to the shelter. No-kill or otherwise, it would ruin me.

I was going to be going to college to be a veterinarian in the fall, so the love of animals was a passion. Seeing them depressed hurt my heart.

Thank goodness, it was like love at first sight and I needn't have worried. I couldn't have been happier, although now I had an entire day left here with nothing to do. I knew staying in the house I would stew on the contents of the trunk.

Aunt Millie had lived in a beautiful rural neighborhood. So, I spent the day exploring. I was outdoorsy and being stuck inside for more than a day gave me anxiety. Nature had always been a soothing outlet for me, like books. My home in North Carolina was the perfect coupling of mountain and sea. I loved it. I was one of the few people that liked their hometown. Granted, people weren't overly nice to me at school, but it could be worse. Being on the swim team had helped me fit in. My parents had been shocked when I'd gotten on the team. Little did they realize I had done it more for them than myself. I wasn't competitive, but I was a good swimmer. I didn't break any records by any means, but I held my own. Some of the people on the swim team had even invited me out after meets. I felt silly for not trying out for the team before my senior year of high school, but building my confidence has been a personal achievement of mine over the past year. The swim team was a major help.

I had taken a mahogany-colored leather-bound book on my walk with me. Old, worn, and out of place in the sea of novels. It looked like a journal.

I found a park bench overlooking a pond to sit and read a while. I opened the first page, and a dried flower fell out. I picked it up off the grass and ran it across my fingertips. It was a pale purple and looked a bit like lavender. I put it to my nose, and the smell was herbal and heady. I set the dried flower down next to me and opened the book again. The first page had a drawing of a key. An ancient-looking key, with a flourishing curling top which feathered out like filigree back to the slender base, with three teeth. Much like the one I had seen engraved on the dagger. Below that was a smaller drawing of a dagger pointed down with two ancient keys, like the one above crossing like an x over it. It looked familiar.

The next page had a drawing of an arched castle gate with wide stone pillars on each side. A crest hung above the gate. My heart sped. A stag with a key between its antlers. Many keys looked alike, but this one was unquestionably the same as the drawing on the first page. That was interesting. This book, the dagger, and the cloak that had a stitched emblem of the dagger and keys too—it all had to be connected somehow. But how? What did it mean?

The next page held slanted handwriting:

I had always known I was different. I always had a tough time making connections.

My eyes skimmed down the page.

When Egret contacted me, I hadn't been overly surprised to find I had a long-lost relative in Scotland. A land of beauty and ancient mystery.

Egret and Lyria explained some insane things to me that I'm just not sure if I can believe.

Stay tuned.

I've felt nothing so exhilarating in my life. The calling for something higher than myself had always sung in my blood, but this? Evirness is majestic. Like a dream. Honestly, I still wonder if I'm living a dream. Evirness feels like the real world, and mine...feels unreal.

Wait. Whose journal was this? Surely not Aunt Millie's. This parchment felt very old. I was no expert on old paper products, so I could be wrong, but it just felt... ancient.

Also, Evirness—I had seen that somewhere—Oh, right. The map in the trunk had been of Evirness.

I skipped ahead a few pages and read:

I had never felt anything like this. This... elation. This passion. I was not a sexual being, had never been, but he made me feel—

Ah, whoa—*No*. I snapped the book shut. This felt very much like a violation. Whose freaking diary was this?

I flipped the cover repeatedly. There was no monogram, initials, or name. Nothing. Just those symbols of the dagger and keys at the beginning which I had no idea what that meant.

I couldn't continue reading this. It was too personal. Too, well, dirty. I laughed aloud. A smut-filled diary was not something I had any interest in, but I *was* interested in the names and places, in connection to the map. I could skim over the personal remarks.

I looked up to see that the sun was dipping below the trees. The night would fall within the hour. Sighing, I gathered the book and made my way back to the house.

At noon the next day, we were officially in our car, seat-belted, with my mom's road trip playlist pouring out of the speakers. I realized as I settled my butt more comfortably into the seat for the long ride home, that I never did find the key to the trunk.

CHAPTER 3

Skimming

The itch on the back of my neck was out of control with the trunk so close. I had no idea what to make of it. I wanted to open the thing but was a little terrified. I wanted to give Aunt Millie the benefit of the doubt that she wouldn't have given me something that could hurt me. There had to be an explanation and the only way to figure it out was to explore the chest's mysteries.

I had tried to tell Mom about the trunk, but she just kept interrupting me as if I wasn't even speaking to her. As soon as I started talking about something else, she heard me. *What the hell was that all about?* It was unnerving, to say the least. It was as if fate, or something higher, didn't want me to tell my parents.

But that was insane, right?

At some point, I had drifted to sleep, my dreams filled with ancient keys and a huge stone wall. I was jostled awake, and out of my dream by my brother.

"We're home, K."

I wiped the sleep out of my eyes as the cat stretched in my lap. The dash clock said it was 10:13 at night. Zena was at a boarding kennel in town, so we wouldn't be able to get her until tomorrow, which was good because I was too tired to work out cat-dog introductions.

"I'll bring in the suitcases, but the rest is staying until morning. I'm toast."

Dad looked exhausted from driving through the night. We all stomped to our rooms for much-needed sleep. I carried my cat with me, quickly setting up his litter box and bowl of water.

"Sorry, no tour, Si. It'll have to wait till tomorrow."

The wonderful cat gave a sleepy meow and settled in.

The next day I was thankful to be home. I breathed in the familiar scents of cedarwood and vanilla. A weight on my legs had me glancing down at the cat curled into a little ball against my leg. I couldn't help but smile as I reached down to stroke his fine fur. He stretched and purred. I was thrilled to have my own pet.

While I went with mom to pick up Zena, Dad put the trunk at the foot of my bed and while it looked as though it belonged there, adding to the flair of my décor, my heart pounded having it in my room. Even though I'd never found a key, the trunk called to me. Just looking at it sent a strange tension through me, and I had no idea why.

I decided that ensuring Zena and Silas were comfortable with each other was far more interesting than being confined in my room with the trunk.

I shouldn't have been worried. Our shepherd was a gentle soul, and by afternoon they were laying together in the sunspots by the slider door.

After dinner that night I went up to my room, but my steps faltered when I remembered the trunk. The back of my neck itched as soon as I walked through the threshold to my room. Unable to handle my anxiety, I grabbed the journal and went out on our deck, the floodlights illuminating my view.

I flipped halfway through, and started to read again:

Rhone and I went riding today and he showed me more of the countryside. Castle Vanstarr is incredible, but it was nice to go beyond the castle and ride in open fields and forests. When first I came here, I didn't understand anything, but now I feel like my other life is slipping away. This is the real me. This is my real life. This is where I am meant to be.

Here, with Rhone, is where I was always meant to be.

Castle Vanstarr had also been on the map in the trunk.

I flipped pages.

The King of Evirness invited me to the ball! I can't believe it. Vera found me an incredible gown and I can't even begin to describe it. The color of thunderclouds and covered with sequins depicting starlight. I feel like a princess in it. If only I was a princess. But I am only a Keeper—revered yes, but not—

I flipped another two pages.

Rhone can never marry me, he must uphold the accords of his kingdom, and marry a regal heiress. A wealthy princess to another country—not a Keeper. King Harrant would never allow it. Rhone needs to unite countries—

I flipped to the next page.

Rhone asked his father! I can't believe it. We both knew he'd be furious, but— I'm not sure what was said. I was dismissed. I had to return home. To my own time. The brand had been itching so bad for days, I couldn't ignore it any longer. Amara had been holed up in my room—

My world no longer feels like home. Home is where Rhone is. I can't stay away.

I set the journal on my lap. This seemed very personal. I was dying to know who the writer was. I tried flipping pages in hopes there would be some indication, to no avail.

The next day I asked my mom if she knew anyone named Rhone, or where Evirness was. Dead end. She'd never heard the names before. At least she could *hear* me when I asked about them. I was beginning to wonder if there was secrecy magic associated with the damn trunk, or something equally insane. I wouldn't even be surprised at this point.

I went back to the journal and read a few more pages. I skipped and skimmed in hopes I would see something—anything—familiar.

This city was made for dreamers, for wishing on stars, for watching the moonlight glitter off the sea. The buildings are phenomenal. The dusky gray of twilight, with rambling—

Blah blah.

It was like taking a step back in time. Incredible.

I flipped closer to the beginning of the journal.

A portal! I went through a portal! I can't even begin to believe what has happened in the last 24 hours. Did I travel through...space? To another realm...a parallel dimension and into... the beautiful country of Evirness.

A portal? What a fantastic imagination this person had!

I skimmed a few sentences, then read:

Keepers are so much more than key keepers. They keep secrets—

Yeah, yeah.

I had been called there by an ancestor, a woman named Lyria.

I skimmed a bit more but saw no useful information. No names jumped out to give me any clue as to what it all meant. Nothing made sense. But again, I had no idea its origins, so it could be old enough to be castle-related. Since this Egret person had been from Scotland—which had been the only part of this journal that I understood—that's likely where this was from.

It mentioned portals... and that was a fantasy or sci-fi thing. These had to be notes for a book or screenplay. Along with the map, it made sense. Had Aunt Millie been a writer, and these were her notes?

I tossed the book on my nightstand and tried to go about my day, but the trunk—*Ugh.*

I couldn't take it anymore. I was going back to school tomorrow, if I was going to check inside the trunk, this was the day. That is if I could get it opened with no key.

Silas wound between my legs. I took a deep breath. The back of my neck prickled, and my heart raced. "We're going to do this." I swallowed, my nerves thrummed. "You're going to stay with me?"

He meowed in answer and stayed against me as I knelt in front of the trunk. My left hand prickled, and I hovered it over the lock and instantly the tingling intensified. I heard the audible mechanisms unlocking each section until finally, it was silent. My heart raced, and the tingling went from my left hand up to the back of my neck.

Why did it feel this way? What was this?

I took a shaky breath and glanced at the cat who was looking at me expectantly. Well, here goes nothing.

I opened the lid slowly as if something was going to jump out at me, but the contents were the same as they had been. The map lay on top. *Not glowing.* Completely ordinary.

I took another steadying breath and grabbed it. My skin tingled where I touched it, and it flashed gold. The light danced across the map, the lines of the map aglow. Then before my very eyes, the lines changed. The country, which had been one massive landform, now had a large black line horizontally across it about three-quarters of the way up. Under the thick black line, it said *The Divide.* Below the line was a large fortress/castle-looking depiction that said *Castle Vanstarr* with a crescent moon and stars symbol. Below that were the words *Silvercrest City,* with house-looking drawings with a wall around it. I noticed the words *Sky Harbor* attached to a drawing of ships at a port.

Above *The Divide* was a cluster of house drawings and castle-like buildings with a hawk depiction above that said *Hawksedge.* It seemed to go with the journal.

If this were notes from a book Aunt Millie had written, I hoped it was— Wait! What if that was what was in this trunk, and why Aunt Millie had left it to me?

Excited now, I set the map down and removed the fabric-wrapped dagger. My body tingled with its nearness, but I moved it directly to the floor away from me. I had already seen its deadly beauty and needed no reminder.

I pulled out the cloak next and it felt incredible in my hands. Heavy and woolen on the outside, and soft and silky on the inside. Beneath the cloak, the trunk was depressingly, surprisingly sparse. I was expecting it to be chock full of interesting stuff—from the way the thing gave me anxiety, or at least have a skull and coin props or something pirate-related. But there was only something wrapped in fabric and a gemstone. I pulled the orange gemstone out. It was cut, as if straight from a mine. Rectangular shaped with rough edges—not polished like most of the gemstones on display in stores. I turned it and it heated up in my hands. The tingling zipped up to the back of my neck.

Unsteadily, I set the gemstone down on the floor beside me and grabbed the wrapped item. It was heavy and the same shape.

Another gemstone?

My body tingled, and my blood hummed.

Why did I react this way?

My left hand prickled. I sat back on my knees with the parcel in my hands. Silas was staring at me, and he seemed eager, which put me on edge.

What was in here?

Silas rubbed against me as I slowly unwrapped the... crystal. It was gorgeous, like amethyst but darker and slightly more polished than the other one. It was rectangular and phallic-shaped, the top coming to a point. It looked, honestly, like something you would see in a sacrificial ceremony—or maybe I had just watched way too many witch movies. I didn't want to feel underwhelmed by the things I had or hadn't found in the trunk.

Why had Aunt Millie left this to me?

I unwrapped the crystal a bit more and it started to hum. It heated and buzzed with energy. I could hear it—like bees. It began to pulsate in my hands. My heart stuttered. The sound increased, and my heartbeat with it. It was as if all this stuff was...alive. Living energy. It was mystifying and terrifying.

How can a crystal be doing this? It looked so ordinary. I held the beautiful stone up to the light and something seemed to be moving inside of it.

No, that was not possible. I brought the stone back down to my lap.

I took a deep breath. My left hand tingled obnoxiously, and I had an overwhelming urge to touch the stone. Hesitantly, I ran the pointer finger of my left hand across the surface. Light flared, and it heated under my touch. A vortex of swirling colors erupted inside it. It continued to pulsate. Terrified, I dropped the stone to the floor, half wrapped in the fabric. Still, it made a dull thud as it hit the ground. I quickly stood and stepped back as purple light flung out, and arced upwards. I stifled a scream as the swirling vortex from inside the stone came outwards, upwards, and began to create an archway. A dusky gray stone-like archway illusion appeared in my bedroom. Swirling purple wrapped around and through it.

Holy crap. It was creating a—portal... *Oh, my goo*—And then I was being sucked into that swirling vortex, and—nothing. Blackness.

CHAPTER 4

This is all just fantasy stuff, right?

When I came to consciousness, I was on the... ground? I smelled earth. My body tingled, and my senses slowly came back to me. Hadn't I just been in my bedroom? Then it all floated back. The trunk, the dagger, the gemstones, the portal... Wait, what? Portal?

There had been a portal in my bedroom...

What the hell? This couldn't be happening. Where was I? What happened? My mind went to the journal. It had spoken of portal travel. That couldn't be what happened. That wasn't possible.

That was all fantasy stuff, right?

But I scanned the dark forest, noticing the trees were like something you would see in California or Washington state, not North Carolina.

Seriously though, where was I?

Something bumped against my thigh. I peered down at...my cat. Silas had made it through the portal—or whatever it had been. I wasn't ready to believe a portal had opened in my bedroom.

"Well, what happened?"

Silas flicked his tail and stared at me with those uncanny eyes of his. He seemed so calm, expectant.

"Did we go through a portal?"

His eyes tracked back to me, and he came over and butted his head against my side then trotted off.

"I don't speak cat. So... not helpful."

He went over to a pile of fabric a few feet away.

It looked familiar. The cloak! Its stunning burgundy color was unmistakable. Well, that was something. The cat walked across it and then toward a dirt path. I stood, picked up the cloak, and felt a weight to it. I checked the folds and discovered the orange-colored gemstone and the dagger. I left both pockets and pulled the cloak on. I was wearing a pair of jeans and a thin shirt—not particularly dressed for portal jumping and traipsing through the forest. At least I had on shoes. Granted, they were running shoes, not hiking shoes, but I was glad I was wearing something on my feet. The cloak would keep me warm, and the dagger could be used to defend myself if need be—not that I knew how to use it.

I looked up at the sky, the sun was dipping low. "Alright, Si, I'll follow you."

He trotted onto the trail as if he knew where he was going. I followed him, as my mind raced. What *had* happened?

I had known that trunk was bad news. Is that what gave me so much anxiety—not the trunk but the gemstone? It was a portal! Had I sensed it? But that would be even weirder.

Soon the trail widened, now large enough for a small car to fit down, and there were tracks. Ruts. Skinny tracks, like...wagon tires or similar.

Where the hell were we? I wanted to get home before dark that's for sure. "Get us home, pal."

Silas looked back over his shoulder at me but continued to walk. I had a bad feeling about this.

"We're not even in North Carolina, are we?"

He looked back at me again, and I had a feeling he was saying *no*. If listening to my cat, then it *had* been a portal. So, where were we?

Dusk settled around us, and I started to panic. Nothing looked familiar. The trees were bigger, the world quieter. An owl hooted, causing me to jump. A turkey crossed our path. I was starting to be unable to see much past the cat.

Trees turn into dark shadows, the path ahead of us became obscured. This was becoming more and more of a nuisance. I just wanted to go home.

I stumbled along in the near darkness, the only thing keeping me from falling was Silas' tail in front of my feet, like a flag. If he stopped quick, I would step on him.

I loved the outdoors, but I had no idea where I was or what I was supposed to do. My stomach knotted, and true fear nagged me.

Then in the distance, I saw a flicker of light. Silas sped up. Civilization. It had to be. Then—a howl cut through the night. I stumbled, fell, and caught myself with my hands, both of which were now skinned with dirt and tiny rocks. I stayed like that a moment and Silas let out a soft mew and rubbed himself against me. Trying to usher me along. Neither of us wanted to be wolf dinner. With a shaky breath, I lifted myself and we headed again toward the light. As I got closer, I realized it was a lamp post—albeit a rustic one. Wooden post with a lantern inside, not a light bulb, but something aflame.

As I look ahead, I could see dozens of them blazing a path toward a wall. About ten-twelve feet high, with a rampart, and I could make out the figures of...guards.

Where the heck was I? It was like I had stepped back in time.

"Name?"

The deep voice made me jump as I approached. "Ah, Kaidyn. Kaidyn Flynn."

"Flynn... Are you Fogdyn's niece?"

Um—what? If I said no, would they keep me out?

"Um... Yes."

"Well, I'll be! Finally, come home!"

I had no idea what else to say or do. I heard mechanical whirring and the door slowly opened just enough to slip my body through.

"Good luck." The man called down to me, but I just stared. Dusky gray cobblestone with chips of glimmering black and veins of purple met me. Tall buildings, white with red doors and molding, and dramatically pitched red roofs sat in front of me. It was warmer within the walls. The row shops and houses were neat and clean. There were bridges and hallways from the second stories of some buildings that ran above the street. Some of the buildings were stone halfway up, with rambling wood on the second story. It was not a bustling town, per se, given the hour, but I could hear a dog bark, children laughing, and the rumble of a wheel on cobblestone.

The path from the gate led to a crossroads. Straight ahead in tall lamp lights a path as far as my eye could see inclined to another wall. Something huge sat in the distance, and lights flickered from various windows. Oh, man. I had read enough fantasy books to know what lay ahead. A castle. Where Cinderella went to the ball, no doubt. The lights were undoubtedly from towers and parapets.

Where the heck was I? My mind whirred. Nothing looked familiar, even in a historical sense. Where do I go from here?

Was I on some set to a movie? Some medieval rendition? It didn't feel like that. This felt...real. Like a portal to another age, but that was not possible.

The shops were closed for the night, but I saw light spill from an open doorway. A tavern? Might as well stay with the times. A tavern meant gossip and people and I could get some answers as to where heck I was.

As I approached, I felt a shiver of trepidation. I was a lone woman walking into a tavern. What would I say?

"Silas, ah..." I had no idea what to do with the cat either. I could pass him off as my...familiar? That was a thing, right? I'd read about them enough, but then again, the books I read about familiars usually came with magic or witchcraft, and I did *not* have that. But as if Silas knew exactly what I was thinking he jumped on the windowsill, made a circle, rubbed his body along the window, and mewed at me.

I huffed a laugh. "You are one smart cookie, aren't you?" He mewed and I raked my fingers down his spine, causing him to arch into my hand.

"You're a good boy. You *are* my familiar, huh?" I smiled. He had saved me tonight by leading me to civilization. I had no idea how a cat had become so smart, but I was thankful for him. "I'll get some answers and be right back."

He meowed and looked in the window.

The tavern was hot and bustling. A few men gave me appreciative glances, but I ignored them and sidled up to the bar. I realized then that I had no money, no way of paying for anything. I had no idea where I was, no food, no water, no money, no identification... Nothing. I had the clothes on my back, the cloak, dagger, gemstone, and my cat. That was all I had in this...world? Country? Time?

In this place—wherever I was.

The barkeep turned to me briefly and lifted a brow.

"Ah, can you tell me anything of..." *Shoot.* It wasn't like I could outright ask, *where the hell am I*, could I?

"Never mind." I had no idea what to say. I should have brought the diary with me. It would have told me more information as to what I should do here. I only remembered a few names. Rhone. Van—something castle, Evirness, and something about the Keeper of Keys or some such. Would someone recognize the dagger if I showed it? Whipping that out couldn't end well though. Not in a damn tavern.

Would someone recognize the cloak's emblem?

"Have you ever heard of the Keeper of the Keys?" I asked timidly when the bartender came back through.

The bartender stopped what he was doing and stared. "Everyone knows of the Keeper. What of them? They abandoned us many years ago."

"I...heard one was back...around."

The big burly man looked me over, his eyes settling on the cloak. "It is said Keeper's wear," he gestured, "a cloak like that—burgundy and gold."

I swallowed. The cloak was potentially this Keeper of the Key's, considering the emblem. I mean seriously, a dagger with two keys, shouted the *keeper* of *keys*. I wished now that I had read the journal word for word, instead of skimming and skipping personal inclusions.

The barkeep's eyes seemed to settle on the emblem and widened. *Perfect.* Hook line and sinker. "Do you know anything about—"

"Ligus, why don't you leave the lovely girl be, huh?"

"Oh, yes, sir. Of course." The burly man bustled around, looking busy. "Your usual?"

My eyes whipped to the newcomer. He sidled up to the barstool next to mine with ease and comfort. He was thick with a round youthful face and brown eyes. He wasn't good-looking, not really, but he had an air about him—arrogance, and charm. He expected others to do for him anything he pleased. For some reason, I took offense to his attitude.

"May I?" He leered.

The bartender fell over himself to get him a drink, and I noted that the man didn't pay or thank him. An air of...higher status. I gritted my teeth and looked around. I needed to find some information, but I was not going to gain that here. The bartender had seemed like he might know something, but with the big guy beside me, I had a feeling the bartender wouldn't say another word.

I went to move on, but a hand on my arm stopped me. I followed the beefy appendage to the face.

"Sit."

"I—"

"Sit," he repeated. "An ale for the lady." He gestured to the bartender who produced a drink for me. I swallowed but grabbed the tin cup. I *was* thirsty. I took a long swig. It tasted bitter and hoppy, but I muddled through the flavors and swallowed it. It did feel nice on my parched throat.

"I heard you ask of the Keeper." His eyes swept my face in earnest, then across my cloak. "That cloak does appear to be similar to that of the Keeper's."

I swallowed. What could I say? He knew the Keepers. I wanted to ask a thousand questions, but I also didn't want this big guy to know anything about me. Something about him seemed dangerous, in a strange, niggling at the back of my neck kind of way.

His eyes roamed my face again, and then landed on the emblem of the dagger and keys and his eyes widened too. Well, at least they recognized it. I had no idea whether that was a good thing or not at this point.

"It...was left to me."

His brows raised. "By a female family member?"

Ah... "Yes," I said softly, unsure how to proceed.

"The dagger as well?"

Holy moly, he knew about the dagger? Indecision must have flashed across my eyes because he looked around. "If the answer is yes, leave when I do. Get in my carriage. I will take you to my father."

"Your father?"

"Aye. The king."

The king? Oh boy, things just got very interesting.

I didn't even know this man's name, but honestly, what other choice did I have?

When he got up to leave, I followed him out. He stood at the door of the carriage, an attendant hovering nearby.

As soon as I marched off the steps Silas meowed and sidled up to me. I scooped him up. The man lifted a brow and smirked. "The last one had a cat too, or so they say."

What? I had taken a gemstone out of a trunk and it had opened a portal. I was not—whatever they think I was. I just wanted to get home.

"Do you know how the Keepers went back to the..." I paused. What did I say? My world, my time, my—

"The other realm?" He offered objectively. He did seem to know quite a bit.

So, I *was* in a different world. A different world! Whoa. This was getting crazier.

He shrugged. "I've only read about the Keepers and heard what Father and Mother have spoken of them. I've never met one. The last one left and never returned years ago. The country has been in an uproar ever since."

"Uproar?"

"Yeah," he waved a hand and gave a haughty look. "The magic has been going wild without the Keeper."

Magic? What?

"Do you remember the last Keeper's name?" I idly stroked Silas' back as he settled into my lap.

The young man glanced at the cat. "Ah, no clue."

"And you are?"

His eyes turned cold. "I am Prince Payson Barthol."

He said it like I should be impressed. "Sorry. Different realm, remember?"

He stared at me a solid minute before he chuckled. "Right. So, you weren't trained as a Keeper?"

"Oh, no, I'm not the Keeper. I just... My aunt left me the cloak, dagger, and stones in a trunk and I'm trying to figure out why a portal opened up and I'm...here."

He lifted a brow and smirked. "Sound's a lot like you're the Keeper."

"I'm *not* the Keeper."

He snickered. "Whatever you say."

Ugh. Even boys in this world were annoying. I was *not* this Keeper. I would know if I was—whatever a Keeper was. A crazy deceased family member had left me some crap in a trunk. Somehow a portal opened, dumped me in this Godforsaken place, and I just wanted to go home.

I watched out the window as we went through the gate. There was a huge tower on each side with a red roof. When we entered the castle grounds, I couldn't see a whole lot in the dark. There was a fountain in a circular courtyard where the carriage stopped. An attendant opened the door, and Payson stepped down and offered me his arm.

At least he was cordial.

"Summon my father," Payson commanded one of the guards.

I noted that above the doors was an engraving of a moon and stars. I remembered seeing that on the map. This was...Vanstarr. Yes. The southern castle on the map. If I recalled correctly there was a harbor southeast of this castle.

Why hadn't the map come through the portal with me like the cloak and dagger? That would have been helpful.

I was lost, anyway, even if I knew where I was on the map. How did I get home? That is the information I needed next. The purple-colored crystal had gotten me here, did the orange crystal bring me home? But first I wanted to know who the Keeper of the Keys was, and how they were connected to my aunt.

A steward—or I guessed something of that effect—trotted up to us. "He will see you in the throne room, my prince."

Payson led me down a hall to a massive onyx marble archway. Above was the same moon symbol with stars and more stars rained down the pillar. I noticed it had veins of indigo and blue like the night sky. Breathtaking. As we passed through, the accents of the place weren't as tasteful and didn't seem cohesive. The thick rug was red, statues of knights in blinding white armor. The light was bright, harsh. Many things about this castle were contradictory. As if it were made for worshiping twilight but they forced it to worship mid-summer sun instead.

Payson walked with purpose, and I had to trot to keep up with him. I tried looking around, but he moved so quickly that I barely had a chance to take much in. For the best; the quicker I got the king to tell me what the hell was going on, the faster I could get my ass out of here.

The throne was impressive. Wide with ebony and deep blue granite that made up a dais. I noticed a shimmery mineral on the stairs and was struck by its magnificence. Then I saw the throne chairs, and again I was conflicted. They were huge with wide, tall backs of deep red. The throne chairs seemed ostentatious and didn't go cohesively with the dais. Who the heck was I to judge on castle décor?

Sitting leisurely at one throne was a thin, older man with blonde hair that swept his shoulders, trim facial hair around his mouth, and small blue eyes.

"Payson, my son." He spread his hands and graced us with a smile that was filled with maternal love and pride.

"Father, I have a fascinating guest." Payson gestured to me. I had no idea whether I should bow or what.

"Oh?" The king's eyes grazed me expectantly, and his brows raised, taking in my attire.

I bowed my head in subservience, but I was not bowing as I had seen in movies. No, thanks.

"She is... *connected* to the Keeper." The prince sent me a mischievous wink and I couldn't decide whether I found it charming or wanted to punch him in the throat. Not that it would affect him much, as thick as it was.

The king's eyes narrowed, and then he looked me over speculatively. "A great fabled Keeper of the Key's gracing *my* castle!" He dramatically put a hand to his heart.

I wanted to retort but held my tongue. Let them think whatever they wanted about me at this point. I was exhausted and thirsty, and I wanted out of these clothes. I continued to hold Silas, too nervous about him wandering to let him down.

The king wasn't tall, nor broad and wide like his son. He didn't look like a warrior king, but a strategic one. This king *used* people. You could see it in his dark blue eyes.

"Your name, girl?"

"Kaidyn Flynn."

"It has been a long time since a Keeper has set foot on our soil."

"So, I hear," I no longer had any interest in correcting them, I was too tired.

"I am King Ainon."

"Charmed," I said before I could stop myself. I shouldn't be a little snot, but I wanted to go home. I wanted to figure out what the crap was going on and go. Throw the trunk, the diary, the cloak, the dang dagger—all of it, directly in the dumpster.

Ainon grinned. "My wife, the queen, will be thrilled to meet you tomorrow."

I nodded. *If I'm still here tomorrow.* "What was the last Keeper's name?" I needed to know something before I fell asleep on my feet.

He gave me an odd look and cocked his head. "You do not know?"

"My aunt left me a trunk with stones and a cloak. I opened a portal, accidentally, that brought me here." I didn't think displaying that I had a dagger hidden on me was the smartest move right at this moment.

"Really?" He leaned forward from his throne chair, his chin on his fist. "No amulet?"

Amulet? I shook my head.

"So, you may not even be the Keeper?"

"I very seriously doubt it." I should be more respectful, but I was freaking tired, and... this place made me emboldened. I had no idea why. Something inside me shifted as soon as I stepped foot on this ground, and it pulsed inside my core. I was trying to be brave, solid, and not freak out, but it was getting harder to accomplish.

He pursed his lips and glanced at his son. Payson shrugged at my side, but his eyes ran over me, and it was clear they were uncertain.

"Her name." He tapped his chin with a finger. "Our records indicate that the previous Keeper of the Key's name was Mildred... No. That's not right. Millicent, I believe." He fluttered a hand. "The queen knows more of it, than I."

My blood ran cold. Millicent? Great-aunt Millie's full name had been Millicent Giles.

I closed my eyes. *Shoot.* Was this happening?

Had Aunt Millie been the owner of the cloak, the dagger, and the journal? Goodness. This changed *everything.* Had she had an entirely different life, here in this world, that no one had known about? Mom had never spoken about any of this. Did she even know? From the weird way my parents had gone deaf every time I spoke of the trunk, I had a feeling no one knew. My quirky great-aunt had kept one hell of a secret.

"You have the look of her—the Keeper woman."

"I do?"

"Certainly. The hair, face shape, the eyes."

Aunt Millie had had green eyes? Yes, now that I remember they were dark green almost brown, but I didn't look like her, did I? I mean she was my blood and all, but I just didn't...she had always just looked *old.* Forlorn. Tired.

"You met her?" I asked, as things still jumped in my head. I didn't want to believe this.

"Oh, no, I never met her, but there is a portrait of her. She has passed the magic to you, yes?"

Nope. "Ah, no. She died. I don't think..."

"It is late. Let us get some rest and reconvene in the morning, shall we?" King Ainon clapped his hands looking caught between distraught and ecstatic. It was a little disconcerting.

This was all so weird!

Would they toss me in a dungeon? I hadn't thought this through. I had no one here, no place to go. Were the Keepers something bad? I knew nothing about them. I knew nothing about my aunt either, it would seem.

My head hurt, and I just wanted to wake up from the messed-up dream. I let out a shaky breath and looked around as three attendants fluttered about.

"But—"

"Payson, why don't you show the Keeper to her quarters?"

Quarters?

Payson jolted beside me. "We have servants for th—"

"I said you. Now." The king's voice changed in octave.

Payson rolled his eyes. "Do we no longer have servants, Father? What is this?"

"But—" I tried to ask more, but again he cut me off.

"We will discuss more tomorrow." King Ainon waved a hand, and I was dismissed. But father and son stared at each other in a battle of wills. Some silent language, I wasn't privy to.

"You will do this, my son. Do not question me."

"Yes, Father. Come along, Keeper." He turned on his heel and strode down the corridor the way we came. I reluctantly followed.

"I do have a name."

Payson chuckled. "Kate, was it?"

I rolled my eyes to the ceiling. "Kai*dyn*."

"Right." Payson offered his left arm, and I took it with my right hand because I couldn't do anything else, and it was on the correct side, at least. His arm was thick but didn't feel as firm as I thought it would. But who was I to care about the guy's physique? I wanted some answers about Millie and then go home.

Payson led me up a flight of stairs, and the mahogany brown wood of the banister gleamed.

"May I see the painting of my aunt?"

He glanced at me. "Tomorrow."

I nodded. I couldn't demand anything, could I? They were housing me, no questions asked.

Were *quarters* just their codeword for the dungeons?

Payson brought me to an alcove that contained a shadowy door. This castle was so interesting and ancient. Some things seemed ageless, filled with starlight and moonbeams, then some things seemed new, obnoxious, ostentatious. It was odd.

The prince put his hand to the small of my back as he led me through another doorway. The touch ignited awareness of him, but it was forgotten entirely, and my heart nearly stopped when I beheld the grand hallway we entered. It was domed at the top and was glass, everywhere, even on the floor. I gasped. It was breathtaking. Phenomenal. Above a tirade of stars twinkled. The middle section had windows that could be opened, and a few had been swiveled outwards allowing the scents of the night to cascade in. I was an outdoorsy girl, and I loved flowers. Call it a weakness but horticulture and plant husbandry were hobbies of mine. I picked up the scent of night-blooming jasmine, Easter lily, and moonflower with a hint of roses. I could also smell a faint salty scent of the ocean and could imagine its glittery surface reflecting the multitude of stars overhead.

I had never seen so many stars before—and *oh, how they shined*! They were brighter, bolder than I had ever seen in my life. I loved the stars. Kial and I used to lay on the grass for hours looking at the stars. During our childhood, we camped in our backyard most weekends if the weather was nice. Just he and I and the stars. My heart ached from missing him. I needed to get out of here.

"Let's move along," Payson said as he ushered me through the hall, not even bothering to glance around. When one has access to this hall every day, perhaps it lost its magic over time. Not that I could see how.

I stared over my shoulder to catch another glimpse of the stars as he shepherded me through. We went down another short hall to a massive spiral staircase.

Where was he taking me? This seemed very... Rapunzel in the tower-like. Was I a prisoner here? My heart skittered, that humming inside my blood intensified, and the back of my neck itched.

He escorted me up and up. The walls were obsidian with veins of gold and gray. As we got even higher, small windows—just large enough to allow moonlight to dance across that obsidian wall and—Gosh! It shimmered, sparkled, and glowed ethereally in the moonlight. I stood, transfixed, and Payson pushed gently on my back.

"Wow, this is—" I fluttered my hands. "It's incredible." I spun in a moonbeam.

He looked at me perplexed. "What is? The tower?"

Tower? So, it was like Rapunzel! I wasn't sure if I was impressed or petrified.

"I meant the walls, the stairs, the moonlight."

He looked as if seeing it for the first time but shrugged.

How could someone not find this all magical?

The shimmering continued as we climbed higher, each tiny window letting in ample light causing little dust particles to dance as if this area had not been swept in years. As we crested the top of the stairs, and he opened an arched door, I was spellbound. Transfixed.

The ceiling was crisscrossed by dark beams and domed, starlight windows slanted moon dusted stars across the dark floors. My eyes traveled from the massive expansion of the ceiling to my right which was dominated by large wide windows, and the biggest window seat I had ever seen. I could have laid on it and easily stretched out. Directly ahead was a large bed with a shimmery blue canopy. Paintings of the moon phases and stars graced the wall, and my eyes alighted on the dagger with two ancient-looking keys crossing over it. The Keepers symbol I had come to assume was painted right here on the wall.

"This was the keeper's tower," Payson said, pulling me from my spellbound gaze of the circular room. "My father never bothered to renovate this part of the castle."

Renovate? My eyes flicked to his. So that was why it felt so new and strange in the castle. It had been remodeled. I had an urge to know what it had looked like before.

This tower was breathtaking. I couldn't wait for princely pants to leave so I could snoop.

"If that is all Keeper."

Just then my stomach decided to grumble—I didn't miss meals, I liked food too much. I set the cat down. Silas stretched, and trotted to a windowsill, not even sparing our princely companion a second look.

The prince watched the cat, then his eyes flicked to me. "I'll send a servant to you for refreshment and anything else you may require."

"Delightful."

He gave me one more long look, and then turned on his heel and fled.

Good. Begone, little princeling. Something about him was unnerving, and I was undecided whether it was good or bad. I wandered to the window where my cat was and peered out. The moon was full and lent glorious light to the city below. We were so high up. It glittered off the stunning cobblestone streets to the sea. Ocean waves rippled and shimmered. I couldn't help but revel in the ethereal beauty, but it still felt like I was stuck in a dream. There was just no way this was all real. A portal opened in my bedroom from a gemstone, taking me to a completely different realm stuck in perpetual medieval times... It was too storybook.

Once upon a time, a melancholy girl named Kaidyn was sucked through a portal into an ancient realm filled with ethereal starlight and moon dusted—

A knock at the door interrupted my internal rambling. "Come in." I was exhausted, mentally, and physically drained, and was in no mood for company.

A small woman stepped into the room. She had skin the color of coffee with just a hint of cream, dark hair, and eyes, and seemed timid as all heck. *Great.*

Payson had said something about servants, it just hadn't seeped into my fuzzy brain. Now it washed over me with a pull of disgust and anger.

"Prince Payson requested I bring you—"

"You don't have to wait on me, I can get myself—"

She bowed and shook her head. "No, no. Please." She hurriedly entered and set the tray down on a low table. There was a sofa next to it. I noted a chair in front of the bookshelf, which looked mighty comfy—or I was so tired that all soft surfaces looked cozy right now.

"Please," she begged again, and I nodded with a deep sigh. This girl looked exotic. I couldn't place the origin, but she was lovely, but her terrified nature made me nervous.

"Are—" Ugh. I didn't want to be rude or scare her with my stupidity or self-righteousness. "The king—does he treat his subjects fairly?" That was subtle.

Her eyes widened, and she bobbed her head. She quickly deposited the tray and water pitcher and hightailed it from the room. *Well, shoot.* That went— honestly about as I suspected and answered far more questions than I had asked.

What had I gotten myself into?

I sat on the chair, which was as comfy as I had hoped, and looked at the tray of food. Hunk of meat, that I was unsure of what exactly, but it smelled amazing. Potatoes, and vegetables. Seemed good enough for me. Better. I was unsure what most medieval-like meals consisted of, but at least I could identify the components.

Silas trotted over to me, and I ripped off a small piece of meat for him. "They aren't going to have Friskies in a grocery store around here, my friend." He scarfed back the food and meowed for more. Our jaunt through the countryside made him hungry too.

I wanted to snoop, but my eyelids drooped. The bed smelled a little musty, but I didn't care. I slung open the smallest window. The smell of night-blooming flowers, and the sea assaulted my senses as I curled up with my cat and drifted into a deep sleep.

CHAPTER 5

Smile, wave, and be hope to the people

I imagined waking up in my bed, all of this being an elaborate dream, but when sunlight slanted into the windows and I heard the bustling of wagon wheels on cobblestone, horses neighing, and men shouting—I quickly realized it was no dream.

I got up, stretched, and went to the window. I was stolen for breath. This was real. This city was magnificent. The cobblestone that had shimmered in the night, seemed subdued by daylight but still beautiful. The stark white buildings with their thatched roofs seemed out of place against the gray veined glistening cobblestone. I wondered if the king had remodeled the buildings but thought it too much of a feat to rip up the street.

I noted watchtowers with needlelike spired roofs, and a high wall keeping the city enclosed. I watched the waterwheels and noted aqueducts and canals around the city. Beyond the city were farms, grasslands, and rolling hills to then be swallowed up by tall trees. If I looked to my right, there was an open causeway leading down to a harbor city. I could see masts of ships on the horizon. Below me, this world was bustling with activity. The city was stunning but the buildings, the paint, the roofs, it all seemed... Flashy? Ostentatious?

It was still all so...*grand*. Beautiful, magnificent, and insane.

A soft knock made my head whip to the door. I looked at Silas, who only flicked the tip of his tail, and continued to stare out the window. "Enter," I said, hoping I could be a bit more friendly to this servant.

It was the same girl.

"My lady, I have your breakfast," she bustled with a tray in hand. She wore a simple brown woolen dress and a band across her brow. I realized my hair and clothes, and—everything about me was a rumpled mess and I completely forgot to hide my left hand from view. I watched her eyes flicker to it, widen and then move away. Exactly what most people did. The nicer people anyway. Others openly stared or backed away.

"I'm sorry if I—"

"It's okay, miss. I will have a bath drawn for you in the bathing chambers below."

"Below?"

"Why yes, the tower has a bathing chamber and library."

No freaking way. "Will you show me?"

"Eat. Eat."

I smiled and hoped to not spook her. "Please, tell me, what is your name?"

"It is Eloise, my lady." She curtsied.

"It's nice to meet you, Eloise. My name is Kaidyn."

She bobbed her head. "You are a Keeper, yes?"

"I... I'm not sure." She cocked her head. "I could be. I don't know." I gave her a genuinely bemused smile. In all honesty, I didn't think I was. I was simply a girl that was given some crazy stuff from her crazy aunt and was swept up in this crazy world.

"But..." She looked around the tower. Her eyes took in the cat, before settling on the cloak I had tossed on the bed, then back to me.

"Do I look like a Keeper?"

She scrutinized me. Her eyes drifted to my hand, but there was no pity, no fear, no curiosity, she simply looked interested. "I—I saw her once. The last Keeper. When I was a girl." She looked quickly to the door as if expecting to be screamed at for talking to me. "I had come here with my mother and father from Stylvane where we had been docked for a season. My father was a textile merchant, and my mother a weaver. He had chartered a ship and crew and we sailed the harbors of the world, trading, bartering. We lived a bit like ocean nomads." Her eyes lost focus, and she looked toward the window, the sea breeze and bustle still drifting in. "We had docked in Sky Harbor, had just gotten off the ship when Ki—Rhone rode by, the Keeper at his side. I remember her jumping off her horse and running up to my father. He had taken ill on our voyage and collapsed as soon as he was off the plank. She performed some strange maneuver on him, pushing his chest, blowing her life into him. I think he would have died if she hadn't helped. Something with his heart. It took him ages to heal. We remained here, my mother did the trading, bartering, and sales, but my father never fully recovered. He was always weak and got winded just walking from our home to the docks. He died three years later, barely able to get out of bed. But we would have lost him that day, if not for her. We had three more years with him—even at half capacity, it was still time."

Time was something one never gets back. It could be taken so quickly, but to have a second chance with someone... My Aunt had saved this woman's father. Despite what had been going on in her own life, she'd been brave, confident, and knowledgeable enough to stop and save a man's life. To give him more time with his family. Borrowed time—but it was still time.

I blew out a breath. I wish I had known my aunt had done these things. I wish I had more time with her.

"What is a Keeper, anyway?" I still had no idea.

"I...I shouldn't—I must go."

Wait, what? "I—"

"I'm needed elsewhere, but I'll ensure the bath is run for you, and have clean clothing sent for."

She gave me a quick nod before she bustled out. I watched her go with mild annoyance. My eyes went to Silas. "Alone again, my friend. But I did learn something." I scratched under his chin and shared some of the milk and mash from the porridge with him. "Aunt Millie was badass."

I ate quickly and then bounded down the stairs. Thoroughly looking forward to a bath. I was met halfway by another girl, this one much younger.

She squeaked and put a hand to her heart with a giggle. "Hi!!"

I laughed. "I'm sorry! I was looking for the b—"

"The bathing chamber is this way," she stated with enthusiasm, and bounded down a few more stairs in front of me, to an alcove behind the stairs. There was a door tucked behind it. I would have never noticed it without help.

Inside was a decent-sized room with a small window filtering sunlight through in slats, but not enough to see out, or in. Candles were lit, and a massive stone tub was filled with steaming water. It was simple and appeared to not have been used in ages. A small fireplace graced one side, which seemed like quite a commodity in these times. The scent wafting from the water was lavender and something else floral. This was magnificent.

"This is wonderful. Thank you."

She smiled brightly, and I was struck a little at how happy she seemed, despite being a servant. Perhaps this was a far better fate than some girls had in this time. There were brothels and other unsavory things a girl could contend with.

"Eloise left some clothes here for you." She gestured to a lavender dress hanging.

A dress? *Really?* "Thank you," is what came out of my mouth, however.

She bounced around me pulling out items and setting them on the side of the tub. "I'll come back and check on you before the next bell." Her eyes stuttered on my deformity. She sucked in a breath but at least she didn't take a step away from me as so many others did. As if a born abnormality could be passed on to them, like the plague or the flu. I was used to every kind of treatment; this was mild in comparison.

"What time—" How did they gauge time here?

"An hour until the noon-day bell."

I nodded, and she bounced off. *Okay, then.*

I stripped out of my clothes—grimy and sweat-covered from the previous day and could only imagine how they smelled.

I sighed in ecstasy as I slipped into the warm stone tub, the fragrant water steaming around me. When was the last time I had taken a bath? Why didn't I do it more often? It was sheer heaven.

I had barely gotten the dress up my chest when the girl came back. I had been in the tub for an hour.

She flounced in and helped lace up the back of the dress. "This color suits you nicely."

I snorted. I couldn't remember the last time I'd worn a dress, but I imagined with my brown hair and green eyes that lavender would suit me well enough. The front was square cut and dipped low enough to show that I was decently endowed in the chest. The laces in the back helped that tenfold. No wonder women wore corsets. Tightened laces certainly gave some oomph to the chest. I realized the cinching also made my waist seem smaller. I had wide hips, and I was not what you would call thin. I was regularly active as idleness made me restless. I liked to hike, bike, and swim, *but* I also really liked junk food. I had a love-hate relationship with Oreos and donuts, so I tended to gather weight in my butt and thighs, but my stomach remained deceivably flat-ish. This dress made me look and feel...womanly. Shapely. And thank goodness it didn't have the petticoats and layers. Ick.

I had been given clean panties and a silk slip for underneath. I wasn't overly thrilled with wearing someone else's underthings, but beggars couldn't be choosers, and mine were disturbingly soiled.

"What is your name?"

"Oh, I'm Feyla," the youthful blonde girl answered.

"That's a beautiful name."

"Oh, thank you!" She grinned exuberantly. "I'm named after my grandmother."

I wanted to ask more personal questions about the servants, about the king, but I would be gone soon enough. I didn't want to care. I *shouldn't* care.

"Have you...worked here long?"

"Only a few years. My mother was a housemaid here before...Well, when the other... Ah." She looked around, then gathered up my wet hair.

"Before?" I prompted.

"Ah, well, years ago. I was eager when my mother secured my position here."

"Are you... Do you get paid?"

"My parents received a stipend when I was accepted."

"Do you li—"

A knock sounded at the door, and we both jumped.

Eloise stuck her head in. "Oh good, my lady. I have your noon-time meal in the tower room, and I brought... I hope it's okay, but I brought some fresh fish for your cat."

I grinned. "I imagine he was thrilled to have that."

The quiet woman gave a small smile. "Indeed."

They were tight-lipped as they finished dressing me. Eloise took my clothes and told me they would be laundered. She had touched the jeans numerous times as if assessing their material. I'm sure denim had not been created yet in this world. I almost laughed at her bemused expression, but I was thankful to have them laundered.

Feyla led me back to my room, and a tray was waiting for me. Fruit and cheese. Yum. As I turned around to say something she was gone, and I was left alone. This time I ate and snooped. There was a trunk, like my own, at the foot of the bed. Locked, of course, but as I ran a finger over the lock my hand vibrated, tingled, and began to blur, and then I heard the telltale sound of a lock mechanism. I stared at my hand, perplexed. The deformity had blurred, and I swear it had turned into an ancient-looking key for a few seconds. My eyes flicked to the cat, who was dutifully cleaning himself at the edge of the bed and ignoring me.

Inside the trunk were a few bundles of fabric. One was a nondescript brown cloak. I went to lift the cloak, and a shirt fell out. A rainbow tie-dyed tank top. Homemade tie-dye from the looks of it and... This could not be from this realm, could it? Tie-dye... No. This world was surely in a time long before tie-dye... I didn't have a clue if it were my aunt's or not, but I fingered the thin fabric. I wanted to take it with me but needed a pack.

Next, I pulled out a brown leather pack. Ha! Check that out. I held it up in the streaming sunlight. It was a decent-sized backpack. Interesting. I was unsure whether these things were Keeper's items or not, but I felt the need to take them. I was stuck in a world where I was no one, I had no one, I was nothing, I had nothing.

There was a navy-blue hairband with silver stars on it—like I had seen Eloise wear for her hair. Heck, that would come in handy too. There were two pairs of tan breaches—like riding breaches—slim fitting and fine, a white and sage tunic, and a sleeveless blouse. Next, I pulled out something that was heavy leather, phallically shaped—Ah. A scabbard for the dagger? I held it up. Yes, definitely a sheath for a dagger. I was unsure whether my own would fit into it, but I set it on the bed to try it later. Then at the very bottom wrapped in another blouse was a necklace. It was a dainty, delicate gold chain with a stunning dark blue gemstone with glittering golden stars inside that shimmered in the sunlight. It was spectacular.

I shoved all the stuff in the pack and left it in the trunk. I would retrieve it when I left. I had every intention of taking those things home with me. I wanted to know if they were Aunt Millie's. It was stealing, but I didn't care at this point.

I checked the rest of the room, but there were few personal artifacts aside from an Edgar Allen Poe book. I assumed Aunt Millie had taken everything when she fled or someone cleaned out the room because I searched high and low to no prevail and I even got dust on the dress for my troubles. I was wiping it off, as a knock sounded at my door. I blew out a breath and pushed my hair back from my face. Ugh.

"My Lady, you—" Eloise cocked her head at my overheated cheeks and dusty dress.

"I was..." There was no point in lying. "Snooping."

She wanted to laugh. I grinned, openly, and she let a smile slip.

"I'm sure this room was cleared when King Ainon was... put on the throne." The way she said it begged a story. A tale I was nervous to understand. From the look in her eyes, the flit of something that passed across her features begged me not to ask, which made me want to know even more. I could tell I was going to get nowhere with her, nor did I want to push. I shouldn't care, anyway. I kept telling myself not to.

Finally, with a long sigh, I asked, "The king?"

Eloise nodded. "In his study."

"Can you show me?"

She nodded. I said goodbye to Silas, who seemed all too happy to remain in the room watching out the window. He showed little interest in venturing with me, which seemed odd since he was my shadow at home. Eloise led me down the stairs, through a door, and down a hall. Enough of the castle was open to suggest it was typically mild weather here. Eloise stopped at a door just past the double doors of the throne room. I knew there was an antechamber that attached the two with a short hallway. Two guards flanked the door and gave me a long once over. I had nowhere to hide my deformed hand—this dress had no pockets. I normally never bought clothes without pockets because of my hand. Hooded sweatshirts with front pockets were my very favorite attire. I held my hand at my hip, hoping to hide the missing fingers.

One, the elder of the two, gave me a scrutinized look, but something moved across his eyes. Respect? Resignation? Hope?

"Keeper," he said, a timbre of his voice matching the emotion in his eyes.

"I'm not…" *Screw it*. Might as well go with this facade. I gave him a nod and a flit of a smile. His chestnut brown eyes flickered, and hope flashed. He gave me a wide smile.

Why did the Keeper bring hope? What exactly *was* a Keeper?

The man opened the door for me, and Eloise left me. The room was sparse, but there was an air to this space… ancient and revered. There were bookshelves on the right wall, broken by stone pillars. Iron sconces adorned the columns, and a red owl banner hung on each. High above the bookshelves were small arched windows. Directly in front of me were skinny windows with slats of metal intersecting them. I could only imagine the moonlight streaming into this room.

I could hear soft voices, and I moved toward them. There was a door between the two bookshelves hidden by the columns, and it was ajar. I would have never known it existed if I'd not heard the voices. This castle was full of alcoves, and hidden doorways. I wasn't surprised, I had read plenty of fantasy novels to understand a well-hidden stairway to a concealed room.

"Such a union would solidify our claim. Legitimize—" Inaudible noises continued, and I stepped just a bit closer, praying I didn't step on a loose floorboard or something.

"If the walls come down, we need some kind of reassurance—"

Then I heard Payson's voice, "The army is ready. They look—" Indistinct continued and I moved another step closer.

"Good," a pause. "This union could mean everything. The people would be overjoyed. There would be no uprising, no cause for discord—" Inaudible voices ensued, and I made another step. I don't know why I was listening, why I didn't announce my presence. I made another step, now nearly at the doorway, almost able to peer inside.

"You would be surprised, my son. He is capable and resourceful. We must be prepared for—"

Honestly, I didn't want to listen anymore. As curious as I was, I just really wanted to go home.

I stomped a little as if walking to the opening and cleared my throat, hoping they would think that I was just coming upon them. "King Ainon?" I called out idiotically.

The voices paused. "Keeper," the king called. "We will be out shortly. Await in my study."

"Of course," I said softly, and moved back from the opening and went to stand at the bookshelves. I read some titles. *Arient's Guide to Liondralite*, *Bastian Bones*... were these just novels? I imagined a king to have... I don't know, battle tactics?

Finally, the king and prince sailed into the room. Payson looked like a linebacker beside his father. His youthful face and his light brown eyes were pleasant today and trained on my...chest. I felt my cheeks heat at his gaze.

Payson swung his eyes down my body, then up again as if just now seeing that I was female. *This damn dress.*

I swallowed and met his eyes when they finally flicked back to my face. I was no longer covered in sweat and grime from my voyage.

King Ainon gave me a knowing grin and glanced at his son with a nod. "I have a few things to attend to. Payson, why don't you show the Keeper the painting of her...aunt, was it?"

I nodded. "Yes."

"Excellent." He smiled at us and swept from the room. I flinched at the idea of being alone with Payson. He hadn't rattled me before, but the way he had looked at me in this dress... It had gone from mild curiosity to an actual interest, and I had no idea if that sent embarrassment, or nerves through me. I didn't want him to be interested in me... Did I?

"Keeper, you look...lovely."

I squinted at him. He had a smile on his face, and his gaze was still on my body. I felt a mixture of appreciation and revulsion.

I curtly whispered my thanks.

He led me from the room, and up a staircase, to what I had to assume was a royal wing of the castle. There was a thick red and gold rug, red banners with a golden owl on them, and a few symbols of the sun. This area looked a little more extravagant. Golden vases graced low tables, paintings depicting ocean scenes and ships. Finally at the end of a hall was a large window, open to let in the ocean breeze and scent of the sea. He waved a hand to our left, and I jerked in astonishment. There was a painting of my aunt and she looked...stunning.

She had long flowing brown waves down her back, much like my own. She was facing to the side, her profile stark and... intense. She reminded me of a hawk, beautiful but deadly. Everything about her said she could take care of herself and looked damn good doing it. She was wearing the same cloak given to me, her hands on her lap holding...the same dagger. I could just see the side of her tranquil dark green eyes that bordered on brown, shrewd, and cunning.

Aunt Millie exuded confidence. A complete conflicting contrast to the quiet, reserved, removed woman that I had come to know. This woman was full of life, radiating power. It was magnetizing. She was menacing in a penetrating, confident way. I was deeply saddened that I hadn't known she was...*this* person. That she had lived in my realm under a different guise.

I wanted to touch the painting, run my hands over her serious brow, the light that winked in her eyes. Those eyes were filled with adventure and fun, and her mouth was set in a smile that I could tell she was trying to hide. Failed to be serious, as if there was someone on the other end of the canvas that was trying to get her to giggle. A smile touched my lips at the probability.

Oh, Aunt Millie, who were you? Why didn't you explain any of this to me? Why did you leave me your things and not mom? I have no idea what the hell I'm supposed to be doing here, what I'm supposed to be accomplishing. I don't even know what a Keeper is. Why couldn't you have explained any of this to me? I'm floundering around in another realm, which should not exist, and here you are looking like a warrior-Goddess. I have no idea what to do!

I glanced at Payson, and he looked at me with mild interest. I exhaled through my nose. "Thank you," I whispered. I was unsure what else to do. I wanted to go home, but I felt like his father was dancing around my need to return. I felt like there was something he wanted from me, it was an impression I had received last night and again during our brief interlude today. I just had no idea what it could be. Plus, I wanted answers. I wanted to know what was going on. I wanted to know how to get home, and then how to ensure that another portal never opened again to take me or anyone else to this place. No one should have the power to portal jump. Portal jumping should not be a thing—at all. Ever.

"I... Can you take me to your father, please? I need to figure out how to get home."

He cocked a brow. "You could stay, you know. The people will be thrilled a Keeper has come again. You are what has been missing for two decades."

I resisted the urge to sigh. "I don't even think I am the Keeper—whatever that is."

"I can't believe you do not know."

I lifted a brow at him. "Do you?"

"Only what my parents told me, or I read."

"Are there books on the Keeper's, what they do—did?"

He shrugged. "I'm sure, somewhere."

Then it dawned on me. Eloise had mentioned a library in the tower. Did the answers lay there? I decided not to request that yet, instead, I let him lead me to the throne room.

Instead of just Ainon, as I expected, the other throne chair was occupied by a woman. His wife, I assumed. The queen. She had straight auburn hair, her face was thin and pale, her eyes a massive sapphire blue, her lips in a permanent frown. She wasn't beautiful in a conventional sense, but something shimmered in the air around her; a power that shivered against me. This woman was dangerous. She was not someone I wished to cross. The back of my neck tingled, and I resisted the urge to scratch it.

"Keeper, this is your queen, Aoife."

Not my queen, my mouth opened and closed soundlessly around the words, but instead, I bowed my head just slightly. I was in *their* world, their kingdom, and I needed to tread lightly no matter how miffed I was in the situation. At least I was clean, fed, and housed, I couldn't ask much more from strangers. Whatever position the Keeper held, it was given to me, and I couldn't exactly be upset about the accommodations.

"Can you help me get home?" My eyes roved Ainon and then his wife, who was staring daggers at me. I couldn't fathom why. Her eyes held disdain as if my very existence pissed her off.

"How are you liking your accommodations?" Ainon's voice was gentle, comely.

"Ah, wonderful. Thank you for everything you have done for me." *Blah blah, what you want to hear.*

"Good, good." He said, his fingers steepled as if he were bored.

I did not like this man, not one bit.

"Do you have any idea how I can get home—to my realm?"

The king arched a brow, finally registering my question. "You do not know how to get home?"

"No."

He turned to his wife, who was staring at me as if assessing a threat, an adversary and it terrified me. When she offered no resolution, not even taking those sapphire eyes off me, he threw me a glance and a shrug. "I've never read as to how that is done in the records."

What good were these freaking people? Ugh. I wanted to scream. "Is there anyone...that knew the last Keeper that may know how it was done?"

Ainon glanced back to his wife. "I am unaware."

I opened my mouth and closed it. Were they going to be of no help to me? "Is there nothing I can do to figure it out?"

"You could go to the wall."

The wall? Was that what appeared on the map as *The Divide*? Ugh. I was so freaking clueless, but I needed to get home. My family was freaking out by now. I had never been away for a night. Every police officer in our district was probably out looking for me.

"Great, can someone direct me there?"

He laughed. "In four days, I will send a procession of men to the wall with you." He gestured to his son. "My son included."

Four days? I'd had enough of this barbaric place, these unhelpful and unfriendly people. "Ah, why so long?"

"Because I wish it so."

"Can you not just send me in that direction?"

He sneered. "No. A carriage will bring you. It will be much faster, I assure you."

I sighed. It wasn't like I had any choice. I didn't feel like wandering the countryside hoping to find the wall, or whatever else may get me home.

"What about my home, my family? They are going to be going crazy wondering where I am."

The king lifted a slender shoulder. "I've no idea about that realm, or how the time of the two places work, but—"

"The two worlds move differently." The queen had not stopped staring at me, open condescension in her features, contradicting her lyrical voice. "The time in each is skewed. Your family won't even know you've gone."

I nodded because just being in the queen's presence terrified me and I wanted the heck out of here.

"We will show you to the wall but first there's something you must do for me." The king's voice held more strength, less boredom.

I did not want to be indebted to this man or his family. I was making a deal with the devil.

"You must make it seem as if you are a willing Keeper. A beacon of hope for the people."

An echo of what Payson had said wallowed in my head. Why?

He must have seen my questions because he sighed. "You will smile, wave. Act as if you are here to right all wrongs that the magic has bestowed on the people in the last twenty-five years."

I cleared my throat. Ah. I wasn't the best public speaker, nor did I know anything about being a Keeper, nor what a Keeper did. "I..."

"I'll do the talking. You smile, and stand at my side."

I could do that... I think.

Smile. Wave. It might be forced, and I could only wave with my right hand, but heck I *could* do it if it meant getting me home and out of this crazy, barbaric, medieval shithole. "Alright." A shiver of dread danced up my spine. I ignored it.

"Tomorrow morning then."

Wait, what? I still hadn't done any research on Keepers.

He grinned. "No need to look so terrified, Keeper. The people will be so thrilled to see the cloak you bear, they will question nothing. Even without the amulet."

The people would believe in a lie, for whatever the keepers did, I could not do. I was not that.

"I don't even know... I—"

"Look the part, girl," the queen's voice lilted to my ears, and I glanced at her. She still hadn't stopped staring at me, and I felt the heat of it from my toes. It slowly made its way up my body.

"Just stand there and look *capable*," she spat.

The king chuckled and put his hand on the queen's arm. She yanked it away without breaking her gaze on me. She was terrifying.

"No need to intimidate her, my love. She will listen."

I glanced at Payson who was looking intrigued by the entire situation. This was weird as hell.

"That's all I need to do, and you'll help me get home?"

"I will send you to the wall. Perhaps, answers lie there."

"But you're not—"

"You'll be fetched in the morning." He waved a hand. "You are dismissed."

"I—" *Ah.* What the—? I wanted to tell them to piss off. I wanted to turn on my heel and get out of here. I wanted away from this woman's blistering gaze that had wound heat up to my stomach now. I was terrified if I stayed another moment, she would continue to barbeque me where I stood.

This was all so strange.

I said nothing, just turned on my heel and strode away. The king and queen spoke quickly to their son, and then he followed me. The guards flickered their gaze back at the prince and didn't open the doors for me. I stood there breathing heavily, but thankfully the blistering heat of the queen's gaze was gone.

*Wh*at if it was magic or something? It had felt damn magical. The farther away I got, the coolness of the stone room licked its way up my legs.

The older guard gave me an apologetic smile, but they waited for the prince. Payson came up on my right side and offered his arm. I didn't take it, not ready to show him my abnormal hand. I just gave him a curt nod. He got the hint and let his arm drop.

He led me back to the tower room, and to my horror, stepped inside with me. Silas hopped down, gave the prince one surly look, and then brushed against my legs. I picked him up with my right hand, still consciously hiding my left.

"I'm sorry if my parents were a little...intense." He sent me a disarming smile.

"Your mother..." I stopped. I didn't want to speak to him as if he were a confidant. A friend. Because he was not. He came with his own set of intensity and contradictions. I didn't even think I liked him.

"Yes, Mother has always been that way. Intense, inscrutable." He grinned. "A little terrifying."

I tried not to, but I smirked. "Oh, yes, certainly that."

He laughed, and the sound made him more amiable.

"You are so... interesting."

"I really am not." My brain and mouth were having some inconceivable miscommunication because I said that aloud.

He chuckled. "I think the fact you don't find yourself interesting, makes you even more so."

He stepped closer, and my heart raced. What was he doing—certainly not flirting with me? I was a deformed stranger. He likely had girls lining the streets just for a smile. I was not even from his world.

"I... You..." I swallowed, and the cat screeched in my arms as Payson took another step closer. My eyes met his and his swept from my toes in the borrowed sandals, up the hint of my ankle that showed below the dress's hem, to my waist, and then chest, finally landing on my eyes. Heat seared my cheeks. I had *never* had a guy check me out this blatantly before. Ever.

Guys at school steered clear of me. Some guys out and about gave me appreciative looks. I guess my face was nice, but once they saw the hand it was usually over. I wasn't into leading someone on without them knowing that part of me. I don't know why I hid it now. It was nice having this big blonde prince look at me like this—like I was edible. It was unsettling but thrilling. What girl didn't want the attention of a *prince*?

Silas wiggled. I subconsciously cooed to him as Payson took another step closer. The orange gemstone and dagger were on the table. If he got too handsy, I could grab the dagger. Not that I knew how to use it.

He advanced again until we were toe-to-toe, and our eyes met. His pale brown eyes were a nice color.

I opened my mouth, then shut it. To warn him I'd never been kissed or touched, despite being nineteen, but that was too embarrassing to share. A boy hadn't gotten this close to me since the fifth grade, and that was only because I had been friends with Markus for ages, and he didn't care about my deformity—and then he'd moved, and the possibility of young romance had gone with him. Not that he'd kissed me or anything, but he'd hugged me a few times and pulled my hair affectionately now and again.

This was new to me. Terrifying and exciting.

Payson put a hand on my arm and began to lean in. Silas let out an obnoxious snarl and screech, and I felt a claw dig in. "Silas!" I yelped.

Payson and I both looked down and I tossed the cat on the ground, because I had no idea why I still held him for one, and for two he was being a dick anyway. I knew exactly when Payson spied my deformed hand from the intake of breath, the disgruntled noise in his throat, and the involuntary step back that ended with him tripping over the table.

As the cat hissed at the man, I watched in horror as Payson's foot teetered the table and caused my gemstone to fall. The sound of it hitting the floor was numbing, the sound of it shattering into several pieces heart-wrenching. I sucked in a breath and tears sprang to my eyes. My aunt had left me a gift and this oaf just broke it. All to get away from me and my deformity.

Payson disentangled himself. When he stood at the door, he looked back at me. I must have worn a horrified expression because I saw remorse flicker in his eyes at his repulsed reaction. "I-I'm sorry, I must go."

Tears spilled as I threw myself to my knees and picked up the pieces of the gemstone. Silas rubbed against me, and I glared at him "Why were you such a jerk?" I hiccupped and he gave me a look that I could only explain as reproachful.

Ugh. Damn cat, damn boy, damn... I scooped up the last fragment. Damn crystal gemstone—thing.

I opened the trunk and set the gemstone pieces in the pack. I pulled out breeches and a tunic and changed. The dress just felt dirty now.

I was at the window seat when I heard a soft knock. I knew who it was, so I stood and said, "Enter."

Eloise carried a small tray, with fish. I smiled and Silas trotted over to her. Good to see he liked someone here.

She knelt and set the tray down with a smile, which turned rueful as she swept my attire and the sadness in my eyes. I wondered if Payson had gone straight to his parents and told them.

"You are going to the wall?"

There was hope in her voice, that mirrored the older guard who had smiled at me.

"Yes, in a few days."

"You think you'll make it through?"

"Through?"

"Yes, the wall... I wish you well, my lady."

"What is the wall? Why—"

She shook her head. "I came to see if you required anything before your dinner was served?"

Was it already dinner time? Goodness, where had the time gone? I had been watching the city below. The people going about their lives never looked up to the girl in the tower from a different world.

"Yes, can you show me the library?"

"The tower library?"

"Yes."

"Of course."

The tiny library was actually below the tower. A skinny horizontal window at the ground level was the only light they cascaded in, the sunbeam sent dust particles dancing. Eloise lit candelabras for me to see in the dim area and then slipped out. The shelves were just as sparse as the ones inside the tower, so I grabbed titles at random and flipped them open. A few were in a language I did not understand, and I quickly scattered those to one side.

One had a passage; *The Keeper quickly opened the doorway, allowing the thing to escape into the forest. We got a glimpse of black hide, wide mouth, horned head, and then it was gone. We chased it for days until we were finally able to get arrows into it. It was a Servine, thought to have been extinct for a hundred years. The cousin of a dragon, but far more elusive and deadly. Its scaled hide was thick with ridges, and its long serpent tail ended with a spiked tip. Its blunt face was set by a massive mouth full of razor-sharp teeth. Ram-like horns swoop back on its head. But it seemed to want to get away more than fight us. The Keeper wished to send it back to another realm, her amulet glinted and she began to chant—but the men heard none of it, and twenty arrows flew. It was soon over.*

The passage ended, and it went on to speak of castle politics and how the situation was handled poorly. It made it seem as though the Keepers opened doorways and have magic—or something like it.

Another passage stated that the Keeper's dagger was forged from fallen starlight. *Yeah, okay.*

And a cryptic passage:

Keepers maintain the magic and balance it. Keepers bear the secrets of kings. They are the holder of forgotten things. The sacred gatekeeper of worlds, realms, creatures, and entire civilizations are hidden in a gate.

They hold the stability of our world in their magic. Without the ancient line of Keepers, our realm will fall into ruin in less than a hundred years, turning all living beings into dust and starlight.

Whoa. Had my aunt truly been one of these individuals that this world held in such high regard?

The balance of an entire world... It was just so unbelievable, but as were portals and magic and different realms—but here I was. Nothing was as it seemed in the world. *Worlds.* Whatever.

There was extraordinarily little about them. I had learned they could wield magic, of a sort, and they safeguarded creatures and gates to other worlds.

"I thought I'd still find you here."

I sent Eloise a grateful smile when she set down a steaming plate of roasted meat and vegetables. The woman moved silent and graceful like an assassin. It was disconcerting, but I was also a little envious.

"A fat lot of good it's doing me. I'm finding..." I fluttered my hand with a sigh. "Very little."

She gave me a sour look and sighed. "Well, even though King Ainon did not remodel this part of the castle doesn't mean when he..." She looked around quickly before. "When he came into power, he purged many...artifacts. Books included."

Purged? "Why?"

"When the Keeper abandoned us and there was no balance of the magic, it did things—wild things. The wall shattered lives, ruined, and ended many but it allowed *some* opportunities otherwise denied to them. Sneaky individuals that seized openings."

The Barthol's? Did they seek opportunity? I could certainly see it in them. But the opportunity of what?

"Who? I know nothing about any of this."

Her brown eyes sparkled with a seething passion that contradicted her next words. "It is treason to speak of such things."

"I would never betray your—"

She waved a hand and gave me a rueful smile. "No matter, I shouldn't speak it."

The little she did say begged more questions. I felt in my bones something dubious was going on here.

"I just want to go home," I whispered.

Eloise patted my arm. "Oh, dear, don't we all?" She said it with so much sadness, I reached out and covered her hand with mine. I felt a swell of bravery in me to figure out what was going on, and get her out. "Come with me," I blurted. "To the wall."

She stood and squeezed my hand. "I must be going. I'll check on you in a while."

I exhaled a shaky breath and wished I would have brought Silas with me. I felt very alone.

I read until the lines blurred in my vision. I learned a little about the Keepers and a bit about this world. The raw magic that trembled in the soil, blossomed in the fields and spiraled to the sky needed balance, or it would weed out all life and run rampant. It needed someone to harness it, stabilize it, to keep some of its darker parts locked up or it would breed them and leach onto this world, sucking it dry of resources, and forcing the people out. The magic wanted to take over, to drain the life from this country, to do with it as it wished. A Keeper was a line of ancient women, dating back a millennium, who were born from another realm, of ancient and powerful magic who could harness the magic and keep it in check.

The Keeper of the Keys.

Once, they just had keys on a chain that went to hidden gates where people could find treasures to help them in their discoveries of this world, then that changed to the Keepers keeping court secrets, and mythical creatures.

Over the years, things progressed and changed, but I found little else. I had no idea what a Keeper's actual role was *now*. Each Keeper changed the course of the magic in their way.

Eloise led me to my room, and I stumbled inside. Silas hopped off the bed and wound his way between my legs and then Eloise's. To my surprise, she handed me a glass of wine.

"It'll take the edge off. Help you rest."

I took the goblet and downed the contents. It burnt a bit going down, but it was delicious. Berries. "Thank you, Eloise."

She gave me a knowing smile. "There's something about you, my lady. Something special."

I almost scoffed, but the way she gazed at me, at my deformed hand, gave me pause. "I am no one," I breathed.

"I think that is what makes you someone," she said with a forlorn smile, and then she was gone.

I didn't dwell on her words, or even on what I had learned. I blanked my mind and slipped into the white nightdress that Eloise had left. I opened the windows, letting in the night breeze. It was late, there was little activity, and only a faint amount of light glowed from buildings. I crawled into bed with Silas, my nose pressed into his furry neck, and fell into a dreamless sleep.

Chapter 6

The city of starlight

"Kaidyn." The voice pulled me from my slumber. "Keeper."

I smiled into my sleepy fog. I liked Eloise. She was nice. Finally, I remembered that I was supposed to be doing something this morning. I just wasn't entirely sure what it was. Then as the fog lifted, I remembered.

Beacon of hope for the people. *Right.*

I opened one lid and saw Eloise rubbing Silas under the chin. He purred and stretched under her hand. She gave me a soft smile when she noticed I was awake.

"I have your breakfast. The king requests your audience in an hour and a quarter, my lady."

Ugh. I nodded. "Thank you, Eloise. How will I ever repay your kindness?"

She gave me a sly smile. "When you balance the magic, and things are restored as they should be, as they *were*, that will be enough."

"I..." I had no idea how to do that, or if I was even the person for the job. I had no amulet, and everyone made it seem like that was how the Keepers drew their magic, without it... I was nothing. "I will do whatever I can," I found myself saying because I would. I'd tell Mom about this when I returned home. Hopefully, she had gained crazy magic and could help these people.

Eloise sent me a hopeful smile and nodded.

No one came for me after what seemed like an hour, so I kissed Silas' head and slipped from the room. I had on a sleeveless tunic and had my left hand wrapped in the cloak. It was too hot to wear it. There was no point in hiding the deformity now, princely pants had told his parents anyway.

Feyla met me at the stairs and smiled. "I shall escort you, my lady."

I sighed deeply, and she looked at me sideways. "Are you anxious for the people to see you, my lady?"

"I am. I'm not the most...sociable person, and I don't do well in crowds."

She grinned. "I would never have guessed."

I lifted a brow, and she sobered. I hadn't expected it, but I chuckled and elbowed her in the arm.

"Couldn't tell, could you?"

She laughed and elbowed me back. The camaraderie felt... nice, and unexpected. I shouldn't like people here.

Some people were annoyingly fake nice, and that was worse than avoiding me. Feyla was genuinely companionable. It made my chest ache. My one friend, Bree, was only friends with me because our parents were close. We had to get along. My brother was the only person who I felt at peace with. Even with my parents, I was different. They tried too hard, spoiled, pampered, and sheltered me. I couldn't fault them for it, but I hid part of myself from them.

It felt different with Feyla and Eloise. Maybe I was meant for this world, not my own? I shook my head. No, I needed to get home.

We teased each other and Feyla told me ridiculous gossip. Saucy things, that she didn't even understand. I think that's why she joked about it. She felt kindred inexperience in me for such matters.

We were still stifling giggles when we came upon the royals and a barrage of guards. Feyla stopped in her tracks and bowed low. I swung my gaze over each of them. Payson gave me a sheepish smile. Queen Aoife openly stared daggers at me. Nothing new there. Heat zipped up my legs from her scorching gaze, and I looked away. She was a witch or something. King Ainon stared at me expectantly. I noted the way he looked over my left side, for the hand that I hid in the material of the cloak. So yes, Payson had told him. No good morning. No good day. Nothing. He simply gestured to the castle doors, and I followed him out into the waiting carriage. The queen and Payson trailed behind us.

"What is it you wish me to do?"

He glanced at me sideways as I shrugged into the cloak. I knew he wanted me to wear it, and they were all dressed in long tunics and fine livery.

"Just smile, wave. Look the part," Ainon said as the carriage lurched forward.

I shook my head. I still didn't understand my role or why I was giving the people hope. "I don't understand."

"You soon will."

I could wave, smile, and all that, but why? I understood that the Keepers balanced the magic, but why did that matter so much? Was the magic openly killing people? The books had said that the magic had that kind of power, but everything seemed right as rain from what I could tell.

I stared out the window as we went through the castle gates into the city. Some people bowed or waved at the carriage. Others flung vegetables. I think one might have even been a rock. I imagined being a monarch not everyone would love you, but whoa. The others didn't seem perturbed. I let my eyes catch the queens, and they were aflame with dislike. I swallowed and quickly looked away. What was her issue? Ugh.

The carriage stopped, and my heart raced. What exactly was the king planning?

"I've called a city meeting, and all who are gathered may witness your favor on my reign."

My *what*?

The king stepped down into the slanting sunlight when the attendant opened the door. I stood up. Payson gave me a small smile and put a hand on my lower back to usher me out.

We were in the lowest part of the town square. From here four wide stone steps led to the square. Dead in the center was a stunning cascading fountain depicting the moon and stars. It was magnificent. The moon was a massive orb of yellow, and dusky purple polished marble. The stars were chunks of deep gray stones chiseled into shape. The pool below it had a mosaic of yellow stars, amongst large chunks of purple, deep blue, and dark gray stones making a night sky. I gravitated towards it. I wanted to sit and listen to the melody of the water rippling over the stars.

There was a raised stone section branching out from each corner for about five feet with climbing star-shaped flowers of the deepest purples. To the far left was a covered gazebo with crawling flowers up each wooden pole, to the right was a covered dais. The king ushered us to it.

A crowd began to gather. Guards kept the leering town folk at bay. Some yelled, but most stared on with contempt or curiosity. I'd never experienced anything like this. There was an expectant hum from the crowd. I wondered how often King Ainon spoke publicly. I had a feeling it was rarely. If the thrown vegetables were any indication our guards had their work cut out for them if the crowd got any rowdier.

My eyes drifted across the city. I stared, open-mouthed. Close up the cobblestones reminded me of starlight. The City of Starlight. I understood the name now.

"It's called Elirian mica."

I snapped my head to the guard at my elbow. He was the older guard from the other day. He was in his early sixties, but hardened muscle showed he'd been a guard for most of it.

"The cobblestone. The stone is mixed with Elirian mica. A hard mineral dug from the mines found on the edge of Sky Harbor and in the borders of Eliria, our neighboring kingdom. Ancient kings named it Elirian mica to honor our ties with our neighbors."

"It's beautiful."

"Indeed. This city—" His voice lowered. "Once all of the roofs in the city were also covered in it. Twenty years ago, this city's beauty inspired awe, near and far. Dreamers, painters, engineers... there was a place for everyone to live in harmony. This city and the harbor were a vision of the future, revered by all kingdoms, even ones across the sea."

"What changed?" I already knew though. I had added a few things together.

His solemn eyes skipped to the king, and he said no more.

Hmm.

We made it to the dais with little fanfare. The king held a smug smile that I wanted to punch off him. Suddenly, I second-guessed my decision to allow the king to use me as a trophy. Because that's what I was, wasn't I? A trophy?

He gestured me forward as he took his place on the dais, the queen stood at his other side, and Payson gave me a passive smile as he urged me forward. I swallowed and resisted the urge to look out at the people. I wanted to puke. Instead, I focused on the steps, then the fountain. The stars and the moon. A fountain for hope, for dreams, for wishes to be answered. It was magical, and just looking at it made an ache settle in my chest.

The king beamed and gave a flourish of his hands. His smile was huge and disturbing. I still had the overwhelming urge to punch him. Goodness, I needed to go home before I was thrown in a dungeon for saying something treasonous.

When I looked out at the sea of people, my hands went clammy, and my heart raced. What had I gotten myself into?

Then my eyes shifted to the port city, the sea glittering in the sun. I noticed a massive ship, like a pirate ship. Did this place have pirates? Is that where my trunk came from? *Hmm.*

The king stretched out his hands. "My subjects."

Silence.

"I will keep this short, so you can get back to your lives. I called you all here to inform you that a Keeper of the Keys has returned to us!"

A hushed whisper swept the crowd and a guard pushed me to the front. I had little choice, but to stumble up next to the king. I glanced to the queen, who was frowning, those piercing eyes on me.

"We've been without a Keeper for a long time. The stability of Evirness has been out of balance, the magic going haywire, but no longer!"

A murmur swept through the crowd, and many who were milling around stopped to listen. More people joined the throng.

"The Keeper, under my command, will rebuild our world."

What?

The crowd whispered.

"She will become a permanent asset here in Silvercrest, working under my tutelage to assist with not only the wall but with all the resources we've been pulled from."

Tentative applause rose, and the king beamed proudly.

Ah, surely not *permanent*. He knew I wanted to get home.

"Some of you have family across the wall in the north that you wish to see again. *I* will make it so."

The crowd murmured for a moment before a smattering of applause ensued. I looked out over the crowd.

"Good girl. *Smile*," he said sternly under his breath.

I tried to. The crowd erupted in cheers. So many smiling faces. The Keeper truly was a beacon of hope. Too bad I was not a Keeper, nor was I to be a permanent fixture. He'd lied to his people for what purpose?

The king touched my right arm and lifted it with his. I swallowed but allowed him to. I continued my fake smile, anything that would get me home, even if it was some bullshit to placate his people.

Payson stepped up and with a hand on my back guided me from the dais. People reached out to touch my cloak as I passed as if just touching me would give them good fortune. It was strangely flattering and didn't bother me as much as it should. I found myself truly smiling at these people now that I wasn't in the king's shadow with his expectations.

I realized as I made it across the beautiful cobblestone, that I wouldn't mind being what these people needed me to be. Not for Ainon, but for them. The city people.

My eyes looked through an alley, and I noticed people filing into a large stone building. People in *chains*.

What the—

Slaves?

No. I stopped in my tracks, and Payson nearly ran into me.

"What is that?" I asked, pointing to the people shuffling into the building.

"Just getting rid of some unwanted riff-raff." He smirked.

I glanced at him incredulously. "Unwanted...what?"

"Some of the peasants, some of th—"

"Payson!" The king summoned and Payson's horrid words were cut off. My goodness, these people were callous! I knew in this world things were as they had been in my own centuries ago, but to live the atrocity after being in my own time was infuriating. I wanted to run over and unlock every manacle.

Sickened, I stood staring in disturbed awe until the queen's penetrating glare made me flick my eyes to her and what I saw got my butt moving. I would have jumped off a cliff to get away.

The king gave me a curt nod once we were situated in the carriage. No decent job, no nice work, no praise—as if he expected nothing less.

I dutifully ignored the smug smile of the king and his son. The queen stared at me, unnervingly. A shiver went through me for fear of what I had just done. I had done something for them to which I was not privy.

As we began our jaunt back to the castle, I noted that there was truly something ancient about the Castle of Vanstarr, with the tumbling green hills at its back and the grand city of starlight sprawled at its feet. It was breathtaking, even with its weirdly painted buildings and remodeled feel. The city was made for the dreamers, the visionaries, and the artists, while the castle was stone and moonlight ingrained in the ancient rawness of this world. It was complex and intriguing, and I hated that it all interested me. I was so damn interested. I wanted to get home, yeah, but I also wanted to know more.

Nothing was said as we exited the carriage and walked to the castle doors. The king turned to me swiftly with a curt nod. "There will be a dinner tonight in your honor Keeper. Dress appropriately."

I gaped at him as he and the queen made their exit. Guards and attendants scattered and trailed in their wake.

Payson stood at my side, and I glanced sideways at him. He looked perplexed as his gaze lingered on me. His eyes edged over my chest and made my stomach coil. A heat that I was baffled with, unsure whether it was embarrassment or annoyance, curled in my belly. I wasn't... attracted to this boy, was I? I couldn't be. That would be asinine considering his reaction upon seeing my deformity.

He opened his mouth to say something, but Eloise rounded the corner. She bowed at him but turned to me. "My lady, I can take you back and prepare dresses for your perusal, if you wish?"

Dresses? Fantastic. *Not.* "Yes, of course, Eloise, thank you."

Payson's eyes swept over her, then me, and he opened his mouth, then closed it. Finally, he gave a half-assed bow in my direction. "I'll see you tonight, Keeper."

I audibly sighed, then turned to Eloise. "Let's go then."

I didn't hide my disdain for this situation. She picked up on it and gave me a solemn smile.

The dresses in question were stunning.

Eloise had chosen some of the finest, lightest dresses I'd ever seen. After trying on three, we decided on the sage green one, with the gold stitching. It was sleeveless, but Eloise—ever-watchful—had procured golden gloves for me. Light, to the wrist, but would take the eye from my abnormal hand. I was shocked and thankful when she handed them to me. I had never thought about wearing gloves to hide my hand, but I had read enough books to know that many ladies wore dainty gloves in my realm in centuries past, and even in more recent years.

I loved the idea of the gloves. It was warm here and wearing the cloak all the time was not going to happen. I hated that my throat constricted as I put them on. Eloise smiled deeply at me. Her dark hair was bound in a simple braid over one shoulder held back at the crown with the brown band. Her dark skin and eyes were serene. She was no more than eight years older than me and stuck in this life of servitude. I wanted to fight, rage, and scream, but it wasn't my place. This was not my place—not my world. I would never see this woman again, but it didn't lessen the innate need to spirit her and Feyla away. In such a brief time they had wormed their way into my heart.

"Tell me about yourself, Eloise. Your family. Your hobbies."

Her brows raised. "My..."

"Please. I will take what you say to my death, I swear it."

She smiled. "I have no doubt, my lady." Something akin to affection shimmered in her eyes and she pursed her lips. "Well, there's not a whole lot to tell that I haven't shared with you. I am originally from Jeheria, a warm island deep in the Vestias sea. My family is full of voyagers, adventurers, and explorers. My father ventured to Evirness to discover they had few trade opportunities. He decided to change that. We rented a ship with a seasoned captain and enlisted my many aunts and cousins to help make clothes and fabrics to sell. We had only been trading for three years before he got sick."

"You still have family in Jeheria?"

"I imagine so. I would send letters, but I have no way of knowing if they would be received. I've sent messages in bottles—" She laughed and looked away. "As foolish as that is. A fanciful girl hoping for her family."

"I don't think it's foolish at all," I emphasized, and she gripped both of my hands. She didn't shy away from the deformity.

"I think they have come looking for us, but—" She shrugged. "My father didn't always tell them our plans, and unless they tracked down the ship and captain that had docked us all those years ago, they'd likely never know our fate."

"I'm sorry to hear that."

She gave me a sad smile. "I knew once magic claimed this land and the wall erected that it was most likely that a tyrant would take the place of King Rhone. I was not wrong."

A tyrant? King Rhone? So, Rhone in the journal had been king before the magic went haywire and raised this wall they spoke of. *The Divide.*

"How did the wall—"

A knock sounded at the door, and Feyla stuck her head. "Dinner is in a quarter-hour, my lady."

The time had flown, and I sighed. "What should I expect at this dinner?"

Eloise patted my hands and stood. "A boring, stuffy affair, I'm afraid."

Feyla giggled as she plunked down on the bed next to me, a brush in her hand. "But I'm still jealous," she said and handed the brush to Eloise, who brushed out my long brown hair.

My eyes whipped to hers. "You can't attend?"

"Oh, no, that would not be—"

"That's outrageous. You are just as integrated into this—"

Eloise lifted a hand to silence me. "My lady, I knew you would rattle the very fabric of our world as soon as I laid eyes on you."

Oh, I don't know about that! But I sure as hell wanted to change things. "It wasn't always like this—the slaves, and such?"

Eloise shook her head. "No. King Rhone *employed* his house staff. They were not indebted to him, nor slaves. They made handsome salaries, were free to marry, and do as they wish."

"Well, if there is anything I can do—"

"Return the magic to its place. Free the northerners. Return commerce and trade and take down the wall."

"I don't think—"

"In doing this, it will reinstate the rightful rulers, and balance the world justly."

My eyes widened in panic. "I can't. I don't know how."

"It will damn us all if you can't."

I groaned. How was it possible that the fate of this world rested on *my* shoulders? "I'm not even the Keeper."

"You are a foolish girl to think you are not."

I stood abruptly. "I'm not," I said angrily.

Eloise just watched me, the brush in her hand. The righteous fire crossed her deep brown eyes. I saw a blaze in her that sparked inside of me, but then it fizzled out. Like a sparkler on the fourth of July, fierce for thirty seconds and then turned to ash. That was my passion and spirit. It sparked and fizzled.

"You are exactly what we need. You are more than a Keeper, more than the balance of magic, you are—"

"I'm not," I said sternly, and jerked my chin. Dismissing them. Tears threatened my eyes, and I clenched a fist. Despite my curiosity, *I wanted to go home.*

With one last beseeching look Eloise turned and strode to the door. Feyla gave me a soft look and followed her.

I swallowed back the tears. I had just alienated the only two people I liked in this realm. The only two people I trusted.

My hair was unbound and fell in waves down my back. My dress was lovely, showcasing some cleavage and its cinched waist displayed the flare of my hips. I wore the golden sandals Eloise had procured for me. The gloves were a little haphazard, but they looked normal enough. Despite our words, it was Eloise who summoned me to dinner. I whispered apologies as we made our descent, but she waved me off.

"Words are one thing, actions another," she said simply, and it made me sigh. She wasn't wrong but I still had no idea what I could do to help. I had no magic, no amulet, no power.

I stepped into the hall to Payson waiting as my escort. I hooked my right hand over his arm. I reminded myself I had to play the part to get home. The dining hall was alit with a dinner for the ages, filled with people I didn't know. Everyone looked at me expectantly, like I would spout keys from my mouth and hand them over. I remained with Payson, but even that seemed fake. He flirted, paraded me, courted me like we were something more and it sent my skin crawling.

Was this a ploy? Everything felt like sand on my skin—every look, touch. Every time the king looked at me, I just felt dirty. An inner voice told me the sooner I was on my way the better.

The king introduced me and told everyone that I would be heading to the wall to investigate and evaluate our collective next move to take it down. Together. Unified.

Yeah right. I almost snickered twice during his speech, but with eyes taking me in, assessing me, I didn't allow myself to. I was still at their mercy and needed to keep up appearances.

Payson sat against my side at dinner. Eloise was my server, and she gave me a reassuring smile. Very few people spoke to me. They sent me nervous glances, stared with open curiosity, or glared, but otherwise, there was little conversation centered towards me. I wondered if the king had told everyone not to speak with me.

After dinner, everyone moved into a large open room with a wall of high skinny windows. The room was aglow with crystal chandeliers, and pillars of light. Payson was deviously attentive and every time he touched me, I was torn between a shiver of trepidation and thrill. He *was* a prince. Not the most handsome, but he did have a presence, and he was paying me single-minded attention as if I was the most interesting person he'd ever met. I earned many scornful glances from impeccably dressed, coifed, and outwardly perfect ladies all evening.

I got a strange feeling that something was going on here, with no one talking to me, King Ainon's little speech, and Payson's annoying attention. I had a disturbing feeling that there was something at play I did not understand.

Payson danced with me, and introduced me to "friends" that I knew were only acquaintances, his hand always at my back or over my shoulders. I wanted to ask what game he was playing, but I remained quiet. I was leaving tomorrow, it didn't matter. There were answers on this wall, and I hoped that tomorrow night I would be sleeping in my bed, in my world, at home with my family.

After the third dance with Payson, his hands too tight against my waist, his body too close, I excused myself. I wanted to sleep so that morning would come faster. Payson offered to escort me. I didn't want him to, I was done with his company, but he insisted. He gave his father a long look as we broke away. I didn't so much as look at the king. I just wanted to get out of this dress, the looks, the hatred from the other women for the unwanted attention from the prince. I was over it.

Payson led me up to my tower. I was hoping he would say his goodbye at the door, but he didn't. Instead, he opened it and stepped inside. Silas growled and launched himself at my feet. I lifted him into my arms and snuggled his soft fur against my neck. I had missed him. He rubbed his face against mine and gave me a strange look with those luminescent eyes of his.

Payson was watching me, and I had no idea how to kindly dismiss him. "Thank you, for all your...help tonight—making it less awkward, or whatever."

He lifted a brow but gave me a slow smile, turning up the charm. "It was no hardship. You are fine company."

"Hmm." I didn't want his company. I wanted him gone so I could figure out how I'd get this dress off.

He stepped closer, and I noted a glint in his eyes that had me gulping. He surely didn't—I hadn't—We weren't...

I couldn't put up a hand, since I was holding the cat, as he leaned toward me. I didn't want to piss him off, but I also did not want him to get the wrong idea. I swallowed and watched him as if out of my body. His head dipped down, and his lips grazed mine. Silas shrieked in my arms.

Payson chuckled and went to pet the cat, but I twisted knowing Silas would scratch him. Payson looked me over briefly, and then leaned in again with that glinting grin—

A knock sounded at the door, and my heart flopped in my chest. Thank goodness! Whoever was on the other side of the door I would hug for saving me.

"My lady," Feyla said, as she opened the door wider. When her eyes met mine and then snagged on the prince she bowed and started barking apologies.

Payson glared at me, then pushed past us and out the door. Feyla watched him go and turned to me.

Had I just made an enemy without intending to? He was supposed to ride with me on what I was told was a solid day's trek tomorrow. Wonderful.

"Did I interrupt—"

"Yes," I said, and she balked. "And thank heavens you did. *Ugh.*" I stroked the cat and then set him down as her eyes rounded.

With her quick fingers, she helped me out of the dress.

I sighed as she looked at me thoughtfully. "I'm not interested in the prince," I said as much to myself as for her.

"As you say, my lady."

CHAPTER 7

The wall

The situation with Payson the previous night had been awkward enough to then have to be stuck in a carriage with him for the day... Not my idea of enjoyable. At dawn, King Ainon and Queen Aoife gave a wave as we set off. No words of luck, no warm goodbyes, no advice, or direction. I found this entire experience to be cold and confusing. I had learned little from them. I'd learned more from the library and the servants.

I carried Silas to the carriage, my pack slung over my shoulders. Payson didn't offer me an arm, but then again, I didn't want one. This was going to be awkward and awful. I wanted out of this realm. Away from these people.

Saying goodbye to Eloise and Feyla had been bittersweet. I was glad to be gone from Castle Vanstarr and the rulers there, but I was saddened to be leaving the two serving girls. I had grown close to them and felt a connection I rarely felt for anyone—even people I'd known for years, never mind days. Someday, if I had the gumption, I would return to this place and do something to help them—that was if I was even the rightful Keeper, of which I was still unsure.

Payson dutifully ignored me as the carriage took off down the sloping courtyard, and over the cobblestones in Silvercrest, at a jovial clip. Soon we were out of the city gates, and into an expanse of large manor houses for the wealthy, that didn't live within the city walls. Those stretched on for some time, followed by a wide expanse of farmland, grassland, and forest.

The trees rose in a dense wall ahead of us. Everything about this forest felt ancient, strong—like sentinels watching over something valuable. As the carriage rumbled along the dirt path, I noticed that it seemed unused. Grass dotted the middle of the road, unlike how it had appeared near the farms; packed and well-traveled. Once we broke into the dark wood, the dense canopy above us blotted out the sun, and the heat along with it, which was a blessed relief. Payson sat across from me; his focus out the window. He looked annoyed with everything.

"What is the plan when we get there?" I asked, stroking Silas in my lap.

His eyes flitted to mine and then back, and he lifted a meaty shoulder with a shrug.

Great. A big broody oaf. Wonderful.

For hours, I watched the world pass. It was while we were on a stretch of farmland that the carriage gave a mighty, massive jostle and lilted to the side. I was launched across the carriage and landed against the window, on top of Payson.

I grunted as he heaved me off the window, and I tumbled into his lap. My eyes searched for Silas and found him on the seat still, his claws dug in. I grumbled at the awkwardness of being in Payson's lap, but it was better than being splayed against the side of the carriage. I was just getting ready to move away when the door opened, and the attendant looked sheepishly at us. I hopped up.

"Your majesty, our wheel has been damaged and will need to be repaired."

Payson scowled but nodded. I leaped out the open door. I blinked at the dipping sunlight. At this rate, we wouldn't make it to the wall before nightfall, but I could see it ahead of us. We had about 2 miles left of grass plains and then there was a dark, dreary forest, two massive watchtowers and then it was the wall. Dark gray stone as far as the eye could see. It was intimidating, and enormous.

I felt fear for the first time. What if I couldn't get answers here? Was there someone there to give me answers?

Payson turned to one of the guards. "Get back to the castle." He looked to the sky. The waning sunlight. "Tell my father what has transpired and seek his counsel."

I didn't want to go into that creepy dark forest at night. I wanted to suggest staying somewhere for the night. Honestly, even sleeping in the carriage until daylight was preferable.

Payson's eyes followed mine to the dark forest and he swallowed. *It made him nervous too.*

With a sigh, he plunked down on the grass.

I followed suit. "What do we do now?"

He shrugged. I sighed again.

After what felt like hours, but was more like twenty minutes, I'd had enough of the silence. "I'm sorry about last night... I—" Did I lie? Ugh. "I was shocked. I... You're a prince. I am... no one."

He looked at me sideways, something played across his eyes. *Humor?* "I know."

Well, thanks, jerk. But what did I expect?

"My father wanted me to appear to the people as more than a spoiled prince and he thinks courting you will change that."

My eyes bulged. "Ah...do you want to...court me?"

His eyes scanned my face, and he shrugged. "You're beautiful and...unusual. Completely different from the Lord's daughters that I usually..." He looked away, sheepish.

"Court?" I finished with a grin.

He waved a hand. "Right."

I shrugged, and we were silent for a time.

"How long will it take the guard to get back to the castle?"

It had taken all day to get to this point with the carriage and the procession of guards.

"Honestly, I have no idea. At least... four hours, less if he rides like a Servine is chasing him."

I had read about the dragon-like creature but had assumed they were extinct. It had to be metaphorical... I shook my head. Back to the matter at hand.

"So, it's going to be well beyond dark before you get an answer from your father?"

"Well, he could send a messenger hawk..."

I sighed and laid back in the grass. The day was clear, the sky the most brilliant blue I had ever seen, with big puffy white clouds. I exhaled deeply through my nose. I was trying not to panic about my family at home, trying to analyze my self-preservation, and live in the moment. It was amazing here. Storybook. No one would ever believe me if I told them about this. I was trying my best to treat this whole insane ordeal as some fanciful vacation.

After several moments, I felt a large arm brush mine. A deep sigh wrenched from him, not in exasperation, but as a release, as he laid next to me. We enjoyed the moment together.

"I haven't done this since I was a kid. When... Before..."

I looked at him. "Before...?"

He swallowed but remained silent.

Hmph. Silas leaped onto me, and curled up on my stomach, sending Payson a dirty glare. I chuckled.

"How old are you?" I blurted.

"Seventeen summers."

Seventeen? No wonder he seemed childish and spoiled. He was so young.

"How old are *you*?" He asked, glancing at me.

"I'm nineteen."

He wiggled his eyebrows. "I like my ladies older."

I giggled. I couldn't help myself. Why hadn't we acted like this before? Had it been his father's influence? Princely duties swaying his actions and motives?

I had a feeling there was more pressure in being a prince than most realized. They saw a spoiled, bratty, rich kid, but never realized how influenced he was by his parents and the structure of monarchy. He was supposed to be something to everyone, but how often was he allowed to be a seventeen-year-old teenager with expressions, dreams, and thoughts all his own? I guaranteed it was few and far between, and that made me a little sad. It made me pity him—just a bit.

I elbowed him in the arm, and he sent me a goofy grin, which made him look kind of cute. "We could hike back a few miles... to the last village before nightfall," I offered.

He looked at me. "That's probably a good idea."

I blinked. "Yeah?"

He leaned up further and gave me an appraising look that ended with a smile. Another cute one. He'd never smiled like that in the castle. His smiles had been cocky sneers, which grated on me.

"Yes. Let's go." He sprang up and offered me a hand. Silas hopped off me to prowl a dandelion a few feet away. I gave Payson my right hand and he pulled me up.

Standing together in the sunlight, I looked up at him. In this light, in this situation, I found him attractive. Far more than I had before. I was not attracted *to* him, but I found him attractive now that he was acting...normal with me.

"To Kinnder Plains."

"Okeydokey."

"What?"

"Ah. I was agreeing. Sure. Let's do it."

Twilight settled against the stones of the watchtower as we passed the first keep and came upon the crossroads. In the distance the plains were flat with yellow grass, a slow-moving river snaked across the land, and the mountain range loomed in the distance. Along the riverbank and creek beds, trees sprouted, but otherwise, the land was sparse until the lush mountain valley in the distance. The village was nestled along the steppes. Wheatfields and cows dotted the surrounding lands. We were just approaching the village center when night descended. There was no castle, just a cluster of small buildings spanning out to a low wall, which housed a beautiful timber home, much larger than the rest. It sported bushes with tiny red berries out front, and I noticed four massive willow trees around the house.

"Newl lives there. Lord of Kinnder Plains," Payson offered at my pointed stare.

"Ah." If it were in my world, I'd have guessed it to be the mayor's house. I would have been close enough.

The inn wasn't large, but it looked clean and welcoming, with a small herb garden and various fruit-bearing trees, with a stone garden of beautiful flat river rocks. Half of the garden was under a balcony, which housed chairs for outdoor dining. Honestly, it was quite beautiful.

The innkeeper was a small, middle-aged man who ran the inn with his wife and teenage daughter, who took one look at Payson and fawned even before he was introduced as the prince. I tried not to roll my eyes. Payson secured us and his men's rooms, and board for the horses in a pleasant manner, which conflicted just a bit with the pampered persona he displayed in the castle.

I freshened up in my sparse, but tidy room. I was starving and I couldn't wait to sleep. I left Silas in my room as I went down for dinner, with a promise to bring him back something.

Dinner consisted of jackrabbit stew, which was surprisingly delicious. Payson was quiet and kept sneaking glances at Jeina, the innkeeper's daughter. She was pretty. Golden waves of blonde hair, and brilliant blue eyes. Her face was lovely and still blossoming into womanhood.

I elbowed him once, as he watched her bend down to get something from a low cupboard, and he choked on his stew, to the point I had to thump him on the back, which caused guffaws from his guards. His cheeks were painted pink, but he sent me a sheepish grin. I laughed. The guards looked at one another with smiles and quiet laughter. It was as though they had not seen this side of the prince, nor laughed with their monarchs in a long time. I felt a strange vibration against my skin as if something shifted in this world. As if something opened an eye and looked at me. I shivered against it, and my eyes searched the windows as if expecting something to be out there. But there was no boogie man or monster. I was crazy.

Dinner was whisked away with a promise of dessert, and I was beyond ecstatic. Dessert didn't seem to be a grandiose thing in Castle Vanstarr, and although I loved the fruit and honeyed bread they offered, I craved something sweet. Delectable. I had a fondness for junk food and knew I had lost a few pounds from not being able to binge on Oreos and French fries.

"Cloudberry pie," Jiena said, with a wide smile. The red filling oozed out enticingly. It tasted like a cross between blueberries and cherries. I sighed as I pushed another forkful into my mouth. This was delicious.

"I've never had anything like this. Where I grew up, we have jack berries, and my nanny used to make a pie. Gods it was incredible," Payson sighed in delight.

I glanced at him as our elbows brushed. "Where did you grow up?"

"Not far from here actually. Closer to the mountains, but on the line of plain and valley. You can see the village from the crossroads. It was called Cahava Valley."

"Was?"

"I think it has been abandoned since my father... When he took sovereign."

I swallowed but didn't press him. He had divulged so much to me this day, and I didn't want to ask a million questions. I didn't *want* to get close to him. It was clear what was between us was platonic, and I liked him, but I didn't want to get close to him. Feeling something for Eloise and Feyla was bad enough. I would miss them, and I didn't want to miss this big oaf too.

Payson led me to my room and stood at the doorway. "This has been shockingly great."

I snickered. "It has. Why couldn't it have been like this before? We could've had fun together instead of being... awkward."

He laughed, the sound coming from deep in his belly. "I don't know. I let my father get in my head and make me uncomfortable. I felt like I had to push you into a conversation, push you into..." He shook his head. "I'm not entirely sure, but I wish I wouldn't have listened." He looked at me with a gentle expression. "I wish I would have just been myself because I think we could have been friends."

I nodded. I thought the same thing. "I guess now we'll never know."

"Who knows what fate has in store for us, Kate." He grinned like a fool, and I punched him in the gut. "*Oomph.*"

Fudge. I just punched a prince. I put my hand to my mouth instantly and backed away. "Payson, I am so s—"

He lunged for me. I squealed and he grabbed me around the middle and then—

Ground his knuckles into my head. A noogie? The prince of Evirness just gave me a noogie... I laughed so hard at the ridiculousness of it, that I snorted, then laughed harder at the sound. The prince chortled right along with me. Guffawing his ass off.

We eyed each other warily, anticipating retaliation. Payson braced his hands on his knees as laughter bubbled up from deep in his belly again, and I giggled into my hand.

We were idiots. It was nice seeing this side of him... I liked him. Truly. I wish we had spent my time in the City of Starlight acting this way. Yes, he was pompous and spoiled and his views of the world were *very* different than mine—slavery and such coming to mind—but I didn't think deep down, that he was cruel. Not in the calculating way of his father. I think Payson could be likable without his father whispering in his ear. He was just naïve, and followed his parents blindly, even if that meant sacrificing his wants.

Finally catching our breath, Payson grinned at me, his eyes bright. Foolish boy. I returned his grin.

"I like you, Keeper. I didn't think I would, but I do. I..." He sobered and looked away. Something deep passed in his eyes, something someone so young shouldn't carry.

I bit my lip and touched his arm. He followed my unmarred appendage to my face, and our eyes met. I felt something for him, not even slightly romantic, but a kinship brought about by our foolishness and the fact that instead of being a stubborn, spoiled jackass, he had taken my suggestions all evening, and followed my guidance. There was hope for change in this mottled world. They didn't need a Keeper, but a ruler to help bring forth change.

Could Payson be that for them when the time came?

"I like you too, Pays." I smiled, and he returned it.

"This reminds me of brighter days. When I hadn't seen... the things I have," his ochre eyes grew sad, haunted.

Things that his father had done, said, envisioned. It plagued me—the look in his eyes—long after we said our goodnights, and I fell into bed.

The next morning, after we had eaten a hearty breakfast, we made our way to our fixed carriage. Payson had told me that morning that sometime in the night his guard had returned with the advice of his father to leave me at the wall and return home. *What a guy*, I thought, sardonically.

Payson gave me a knowing smile at my sour look and bumped his shoulder to mine. "I won't leave you until I know you'll be okay."

"You really think the wall will give me answers?"

"Honestly, Ka*t*e, I have no idea."

I slapped his arm at the name, which he said with a very obnoxiously pronounced T instead of D.

"I don't know a lot about the wall, only that it cut off trade routes, waterways, resources, and people from families. It divided the country and is *impenetrable*. There are ways around it, across the ocean and far out to the west past the borders of our kingdom. I've heard both voyages are perilous and take longer than they're worth. I don't claim to know any of it for certain."

"But what am I to do at the wall if it is impenetrable? Can I come back to the castle with you if I can't figure it out?" *And find another way home.*

"Of course," he waved a hand. "I won't just leave you there, despite what my father suggests. You will come back with me. Damn his consequences."

I smiled at him. Our newfound friendship ran deep enough that he was willing to deal with his father's wrath for me. I leaned over and kissed his cheek after we mounted the steps to our carriage. His eyes widened at my affection, and he touched the spot with his fingertips. He gave me a warm smile.

The watchtower waved us on, signaling nothing amiss. As we entered the forest, we held our breath and a fine mist enveloped us. After another hour, our carriage jostled to a stop. Payson gripped both of my hands before giving me a disarming smile. "Whatever happens, I'm with you."

I smiled at him gratefully. It was hard to believe he was only seventeen. He seemed ages older. I squeezed his hands back. To think I had disliked him all this time. It truly was a pity.

I had no idea what to expect, but as I stepped out of the carriage and got a good look at the wall all thoughts dissipated. It was massive. Moss and vines covered the stone for about six feet, and then it just soared up to the sky. Close to three stories high. Opaque and terrifying. What superfluous use of stone.

It was said that the magic of Evirness had done this when the Keeper had abandoned them. There were no grouted spots of fusion, as you would see in a manmade structure. This was a sheer, solid wall. No gaps, no grout—just a rough mountain of stone. I wondered where the stone had come from, if it was magic that had created it or if the magic took the stone from another place and put it here.

The back of my neck tingled, my left hand vibrated with sensation, and I exhaled shakily. My Spidey senses or whatever the hell they were, were on high alert. My body thrummed with energy. Heat shivered across me, similar in feeling to what Aoife's searing glares did to me. I stamped down the fear it created and looked around clinically.

Nothing grew for four or five feet in front of the wall, save for the moss and climbing vines. Even the forest was silent, with no chirping birds, or scurrying animals. No wonder there was no light in the forest, the wall drowned out the sun. It engulfed the world in darkness.

I gulped past my trepidation and walked up to it. My senses leaped and my left hand vibrated. I glanced back at Payson; he stood alert in front of the horses, guards fanned out around him, their hands on the hilts of their swords. Payson's eyes were wide and wandering the wall as mine had. When they met mine, he gave me a slow nod. He would give me space unless I needed him. He expected me to find nothing and return with him. I saw resolve flit across his features.

I looked down at Silas who sat at my feet. I bent down and rubbed his head. "Stay with me," I whispered, needing his reassurance as much as I feared that if something were to happen, he would be lost to me.

Finally, I lifted my left hand. The thumb and forefinger shook, and my body tensed, ready to spring—back or forward, I was uncertain. The back of my neck itched so badly, but I refused to scratch it. Instead, I slowly extended my left hand, doing what it wanted, to touch the wall. My eyes widened as my hand vibrated with such intensity, like a hummingbird's wings, that it began to blur and took the shape of a...key and then—

I screeched as I was sucked through the wall and popped out the other side, landing on my knees on the moss-covered ground. I gasped for breath. Silas mewed at my side. I whipped my head around but saw nothing but the wall.

Had I just gone through it? That was not *possible!*

"Payson!" I screamed, again and again. I went to the wall, pounding my fists against it until they ached. I screamed his name a handful more times. A tear streamed down my cheek, but I hastily wiped it away.

I stepped back and adjusted the pack on my back, pushed the braid back over my shoulder, looked down at the cat who watched me with mild interest and then surveyed the forest I had ended up in.

Shit. I was not getting back to Payson, or Silvercrest, or home from the looks of it, because these towering pines did not scream *North Carolina* to me. Although I had to admit this side of the forest seemed more welcoming. It was not dark or dreary but bursting with life. Birds chirped and sang, small animals scurried from the mossy undergrowth, and even flowers sprung up. Dappled sunlight filtered in through openings in the pine boughs and birch branches. The smell of honeysuckle and lichen trickled into my nose, and I inhaled deeply. It looked like an enchanted fairytale forest. Now, this I could handle. It didn't send a shiver of trepidation up my spine but calmed me. This reminded me of the forests at home, not that I had any delusion I was home.

I was on the other side of the wall. Whatever that meant.

"Alright, bud, ready for another jovial jaunt through the woods?"

In answer, Silas mewed and trotted on ahead of me. There was a path directly ahead of us as if the road I'd been on had met this one before the divide. This one appeared just as infrequently used as the other side, but it was still a blatant path. I started when I looked over and saw two deer foraging to the right of us. They ambled off as soon as we got too close, but they had been magnificent and larger than any deer I had ever seen.

We carried on. Sweat clung to my back as the sun heated my face and shoulders. I felt myself burning in the blotchy swatches of sunlight, and I had to stop periodically to take sips from the skein of water I had smuggled into my pack. Thank goodness I had been smart enough to do so.

The sun was at its highest in the sky, marking it to be early afternoon. I had been hiking for a few hours when Silas stopped dead ahead and turned to me. *Shoot.* That was never good. Then I heard it. Hoofbeats. Did I hide? Jump out and ask for directions? Where the hell was I and how did I summon a portal to get me home?

I'm not sure anyone, including myself, thought I'd be able to unlock and walk through the wall, and it granted me no answers aside from... Well, I had made it through an *impenetrable* wall out of no apparent gate or door. My hand had turned into a magical key... I was trying to ignore that fact—because it was insanity.

Instead of running and hiding, I simply stepped off the path, giving the horses ample room to go by.

They stopped as they saw me. My cat postured ahead of me, his tail flicking.

One man hopped off his horse, the others followed suit. This man ate up the ground as he stalked toward me, and it was all I had in me not to balk at his menacing presence. To say I was intimidated was an understatement. Silas let out a short mew and trotted to my side, but he didn't seem perturbed. I prayed he was a good judge of character. He had hated the Barthol's but seemed completely fine with the terrifyingly threatening man stalking towards me.

Panic seized me and rooted me to the spot. I saw my death looming. His sword was unsheathed in his hand, not raised but it would take only seconds to cut off my head. My eyes swept across the gleaming blade.

When the man reached me, I had to look up at him. He was tall with a powerful frame. Not beefy like Payson. He had the air of an authority figure. He was dressed in all black. Daggers glinted from the leather vest over his broad chest, and armguards of dark blue and glinting silver graced his arms. Was this sneering, menacing man an assassin? With that lean, powerful frame... It was possible. A mercenary sent to kill me on Ainon's orders?

My mind raced. What did I say? What did I do?

My heart sprinted in my chest; a heat of panic simmered in my throat. Could I talk my way out of this? I had never been good at talking, so doubtful. I closed my eyes to the strike of metal that was sure to come. After a few seconds of nothing, I looked up into the eyes of the darkest blue I'd ever seen, almost violet. His face was... interesting. Dark hair, thickly lashed midnight eyes, and a straight nose, on a perfectly symmetrical face with a full mouth. The shadow of facial hair growth on his face was the only thing that stopped him from being *pretty*.

Stop ogling him, dumbass, he's going to fucking kill you.

"Who, in the stars, are you?"

"What—"

"Are you daft? Who are you and what are you doing?"

Hostile much, asshole? Sheesh. "I'm Kaidyn Flynn, apparently the Key Keeper."

His eyes narrowed. "You expect us to believe that?" But he sheathed his brilliant sword.

Piss off, is what I really wanted to say, but I decided that a semblance of truth was the smartest route. "King Ainon sent me to the wall to find answers. I..."

How could I explain? I had a weird sensation in my left hand, and when I put it against the wall it turned into a key, to which the wall popped me through to...this side.

I needed to get to wherever I needed to go to get home. Let them think me insane, so long as they didn't see me as a threat and murder me. King Ainon had claimed that I would have safe passage anywhere in Evirness because of *what* I was. Had he been lying to me? Hoping I would get killed?

"I touched the wall and it dumped me onto this side."

"It—You..." He turned to the man with the bow. This guy was smaller with a dark green hat with feathers on it. He looked like someone I would cast to play Robin Hood. Even his attire was spot on. *Where the hell am I?*

"I mean she looks like a Keeper."

The tall man rolled his eyes. "Because you've seen so many Keepers, Aven."

The Robin Hood wannabe chuckled. "Okay, well from what I've read she certainly seems to fit the profile."

They were talking about me as if I weren't in front of them.

"Hadn't the last one had a cat too?"

Wait—what? Then my heart skipped a beat. Amara. I do think the cat's name had been in it. Oh my gosh. It had never added up before.

"I...You might be right, Av."

I'm right here, dicks. I'd obsess over whether the white cat had been a portal jumping feline later.

"Well, might as well get her to Rhone. He'll know what to do."

The proclaimed King of the North—as the Barthol's called him. Although Eloise insisted that wasn't true, it was actually the opposite. I wasn't sure what to believe. I didn't care who or what was right—at least I tried telling myself that. Although the deeper part of the story held my curiosity.

Payson had said that no one in the realm would ever hurt me. I was sacred territory. A beacon of hope so powerful, I was revered as highly as a Goddess. Not that I wanted any of that, but he had insisted I would have safe passage no matter where I went. I prayed he was right, as these men scrutinized me.

"Alright. Let's get you to the king."

This sounded all too familiar. I rolled my eyes at the absurdity of it all.

I looked at the horses with wonder and apprehension. The dark man had dismounted a massive gray dappled horse with fur on its feet. The large horse was beautiful, regal, and sturdy looking. I loved horses, but I'd never ridden. My mom had taken me to a barn when I was about twelve to learn to ride. I'd loved the barn; the sweet smell of hay, the gentle sounds of the horses, their warm muzzles against my hands, but then I had overheard the other girls making remarks about how I could never be a good rider. I could never jump or show a horse with one hand, even though I had seen countless cowboys ride with no problem one-handed. I had called my mom to get me after only being there for a few hours. If I was going to fail at something, why try? I had been young and hadn't learned yet that I could do anything anyone else could do if I tried hard enough. I had just found so few things that required both hands that I was willing to be challenged with, to fail at, and still be worth me continuing to try. I hadn't liked a challenge, especially one people could make fun of me for. Being the brunt of jokes and bullying was something I avoided. Did I miss out on a lot in life because of that fear? Yes. Absolutely. But I'd never been pushed to try to do anything. I was a bit spoiled and privileged in that sense, but as I got older that immaturity had become a slow burn of annoyance. As I aged, I realized I wanted to be challenged, but then I wondered if I was too old for such things. Becoming a vet tech would be a massive challenge with one hand, but it was worth the try. My parents had tried to talk me out of it, for fear of rejection and failure—so came my life of privilege and indulgence, but I would face the challenge come fall when college classes began.

So, the horses fascinated me, but I didn't think I could be a successful rider, or I hadn't in my youth. It was on my list of things to revisit from my past. Things I hadn't bothered to be challenged by, but now wished to be.

I knew enough now that some riding styles required only one hand to hold the reins, and cues could be given with your legs. I think I could ride if given direction, but now was not the time to overcome a challenge from the past.

The dark man watched me then rolled his eyes to the sky. "You're kidding. You can't ride?"

"I…" I was embarrassed. In this world horses were the primary mode of transportation, but I mean there *were* carriages. I hadn't had to ride in the days I had been here. *Riding* wasn't the only means with which to travel, but I saw no carriages now.

"Gods, why…are *you* the Keeper?" He snarled in exasperation.

His words stung. I didn't care if I *were* the Keeper, I just wanted to go home. But just as the journal suggested things were beginning to blur. Eloise telling me her backstory had made me feel invested, her words to right the world burned in the back of my mind. Haunted me.

"I…"

He growled in frustration and before I could even blink his hands were at my waist.

"Hey!" I bellowed and thrashed as he picked me up like I weighed nothing and set me on the huge gray horse I had been admiring. My right hand gripped the saddle as my legs found their balance. My eyes met his midnight ones, and I swallowed. Well, I was on a horse.

I watched as he bent down and picked up Silas gingerly. Silas didn't even bat an eye, or a claw for that matter, unlike I had expected. No, my cat purred and bumped his head against the man's chin. *Traitor!*

The man rubbed my gray furball's cheek kindly with his knuckle and rubbed his chin back against the cat as he held him gently. What the hell.

Then he set Silas on my lap. I swallowed and wrapped my arms around Silas' body. Would my cat ride on a horse? Did cats ride on horses?

I didn't think this was going to work, but in a quick, graceful movement, the powerful man was on the horse behind me.

"What the h—"

His body went flush against mine, my back to his front. One arm snaked around me to collect the reins, the other secured me around my waist. I squeaked at his nearness, but he gave me no time to do anything else. I felt his thighs apply pressure, his tongue clicked, and the horse moved forward. His arm around me kept me in place, giving me the ability to worry about holding the cat instead of myself.

I was shocked and speechless for several moments as my body adjusted to the horse's movements and his arm around me. Once my wits were about me, I demanded, "What in the hell do you think you—"

"Keeper, we have places to be and no time for your bullshit."

My mouth snapped shut. *My bullshit!?* He was such a dick. This whole situation was *bullshit* and I had no control over it. It wasn't my fault I was expected to ride a horse in this Godforsaken place. I didn't ask to be here. I didn't *want* to be here.

The man with the green hat grinned openly at me. I almost stuck my tongue out at him as we passed but resisted the urge. I simply stared. His grin deepened; dimples flashed.

Damn it. Damn all of this. Where were these people taking me? How long would we be traveling?

I looked at the Robin Hood look-alike again. He looked in every direction, scouring as if looking for a threat. His horse was a burst of gorgeous sunshine gold. The horses moved steadily, the gait gentle and lulling. I realized I liked being on horseback. Not against this man's body. Not at all. I felt...embarrassed that I needed to ride with him, but thankful they hadn't just left me, or made me walk. Silas was asleep in my arms lulled by the movements and was a complete deadweight.

"Where are we going?" A silent moment passed where I resisted the urge to look over my shoulder.

"Hawksedge." His voice was a husky, deep timbre, and vibrated against my body.

I had seen that on the map. A castle on the northern tip of Evirness. The map had seemed thus far to be accurate.

Silence hushed over the group as we made our way steadily out of the forest to open grassland. Dark green highlands swept on for miles. Long grass swayed in the breeze, dotted by rocky outcrops and tall rolling hills. To the left, I could see ridges and tall spires of jagged mountain ranges. A wind blew continuously, but it wasn't frigid. I had hiked enough to know what the wind felt like at a high elevation. We were surrounded by mountain ranges. This looked very much like moorlands. Harsh, but incredible.

The horses picked a path up and over a ridge, and as I looked out, a breeze ruffled my hair. This really was incredible.

We were headed through the center of the small expanse of green mountains. No one spoke as we made our way down the ridge and through the green world that shimmered emerald in the sunlight. I rubbed Silas beneath his chin as we steadily trotted through the pass. Two tall watchtowers greeted us.

"Oi, Captain!"

The man behind me did some gesture I couldn't see.

Captain? What kind of captain?

His body was warm, and solid against my back. I didn't *want* to notice, but I did. I tried to think of anything else, and my mind drifted to Payson. Was he worried about me? Did he understand I had gone *through* the wall?

Once through the pass, supple farmland rushed to greet us. Fluffy, longhaired cows stopped their chewing to stare. Massive stone buildings with thatched roofs came into view. Goats bleated, dogs barked, and horses nickered as we passed. We came to a jagged mountain ridge to the right of us, and a swath of dark forest. Skinny waterfalls cascaded from the mountainside and little bridges had been erected in their path, the horses plodded confidently.

A blonde woman came up beside us. My eyes scanned her. She was tall, athletically built, like the man I sat in front of. These were warriors. She had on dark breeches and a sword at her hip. There was iron armor at her shoulders, and she had gloves that covered her hands, but not her fingers. She was beautiful with pale blue eyes, and high cheekbones. Her white-blonde hair was braided along the side of her head.

"Reid," her voice was strong and confident.

I felt the man behind me shift.

"Yes, Bronwen?" *Was that annoyance in his voice?*

"What are we doing with the girl?"

"Bringing her to Rhone." *Definitely annoyance.*

"Is she truly the Keeper?" *I'm right here.*

"Appears that way." His voice was gruff.

It does appear that way, I thought grimly.

"Can we trust—"

"Back in line, Bronwen. It is already decided."

"But Hawksedge—"

"Enough." I felt him shift again and knew he was giving the blond woman a pointed glare. She got the message and stilled her horse so that Reid's big gray moved alone. He clicked his tongue, and I felt his thighs press into the outside of mine as he urged his steed into a gentle trot. As the land leveled out, he urged the horse faster, to a rolling canter. I didn't bounce around like I thought I would as the horse shifted, its furry feet gliding across the packed dirt path. We passed a wagon filled with hay, and the wagon driver saluted Reid and the others.

The Robin Hood bowman urged his horse next to ours when we slowed. Cliffs and mountains spired to the sky on our left again, and I felt something shift in the air. The back of my neck tingled, and the thing I had felt back at the inn—like I was being watched by some big bad monster—surged inside me. Tension radiated, and crawled against my skin.

I looked around frantically for the source.

"What is it, Keeper?"

"I... I don't know." I didn't, but the feeling put me on edge.

Reid shifted his gaze to the bowman and some silent communication stretched between them.

How did all the people in this world seem to talk silently to each other? Was there some magic at play that they could speak inside each other's minds, or was it just that much intuition for each other to know what the other is asking? In my time technology dulled our intuition for other people.

The bowman nodded and shifted his horse away.

"Where is he going?"

"To check the area," the captain's rumbling voice rippled against my back. For some reason, being with him made me feel safe—which was disturbingly conflicted with the menacing intimidation I had felt when he'd approached me earlier.

The feeling of something lingering against my skin faded as we made our way to a cluster of stone homes that fanned out to the river, flanked by watchtowers. The captain stopped their procession when a rider returned.

"Spiders, Captain. Only a few. We've despatched them, but a doorway must be close by. Aven awaits your orders."

Spiders? Why did spiders matter? Were they a bad omen?

The captain cursed. "Four men will remain to ensure no more creatures are lurking to attack livestock."

Livestock... They were worried about spiders going after their farm animals. Spiders had to mean something different in this realm than mine. That or they were poisonous.

"Of course, sir."

I felt Reid's assessing gaze against my neck and it prickled with his intensity.

"How did you know?"

Huh? I swallowed. "About what?"

"The spiders. The doorway."

"I didn't."

"No? Your whole body tensing in awareness and us finding the spiders were mere coincidence?"

"Yeah." But the answer sounded silly to *my* ears. I had felt something and knew it wasn't right. Had I sensed the open doorway they spoke of? I didn't understand what that meant exactly, but what I'd read about the Keepers said they sensed doorways and were able to open and close them—but I had wanted to believe I was *not* the Keeper. I had banked my pleas for home on that improbability. But now...

Reid scoffed, then sighed. I felt him put pressure on the horse's sides and we moved steadily onward.

At some point in our journey, Robin Hood returned. I eyed him. He looked no worse for wear—if anything his eyes were brighter. He caught my stare and gave me a wicked grin, dimples flashing. My eyes snapped back to the front. No man should have a smile like that. It was sinful and...Why was my face wanting to smile in answer? What was wrong with me?

Hours passed. We rode fast, far faster than the carriage ride from Silvercrest, but we were still chasing the sunlight.

"We're going to be entering the city of Hawksedge."

Reid must have glared at him, but Robin Hood just shrugged and pointed out Eagle Ridge to the right.

The cluster of cottages grew, and then I noticed a wall spanning out, a rampart above, with more watchtowers. There was a massive crest of a hawk etched into the door. Its wings wide, its eyes an orange-colored orb.

The gates slowly opened with a mechanism, like Silvercrest. Inside the buildings were massive and made of dark gray weathered stone and wood. There were raised stone garden beds next to each building filled with herbs, vegetables, and flowers. The center of the city had a small fountain, the same as the one in Silvercrest. Next to it was a statue depicting a warrior woman. She had a long braid over one shoulder, and light armor etched into the stone. Her face was otherworldly beautiful, with succulent lips and large almond-shaped eyes. At her feet was a massive dog that I thought looked like a Wolfhound. The enormous square pool that the water cascaded into had lily pads and golden fan-tailed fish in it.

"The sculpture is of Henna, the goddess of the night, the moon, and stars. She guides our warriors—"

"Aven," Reid's voice cut through my avid attention.

"What?" Aven looked at him innocently.

"There's no point explaining any of this to her until Rho—"

"But she should know where she is—"

"No matter."

Aven huffed and sent an annoyed glare at the captain. I almost smiled at him for it. Their connection was apparent. Were they brothers? Although opposite sides of a coin. The captain all height, bulk, and darkness. The bowman was small, light, and mischievous.

The city stretched out before us. I hated to admit that both Silvercrest and Hawkspire were gorgeous. Similar in architecture and structure, but unique for the different environment and materials.

Soon we hit the end of the wall where a gigantic gate awaited, a gatehouse and a tower on each side.

"Liamara." Reid hollered up to the guards, and the gate creaked open.

To the left were crumbling stone walls and slate rock faces. The path swept against the rocky ledge. A small dense forest to the right, then pastureland. Stone posts and wooden fencing stretched across it, bordering a river, and then looped straight ahead. It was broken with smaller fences, paddocks, and buildings.

"The barracks," Aven said as he pointed to a large building, with a stable. Horses whickered and trotted up to the fence as we made our way into the courtyard. In the middle of it was a beautiful, towering sculpture of a hawk. Beyond that was a short bridge, a tiny rivulet of water runoff from the mountain against the castle beneath and connected with the indoor plumbing of the castle. I had read a lot of fantasy books; I knew most of what I was looking at. Being an avid reader made me not as shocked, but I was still a child of another realm and had been born and bred there, not here. I had been deceptively adept at picking up on the language and mannerisms to hide my ignorance.

My eyes swept over the ancient stones of the castle. It was less grand than the one in the south but just as impressive. This one was more like a wizened, battle-worn warrior slumbering quietly. The southern castle had been tall, full of towers, parapets, and spires reaching up to the sky, this castle was wide and stout. Ready to weather the winter storms. It seemed fitting with the landscape.

Stable hands came out and grasped the horse's reins. I felt Reid shift, and one minute he was behind me, the next he was on the ground.

"Tomorrow you will learn to ride," he said as he gripped my waist and pulled me down—cat and all before I could protest.

He was such an arrogant prick. I glared since he had set me in front of him. I had to look up, but still. He returned it and after a few minutes of us glaring at each, a battle of wills for the ages, Aven cleared his throat with a sly smile. I glared at him too, and he threw up his hands in defeat. The captain and I still stood toe to toe, and I noted Bronwen loitered nearby. Most of the guards had fled to the barracks, but a few lingered. Reid stepped back, dismissed the guards with a wave of his hand, and sauntered over the bridge to the wide steps of the castle. Massive red poppies and climbing vines covered each side of the covered archway. The aesthetics of this castle were more well-kept than Vanstarr.

Torches of light began filtering across the buildings, casting amber over the courtyard. It was...magical. I pinched myself, for at least the hundredth time.

Aven, with his tapered hat, tipped to show his unnervingly sexy dimples and green and topaz eyes. He offered his arm, I gave him a small smile as I took it.

There were carvings of hawks and stars on the doors, and four guards stood before them. This place seemed well fortified, even more than the castle of the south.

Flaming torches and lanterns stuttered to life as we stepped to the door. We had raced the night and won.

This castle was simple, but it felt *lived in*, warmer, and far more welcoming. Directly ahead was a raised stone bed filled with herbs. Probably grown inside so they could be plucked throughout the year, even in the cold. Beside that was a small water fountain the same as the one I had seen in Silvercrest with the moon and stars. The moon was a dusky yellow orb, and the stars were carved from polished stone. To the direct right appeared to be a hall of some kind with tall, skinny, arched windows and I could just make out a long table.

"The great hall and kitchens," Aven offered. The arched doors were flanked by one massive stone fireplace, which was easily as large as my Dad's SUV.

"Inner courtyard, solarium, interior gardens," Aven said and pointed to those arched openings on the left. Windows were everywhere letting the darkness seep in.

Past the fountain was a massive double door, engraved with birch branches and the hawk sigil. Next to the door were staircases that looped upward.

Hawksedge held an ancient air of strapping warrior. The many harsh winters emphasized the worn stone. Everywhere I looked was a plant or painting or something beautiful. It made the dusky gray stones come to life, to feel like a home. It felt friendly and hospitable.

The captain's boots echoed on the floor as he stalked to the doors, and two guards stepped out to open them for him.

Aven, my hand still on his arm, followed him.

CHAPTER 8

One too many kings

They were taking me to the man from the journal. The one that the journal owner—which I was leaning towards being my aunt—had been in love with, and I had gathered he'd broken her heart. I already hated the old man and hadn't even met him yet.

Reid ate up the hall with his long legs, and I was so focused on not falling I didn't quite register that at the end of the hall was a throne.

"Your majesties," Reid stepped up to the wide stairs, where three worn and comfortable gray cushioned chairs with high backs sat on a dais.

Three people sat on them. The woman in the middle was small-boned with raven hair and pale skin. She was lovely in a regal way. Not terrifying like Aoife, but still intimidating.

The man in the next chair was young and handsome. Brown hair, light eyes. The next chair held the older man. The northern *king*. He was identical in facial structure to the youth, but his hair was lighter, his eyes a pale brown.

That answered that. My aunt couldn't have been the journal writer, speaking of Rhone as if they were lovers because this man was far too young. Aunt Millie had been in her seventies when she passed away, this man only looked to be about forty. I was further stumped by that revelation.

That also meant that the Amara spoken of in the journal was not the cat my aunt had in my realm. Interesting.

Aven bowed, and I stood awkwardly.

"Sire, I have a girl here who claims she is related to the Keeper," Reid stated with contempt.

The older man stood abruptly, his eyes wide and brilliant. He stepped to the edge of the dais and surveyed me, his eyes holding on Silas in my arms.

"Is that so?" He scrutinized me. "Your name?" His voice held an edge of excitement.

"Kaidyn Flynn."

"I am King Rhone Celestria." He gestured. "My wife, Eranora. My son and heir, Kavall."

I tipped my head to them. Kavall did the same to me. Eranora continued a cold gaze, but it was pained and nothing like Aoife's glares and heat.

"So, how did you come to the north, Kaidyn Flynn?" Reid blurted. I could tell he wanted to interrogate me further but held himself in check.

"Ki... Ainon sent me with a procession to the wall. He told me answers on how to get home would lie there. I touched the wall, and fell through it."

The guard captain cocked his head. Rhone sucked in a breath. I noticed his eyes were the color of polished bronze, and they were lovely.

Rhone whispered, *fell through,* under his breath.

"Well, girl, please continue."

I resisted the urge to grumble *piss off* to the captain. It was on the tip of my tongue, but I was too tired for snarky retorts. "My aunt was, apparently, the last Keeper here."

"Has... Did your aunt pass the artifacts to you?" Rhone asked, and I noted there was something in his expression, some anticipation.

I nodded.

"Do you have an amulet?"

I shook my head. "Ainon asked as well. I was not left a necklace."

Wait! My eyes widened. I had found that gemstone necklace in the trunk in the Keeper tower. It had appeared very amulet-*like.* I tried to remain passive. I wasn't sure if I wanted to display all my cards upfront. I'd rather discover what the amulet did before revealing that I had it—if that were even the one, they spoke about.

His eyes beseeched me. "Left?"

"Yes, when Aunt Millie passed away."

"Millicent has passed to the stars?"

I had no idea what that meant. "Yes..." His look was one of sadness and memory. I bit my lip. "My Aunt Millie was the last Keeper, then, truly?"

Rhone's eyes turned distant, their bronze coloring darkening to amber. "Yes," he said hollowly.

"She left me a trunk with a cloak, dagger, gemstones, and a map."

His eyes bored into mine. He had to have known Millie with the emotions on his features. There was true sadness there, private, and deep. It was a long moment before he schooled his features. "I wonder why she did not leave the necklace..." He tapped his lip with a finger.

"So does that mean I'm not the Keeper?"

"Has the magic passed to you?"

"Ah... I don't think so?"

He cocked his head and came down one step. I noticed the captain tense at my side, his hand going to his sword. The guards around us each put a hand to the hilts of their swords as if I were a threat. My dagger was in my pack, I held a cat in my arms, what kind of threat could I pose?

Rhone's eyes snagged on Silas. "She had a cat. Amara."

"Yes," I said, but didn't wish to explain to him the adoption and all that.

The journal... No, no, the age thing didn't make sense. None of this made sense. How had he known Amara then?

"Why—" He sucked in a breath, and his eyes slowly flicked back to the throne chairs, and he cleared his throat. "You must be exhausted."

I exhaled a deep breath. *You have no idea.*

"Your aunt leaving had terrible magical repercussions that ruined a once prosperous country," Reid chimed in, like the asshole he was.

My eyes narrowed as I turned to him. "My aunt had good reason to leave, I'm s—"

"Stand down, Captain," Rhone's voice was strong with authority and thick with emotion.

Reid exhaled noisily and looked to the ceiling.

"We aren't saying she didn't have her reasons, Kaidyn. I know she did." He gave me a look that said he knew far more than he could say. "But it doesn't change anything. The captain is right. This divide has ruined lives. Evirness was once a revered country. It had bountiful farmlands, rich trade, and prosperous and wealthy commerce. Waterways were abundant with goods. We now hear that most of the lands beyond the sea refuse to do business with Ainon. He's let the ports, and harbor cities become poor because he's too prideful to negotiate tactfully."

I lifted a shoulder. I knew little about the city, but I had to admit the people did seem to be poverty-stricken and discorded. The bits of information I had gathered from Eloise and the guard suggested that Ainon was putting funds into remodeling instead of progression.

"Does the city look in despair?"

I shrugged. "Yes, the city—with what little I saw, and understood—looked impoverished. There was discord. Some threw fruit at the carriage."

I watched Rhone's throat bob with emotion. "Alas, the rumors are true then." He sighed. "I've heard that Ainon has even changed the look of Silvercrest."

I cocked my head. "The buildings are obnoxiously bright white with red roofs." I'm unsure if this is what he meant by 'the look' but that's what stood out to me.

"Ah." He took a deep breath. "It was not always so." He looked to his wife, who was taking it all in with—I noticed with a start—a tear in her eye. The cold look she had cast me was gone, replaced with one of sorrow and fraught with a pain I could not comprehend.

"The colors were pale yellow, shining silver, dark purple, dusky gray—to replicate a starry sky."

That made sense. City of *Starlight*—those colors. More sense than the unpleasant white and red. The older guard had been right when he said that the mica on the cobblestones had matched the rest of the city.

"I'm sorry I did not see *that*."

He surprised me with a small chuckle. "Indeed, little Keeper, indeed." He looked again at my cat, and without hesitation came up and ran a finger over the cat's head. Reid tensed beside me and stepped closer, but I stood still. I didn't want to be run through with a sword, and I imagined that Silas would scratch the king anyway, and I'd have to deal with *that*. But to my surprise, the cat rubbed his cheek against his finger.

The king gave a small smile. "Millicent was..."

There was so much more in his face, his emotions, which begged questions from me. His eyes still seemed far away, like I was intruding on a memory. I had a feeling that confirmation the journal was Millie's was right here, but the age difference... I couldn't understand that.

My eyes skimmed over Rhone's stoic wife. She was looking dutifully away as if she knew there had been something between the last keeper and her husband, but I was not convinced. The age thing just really threw me off.

"If she left those things to you, she must have assumed the magic passed to you. But she never explained anything to you? Trained you before her passing?"

"No, nothing."

He sighed and dropped his hands from the cat. "No matter, we will—"

"Did you know her... well?" I knew he did, but I wanted to hear what he had to say about his relationship with her.

"I...Yes, I knew her well."

I could see the loss of great love, but Rhone was silent.

"I...I'm not sure why I'm here or what it is I can do. But I *must* get home."

Reid groaned. "Keeper, you must bring down the wall!"

"I'm not the Keeper!" My eyes whipped to his. Softer, I stated, "At least I don't *want* to be." Because honestly, I wasn't so sure anymore if I was or wasn't, but it didn't change my need to get home.

"Do you have the brand?" *Brand?* "On the back of your neck," Rhone offered at my quizzical expression.

I remembered the tremendous tingling on the back of my neck when I had touched the trunk and the dagger. I had checked numerous times and hadn't seen a *brand*. Discoloration, sure. I hadn't checked since I had been here, but it still did tingle from time to time and I recalled something from the diary that had mentioned a brand, but I had skimmed so much that little had stuck, aside from a few names and the personal bits that were imprinted to my brain.

"No." I didn't think I had a brand, but either way, I wasn't showing them. The nape of my neck seemed too intimate like a breach of my security.

"I am unsure, but you made it through the wall…"

Did I tell them about my deformed hand and how it had turned into a key? It wasn't the first time it had done it, either, so it was most definitely *something*.

"Yes," I said simply.

He looked at me with interest and intrigue as if he knew there were things I was hiding.

"You must take down the wall," Reid said. Rhone's eyes shuttered.

"Before I can go home?" My eyes held Rhone's, not looking at the imposing captain.

Rhone's eyes pinched together. "That *would* be preferable."

"Why the wall?" Not that I was agreeing. There was no way *I* could bring down that wall. No one could. It was solid stone.

Rhone cocked his head. "Did Ainon explain nothing to you?"

I gave a short laugh. "Not much."

He sighed. "He knows little of the Keepers, as he stepped in well after the wall divided our land."

I exhaled a breath. I needed to learn more. I glanced at the woman—the true queen. Then at the younger man at her side. He wore a frown, but his eyes held curiosity. Aven was staring at me in open interest, and the captain—I didn't look at him. His presence beside me was more than enough. I could feel the heat of his commanding body from here.

"I need to get home. Ki—Ainon wasn't very forthright with information. He housed me, paraded me around, and then tossed me at the wall. I don't think he knew I'd be able to get through it."

"That bastard," Aven said, his voice making me jump. Rhone cut him a sharp glance and Aven looked away.

"But you have no amulet?"

I shook my head.

"Then how..."

"I just pushed my hand." And against my better judgment, I gestured with my abnormal hand. I wanted to get it over with. He had known Aunt Millie. With all the information, he could help me. Hopefully.

His eyes widened—not with repulsion, but something akin to wonder. That was a new one.

"The stones?" He said, his eyes flicking from my hand to my face. The wonder in his bronze eyes was obvious.

"Ah, I used an orange one at home that brought me... here. The purple one was broken."

He arched a brow. "I'm not sure how it is possible with no amulet, but I'm sure things have changed with the magic in the Keeper's over the years."

Magic in me? No way. Although how else did I explain my left hand turning into a key? Or going through a wall?

"Ainon must be confident in his position and with his troops to allow you to bring down the wall. I'm shocked he didn't kill you on sight." Rhone's son stated calmly. My blood ran cold at the thought.

"That or he thinks she will fail," Reid piped up.

Rhone nodded slowly. "Perhaps. I think there is much more courage and tenacity in Miss Kaidyn than she lets on."

He did not know me.

Rhone gave me a slow once over. Not in a creepy way, but I felt his gaze in my soul—into a part of me I didn't understand. He saw more in me than I saw in myself, that much was clear as he gave me a wide smile. "With Millicent's blood, there is surely more to her than meets the eye."

"Sir, I—"

"You need to find yourself, dear girl. There is a part of you, a primal element, you must get accustomed to. That is the only way to bring down the wall. You hold the key to do so..." He looked at my appendage and I resisted the urge to tuck it into the folds of my cloak.

"I don't understand."

"Tour the castle, the grounds, the city, the mountains. The inner strength you need to possess will come to you."

"I don't have that kind of time! My parents must be worried sick!" Unless what Aoife suggested was true and time moved slower in my world. But they didn't need to know I knew that was a possibility.

"Your...? Ah. You weren't even told how our world works in comparison to yours?"

I shook my head.

"Do not fear, darling. All will be well in your realm. The Keeper's magic will ensure that time remains still."

Wonderful. But insane. I began to concede, but a random question popped into my mind. One that had been plaguing me. "Why did the portal take me on that side then, if *you* are the real king?"

"That is not—"

The king held up a hand to his guard captain. "Reid." His voice was stern but laced with... love? Pride? There was certainly familiarity. "The portal opens in the last place it was used. There may be a way to harness where it takes you, but I have no idea. Marida may," he paused. "Dinner is in an hour, but you may not wish to attend. At breakfast, I will explain more, but do not fret about your world, Kaidyn."

"I... Okay. Sire."

He chuckled. "Rhone is sufficient."

Rhone nodded to Reid, who barely contained a groan. "Reid, will you show Kaidyn around?" His eyes held mine. "Or, of course, if you wish to go straight to your suite..."

"Your Majesty, I—" A look passed between them. Reid's deep blue eyes flashed on me, and I shrank back from their intensity. "Of course." He gave a small bow to the king and strode down the hall.

I glanced at the king who was staring at me. With a huff, I tightened my grip on Silas and stalked after the guard captain. This was surreal. All of this. A part of me still thought I might wake up from an insane, elaborate dream. Or to find that I had been in a coma from a car accident or something, and I dreamed up this fantasy. But right now, my mind snapped back to the present, and the stiff lines of the captain's body. It wasn't hard to see that he had better places to be.

He waited for me at the door, two guards looking on with interest. Reid flourished a hand when the guards opened the door, and I walked out into the hall with him at my heels.

This felt like it had with Payson and Ainon. Ainon passed off the duty of tour guide to his son, this king to his guard captain.

"Is there no butler or servant that can show me around, why you?"

He quirked a brow at me. "As painful as this is to say, you are far too valuable, and... revered."

Me, valuable? Unreal. I had never considered myself valuable before. Certainly not revered, but the deep timbre of his voice sent a shiver down my center and a blush to my cheeks. "That's preposterous."

"A Keeper of the Keys is precious to the kingdom. Nearly as valued as the king."

Who would not be flattered at that?

Then he said, "Not personal, of course, the *title* of Keeper is esteemed. Whether you are the Keeper or not is still to be seen." He looked me over with scrutiny. "Plus, I don't trust you."

There it was. My smile fell. This man *was* an asshole. But I couldn't be upset.

Was I intrigued being here? Yes. I was a curious person by nature, I would have to be dead not to be intrigued, but I also didn't want to be a beacon of hope or take down a wall. I didn't want to be anything but home.

"My room is fine," I said.

"What?"

"You can show me to my room and go do—" I waved a hand. "Whatever it is you wish to do."

He glanced at me slowly. Instead, he showed me the dining hall. "If you wish to dine with everyone, you will know what the dining hall entails."

It looked very much the same as the one in the southern castle. Floor to ceiling windows along the right wall, pillars of stone, and flames of light. To the left, to my surprise, was an open window that peeked into the kitchens, affording a view of the cook and two other assistants hard at work creating a dinner that—from the smells wafting from the opening—was going to be amazing.

"So, the cook can see the smiling faces of those enjoying his creations. And so that the kitchens don't get too stuffy for the staff." Reid offered when he caught my blatant stare.

Clever. And how he said staff instead of servants... Was what Eloise said true; that Rhone employed his staff and had no servants?

A scarred table had a runner of deep blue with pale silver lining and gold stars. The back wall held a massive stone fireplace, chips of blue mineral shimmered inside the stone. They really liked shimmery minerals in this realm.

Around the back of the room was an arched doorway that led to the common room. He took me there next. It was kind of a study/library/living room. On the right was a wall of windows, straight ahead was another massive fireplace, the same as the others—blue and gray stone that had veins of shimmery silver speckles. Low back couches and comfortable-looking chairs along with several bookcases containing books and baubles, and paintings were dispersed for décor.

Then he led me to the kitchen, in which a large man was baking bread. The smell was heavenly. The man grunted as Reid swiped a roll and handed it to me. At least I learned he might not be a *total* jackass. The cook gave me a wink, but Reid gave no introductions, so I was unsure whether the man knew who I was, or if it was common for the Captain of the Guard to bring young women to the kitchens and steal food.

As soon as we exited the kitchen, he led me up the staircase and I had to quicken my pace to keep up with him. I felt the weariness of the day seep into my bones. Muscles ached from riding all day, and sore chafing on my thighs made me ecstatic with the prospect of rest. Plus. Silas was heavy in my arms.

"Reid," a high, musical voice yelled at the end of a hall.

That stopped us, and we turned to the woman. She was stunning. Long auburn hair falling in loose waves. She was tall, willowy, and curvy in all the ways that made someone as average as me feel intimidated and a little envious.

Silas sprang out of my arms. I didn't think he'd wander too far from me at this point, and it was blessed relief to not carry him, if even for a few moments.

"Marida," Reid said with exasperation.

She was the embodiment of beauty. I had a bit of a girl crush already. How were all these men not falling at her feet?

"It is true then," she stated with wonder as her eyes swept over me; taking in the cloak, the cat, the appendage I didn't hide here like I had in Vanstarr. Why I wasn't sure.

Marida bent down, and Silas trotted over to rub himself on her. He was quite the little traitor with these people.

"Cats have always been the Keepers companions, since Kaliya." She glanced at me, seeing my blank expression, she offered a bright smile. "She was the first Keeper of the Keys, centuries ago."

"Marida, this is Kaidyn. Kaidyn, Marida."

I looked at her with renewed interest. "You know about the Keepers?"

"Oh, yes. They are fascinating and those of magical standings tend to...gravitate towards each other."

"Magical..."

"I'm what you would consider a sorceress."

"No way." My face held a slack-jawed expression.

She laughed, the sound like a harp expertly strung. "Yes...way."

"That's—"

"The Keeper is tired, Mar, so can we pick this up later?"

"I... Oh. Yes." She looked between him and me, then smiled softly. "Tomorrow, Kaidyn?"

"I'd like that."

She bent and rubbed the cat again. My cat rubbed against her, then sat at her side looking at me. I glared at him before my eyes wandered back to hers.

"Nice to meet you, Kaidyn. I hope we get to spend some time together while you're here."

I nodded but said nothing. She must have gotten the hint because she looked down at Silas and gave him a conspirator's smile. "Nice to meet you too, Silas."

Wait—*What*? I hadn't mentioned his name. To anyone. I hadn't told a single soul his name since coming to this realm. Had I? Had I said his name... *No*. I definitely hadn't.

"How did you—"

She grinned. "See you later, Kaidyn. Reid."

I watched her walk away, mystified. Silas mewed and flicked his tail. "Who—What—"

Reid chuckled. "Marida... knows things."

He continued down the hall. After staring after the red-haired beauty another minute, I trotted after him. He stopped at a door. My eyes met his. His imposing strength dominated the space, but he was gorgeous. Frightening, though. He opened the door for me and stepped aside. Inside was a spacious room. Not like the Keeper's tower in castle Vanstarr, but still expansive and beautiful. The back wall was floor-to-ceiling windows with a glass door, leading to a balcony. The bed was a massive four-poster, a rug like the others covered the floor beside it. There was a fireplace, and two short couches. Two tall, thin bookshelves were divided by a stone pillar, flames of light danced across the stone and lit the room in a golden glow. A painting of the night sky sat above the bed.

Reid gestured to a doorway. "Bathing chamber, lavatory." Silas wound his way between Reid's legs, and the tall man scooped him up and rubbed his fingers against Silas' chin.

I watched in idle fascination at the captain's gentleness. He was a jerk when it came to me, but at least he was nice to my cat. I wrenched my eyes from his fingers caressing my cat, to his deep blue eyes. In the golden glow of the room, they shimmered purple.

I swallowed. This was a lot to take in. One city, one ruling family, and one castle had been a lot. Another one only a few days later to now deal with. *Ugh.* Exhaustion seeped into my bones, weighing me down. "Thank you. I'm going to retire."

"I'll have some food sent when dinner is served. I'll ensure your attendant doesn't disturb you." He rubbed the cat again, then set him down. "I'll make sure something is brought for him, as well."

I nodded because I had already retreated inside myself. I slung the backpack off and tossed it on the bed.

Reid hesitated at the doorway, his eyes looking me over before he opened the door. I paid him no more attention as he saw himself out. I undressed quickly, slithered into the soft nightgown I had stolen from Vanstarr, and tucked into bed. Silas was already curled into a tight ball on a pillow, and I quickly faded into the oblivion of sleep.

When I awoke at dawn, I stretched and hummed at the comfortableness of the bed. I had been too tired to appreciate it last night. The room too was far more impressive than I had originally thought. The golden glow turned to a silvery purple of dawn's pre-light. I whistled between my teeth as the soft light caught on some of the stones that graced the bookshelves.

I needed to ask Rhone about the necklace. I needed to tell them everything so they could help me. First, I needed to know if the necklace in my pack was *the* amulet.

My eyes roved around the room again, landing on a plate of food. I got up and ambled over to it, as my stomach let out a rumble. Dried meat, biscuits that appeared to have been baked with nuts and dried fruit, and a pitcher of water. Things that would keep if left out. It wasn't much, but I scarfed it all down. There were a few of the biscuits left plain, broken into tiny pieces, and I gave them to Silas, who devoured them. He was as hungry as me. Reid had delivered on getting something for my cat. I hated that it made me appreciate him—just a tiny bit. He was still a terrifying asshole.

The balcony beckoned me, and I opened the door. My breath caught before I even stepped fully onto the stone balcony. In all my life I've never seen anything this breathtaking. Nowhere and nothing could compare. My breath was so completely stolen from my throat, that my fingers went to it as if to hold it there. There was an emerald-green expanse of flatlands met by a gentle ridge, waterfalls cascaded down the base of two intersecting mountain ranges.

I took a deep breath, my hand still at my throat, and sucked in the glorious mountain breeze, and the drifted scents of the flowers. I exhaled, and my mind began to filter all the things that had transpired over... a week? Two? I had lost track at this point. Whose story was the truth? Eloise made it seem as though Rhone was the rightful king, and the diary also mentioned Rhone—that his father *had* been king, and nothing of Ainon—not that I had *skimmed,* anyway.

I wanted to hear what Rhone had to say, and I had a feeling he could lead me in a better direction with getting home, learning more about my aunt, than Ainon had.

I snooped in the armoire and found several articles of clothing. All finely tailored with thick, soft materials. Most of the pants were heavy, some were even lined with fur. There was a barrage of different colored shirts, varying in fashion and cuts. I had no idea whether I was at liberty to wear these or not. A soft knock shattered my thoughts. I looked down. I was still in my nightgown.

"Who is it?"

"Vera, your attendant, my lady."

"Enter." Another *attendant.* Goodie.

But this woman did not look like a despondent servant in muted colors. She was older, plump, and in a bright purple and white dress. She looked severe, and a little ornery.

"I see you've found the clothes."

"Err. I... Are they—Can I use them?"

"Of course, of course," she waved at me.

"I... I'm going to be riding today..." I had no idea why I said that nor why the thought sent a massive tremor of excitement through me. That was, of course, if Reid had been serious.

"There should be an array of riding habits. Millicent and the other Keepers were natural riders."

"My aunt was a rider?"

"Oh, yes. A fine one." Vera pulled a brush from atop the vanity and turned to me.

With wide eyes I stared at her, dumbfounded. She must be far older than she looked. I didn't understand how these people had known Aunt Millie; she was well into her seventies when she passed away.

Vera arched a brow and plucked a few items from the armoire. She held them up to me, assessing the cut and colors against my complexion. With a critical eye, she tossed something back and retrieved something else.

Finally, happy with her choices, she arranged them on the bed. "I'll have these adjusted for you. You are a bit wider at the waist and larger at the rear and chest than Millicent, but about the same height and build. So, her things will work for you."

"I..." I felt a bit invasive, but she was gone after all, and I needed clothes. "Okay," I said finally, and the woman looked me over again. Her eyes snagged on my deformed hand, but before I could tuck it against my side, her eyes moved back to the clothing arranged. I had seen nothing akin to repulse in her eyes, but simple clinical accession. Interesting. None of these people seemed to care one way or another about my hand. I wished people at home felt the same.

"Would you like to wash up? I'll grab the pot from the fire."

"Ah..."

She smiled, casually. "If I had to guess the captain will have you getting dusty enough today that we'll wait on the full bath until tonight?"

I gulped. Great, even she knew I was in for it today. "Right," I whispered.

She gave me another smile and went to the small fire burning in the fireplace. Efficiently she took a pot from the fire and into the bathing chamber. When she came out, I finally had my wits about me enough to glance at the clothes she'd chosen. Brown breeches, a white tunic, and a leather vest, which looked more like a corset...

She waved a hand and sent me into the bathing chamber. It was simple. A rectangular stone tub with flat rocks across the top, a pump, and handle that pulled water up and into the tub, a cabinet with an oval-shaped washbasin, and a stone bench with a toilet. Rudimentary, primitive, but reasonable, private, and beautiful. A nice touch of candles and several potted plants, not to mention the windows that pooled silvery light into the room.

Two small hand towels and another linen towel were laid out for me, and the washbasin was filled with citrus-scented water. I dipped the small towel in and washed my face, neck, and armpits. I used the toilet, then removed my sleep gown, and grabbed the other hand towel, I ran it over my body quickly. My thighs still felt chafed, and my butt was sore from the hard riding we'd done.

"I have clean undergarments. I can toss them through the door if you wish." Vera opened the door just slightly and tossed in the clean underwear and a bra band.

I walked out with the panties and band on, and she held up the white tunic. I quickly dressed, and then she held out the corset vest. It was beautiful and laced up the front. I could only imagine what it would do to my moderate chest size. I almost waved her off, but I saw the look in her eye and realized that she wouldn't take no for an answer. I had a feeling Vera was not someone to cross. I huffed a laugh as she put it on me and laced it up. Vera brushed my long brown hair and plaited it in one braid. She pulled a few tendrils by my temple free, and then pulled over a small box of cosmetics.

"Oh, no." I shook my head, vehemently. "I don't—" But I ceased my protests as she lifted a brow. I swallowed and sat at the chair she gestured. I was riding a horse, not attending a ball.

She ran something over my eyelids, against my lashes, and brushed something over my lips. A quick splash of perfume at my throat, and she deemed me done in record time.

Okay, well that wasn't so bad. I had envisioned powders and whatever other horrors women did to their faces. I'd never been one for makeup.

Vera handed me tall brown boots, which were supple, and fit perfectly. She showed me to a full-length mirror, and I barely recognized the woman that looked back at me. I seemed older. Different, in an alluring way. The clothing made me look imposing. I'd been concerned the corset vest would make me look a bit...slutty, but it didn't. I looked like a badass.

The clothes made me look attractive in a powerful way. Something I'd never felt. The makeup was barely discernable, but it made my green eyes stand out.

I gave her a small smile. "Wow, I look..."

"Like a little warrior," she said simply, and I shrugged. More like one of Robin Hood's merry men.

A knock came at the door, and Vera glanced at me. I gave a nod, and she hollered a welcome.

Aven stepped onto the threshold.

Well, there was my Robin Hood! My assessment was right, I certainly looked like I belonged at his side.

He wore a green tunic with a vest over his chest, his silly green hat over his sandy blonde hair, and his boots were similar but darker in color than mine. As I ran my eyes over him, he ran his eyes up and down me, and a slow, lazy grin etched his face. Dimples flashed.

"Well, damn."

Vera chuckled and slipped out the door.

He sent me another searing look and winked. I shook my head when he wagged his eyebrows at me, and Silas trotted over to us. Aven bent and petted him, and I exhaled.

Silas already loved every one of these people, which made absolutely no sense considering he had hated the Barthol's.

"So, strap on your dagger, I have to get you to the king for breakfast, and then we'll head to the stables."

"Are you instructing me?"

He whistled. "Oh, gods, no. I wouldn't dare take that pleasure from Reid."

Ugh.

He gestured to me again. "Dagger?"

"I..." I looked down at myself. Where the heck would I put it? It had a little scabbard, but...

He cocked his head. "There's usually..." He gestured to my chest. "In ladies' clothes, there's typically a hidden pocket."

I lifted my arms and twirled. "Ah... I don't think so."

He gave me a lazy grin that showed confidence and swagger. I scowled at him. "Come find it then," I said boldly. I was not flirting—it was simply a challenge.

A twinkle flashed in his eyes. The emerald sparkled with mischief. He was boyishly attractive. Unlike the captain, who was mysteriously, darkly beautiful.

Aven circled me, a knuckle curled against his chin. "Inside, against your... left rib. Your aunt must have been left-handed."

I started. I had no idea.

"You are right dominant. Yes?" His eyes grazed my deformed hand with that same clinical assessment. As if evaluating its weakness but taking stock in its strength. Something about that look sent a shiver down my spine. I had a feeling they would look at me, at my hand, as a challenge and never a weakness. That thought sent an arrow into my heart. No one had looked at it that way before, including me.

"We'll have to get that stitched differently for you but go ahead." He gestured with a chin. "See if I'm right."

I huffed but stuck my hand inside and felt... a *pocket*. A spot for a sheathed dagger. Well damn. It would fit along the length of my side and the leather was thick enough that it wouldn't even bulge out. It would be perfectly concealed, with just the hilt sticking out for easy access. Clever.

I retrieved the dagger and Aven helped me slip it into the pocket and watched me pull it out twice before deeming it fit for me.

"Alright, now that's settled. Although a thigh belt... Well. Hmm. I still think we'll have to refit some clothes for your dominant hand, but—" His eyes roved me with a grin. "I think you'll do."

I gave a short laugh. "Why must I carry the dagger—are we in danger?"

"You don't need apparent peril to carry weapons around here, my lady. One must always be prepared."

"Well, it would be one thing if I knew how to use it."

"Those idiots didn't even show you how to use the dagger?"

"Ah... No."

"Well, may a fire drake strike those fuckers."

I startled myself with a laugh. I had no clue what he was saying, but it was said with such vehemence.

"I can't ride a horse or wield a weapon. I'm pretty useless in this world."

"Oh, I seriously doubt that." He winked and gave me a genuine smile. A flutter settled in me at the sincerity of it.

Aven led me to the dining hall. I noted in the morning light that Hawksedge felt even more mighty and formidable, like the battle-worn warrior I had thought of before but with a gentle laugh and a warmth never dimmed by those his sword met. I liked it here—the warmth, the feeling it gave off.

CHAPTER 9

Dawn of freedom

I took a moment to marvel at the beauty of the landscape when Aven led me to the stables. Guards saluted, and I took a sidelong glance at him. He was lithely built. Not like Reid who was massive, imposing, and musclebound. Even Kavall was built like... a warrior. Aven was graceful. Sort of... elvish. Were there elves here? Damn, it was possible considering they had *dragons*.

"Are you studying me because I am exceptionally handsome?"

I laughed; it bubbled out of me unbidden, and he grinned massively. Dimples flashed conspicuously.

"Wouldn't you like to know?" I purred with a smirk.

He barked a laugh. "Oh, I do like you. You're going to make things far more interesting around here."

I scoffed but continued to smile as he led me to a pasture.

"I'm a scout, in case you were curious. Before the wall, I was training as a messenger for Rhone. I've always been fast, light on my feet, and a good rider. So, I had plans to be a mounted messenger, an out-rider. Now—Well, since I can't get through the wall, I'm still a messenger but only for the coastal villages and mountain passes."

As soon as Aven walked up to the fence and leaned over I noticed a pair of horses break off from the others. His golden mare trotted to the fence, a gangly youth at her side. The colt was slightly taller than her but less bulky. His coat was two shades paler than the mare, and where she had a thin white strip down her face, this guy had a full blaze. He was gorgeous.

Aven grinned with deep affection as his mare nudged against his shoulder. I couldn't help but smile too. His obvious joy was infectious, as was their love for each other.

"How long have you been together?"

"Seven years now."

I nodded my chin to the youngster, who stayed just behind. "Is he hers?"

"Aye. He's three. I've been trying to break him, but he has an attitude." Aven must have seen my horrified expression because he chuckled. "Break, as in teaching him to allow a rider on his back. I don't wish to break his spirit, simply ensure he's safe around people. If he doesn't accept a rider within the next year, we'll turn him loose. We don't keep horses that can't be broken. If a horse doesn't wish for a rider or stand for a carriage, there's no point in us keeping them."

He ran a hand over the mare's nose, and she leaned into him. What was it about men who loved animals that was such a turn-on? Not that I was turned on by Aven. He was cute, but I didn't feel attracted to him. Not really. I would have to be cold-blooded not to feel a little attraction. He was golden and gorgeous, and the way he was caressing his horse? Hello.

I shook myself. No ogling! *Bad Kaidyn.*

The younger horse nosed me, snapping me from my thoughts that were far saucier than they ever should have been, and I tentatively held out my hand. He sniffed me and lipped the edge of my sleeve, then my hair. He let me scratch his ears and nuzzled me.

Aven grinned. "He hasn't been that interested in anyone since he was born."

I smiled, and ran a hand down the horse's cheek, feeling my confidence grow. The horse lipped at my left hand, and I held it up for him to smell. His warm breath skittered across the abnormal appendage.

I caught Aven looking at the gesture with a smile. "His name is Dh'evfaineser, which in old language means Dancer of Dawn."

At my lifted brows, he chuckled. "Rhone named him. We just call him Fain. Fain's father is Rhone's white stallion, Vesmire." He pointed to the tall, beautiful white stallion.

I smiled and patted Aven's mare on the nose. Fain ran his nostril up my cheek. As if he didn't want my attention on the others, it made me giggle. Aven pointed out a few of the other horses, telling me their names, but I found myself gravitating back to the colt.

"Grab his muzzle and blow softly into his nose."

I whipped my head to him, perplexed. "Do what?"

He chuckled and showed me, softly lifting Alida's nose and blowing gently into her nostril. I followed Aven's example and blew into a nosy bay horse's muzzle. He snorted and pranced away. I laughed. Fain pushed his way back to me, and I was gentler with him since he seemed less tame than the others, but I did the same to him. He didn't snort or prance away, he just gazed at me with soulful brown eyes.

"Reid made me do that when it was time for me to have a horse of my own. It was strange, but the next day I came out and he said to blow into the wind and the first horse to come to me was mine. They choose their rider. As soon as I blew in the wind Alida picked her head up and came over to me. She's been my loyal companion ever since." He kissed the horse's cheek.

Well, damn, if scary Reid wasn't clever. Eck.

"It works?"

Aven grinned. "I know it sounds bizarre, but it's what riders have been doing for eons. It's how the guards have gotten their mounts since Reid has been captain and honestly all the men love their horses as much as their wives and children."

Aven made me do the same thing to five other horses. "See, when Reid makes you do this, you'll be ahead of the game."

I wondered if Reid would have even bothered doing this for me, or if he'd have just tossed me on the first ornery horse he could find, just to watch it buck me off. He still could.

"I'm not so sure it matters. I'm not sticking around very long."

"No?" Aven prodded. His eyes begged to differ. I shook my head.

We heard hoofbeats and turned to see Reid's big gray stallion trot up to us. The horse pranced sideways, and Reid gentled him with a stroke of his hand. I felt a little envious of the ease he had with horses.

"It's good to see you can be around horses, at least."

I grimaced. He elicited annoyance from me. My pulse jumped just at the sight of him, and I wasn't sure if I wanted to run or punch him in the throat. A bit of both. He didn't deserve a response.

He slowly dismounted, his eyes running over Fain who was lipping at me for more attention. Then his attention shifted to Aven. There was a silent communication between them, as Reid sauntered over to us. He wore dark clothing. His vest had a crescent moon and star sigil I didn't notice before. The same one at Castle Vanstarr. I pried my eyes away from the captain and ran a hand over Fain's nose. My gaze caught Aven, who held a mirth-filled grin. I wanted to elbow him in the gut. He sensed how unnerved the captain made me. I tried to ignore the unsettling shiver at Reid's towering height and commanding power.

How was I supposed to get through a riding lesson if I couldn't even be in his vicinity? I swallowed, and Aven noticed it. It spread his grin, and I didn't resist the urge any longer, I elbowed him in the ribs. He choked on his laugh, a hand on his side, eyes shining. It was easy bantering with Aven. Like it had been with Payson toward the end of our time together. I wondered how he was faring. I wondered what he'd told his father.

During my inner thoughts, a few more guards had strolled over, and they talked amongst themselves as if I weren't even there. Finally, I snapped back into the present when I felt the heat of a gaze and looked up at violet-blue eyes. A shiver of apprehension and awareness skated across me, and I wondered why he hated me so. It's not as if I had done anything to him, but the look he sent me was obvious dislike. I quickly glanced away, back to the horses, and tried to forget the wall of muscled men at my back. Another man rode up, and he commandeered space like Reid did. He was huge, with ebony skin against dusky gray clothing. His head was bald, and he had enigmatic golden eyes.

There was a daring scar from the side of his mouth, across his cheek, to the side of his ear. He was otherworldly formidable in appearance and intimidating.

"Saul," Aven and Reid greeted him.

"War commander," Aven offered at my blatant stare. I grunted as the big man rode past. "Saul is the war commander for Hawksedge and a legend."

"Really?" My eyes finally left the commander to flick to Aven.

"Aye. He's battled a dragon. That's where he got the scar." Aven gestured to his face to depict where Saul's scar ran.

"A dragon?" Holy mother of pearl.

"Not just any dragon either, a *frost* dragon."

"Dragons are real?"

He cocked a brow. "Aye."

"And there's more than one... type?"

"Of course. We mainly see Drake's but the occas—"

"Av." Reid shot Aven a look, and Aven conceded with a frown.

"Keeper, why don't you—" Reid gestured to a guard who meandered over. "This is Holt. He can show you back to the castle. I'll be along shortly for..." His eyes pierced mine and then moved down my body. "Your riding lesson."

I couldn't argue, they had some kind of meeting taking place that I had no part in. Aven touched my arm, and I gave him a tight smile. He returned it, but his eyes went to the captain, and he dropped his hand. I followed Holt back to the castle resignedly.

I didn't see any of the royal family as I crested the stairs. Vera stood at my door as if she'd known I was coming.

"Do you require anything, my lady? I dropped off a few items for you. Altered clothing, some fruit, and a few snacks for your cat."

"That's wonderful Vera, thank you. No, I'm all set."

She dipped her chin in farewell.

Silas trotted over to me when I stepped into my room, and I dropped to one knee to scratch his back and behind his ears. He went back to his meal. There was a basket of various fruits, a platter of cooked meat, cheese, and a blueberry tart. *Screw it.* As a lover of all food, I sat. Despite my hearty breakfast, I ravished the dainty blueberry tart in two bites. I shared the meat with Silas.

I paced after my fill, then rearranged my pack and pulled out the necklace. The dark blue gemstone glinted in the sunlight streaming in from the balcony, the glittering golden stars winked, and my breath caught just as it had done the last time. Could this be the missing amulet? I would show it to Rhone. I had a feeling he knew a lot more about my aunt than he was willing to say in front of his wife, especially now knowing the way time was in comparison to this world and mine. It had to be *her* journal, which meant she and Rhone *had* been lovers. Ick.

I was glad I had ignored those pages. I don't think I could have looked at him with a straight face had I read more.

Then it hit me. Something unraveled and my heart ached.

Rhone was the man Aunt Millie had loved but could never have. He had been the man that she'd pined for all those years, the reason she hadn't married or had children. She'd said she had a great love once, but he'd been unattainable. Rhone was that. There was love between him and his wife. You could see their respect and unity, but had Aunt Millie been *his* great love too? Had he and Eranora married after my aunt left? I couldn't see Aunt Millie being the type to dally with a married man.

I suddenly remembered the diary had spoken of Rhone asking his father about marriage to her.

So, what had happened?

My head spun, and my heart ached for my aunt. For the life she'd led without him. It didn't make any sense. Why had she left? Why had Rhone married another? Was it an arranged marriage?

The torture of not being with the one you were in love with. I hoped I never loved and lost like that. I couldn't pretend to grasp what she went through, and I tried to find it in me to hate Rhone for doing that to her, but I didn't know his story. I didn't know his reasoning, why they hadn't remained together. I had a feeling it had something to do with regal duties, or that monarchs of

Evirness just weren't allowed to marry a Keeper. Perhaps there was an ancient law against it. In this crazy world, such would not surprise me. I felt bitterness surge and wrapped the necklace back up in a blouse. I would show Rhone another time when my annoyance at him had lessened. With a sigh, I went to the balcony doors and pushed them open, allowing the crisp mountain breeze to lift my spirits.

After taking in the beautiful view, I got edgy. Idleness had never done me any favors, and I decided it was time to have a chat with Marida. I could find her somewhere in this castle, I was sure of it.

After bidding my cat goodbye with a promise for more food later, I stepped from my room and then jumped in fright. My hand went to my heart which seemed to leap from my chest. Across the hall from my room, the Guard Captain leaned against the wall, his arms over his chest, ankles crossed. He gave me an annoyed glare before pushing off the wall and walking ahead of me.

I stayed rooted for a second. Did I wish to follow this impossible asshole for a riding lesson? He seemed annoyed I wasn't harnessing attitude or simpering sullen in a corner. Part of me wanted to, but it wouldn't get me anywhere. It wouldn't get me home.

After getting confirmation that my own time would stand still until my return, I realized I wanted to make the most of being here. Learn what I could, find the gemstone, and go home. I wanted to learn how to ride, and I had a feeling if I wanted to learn quickly, he was the guy. From the dead set seriousness in his eyes, he would make damn sure my deformed hand wasn't a hindrance. It sent a shiver down my spine, whether of thrill or fear I was unsure, but my eyes held his. Something flashed in his indigo eyes that I couldn't quite decipher, but I wanted to know what he thought. I imagined it was nothing good.

I followed him wordlessly as he strode down the stairs and passed the atrium. My eyes tried to take it all in at once. The sparkle of the lights bouncing off crystals scattered on tables and shelves, the glistening of water drops.

Marida strode from an open arched doorway to the left and met us by the door. "Lady Kaidyn! After your riding lesson, I would love to speak with you."

I had wanted to speak with her anyway. I went to open my mouth, but Reid sent her a glare, that she wholeheartedly returned. Damn. She even made a glare look sexy. How was that possible? Hell, Reid made a glare look sexy too in all honesty—not that I wanted to dwell on *that*. I wondered if they were dating with that kind of familiarity.

Reid sighed through his nose but conceded with an eye roll. Marida beamed as if no power play had just taken place. I was intrigued. This willowy woman that looked like she should be a supermodel had just overpowered the captain of the guard.

They *must* be sleeping together.

"Come find me later!" She gave me a wink. I hated myself for watching her walk away. Damn, she was freaking beautiful.

"Are all of you people that... beautiful?"

He snapped his head to me. "What?"

"You people." I waved to him, back to Marida. "Are you all gorgeous?"

Reid snorted. "*You* people?"

"Oh, please. You're a *man,* you can't possibly tell me you don't think she's gorgeous?"

He looked over his shoulder even though Marida was long gone and sent me a perplexed look before shaking his head. "I suppose."

Okay, they weren't sleeping together. Weird. I shrugged. These people were weird. I was thankful that he had completely ignored the fact that I had called him gorgeous. To his face.

What was wrong with me?

At the stables, to my utmost surprise and pleasure, Aven greeted me with a saddled Alida. Was he to be my instructor...? Then I noticed the big, dappled stallion was also tacked. Nope, it was still going to be the captain.

"Since you've gotten acquainted with Alida, Aven offered her for your lesson."

I smiled at Aven and rushed over to him and Alida. The mare gave a soft whicker and I pulled out an apple that I had swiped from the fruit basket Vera left me. She took it greedily and Aven grinned.

He laughed as Alida nudged me for more. "Nice touch, Keeper."

Greedy mare. I returned Aven's smile.

"Bridle. Reins," Aven said as he gestured to each piece of tack.

I knew this, but I let him lead me through the basics. "Saddle. Stirrups. We'll adjust them with this cinch once you're seated." I had noted when I was astride Reid's horse the day before, that there was no saddle horn to hold onto.

Aven continued, "Alida is gentle, but also a spirited girl. I had a chat with her to take it easy on you, but she likes to run. So, you'll need to keep her reined in if you encounter any open fields. I didn't want to see—" His eyes flicked to Reid, and his voice dipped conspiratorially, "I didn't want to see Reid give you one of those sod back old-timers, one hoof in the grav—"

"Okay, Aven, I think she gets it."

Aven chuckled. My eyes flicked to Reid, but his face was upturned to the sky. Noting the time, sun, wind direction, trying to hold in a laugh—I wasn't sure, but then he dipped his head back down and his eyes met mine. They sparkled like the sky at twilight. I swallowed and turned back to Aven. It was a lot easier looking at the lighter man than the imposing guard captain.

"Alright, up you go," Reid stated with a sneer.

"Wait, what? I'm..." I balked. "Where's the lesson?"

"I'm more of a throw you to the wolves, and see you fight your way out type of instructor," Reid said smoothly.

My eyes whipped to him as his full lips pulled into a mirthful grin. A mouth like that did not belong on such a jerk. It wasn't fair.

Aven put two hands down, interlocking his fingers. I bit my lip.

"Up, Keeper." Reid's voice held no more teasing, and I squirmed from his tone. This was going to be torture. I wasn't sure if I was ready for it, but I *did* want to learn how to ride.

I ran a hand down Alida's nose and kissed her cheek. "Take it easy on me, pretty girl."

"She loves flattery," Aven said with a wink, as he gestured with his hands. I sighed and with my right hand at his shoulder, my finger and thumb at the front lip of the saddle, I allowed him to guide me up and over, and he fixed the stirrups for my height.

I felt... comfortable. Safe. Right. I shouldn't have let those bitchy barn girls get in my head and miss out on this. I could feel Alida's muscles beneath my thighs, her flaxen mane in my fingers. There was a certain power on horseback. You became part of them. You gained their muscles, their size, their speed. The power of freedom simmered over me, and I was delighted.

I tipped my head to Aven and gave him a beaming smile. Aven patted my thigh. "Aye, you'll do fine, love. Just fine."

I nodded, my smile holding, and picked up the reins. I knew how to hold them, and had studied how to ride despite never having done so physically. There wasn't an ounce of fear in me. Horses *could* be reined with one hand. Maybe only well-trained horses, but I would make it work.

This was perfect. A grin was still plastered on my lips as my eyes skimmed to the captain. His lips twitched and he gave a slow nod.

"Now, I want you to squeeze with your thighs just a bit. Loosen the reins. You're welcome to say something like *walk on*."

I did as he requested, and Alida instantly responded and began walking.

"Now rein her over to me by shifting your body and lightly tugging the reins to the left. Not hard, Alida has a gentle mouth and responds to the shift of your weight. With her, you don't even need to rein, but I'll show you how regardless."

I did as he requested and Alida moved to the left for me. He had me go back and forth near the stables for a while before he gave a nod. "Nicely done. Let's go."

I looked around with a shiver of excitement. Reid clicked to his stallion, and I did the same with Alida. He opened the gate and gestured me through. Once he was back on his stallion, the gate closed, and I resumed following him.

We remained like that for a long while. I let my eyes wander over our surroundings, and as always, the expanse of green amazed me. He veered to the right and my view expanded. There was a ridge over rolling hills, and I remembered Aven saying that was Eagle Ridge. We plodded on at a gentle walk. No trees, no rocks, no distractions, just open grassland. The kind that made you want to run. I felt Alida's muscles bunch beneath me and knew all I needed to do was squeeze my thighs and give her some slack and we would be gone, leaving the captain to eat our dust, or grass, or whatever. The thought sent a sick thrill through me. He'd be so pissed.

As if sensing my thoughts, he stopped and gestured to his side. I reined Alida in next to him. He sent me a smirk. "Think you're ready to pick up the pace?"

"Hell yeah." I hadn't meant to blurt it out so excitedly, but it was getting harder to hide my delight.

He tried not to smile at my enthusiasm. His eyes roved over my form. "Spine is relaxed; very good. Tighten the reins just a bit—Good. You have a very natural seat. You look..." He looked away and fell silent.

Was he going to compliment me? "I look...?"

His eyes flickered to me again, and I saw something flash, at my impertinence or at what he was going to say, I'm not sure. "You look good up there, Keeper that doesn't want to be a Keeper."

Hell has frozen over! I would have preened at his compliment if it hadn't been laced on the back edge with a dig.

"Thanks," I said sweetly, deciding to ignore the barb.

His eyes roved over me again, then looked forward. Instead of telling me what to do, or how to do it, he simply clicked to his stallion who trotted ahead.

I gritted my teeth, praying I was ready for this, and did the same with Alida. I tightened my thighs, gestured with the reins, and clicked my tongue. Alida neatly trotted along after them, and I found myself moving with the rhythm naturally.

I soon caught up, and the mare fell into step beside the stallion.

Reid looked over at me critically and gestured. "Heel down, just a bit. Yes, that's good."

I felt like he wanted to criticize me more, but I turned on every bit of horsey knowledge I had accrued in my childhood and made it impossible for him to. I felt alive on Alida's back. More alive than I ever had before. I liked to swim, I was good at it, but I had chosen swimming to appease my parents. I was on the team to please them not because I loved it. I didn't. Not competitively anyway. But this? This was what I should have been doing. *This was freedom.* Nothing else mattered. Not my deformity, not missing my family, not the company at my side. Just me and the horse mattered, the grassy ground beneath her hooves, my deformed hand put to use with the reins. My thighs itched to push the horse into a faster gait, my heart matched the rhythm set by her hooves, and the breeze captured my braided hair, sending the loosened tendrils dancing across my face.

This was magic. Unadulterated, spanning the realms of the world, pure magic.

"Why have you never ridden before?"

"I..." He slowed the pace to a walk again, and honesty slipped from my tongue without my consent. "I tried once. My mom bought me lessons at this local stable, but the girls..." I gave a cruel laugh. "Snobby, rich, horse girls wouldn't accept me. They teased me about my hand and insisted I would never be a jumper, which was the focal point of that stable. Showjumping. I let their words beat me down before I even got on a horse. I didn't even give it a chance. I sulked and called my mom to get me. I never... I didn't bother again with horses, despite my love for them."

His eyes bored into mine. I looked quickly away, toward the horizon unfolding in front of us. His eyes noticed too much.

"Well, I don't understand some of what you said, but the intimidation? Having others make you feel weak? I get that. I also understand that you've always thought of your deformity as a weakness. I see every time you hide it, every careful gesture."

I swallowed, and my eyes flickered. His midnight eyes held mine. "I think the problem with you, Kaidyn Flynn, is you see your deformity as a vulnerability, not a strength, and therein lies your problem."

"It *is* a weakness."

"No, it is not. *You* are weak. *You* allow that," he gestured to my deformed hand that had no problem holding the reins, feeling Alida's movements and controlling them just as easily as my other hand. "To be a scapegoat because you have no backbone."

What? "You son of a bitch. How dare you! You know nothing about me!" The curse bubbled out, shocking me. I seethed, but I saw a flash of teeth as Reid grinned. My nostrils flared, and I growled in frustration. I wanted to punch him. Something about this place made me bold. Made me *want* to do things I would never even consider at home. Perhaps it was the freedom of being anyone I wanted without consequence because I knew no one here. It felt horrible but wonderful all at once.

"Prove it. Aven says you can't use your dagger. I'll teach you."

He didn't wait for my response before he jumped from the saddle to unlatch the gate we'd come to without my notice. I had been guiding Alida beside Reid without a thought as if it were as natural as breathing. I urged her easily through the opening, and he led his stallion through, closing it at our backs.

He was back next to me before I had time to process his offer. "So?"

"I..." I wanted to learn. I wanted all of it, just because I knew they would teach me. This gruff man beside me would ensure I never thought of my deformity as a weakness again, but I would hate him for it. He would press and challenge me. I would have to face the fact that I was weak and pampered. I would be pushed in ways I never had before. But... I liked the thought of it. I liked the idea of having a challenge.

The tall swaying grass of the hayfield we rode through came alive with a cacophony of the thousands of bugs that called it home. I thought over his offer, on the strong set of his jaw as he awaited my answer.

There comes a time when one must choose to take on a challenge, to be willing to make mistakes, to be willing to fail, to have anything worthwhile in life. To *be* anything. I was choosing that time, in this place, to find myself. To no longer be weak. To persevere through challenges, face my fears, and change my view of myself. I'd rather take the chance and risk failure than never try at all. I had missed out on so much already by letting others dictate and manipulate my life.

My eyes rested on Reid's face. His eyes met mine and it was as if he read my thoughts because his eyes flashed a clear challenge.

"You're really willing to teach me?"

His face set in a firm line. "If you're willing to rise to the challenge. To listen to me. To put in the time and effort I expect. I will push you, pull you, make you face every doubt, every weakness. I will make you rise from it."

It would suck. Majorly. But I would rise, as he put it. I felt the certainty of it in every impossibly powerful inch of him, that rigid set of his brow. "I don't want to be treated differently—"

"Oh, trust me, Keeper, there is no chance at that. You'll leave your spoiled, bratty demeanor outside my training area."

I smiled at that, having expected no less. His face faltered at my smile, and he cocked his head. Assessing, wondering, calculating, evaluating me.

"Well then *yes*, Captain, I want you to train me. Make me see this hand," I gestured with it, "as an equal. But... more importantly, Captain," my eyes met his and he must have seen something in them as I finished, *"keep up."*

"*Keep up?*" Confusion clouded his features a full second before I clicked my tongue and spurred Alida forward. I had to hold onto her mane, but a thrill raced up my spine and settled in my heart. Joy shot through me, and I laughed. I heard Reid's curse and then the pounding of his stallion's massive hooves behind us.

Ecstasy. This was pure ecstasy. We gobbled up the greenery with every pounding hoofbeat. Grassy hills sped by. Alida's muscles bunched beneath me, and I marveled at her gentle strength and fine limbs.

I laughed again as I heard Reid encourage his stallion, but he couldn't catch us. We were wind. We were speed and freedom, and it felt glorious. The wind snapped my hair. My deformed hand was holding tight to Alida's mane and my other held the reins loosely, my thighs held me in place. As Alida galloped along a low ridge, I extended my hands, letting my thighs hold me on her back. I threw my face to the sky, my arms still extended. I felt free as if my golden steed could fly.

How had I ever been afraid to ride? I had let those mean girls take this away from me. I never wanted to stop riding.

As we slowed at the top of the rise, Reid's gray stallion edged next to us a full twenty seconds later. I grinned. I couldn't help myself. I was so happy, so content, in this magnificent freedom.

When my eyes grazed Reid's, he grinned. A full-on, full-mouthed grin and I realized it took my breath away as much as the view.

We slowed the horses to a walk, and he looked me over, contemplatively. "You sure you've never ridden before? I feel like I've been toyed with."

I laughed. It burst forth from so deep in my belly, that I snorted trying to keep it in, and then laughed harder. He grinned, and I watched him try to hide his humor, but a small chuckle broke through.

"Drake!"

"What?" I asked, still giggling.

He chuckled. "It's an old curse word."

"I thought it was a type of dragon?"

"It is," he said with a laugh.

"I see." He still looked at me expectantly and I giggled again. "I promise you, I have never ridden before."

"Well, you sure could have fooled me. If you're as quick a study with everything else as you are with riding, I don't think there will be a problem here one bit."

Our matching grins spread. I still didn't like him, but at this moment he didn't seem as intimidating as he had the previous day.

CHAPTER 10

Giant metallic dragons

"I hear that in the human realm there are giant metal dragons."

"Giant met—Oh." I laughed, not at her, but just...Well. It was funny. "Airplanes?"

"People ride on them?" Her dainty brows were pinched.

"Inside them. Yeah."

After my gallop across the fields, Reid and I rode back to the castle in relative silence. A truce had been struck between us, tentative, and filled with a renewed challenge. I had agreed to let him train me in all manner of things. Things that I would have never imagined in my world, let alone in this one because of my deformity, but his confidence... Goodness, the man exuded confidence. Not arrogance, as I'd originally thought, but confidence in himself, his abilities, his people, and their abilities. It was astounding and kind of endearing.

He'd left me at the dining hall with parting words; *"I will be along later to produce a schedule. And if you lose your nerve, I'll drag you out of your bed-chamber."*

He was such a dick.

I tried not to think of Reid as Marida, and I chatted about my realm. She asked me questions about things she'd heard. We both tried not to allow the seriousness of the gemstones to taint our conversation. I tried to be friendly without the looming need to rush home. I wasn't sure I wanted to talk about the gemstones and everything that came along with going home just yet, as the things that Reid promised trounced my mind.

I was in an armchair next to Marida's bed, my feet kicked up on a plush gold ottoman, a book open in my lap, and next to me a goblet of spiced apple cider, which I quickly learned I loved. Marida was on her stomach next to me, head dangling next to my arm. It felt so...*normal*. Two people spending time together, getting to know each other with no pressure or awkwardness. I felt a kindred connection to her, a longing for that soul friend I'd never had. This connection—no cattiness, just pure friendship. I had never connected with any girl before. Not even Bree. In my experience, girls were cruel and unwelcoming. They used their words to tear me down, and their scathing glances to *keep* me down, but with Marida that wasn't the case. She looked at me like I was just... me. Granted, her interest in me was because I was the Keeper, but throughout the last—I glanced out the window at the ebbing darkness—several hours, we had passed well beyond Keeper and Sorceress and charted into just Marida and Kaidyn territory. Confiding in her came easy, and speaking with her was fun. She was full of light, laughter, and brightness that brushed against my soul. It opened me up, took a piece of me out, and laid it bare. I was enchanted by her openness, her ability to just be. Nothing more, nothing less, just herself. I had always wanted to be that—just me.

Night descended, and Marida offered dinner to be brought up to us. I liked that idea, not ready to face anyone. I'd spent a day here and already I was looking forward to more, I didn't want that convoluted with expectation as a Keeper. I didn't want the repercussions of me not taking on responsibilities. I was still cresting the high of learning how to ride. I was no master equestrian, but I *could* ride now, and that was more than I had accomplished in my realm, and it boosted my confidence magnificently.

Venison pie, fried potatoes, and fresh vegetables.

"Vern knows what he's doing in the kitchen, yes?" Marida asked with a knowing grin at my hundredth moan.

"Gosh, yeah." I heaped another generous portion of the pie on my plate. The crust was golden, perfectly crusted.

The man was a genius.

We had avoided speaking of Keepers, but I was ready for a few answers—not about Keeper's specifically, but this place. These people. Her.

"You have magic?"

She licked her lips. "I do. When the wall erupted, most of the magic became subdued. I only have a fraction of the magic I should have for my age. Around puberty one with magic develops a large well of it, but with the wall taking most of the lands magic with its bulk and blocking the reserves, it has dampened magic users—what few of us there are left."

I sucked in a breath. "You should be more powerful?"

She gave me a solemn smile. "Yes. Magic users have a well of inner magic, but it has always been tied to the land. It can be advanced and heightened with objects made with magic. Like your portal gemstones. Those were created from the earth of Evirness, so they are infused with the land's magic. I have no idea why Evirness chose to give magic to me. No one knows how magic use is granted. A blessing from the gods, or Evirness' choice, the answer is unclear."

"It is not hereditary?"

Marida shook her head. "Completely random, but I'd imagine there's some archaic reasoning." She gave me a long, assessing look. "Except the Keepers. That is the only magic that is passed through lineage."

"The wall interferes with your magic?"

"It does. It dampens it. I can feel the depth of my well of power, but I can't even grasp half of it. I can only do simple things unless I have a magical object."

"Like a staff?" I had seen a lot of movies with sorcerers and wizards using staffs.

She cocked her head and sent me a small smile. "Yes, actually staffs are a terrific way to conduct magic because they are made from the wood of the land, and generally a gemstone or crystal—a double potency of magic."

"Cool," I said before I could stop myself.

Marida smiled, unfamiliar with the term but making an educated guess that it was a good thing.

I nodded. "It's a lot to take in," I said with a sigh.

"I can only imagine. You're the first Keeper since the divide, so none of us are quite sure what it is you should be doing either. I know you think you are, but you're not alone in this, Kaid."

"What do you mean?"

"Well, of course, we want you to get rid of the despicable wall, but that'll bring a whole new barrage of problems. Especially with Ainon. We need help here in the north, with doorways cutting off resources. We don't even know the extent of that issue, and only know what our scouts discover. Sometimes the doors show up for a day or two and then are gone. Most don't present a major problem, but it's as if... as if each doorway becomes just a little more sinister." She exhaled a deep breath and met my eyes. "A few months ago, a doorway erupted at a farmer's cottage. It blocked the exits, and the man died inside before anyone knew. He was a widower, and his son found him. The doorway evaporated as soon as his son touched it. The magic had cut off the man inside for weeks, leaving him with no source of water, or food. He had tried to break through the wood of his door, but somehow the magic had sealed it, making it unbreakable. Reid and a team investigated the horrific incident, but we're afraid it's only the first of many more attacks."

I turned away. That was horrible. I couldn't imagine magic so sinister it could do something that vile.

What was I getting myself into?

"Do you have the brand?"

I sucked in a breath. I had forgotten about the so-called brand everyone stated the Keepers would have at the back of their neck. "I...don't know," I answered honestly. I hadn't checked still.

"May I...?"

Having Marida check the back of my neck seemed far less intimate than allowing Rhone or anyone else, so I nodded.

She moved over to me, and I pulled my hair over my shoulder. She gingerly brushed more hair from my nape and ran a finger down the back of my skull. I shivered. Marida blew out a deep breath that fanned across my neck sending another shiver.

I swallowed. "So?" I whispered when she sat back.

"It's there."

My eyes whipped to hers. "What's there?"

"The Keepers are known to have a unique key brand on the back of their neck. Each different from the others."

My eyes rounded. "And I have one?"

"Yes. It's beautiful. Filigreed flourishes and hoofprints."

"Hoofprints?"

"Yes. Each Keeper has a key specifically for them. There are illustrative drawings of a few from some of the Keeper's records. I can show you them if you wish."

I swallowed again. So, I had a brand. A legitimate brand on the back of my neck. "At some point, yeah."

Marida was quiet for a long moment. "As I said, even we aren't completely sure what path to follow, and wouldn't push you into anything blind."

But I would be blind, regardless of what path, because I didn't quite understand what was at play here. I couldn't talk about it anymore, couldn't handle it.

We were silent for a long while in each other's company, eating our dinner, and petting my cat. I let the horrors she spoke of seep into my soul—and light a fire there.

If I *could* fix this world, would I?

I tried ignoring the fact that I had a brand and continued to ask questions. "So, your parents are technically the rulers of Hawksedge?"

Marida wiped her mouth daintily on a napkin. "They are Lord and Lady of Hawksedge." She cocked her head at me. "Once the wall appeared and cut their return to the south, my parents moved aside for Rhone and Eranora and the north was thrilled to have them. But my parents didn't step down for them.

Rhone and Eranora wouldn't allow them to. They wouldn't even let my parents give up their room suite. They seek council as a foursome. These are unprecedented times, with the wall and fluctuation of magic. They are doing everything they can."

I had never suggested there was animosity, hadn't felt it, but she must have seen something on my face to feel the need to placate that curiosity. It wasn't a question of enmity, more a need to ensure power was stable, not taken and it made me respect Rhone and Eranora a great deal more, knowing that.

"And you... will rule someday?"

She laughed, the sound tinkling on the stones of the room. "Goddesses help me, but yes, I suppose so."

I pursed my lips. So, she was a princess, of a sort. Interesting. I wondered... "You and Prince Kavall..."

Marida laughed breathily. "There *was* some interest there. We were youthful, hormones raging and all..."

My eyes bulged. I could see them together. The handsome prince and the beautiful sorceress. "Did you..."

"There was some... heavy kissing, but nothing else."

"Oh my!" I had never spoken about kissing or sex with a friend. Ever. My parents had talked with me about consensual but talking about it with Marida felt *good.* Normal. Girly. It was such a simple thing I had never experienced. A coming-of-age event I'd never had. I mentally shook my head trying not to get too caught up.

She gave me smile and a wink. "I will say, I wish I'd felt that calling in my blood, my soul, for him because his kisses? Goddess divine!" She touched her plump lips in memory, and I howled with laughter. It erupted from me. That happened a lot around these people. Silas gave an annoyed mewl and hopped on the bed to settle in Marida's lap.

"He is a beautiful man," I said with a grin.

"Oh yes. He seems a little stuffy—princely duty and all that, but the passion he has for his beliefs and Evirness makes him sexy."

My grin deepened because I could agree. My mind wandered, out of its own accord, from the prince's handsome face to a darker one.

"What of Reid?" I wasn't *interested* in the captain like that. I *wasn't*. I just wanted to have some leverage over him.

A dangerous smirk crossed her face and brightened her eyes. "What about him?"

"You and he... He—"

Her sly smirk erupted into a mocking grin. "Thinking of the captain being rom—"

"No!" I screeched.

Her grin widened, and I blew out an annoyed huff.

"Reid, Aven, and Kavall have been best friends since they were babes. They were an impenetrable trio. When they were younger, before Kavall had his crown prince duties, they were wild, rambunctious boys. Constantly sword fighting, playing pranks, getting into mischief. As Kavall got older and his parents conceived no more children, he settled down. He asked Reid to be his guard. Aven had always wanted to be a scout, like his father before him. Once they became teens, they stopped horsing around and became duty-bound. Although they're still mischievous and best friends. Reid may seem imposing, but he's always been driven to protect Kavall and the Celestria's. It was always his calling."

I'm not sure why she told me that.

"And, yes, Reid's gorgeous. *Yes,* every hot-blooded person has noticed. It's hard not to. Those eyes of his—Goddess save us."

I snorted and immediate laughter bubbled over. I saw in her eyes the need to defend Reid. So, there was a connection, even if it was platonic. They were Marida's friends, and she protected their names and defended their decisions. That kind of loyalty was forged through mutual respect, understanding, and a deep level of love. I felt envious of it—that connection. That circle. The kind of devotion that I felt with my brother but had never felt for another person. I wish I had a friend I could share that kind of bond.

"Reid and I never had a connection of desire or attraction. Not that I don't find him attractive, but even as a girl I was always more drawn to Kavall."

I bit my lip in contemplation. "And Aven?"

Her grin was massive when she turned back to me. "Aven is a handsome goofball. I never looked at him with attraction, but I love him. It's hard not to. He's funny, kind, and easy-going in a way that makes the world a better place. *He* makes the world a better place."

My heart constricted with that heartfelt statement. I agreed with her. There was something about Aven that made it hard not to like him. Marida and Aven were cast from the same mold. In a sense. There was a brightness to them, a softness in their souls that was unmarred by cruelty and hardships. Nothing had dimmed them, and that was a marvel.

Marida gave me a knowing smirk, and her voice dipped. "Now about the captain! Reid is—"

A knock at her door, had us snapping our heads to it. A grin plastered her face. "Speaking of." She bolstered a greeting.

Reid breezed in like an advancing storm. All darkness and intensity. Those impossible violet-blue eyes settled on me, and I found my heart stuttering in fear. Definitely fear. Most assuredly *nothing* else.

"Keeper."

"Captain," I retorted.

His eyes flashed, but a twitch of his lips was all that set apart his rigid stance and thunderous presence. "At dawn, you'll meet me at the castle door, and we'll begin training."

"On what?"

"I have no care if you're a master of anything, I only wish you to be adequate. So, we'll begin with your dagger."

I swallowed. "O—" But before I finished, he strode to the door.

"Good to see you, as always, Reid!" Marida's singsong voice cut through the tension, and he sent her a slow nod before his large body sauntered through the doorframe.

"Goodness, he *is* bristly these days."

"He's not usually like that?"

"Well, I mean somewhat, but not—" She gestured with a leer. "Perhaps he needs to get laid."

I snorted and we giggled together.

We spent the rest of the evening enjoying each other's company. By the time I staggered to my bed-chamber, far later than I should have, I was convinced I may have just made my first ever real friend.

I woke before dawn, anticipation and trepidation gnawing at me with what was to come. I was going to be trained with a dagger. Who would have thought! I stepped onto the balcony and watched as gray light filtered across the mountains, the sun slowly ebbed its way towards us from the east. I was dressed in similar attire to the previous day. I was unsure what my training would entail exactly, so I took several deep, soothing breathes to calm my racing nerves. I heard the clop of hooves below me. Riding along the east pasture was Reid, at his side were Bronwen and two others. As they crept closer, I glimpsed the familiar visage of Aven riding away from them, back towards the city. The two other guards broke away leaving only the captain and Bronwen. I watched Bronwen lean her chestnut horse toward Reid, and her voice drifted up to me.

"You've been so tense, Reid, why don't you visit me tonight, after your patrol?"

"I can't Bron."

"Why?"

"Because I can't. I—"

The voices lowered and I heard nothing more as their horse's hooves clopped across the courtyard, and around the side of the castle to the stables, where I could no longer see. Well, the issue with Reid *was* that he needed to get laid. I found myself snickering at that and couldn't wait to share that toasty tidbit with Marida.

Without someone leading me, I drifted around the atrium for a moment enjoying the scents of the flowers, and the tinkle of the water on the rocks. When I heard the castle doors open, I looked up as Reid strode inside. I saw his eyes flicker around the hall before they landed on me. Bet he thought he was going to have to come searching for me. Phooey on him.

I straightened as he leaned against the wall, his ankles and arms crossed. He waited, a cock of his brow the only indicator that he was surprised I had shown up. I swear he expected that I was some simpering female that would cower to his dominance—and in my world, he would have been right, but being here gave me an inner strength I'd never known I had. I reveled in it, but I knew at the drop of a hat, it would fade. If I squandered it, it would fizzle my resolve, and doubt could swallow me whole. I needed to not allow doubt to tear me down.

I tried to hide how much he intimidated me as I slowly walked up to him. His eyes darted over me, and heat crept up my neck. I knew he wasn't checking me out, but I had never seen anyone do such a thing so blatantly until I entered this realm. Men here were daring. But the women—like Marida and Bronwen—could be too. So, I tilted my head and assessed him with the same scrutiny. He was encased in black leather and the scent of the forest. Wind and mountain crisp air. It was potent and heady, and I *liked* it. He was tall, even leaning against the wall with muscles at ease, he was undiluted strength and capability.

My cheeks heated as my eyes boldly caressed his worn but polished boots, the black pants that molded against his muscled thighs, the tunic and vest that ran against his trim waist and broad chest, and the stubble that stood dark against his face. I took in the strong chin, straight nose, his brow that had a scar that slashed across his left eyebrow. He was ruggedly handsome, beautiful in a way men shouldn't be. With that overpowering strength, he shouldn't be blessed with beauty too. Then my eyes flicked to his violet-blue ones. They were stunning and added to his good looks.

"Like the view, Keeper?" His voice was tantalizingly husky.

My whole body spiraled into a heat that I knew flushed my cheeks, and chest, but I swallowed. "You're young for a Guard Captain."

His brow kicked up a notch higher. "You're young for a Keeper."

"Am I?"

"Not just in age, but naïveté and ignorance."

Asshole. My eyes must have told of my inner outburst because his eyes sparkled in response and his lips kicked up to the side.

He led me through the barracks. Some doors spawned off a covered hall, but the interior was open and in the center was a dusty training ring. Weapons racks and targets were scattered.

I swallowed. He was legitimately training me.

He led me over to a straw dummy. My vest held my dagger and he gestured to it. I slowly took it out.

Reid sighed. "The Keeper of the Keys is a figurehead, but one should know how to defend themselves."

"I..." I would love to learn how to use the dagger, but could I with one hand? Yeah, it was a one-handed weapon, but I still had doubts. "I agree," I said simply.

He lifted a brow as if he had expected me to quarrel with him, but on this... Not today.

"We'll alternate sword and bow as well."

"A... bow? A sword?"

He cocked his head like I was an idiot. "Yes, you've heard of a bow and arrow, have you not?"

I bared my teeth. "Yes, there is archery in my realm, Reid."

His eyes met mine when I said his name, and something flared. I had never called him his name. I usually called him Captain, as everyone else did. In my head, however, he was usually just an *asshole*. I grinned at the thought.

When he continued to stare, I wrenched a sigh. "Show me."

And he did. The proper placement of my fingers, the way it felt to attack with a dagger against a dummy, the thrust I needed, the wrist movements. I was covered in sweat and hating him after the sun had well and risen. Guards came in and out. Some threw out praise, innuendos, and advice. I let most of the chatter go in one ear and out the other. Some of the advice I took and tried.

Reid expected me to sink into the distraction, but I didn't. I remained focused. He had told me he'd only train me if I had the focus he desired, and I tried to prove to him I did.

"Do you want to stop for breakfast?" His voice was gentle.

"Fifteen more minutes," I said as I thrust the dagger into the dummy for, at least, the hundredth time.

"I need to speak with my men a moment."

I ignored him and shook out my arms. He cleared his throat and moved away. Without his strength at my back bellowing orders, adjusting my stance, the soreness punching through my limbs gripped me, but I gritted my teeth and thrust again.

"Damn, you have a nice form—I mean, *nice form*!"

I recognized Aven's teasing and turned to him.

"I was so *not* talking about your ass."

A laugh bubbled out of me. I grunted with the effort it took to lower my arms. "I have a *great* ass," I stated with a grin.

He ruthlessly matched my smirk. "I wholeheartedly agree."

I was kidding, but I had a feeling he *wasn't*, which caused heat to creep over my neck. I had never had someone tell me I had a great ass. Even in teasing, no one had said anything like that to me.

I continued to grin at him, as he gestured with his bow. "Getting the hang of the dagger, are you?"

"Yes. It fits well in my hand and is easier to handle than I anticipated."

"Good."

I looked over his bow, and something about it called to me. I couldn't use a bow, though, with one hand and two fingers, could I? Reid had mentioned the bow, but I had a feeling I'd fail at that. It was a definite two-handed weapon.

"Want to watch me shoot, get a feel for the stance?"

"Yes, please." I needed the break.

He walked me through the stance, the string, the nock, the arrow. He showed me his stance, and where to put each finger. I would have to hold the bow with my thumb and forefinger, which I discovered was a proper handling hold. My hand may tire, but I *could* do it.

"Here."

He handed me the bow and guided my deformed hand and fingers. He never balked at touching it, and I shivered when his callused fingers touched the mottled flesh.

His eyes flicked to mine at my shiver. "I'm sorry, does... Did—"

I exhaled a shaky breath. No one touched my hand, not even my parents. I couldn't remember the last person to touch the flesh there. Probably a doctor.

"No," my voice came out soft. "It doesn't hurt, but people tend to... not touch it. Ever."

He narrowed his eyes. "Why ever not?"

"It's not—Ah. My world is... full of horrible people."

His mouth ticked up. "All worlds have horrible people. Don't let them get to you. Every part of you is beautiful, your hand included."

I knew that. I did. But I still let them get to me. Beautiful though... His sincere words gripped my belly.

Instead of moving away, he simply moved my two fingers where he thought they would work best. "Those fingers are going to be strong as a Drake once you're through."

Laughter bubbled up my throat. "Probably."

I felt a zip of energy, and my head swiveled behind us. Bronwen was speaking to Reid, who watched us contemplatively and nodded to Aven.

"I am needed elsewhere, my lady." Aven gave a little bow.

I grinned, and he answered it with his deliciously mischievous one. His bow was still in my hand. Aven and Reid spoke in hushed tones. Bronwen moseyed over to me. I was instantly unnerved by her. She was tall, muscled, and golden. Beautiful in a badass way.

"This world is a lot different than yours, yes?"

"Oh, yeah." I scanned her from the side of my eyes, from head to toe. "I envy you."

She cocked her head. "Oh? And why is that?"

"Your easy confidence. I've seen you train; you're a vision."

Bronwen grinned. "Thanks. I've always wanted to be a guard. I trained as a soldier but always knew I wanted to work closely with the royal house. When Reid became Captain, Saul let him choose his guards. I don't think anyone expected him to choose so many women, but here I am. I'm grateful for whatever he saw."

I nodded. I knew she and Reid had a romantic relationship after what I'd heard from my balcony, and I tried not to let that sway my judgment of her.

"King Rhone has done much for women. Just twenty years ago women couldn't even be guards. Some snuck in, of course, but they weren't always welcomed. For a woman, being anything aside from lying on her back, pleasuring men, and taking care of the little children they insist on having, is difficult. That's always what women were good for. Now we all have a fighting chance to be whatever we want."

I didn't know where she was going with this, but I sighed loudly. "I'm not like you. I'm not a warrior. I'm a fraud."

"No," she said gently and pushed her long braid back over her shoulder. "That girl I saw in the training circle trying to learn how to use a dagger, how to hold a blade, how to stand correctly—that girl was striving to fit in, to be something, to be someone more than they are. To learn, to transcend. In my opinion, that's as close to being a warrior as some can ever get. What I saw in your eyes was the need to prove yourself. You could just be a pretty, empty-headed ninny sitting in a tower, but you're out here in the dirt. Struggling, but you're still trying. That means *everything*, Keeper. It's pretty warrior-like to me."

I wanted to scoff. I wanted to tell her she was crazy, but my heart felt light, and I liked the way *warrior* sounded.

"I think," she said as she began to walk off, Reid and Aven's conversation ending, "you have to decide what *you* want to be. A female who just lies on her back in your world, or a fucking warrior, revered and loved, in this world."

"Why can't I just be me, in both worlds?"

"What is it you want to be?"

I bit my lip as she walked further away. "A fucking warrior."

She grinned at me over her shoulder, her blue eyes danced with self-confidence and... respect. For me. "Then be one."

"It's not that simple."

"No?" And then she was gone, but I was quite sure I may have just gained another friend. I already had a multitude of respect for her, but those words... Damn if it didn't stir something in my blood. I had always feared the unknown, now I wanted to embrace it.

Reid sidled up to me. "What was all that about?"

"Oh, just us ladies talking about not wanting to just lie on our back for men."

His eyes went wide, his mouth gaped like a fish. I sent him a devilish grin and gestured with Aven's bow. Ready for another lesson.

"I-I—" He stuttered, floundering for something to say.

I laughed and found myself patting him on the cheek—no freaking clue where I grew the balls for that—but I did it. Bronwen's words, this place, the strength I felt simmering in my core, through my limbs and bones made me *audacious*. Foolishly, audacious.

"Going to teach me how to use this or not, Captain?" I batted my lashes at him.

He bit his lip, the gesture hatefully sexy, and finally nodded.

After another beat of him staring at me, I attempted to step into the stance I had seen Aven use.

"Let me show you," his voice dipped softer than I'd ever heard, and he pushed a hand against my hip. I squeaked at the invasion and sidestepped.

His eyes flashed. "I was going to show you how to stand."

"Oh, I... I'm not used... Sorry. Yeah." I may have acted boldly, but I wasn't. Not really. Men—people, in general—had touched me more in the past... however long I'd been here than in my nineteen years of life.

His head cocked, and his eyes went down my body and across my hand that still held the bow. As if he understood what I wasn't saying. I had never been touched, wasn't used to being touched. Something dark fluttered in his eyes, but it was gone with resolve.

"Get used to it, Keeper. It's part of training. Allowing me to touch you, appropriately, is a conduit to training."

I flared my nostrils but said nothing.

He took a careful breath. "We'll break for breakfast in a few."

"Deal," I said, and he touched my hip again. His fingers at my waist were warm, and I gulped down the nerves that came with his touch. I blew out an unsteady breath.

Once he moved my body into position, he came to my hands and showed me how to knock an arrow, and how to draw the string. Where my fingers went, my arms, and he too touched my mottled hand, moving the fingers into place without hesitation. I shivered at his touch, and he eyed me from the corner of his. I gulped it down but felt the touch down my spine and across my belly. It was different from Aven's touch. More of a linger, less innocent. Aven had thought nothing of it, but Reid did it slowly, on purpose, to get me used to the touch as much as to prove a point. I just had no idea what that point was.

Chapter 11

Rise with me

The next morning at dawn, Reid awaited me. This time I had left him waiting on purpose. His nostrils flaring was the only indication of his annoyance. I'd had dinner last night with the Celestria's, Aven, Marida, and her parents. Rhone had asked how I was faring, and I'd told him his captain was training me, but I didn't elaborate. I'm sure the captain reported my every move to the king anyway so there was no point wasting my breath. I needed to show Rhone the necklace, and I needed to ask him questions, but I was still internally angry with him for allowing my aunt to live the rest of her life heartbroken. I childishly wanted him to seethe a bit.

Childish, I know, but whatever.

The look on Reid's face—a predator assessing prey, snapped me back to the present with no lingering thoughts of Rhone, or anything else. There was only Reid and the torturous smile he sent me. It was terrifying.

But when we entered the training ring, he picked up a parcel laying across a wooden chair and handed it to me.

"What's this?" I asked.

"It's nothing. Just," he gestured vaguely, "might help..."

I opened the parcel and saw a strap. "Ah..."

"It's a thigh strap. So, you don't have to deal with the left-handed vests anymore. You can strap it to either thigh, making pulling your dagger out easier."

"I... Wow. That's clever." It wasn't just a strap either, the sheath was new, supple, and finely made. The one I had for the dagger was stiff and old, cracked in some places. This was made from something softer, featherlight, and super flexible.

"This is—" I noticed in the leather was stitching of roses, keys, a crescent moon, and an array of stars. The sheath had a flourishing K on it. I grinned. It was gorgeous and personal... *very personal.*

My eyes lifted to his and I felt a sting at the back of my throat. It was so thoughtful and very Reid-like in its functionality. He was ensuring my deformity wasn't a weakness even with what I wore.

"Did you—Is—"

"It's nothing."

"I..." I tried to convey how much it meant that he thought to get me something like this, but all I could say was, "Thank you, Reid."

He nodded, and I quickly strapped it on.

It was perfect. I barely noticed it was there, and the movement was effortless to get my dagger out with my right hand on my thigh. Reid watched me silently, assessing my movements. There was a small smile on his mouth, and I tried my best not to stare.

Swords. He wanted to teach me how to use a sword. "Can't we go riding again?" Something I excelled at. He laughed.

What an asshole.

"Oh, no, I want to flood you so much with weaponry you smell iron in your sleep."

Well, shit. What had I expected when I agreed to let *him* train me, he was a *guard captain*!

I tried to fake a strike and twist, but his sword came down on my arm. He held it back, of course, so it didn't slice me. Instead, he rapped me with it, and it stung.

"You're using this training to pummel me for your own sick, twisted enjoyment!"

He scoffed. "I get no enjoyment from this, I assure you."

Liar, I wanted to spit, but I was too sore and tired. He tossed me a water skein. I seethed but plunked my ass on the ground. We'd been at this for hours and hours and days and days, and still, I felt no closer to learning the sword. Granted, I could at least hold the thing now. I had strengthened my right hand to hold the sword, my wrist to twist. Now I could strike and block, but I had a long way to go before I could even remotely use it with proficiency.

I glanced at Reid who swung his sword and danced near me. It was awesome. His movements were beautiful and graceful, and it made me jealous, but then again, the guy was a guard captain. He ate, slept, and breathed sword fighting.

I know he took it easy on me. My lack of knowledge, and strength, even because I was a girl. I know he did. I saw it in his temper, his flash of annoyance when I did something insanely stupid, but I was *trying.* I had not run back to my bedroom with my tail between my legs. I didn't even really balk at his touch anymore when he moved my legs to better plant my feet or rotate my hips.

If I was disturbingly honest, his touch was foreign in an alarmingly appealing way.

"You can fight easily with your hands because your hand makes a fist already, you know that?"

Funny. Was he trying to be *funny?*

I tsked with my lips, in distaste and he chuckled. "What, not used to people teasing you?"

"Oh, no, Captain, *that* I am plenty used to."

His eyes flashed with fury—not at me, but my words. I don't know why he would care but his face showed it. "I meant in a joking manner."

"It's either cruelty or silence when it comes to my hand," I said with a bite, as I watched Aven extend the bow, and loose an arrow. I longed for that. I wanted to learn the bow. The swords just weren't for me, and I didn't have the power to use them, but Reid was persistent.

"I meant no offense."

My eyes flashed across his face, his stance, the way he had stopped showing me the sword techniques and stood still. I know he didn't mean to offend, but he thought me a pompous little damsel, spoiled and bratty and he may have been right, to some degree, but not about that. Not about the teasing, the bullying—with that I was no stranger to cruel treatment. "Sure," I said, trying to quell this.

"I'm serious."

"I'm sure."

"Kaidyn." His voice went strangely soft, and my eyes flickered to his. The fury in his blue eyes had dissipated and in them was a softness to match his voice. I swallowed and glanced away.

"Okay," I finally said, hoping he would drop it.

He did. He gestured to Aven. "Av, why don't you teach Kaidyn how to use the bow. She's looking at it like it's a long-lost friend."

My eyes darted to his, and he gave me a tiny smile. He'd noticed?

"Oh! Always happy to show a pretty lady my... *weapons*."

I rolled my eyes, and Reid copied the gesture. We shared a look, our eyes fused before he looked away. "I have a few things to attend to. I'll be back later."

We'd missed breakfast, but Reid had stopped us for lunch and my sore muscles had barked at the break in pace and movement. I had been rubbing on a salve Marida gave me each night that made the ache lessen. I had no clue what was in the salve, but it smelled a bit like cat urine. She also gave me a glorious lavender-scented one to put on in the morning before I started training and that seemed to chase away any lingering aches and hopefully covered up the cat piss scent.

For eight days I had been training with Reid. Every day. From dawn to dusk. Sometimes he'd leave midday, and not return for a few hours, going out on patrol or handling a guard matter, in which case I was allowed a reprieve and dined with Marida in the gardens. I loved those times, but I also loved the feeling of my muscles toning, my arms, legs, and core gaining strength. I know Reid was taking it easy on me, and only showing me the basics. He was persistent on the fact he didn't care if I mastered anything, he just wanted me to be competent enough to handle myself. I could manage that, but I had a feeling at some point he was going to push harder, and challenge me, but for now, he was familiarizing me with words, knowledge, and weapons, that I would have only ever dreamed of hearing and seeing never mind using. This was a dream, and every day I was thankful. This was a once-in-a-lifetime experience, and I was taking it in stride. I felt guilt—it seeped into my pores every night as I lay in bed, but I dutifully ignored it during the day. Yes, I missed my family. I missed my brother the most, but this was insane and unbelievable.

Sometimes I cried at night at how right it felt here. How quickly I fit in, how quickly I accepted a life here. I hadn't been pressured to be a Keeper. I hadn't been pressured to *be* anything except strong. Reid insisted I be strong, and I think I would forever be grateful to him for that. We both had thought I would hate him for pushing and challenging me, but I was afraid that wasn't the case. I was a little terrified of that revelation.

As I watched a guard mount his horse, I had the overwhelming urge to ride.

Could I just ride if I wished it? Would I be allowed?

Aven, sensing my distraction, touched my arm. "We can go riding later if you want. I'll make Reid cut your training short."

"Really?"

"Aye," he said confidently with a shrug.

Aven put me at ease. He made me feel at home and that was a dangerous feeling for a place I was supposed to leave behind. A place I wasn't supposed to be connected to. A place I shouldn't feel anything for. I needed to get home before this place became ingrained in my soul.

"You fit here, Kaidyn."

My eyes flickered to him. It was as if he had sensed my thoughts. "I don't. I'm supposed to be something I'm not. I'm not the Keeper—or at least, I don't want to be. I just want to find the stone so I can go home."

"You have become important to us. Not because you're the Keeper. That might be why we were all accommodating at first, but not now. Now you are ours, and *we* are *yours.*"

My heart leaped at his words. "What changed?" I whispered.

"You did."

I blew out a deep breath. *You fit here. You are ours and we are yours.* My soul shattered at his words, burning tears tore at my throat and settled in my eyes. I didn't want to fit here, I wanted to go home... Didn't I? I had no right feeling so full of life here; so complete. My family wasn't here. These people weren't my friends. They wanted something from me and hoped that once I was through floundering around, I would get on with it, and I was due to remembering that.

"Will he let me go riding?"

He noted my refusal to finish our conversation. "He's not as heartless as he seems. I promise you."

"Well then, show me how to use this bow, and let's go."

Aven grinned. Dropping the conversation. Smart man.

"Teach a girl a little about weapons and she becomes so *bossy.*"

I elbowed him.

He let me fire a few arrows. I wasn't great at it, but I didn't necessarily suck either. Moderate suck, to be fair. After three hours my arms felt like jelly. This was different than the dagger and sword because it was the same movements, the same muscles being used over and over, and it wore on me, but it felt good. I almost hit the target. Almost. I was so close, and Aven was impressed with my progression.

Neither Aven nor Reid thought of my hand as a weakness and it showed with the way they taught me as if I were no different from them, and that...

that was a beautiful thing. Something I had lacked all my life; to belong, to be treated as if I was a complete person not someone with a mostly missing hand.

Reid returned finally, and he could see the strain on my muscles, my need for a reprieve and it was as if he read my mind when he asked before anyone had the chance to speak, "Want to find yourself a horse?"

My eyes flicked to Aven's and I wondered if he had sent word to Reid of my request. I swallowed as my eyes went back to Reid.

His brow lifted. "No? I just thought—"

"Yes. Please." I resisted the urge to do a happy dance—partially because my muscles ached too much for it, partially because of how embarrassing that would be in front of these two.

Reid cocked his head, and his eyes shifted from me to Aven.

"She's already asked, but she—*we*—thought we'd have to... persuade you."

Reid gave one curt nod, and his eyes flickered across mine again. "I'm not a complete asshole. I can tell your muscles are sore, and you've made a lot of progress in the past week. Think of it as a... *reward*."

"For not being a whiny little bitch?" I asked, sweetly.

Aven cackled at my side, and Reid stared at me a full second before he threw his head back and laughed. "Yes, Keeper, for not being a complete whiny little bitch. A bit whiny at times, but... manageable."

"Great!" I grinned and followed them to the pasture.

As soon as we stepped to the gate, Alida broke off from the foraging group and galloped over to Aven.

"Where's Javarr?" I asked, not seeing Reid's gray stallion.

"He..." Reid cocked his head as his eyes met mine. "You know my horse's name?"

"I've ridden with you before, remember?"

"Yes, but... You—Ah. He's in the stables resting. We had a hard patrol at the coast, and it was a long run." Reid scratched the back of his neck and surveyed me.

I nodded, but thoughts of Reid simpered at the back of my mind as Fain trotted over to me.

"Hi, boy." I crooned as he lipped my hair. I rubbed my hands down his face. He had filled out some since I had been training, as had Silas. Marida and Vera spoiled my cat rotten and fed him everything under the sun. He was starting to get a belly, and I think he liked Marida more than me. But that was okay, I liked Marida more than me, too.

Aven shot Reid a look, and Reid watched the horse and me so long that I swallowed and met his eyes as Fain nuzzled down my cheek. I giggled and pushed the horse's face away so that I could seriously look at the captain.

His eyes darted across Fain and then back to me. "I see a horse has already chosen."

"I... I don't know... is—"

"Fain hasn't gotten close to anyone. He hasn't trusted any of us to get close to him. I've voiced to Leiri that he'd be turned loose next spring if he's not bonded." Reid sighed heavily. "I... I was hoping you'd bond with a gentler, already trained horse, but..."

I lifted a brow because there was a smirk on his lips. "You're insufferable, as always."

I opened my mouth to retort, but Fain nudged me for attention, and Aven gestured. "Why don't you go and see if he'll follow you?"

"Ah. Follow me? Inside the pasture?"

"Yes," Reid said before Aven could answer.

I clambered over the fence. Fain stepped back, but I extended my hand and he sniffed it. I blew out a breath at him, as Aven had suggested, and he flared his nostrils and swung his head back to the others.

Finally, as if he'd made me wait long enough, he nuzzled my outstretched hand, and then came to my front. I scratched his ears and ran a hand down his neck and along his side. He quivered under my touch but didn't step away.

"Amazing." I heard Aven say, but I tuned them out as I touched the blond horse. It was just him and me, and I loved him instantly. He flicked his tail in my face as I walked by, and I sputtered.

I heard masculine laughter and I grumbled, "Men." I pointed a finger at the horse's face. "Watch it, buster."

Fain seemed surprised by this, and snorted at me, but nudged my chest with his head. I conceded and rubbed. I leaned into his neck and hugged him.

I did as Aven had suggested and walked about ten feet away, and the horse followed my every move without prompting. I walked back to the fence, and he did the same.

Reid cleared his throat and said my name. When I looked over at him, he gestured with a bridle. "See if he'll let you put this on him."

I swallowed but grabbed the leather straps. I extended it to the horse, who shied away. I waited, patiently. After a few moments, he came back and sniffed at the leather.

"For me to ride you, we need to do this. Okay?" He snorted and moved closer. "Want to run together?" His ears swiveled at my voice. "You and me. We can ride together across the highlands. We can be *free*." I brought the bridle against his nose, and rubbed it along his face, his neck, and his back, familiarizing him with the foreign touch of something on his body.

"Glorious freedom. Sounds good, doesn't it?"

I had forgotten again the men at the other side of the fence. It was just the horse and me, and the freedom of the moors that called to me. To us.

"You have to trust me, Fain, and I must trust you. We need to rely on one another to make this work. I've only ridden a few times in my life, and I need you to take it easy on me. I'll give you the freedom we both desire if you can trust me."

He whickered at me as if answering my plea. I rubbed my face against his neck, and whispered, "I've been so bottled up my entire life. Held back from everything I ever dreamed of because of fear, because of distrust placed there by the people around me, by doubt. But I want to change. I want to rise. Rise with me, and it'll be *magic*." I felt him quiver and his soulful brown eyes descended on me. He rubbed his nose along my cheek, pushing his warm, sweet air against my skin. I smiled and blew into his nose, and he swung his head and snorted. I grinned and brought the bridle up to his face. He met my eyes, and let me slip the bridle over his head, his ears and I slowly cinched it against his cheek. Those eyes never left mine and I smiled. "That's a good boy."

I rubbed his cheek beneath the bridle. "No big deal, is it?" I crooned and then turned to the men.

They both stared openmouthed at me, and I felt a little self-conscious at the things I had said and done. I gulped and the horse nudged my arm.

"Ah," Aven exclaimed.

Had I done something wrong?

Reid arched a dark brow. His stare was full of wonder, and my cheeks heated. "Yes, well... Well done, Keeper, that was..."

"Fucking incredible?" Aven offered and the awe and respect in his eyes flashed through me so thoroughly I felt the strength of it flutter in my heart.

I felt a glimmer of pride. Something I had rarely felt in my life.

"Yes," Reid agreed. His eyes were on mine. I had a feeling he'd heard my whispered words to the horse, because there was something undecipherable in his eyes, and I tried my best to ignore the warmth that spread through me at whatever it was.

They encouraged me to lead Fain around and he was as docile as a tired puppy. Not once did he act up, nor even toss his head. He was a perfect gentleman.

Finally, Reid told me to take it off him and come out of the pasture. I did so with some reluctance. I said my goodbyes to Fain, and we walked back to the stables.

"My men have been picking up my slack while I train you, but now that you're proficient enough, I'll have you train with Aven in archery and Holt with a sword, and every morning after an hour with Holt, I want you to train with Leiri in the stables. She is the stablemaster and horse trainer. She'll work with you and Fain to get him ready for riding. If you wish to ride you can use any of the other horses that are broken, but I want to ensure Fain is safe before you and he rides *freely* together. Understood?"

"Yes." I didn't miss his use of the word *freely*. He had heard my whispered words to the horse. Damn.

"After that training, you will have lunch as you see fit and then I will train you in one manner or another for a few hours and give you a little more... leisure time before dinner. Sufficient?"

I nodded because there was a tiny lump in my throat. I had been given so much more respect here than I ever had in my world. They were doing so much for me, and I was giving them *nothing*. I had promised them *nothing*. I had even told Rhone I wouldn't help them. I hadn't even given Rhone the respect of a council with him, nor shown him the necklace.

"Once Leiri deems you *both* fit, I will conclude if he is the right fit for you," Reid finished.

It didn't matter what he said. He was giving me a horse. Fain would be mine—sort of. Mine while I was here, anyway. The lump in my throat collapsed and I took a shuddering breath as my eyes met his. I tried to say thank you, but it came out as another shuddering breath. His brows pinched together, and he quickly looked away. It gave me enough time to compose myself. I squeaked, *thank you.* But it was fairly indecipherable.

He gave a quick nod. "I'll introduce you to Leiri, and she can show you her training ring."

As we were leaving the stables, Bronwen trotted over to us. She and Reid stepped away from me and spoke in hushed undertones. I caught a few things about disturbances and coastal issues. Reid gestured to a few men and sent a regiment to the coast. I nearly walked back to the castle, not wanting him to think I needed him to show me back, but as I stepped away, he walked beside me.

"You can go, you know."

He looked me over quickly. "I know. Bronwen can head the team just as easily as me."

We walked a moment and I chewed the inside of my lip. Finally, I blurted, "Are you and Bronwen... Ah."

His eyes cut to mine and I looked away. I had heard them beneath my balcony. I had seen Bronwen giving him appreciative glances. It didn't surprise me. She was beautiful, powerful—the same as he. Despite the amount of time he spent with me, he had a life. He'd had one well before I came into it, and he'd have one after I left.

He swallowed, and I could tell he wanted to ignore my insinuation, but after a long moment, he said, "We were once, but I never gave her permanence. We…"

"She just warmed your bed." I found my words were beginning to sound like theirs. In my world, I'd have said, *you were hooking up*. But saying that would be lost on him.

Bronwen's words came back about being a warm spot for a man or being something else, and I knew she was something else. She would never allow herself to get caught up in the pretense of being Reid's warm bed. She was a warrior first, and there would be no hurt feelings with no permanence. There was such a thing as casual sex in my world too.

He sighed. It began deep in his muscled chest and out his nose as if the world rested upon his shoulders. He *did* need to get laid. I snorted at the prospect. Marida had gotten so many things caught in my head. I couldn't even look at Kavall with a straight face anymore without envisioning him and Marida's *heavy kissing*.

"For a time," he stated, denying nothing.

It drew me back to the present. "What happened?"

His eyes flashed, but there was a hint of a smile on his face. "A Keeper came into my life and took all my free time away."

I laughed. "Not in the middle of the night."

His eyes gained a dark heat, which sent warmth coiling far too low in my abdomen for my liking.

I swallowed the torrent that heated look caused.

Reid bit his lip, and I followed the movement. His mouth was so… tasty looking. What? No. No. I did not just think that.

"You don't think so?" He whispered.

I had been so wrapped up in thinking about what those lips would taste like, if his mouth was as soft as it looked, I completely forgot what I had asked, what had been said to follow this conversation anymore.

He left me at the door, feigning somewhere to be. I couldn't blame him. My face was heated with our exchange, and I was really not sure what had just happened.

After dinner that night, which I had eaten with everyone at the dining hall, I asked for a private audience with Rhone. For some reason, I didn't want to share the necklace with the others.

Rhone gasped as I held the necklace out to him, and his eyes grew misted. I swallowed back the lump in my throat, as I watched him slowly reach for it. I placed it into his palm, and I wished to evaporate onto the floor with the harrowed look he wore.

"I gave this to Millicent as a betrothal present. I..."

I didn't dare tell him I had found it in a trunk in Vanstarr Castle. Aunt Millie hadn't even taken it with her from her quarters when she'd left Evirness to go home. I didn't know why she hadn't taken it, but it wasn't my business. It begged the question again though as to the story.

"I was so angry with you," I whispered, and his eyes flickered from the necklace to mine. I glanced away. "My aunt lived a life of solitude. She never married, never had kids. She lived alone with her cats and stories. I had asked her once about herself and she told me she had loved a man, just once, and that he was not to be hers. But I had seen that bottomless love in her eyes." My eyes flickered to his again and I noticed they were swimming with tears, they dripped down his cheeks and my cheeks were wet too.

I shuddered out a breath. "I skimmed her diary because much of it was the spouting of her love for you."

He looked away and walked to the windows. Night had descended, and only the flickering of moonlight and the wink of stars could be seen out of the high windows.

He was silent for so long that I was afraid I might need to slip out, but then he spoke. "I loved Millicent. We were young and in love and I wanted nothing but her. I would have given up my crown, my ancestral rights, *everything* for her, but my father would hear none of it. He had already arranged my marriage and hid it from me. I had tried to sway him on how wonderful a union with a Keeper would be for my reign, but he ignored every word. He pronounced my engagement to Eranora the next day after I had asked for his blessing on my betrothal to Millie. Millicent heard of it the same time as I, but I couldn't get to her in time before she fled. I would have run away with her, even gone to your realm if I could have. I'd have given up my throne without a thought. My father had no right to do that before I even had the chance to tell her. She thought, of course, that I had agreed. *I hadn't.* It was five years after she had left before I finally agreed to my father's wishes, and that was only because he had fallen gravely ill. No mender could help him. He had an infection in his bones that could not be cured, and on his death bed asked me to solidify a marriage with an Elirian princess, joining our friendly neighbors in matrimony." He dashed another tear away. "If Millie had stayed, I would have never married Eranora. I would have defied my father. She... Millicent was the love of my life, the match of my soul. I married for duty, and have grown to love Eranora, but she and I both know she is not... that for me. It wears you down when someone lies deeply in your heart but cannot be in your arms." His eyes held such pain, I felt a deep ache in my chest.

"I'm so sorry, Rhone." Because I didn't know what else to say. There was nothing else *to* say. I wished Aunt Millie would have known. I wish she hadn't been so stubborn, but then again that was a family trait. I, too, was that stubborn. Aunt Millie had missed out on a lifetime of love, a chance at the real thing, the soul-blending kind of love that this man had for her, the kind that one defies all laws of duty for. She could have had that if only she'd stayed, had listened to him, but she hadn't. She'd fled for her world and then existed in it for the rest of her years. Not truly living. My heart ached for her, for him, for all of it.

Despite his insistence that I keep the necklace, I could tell he wanted it. That token of her. So, I made him keep it.

I cried myself to sleep that night, Silas curled against me. I finally grieved for Aunt Millie, but not the grief of losing her. I cried in grief for not being with the man that had been her soul's reflection of love. I cried for the loss of a love that could have set this world on fire. The love that could have changed *everything*.

Because none of this would have happened if she'd stayed. The magic wouldn't have gone haywire, the wall never erected.

I... I wouldn't be here, in Evirness, at all, would I?

CHAPTER 12

Prickly and beautiful like a rose.

"You are nothing but a coward," Reid growled.

He wasn't wrong but it pissed me off. I used the anger and my burning thighs and launched myself at him. My small sword struck him, but I moved again. I was not fluid grace, but I was fast. I had strong thighs and legs from swimming and hiking. My arms were tired before anything else. I rarely used my arms for anything before now—and it showed.

Reid was right, but I used it as fuel to push past the burning in my arms and tread around him. Pushing back at him as he did me. I was in no mood today for his jabs. Marida and I had finally started doing some research on how to portal me home, and I had mixed emotions about it. I needed to go home, but I was downright pissed with the fact that I wanted to stay. I wanted to stay so badly that it was hard to breathe when I thought about leaving. And that *pissed me off.* I had never wanted to get wrapped up in these people, this place, to want to stay. But it happened anyway.

"A spoiled *little* girl."

I wanted to spit in his face, but I saw the burning of his blue eyes and I growled and pushed harder against his sword. Pushing him back just enough to spin away, gather myself, and go on the offensive. I pivoted and swung my lighter sword towards him. He came up to parry, but he had a smile on his face. I wanted to hit him. Hard. With the sword. And not in the rump like Aven did with me. The thought had me smiling and I saw the captain's eyes flash.

"You're insufferable," he said with a rumble.

"So..." I ducked under his sword arc and wrenched my small sword up to his rib. Grazing the leather armor there. "Are. *You*."

Those blue eyes danced, and a smile brushed his lips again. His sword slid the length of mine until it hit the crossguard. Then he heaved once and toppled me back on my rear. My sword clanged on the dirt.

I flopped back exhausted, frustrated, and miffed. The captain smiled broadly, it lightened his face and made him less stoic, and more human. Approachable. Sexier. I hated that my insides heated at the kick-up of his lips.

When he grinned like that, partly in amusement, partly a threat... My insides reacted. I growled and leaped up.

We traded barbs again, and he thrust his sword at me. I spun away again but he advanced, pushing me back against the inner circle, then he drove me to the outer circle. I tried to shove against him, but it was no use, he was a stone wall. Hard. Unmovable. I strained and sweat beaded across my upper lip and dripped down my spine.

With Aven, it was fun, giggling, and simple instructions. I tended to somehow get spun around so he could stare at my ass and smack the flat of his sword against it. It was a game to him. The guy was obsessed with my rear end. Apparently, I was *more endowed* than most women. It was his subtle way of saying my ass was fat, which with anyone else, in any other place, I would have been embarrassed and deeply offended, but with Aven, there was no offense. He liked it and exploited that fact. It *had* embarrassed me at first, but now I realized I could use it against him. Tight booty-fitting clothes made him lose concentration. It was funny. Despite not having attraction between us to act on, it didn't mean both of us didn't find the other attractive. Aven had called me beautiful enough times in the past few weeks that I knew it was the truth— to him. He thought my body was erotic curves, and my face appealing—he'd told me plenty. It didn't embarrass me anymore, instead, it was *flattering*. That's how a woman should take such a compliment from an incredibly attractive man that would never touch her that way said nice things. *Take the compliment*. He meant it, so I took it as such. He liked to smack me on the rump with the flat of his sword. We teased each other like siblings yet topped it with goofy sexual innuendos.

I won't lie, though, when Aven had his shirt off while training, I was distracted too. He was lean and muscled, and I had rarely seen any man with a shirt off, especially men with muscles like these men. I'd seen plenty of the guards over the past few weeks with their shirts off too, and it was a sight to behold. Muscles like that didn't happen in my world.

Marida had even come out with Aven and me and done some sword work. She had a short sword like mine, and she was all fluid grace and twirling movements. I was epically awed by her. It was like watching a magnificent dancer, yet she held a sharp-edged weapon in her hands. She and Aven— watching them dance around each other with the blade was almost erotic in its choreographed beauty. He bested her most of the time, but now and again he would land flat on his ass, and she would put the sword tip to his heart, her foot on his chest, and he would send a crude comment spinning from his sinful mouth, and she'd laugh that tinkling laugh of hers. I wished, in my heart, for them to fall in love because that would blaze the world in its beauty, but that was my little fantasy because I *loved* them. Separately. Together. Training me or sitting at a table eating with me or hanging on Marida's bed gossiping, which Aven did sometimes too. I loved them. They were *my* people now, and I think...I dared to think they loved me too. It caused friction in my heart, an ache. I wasn't supposed to feel connected.

My thoughts snapped to Reid. Holt and Reid were more civilized, more professional when they trained me. Holt was all polite, gentle, and by the book. Everything he did was with precision. Holt showed me a lot with my dagger, and even let me throw his daggers a few times. That was fun as hell, and an effective way to unwind. I wasn't overly good at it—rarely even hit the target, but when the captain pissed me off, or I started to get nervy about going home, or Keeper duties had been brought up and I had tried to ignore it—I slung a dagger at a target. Wonders what a dagger being thrown from your fingers would do to one's psyche.

It was with Reid though that I was challenged. Not just with the weapons, the footwork, and focus but with *him*, in general. He pissed me off, and pushed me and it was effective. But I was beginning to enjoy our banter, our verbal sparring. I looked forward to it each day. I would miss him when I left, and that terrified me.

"You're holding back!" His angry voice pulled me from my thoughts.

"I'm not!" I bellowed because I didn't know what else to say. I was at the edge of the outer circle, and I was only not over it because he had stopped pushing me.

"You—"

"You out-weigh me by like a hundred pounds, you big oaf! Not only that—" I spit out, angered. "But you've been training since before you could walk!"

His blue eyes blazed and widened and then he threw his head back and howled up to the sky in laughter. Effectively pulling his sword away from me, I took the chance to spin away.

I stood there heaving breath as his laughter drifted over me. My lips kicked up. I was winded but pleased with myself. I held my own against Reid. Sort of. I'm not sure if that was my skill increasing or that he was going easier on me but either way, I felt pride in myself.

He stopped howling in laughter, but his grin was still wide, his eyes bright. "Stars Above. I've never been called a big oaf before."

"Well, you *are*!" My voice held no mirth, but the spiritedness of it shimmered in the air between us.

We grinned at each other for far longer than was appropriate.

He turned away first, his eyes slanting to the sun's dip in the sky. His eyes traveled back to me. "It's nearly dinner."

My hair was in a plaited braid across my shoulder—a look I had adopted from Bronwen. I felt his gaze snag on it, then dip lower. Sweat had plastered my blouse to my chest. I could feel his eyes gather across the swell of my breasts and my muscles tightened in my core and lower, to places I had no idea even existed. A spiraling heat rolled across my chest to sit low in my belly. His eyes razed down the rest of my body, then back to mine. At this point, I was looking at him through my lashes, because the heat had slashed a trail from my center to my cheeks.

"You did well today," his husky voice exclaimed.

I preened—

"But." *There it is.* "You still see your deformity as a weakness. It causes you to falter."

"It's half a fucking hand, Reid. I—"

"It's *perfect*. A part of you. Just like your adorable freckles, your big heart, and your stunning green eyes."

What? "My—heart. Ador—What?"

He groaned. "You see your deformity as a flaw, Kaid. No one else does until you make it one. *Don't make it one.* Give no one a reason to see it or you, as weak. Learn to carry yourself with confidence. Your self-esteem is how you present and hold yourself and how others will see you. Your left hand is as strong as your right. Stronger given what it can do. It is an incredible extension of you. A magnificent sign of your birthright."

I sighed. The exhale came from deep inside, but I felt something reaching up, stretching, some inner strength. It liked his praise.

I *was* slowly growing stronger, seeing my deformity not as a flaw, not as a weakness. It was just taking years of feeling different, not good enough, and fragile to get through before I could fully embrace it.

"I think I've figured you out Kaidyn Flynn, esteemed Keeper of the Keys, a lineage of ancient—"

"Oh, get the hell on with it!" I waved my hand, and his grin was broad and belligerent.

"I think I have your training figured out."

"Oh really?" I rolled my eyes skyward.

"When you train with Aven, Marida, or even Holt, you're soft on them, and they are on you because you like them."

"I like them, yes." It was true, I did. But I had no idea what that had to do with anything.

"With me, there is a fire in your belly, passion in your spirit. I see it and can push it. The others can't."

"You think it's because *I like* them?"

"Yes. You have no sense of self-preservation, but you are motivated, or *not* motivated in this sense by... love."

I shook my head, perplexed. "Love?"

"Well, in a sense. Because you like them, I can't let you train with them any longer."

I groaned. "That is the dumbest thing I have ever heard."

"That is why I suppose your training falls to me. Solely. Again."

Awesome. Not. "But I like learning different things..."

"You will."

I had enjoyed training with the others because it was a fun reprieve, but also because being around Reid was starting to get... heated. I was attracted *to* him and it was mortifying.

"That makes no sense..."

He chuckled. "*We* can fight. Brawl. You try harder. I see the fighting spirit, that inner fire in you. I want to exploit it."

"I..." I had no idea what to say to that.

"But first I need to take you somewhere."

"Take...Take me somewhere?"

"Yes. Meet me at the stables in an hour."

"I... Okay..." He sent me a smirk.

He seemed so sure of himself, so positive in his thoughts towards my training. He seemed so confident in *me*.

Alida was saddled for me when I met Reid. He was already astride Javarr looking miffed. Typical. But his eyes scanned me, resting for a long moment on my thigh, and my cheeks burned from the attention in such an intimate spot. I had worn the thigh sheath with my dagger every single moment of every day since he'd given it to me. Before that I had only worn the dagger if I knew we were training with the dagger, otherwise, it remained in my room. But since he had given me the strap, I never took it off, but to sleep and bathe. It was because it was comfortable, not because of who gave it to me. Not to mention it was beautiful and made me feel empowered.

Reid jerked his head, and I hurriedly mounted Alida, who stood still and waited. I wished I could have ridden Fain. We had made so much progress, but since Alida was already saddled, I didn't dare ask.

From the strange look in his eyes, I had no idea what he was up to, I had a feeling I was going to hate it.

"Where are we going?" I asked as we made our way to the castle gates, which led to the city below.

"Patience," Reid said simply, and I seethed.

How could he annoy me so much with a simple word, yet send my heart racing too?

I smiled just for a second because I had noted, with some dismay, that this morning Silas had not been in my room. Not that I cared because he often wandered from my room to Marida's, but when I called for him, he'd come from Reid's room. My traitorous cat was now visiting the guard captain at night, and clearly, the captain was allowing it since I had never seen his door left ajar until recently. It had all added up, as the cat sauntered over to me as if nothing had happened. Embarrassingly, I'd picked Silas up and rubbed my nose against his fur. It smelled of Reid—mountain air and leather.

"Tell me about the doorways." I was surprised I had the gall to ask aloud, but it took my mind off my cat and my mortifying reaction to him coming from Reid's room.

"The... what?"

"Marida explained the doorways to me, and I heard Rhone speaking about new ones opening this morning at breakfast. They're a Keeper thing, right?"

He cut me a sideways scowl and I glared back. Reid would give me the most direct, no-bullshit answer. Plus, he didn't care about not pressuring me. I had been insistent on not being compelled, but I was at the point where... I wanted to be pressured a little, and it was Reid's fault. His training and words gave me confidence.

"Never mind." I already regretted asking him.

His glower turned into a long sigh, as he glanced away. "The magic of Evirness is erratic, unpredictable unless it's harnessed. It has been that way since the dawn of time in this sliver of the world. There's a well of power here that no one can find, nor understand. I won't pretend to comprehend the Keeper's role, entirely, nor how they balance the magic, but they push the magic into doorways, locks, and other worlds, and pull the magic into themselves, thus balancing it. I'm sure there's far more to it than that." He sucked in a breath, and we made our way steadily down into the village. "Without a Keeper, doorways are popping up at random. It's been happening for years, but lately, the doorways have been cutting off villages from resources, trade routes, mountain passes, and waterways. People are forced to make do with what few resources they can acquire on their own but..." He glanced at me, those flecks of dark sapphire and violet flashed. "I know you don't want to hear this, and everyone else will dance around the truth for your sensitivity, but I have a feeling since you asked *me,* you're willing to hear it. We need a Keeper, Kaid. We need someone to return the balance or the doorways will exceed our resources, murder us all before we have a chance to fight back." He graced me with a vulnerable glance. "I am supposed to protect the Celestria's with my life and I will do so without hesitation, but even I... can't protect them from this. I can't *fight* this."

I needed a boot in the ass. I had fallen in love with this place, these people, and my soul felt the call to help them—if I could. But it was Reid's staggering vulnerable words that resonated deep in my soul. It made something rise.

I gave him my best-guarded expression, but I know he could see it—that fire he so brazenly told me I had. His eyes lit up; his rigid set relaxed. It was as if he could read my mind, my heart, my soul, and saw that I wanted to help. That I *would* help them in whatever way I could. I swear he felt my resolve settle over me, as I did.

"There's that fire, Keeper. That beautiful fire that you keep hidden from everyone, including yourself. But I see it, and it is *staggering*."

My stomach twisted at his words, and I felt hot all over. Heat drifted across me as my eyes met his. In those remarkable eyes of his, there was a flame to match what I felt, a fire that matched mine.

A grin curled his sensual mouth and I had to look away. I told myself it was all so that I would balance their magic, close some doorways—that was the only reason he looked at me that way, said those words that shattered my heart, and opened my soul. No one had spoken to me like this. It made me yearn.

Fuck. I had to stop this way of thinking.

"We're here," Reid said, and I glanced around.

We were in the market square in front of a massive stone building, which swept around the corner, and was open on the sides. I smelled leather and heated metal.

A blacksmith shop?

Reid dismounted and tied Javarr to a post. With a swallow, I did the same. My eyes scoured the storefront and then ran up Reid's chest to his face. What were we doing here?

Above the door were two signs; one held an anvil, the other a bridle. Were we buying Fain a bridle? That would be excellent, although I had no funds.

"What—"

"This is the tanner, leathermaker, blade maker, and blacksmith. A husband, wife, and son trio. It's where—" He cleared his throat. "I commissioned your thigh strap."

Oh. I glanced at him, but he was already striding to the door. It jingled happily as we entered, and I looked around. The walls were covered in tools, and workbenches dominated the space, along with an open, round stone fire pit, wooden keg-like barrels, and a few dried herbs. The windows slanted in the sunlight, illuminating the shimmer of blades. So many swords, bows, daggers, and numerous manners of weapons and tools. Then I noted another wall held saddles, bridles, straps, backs, and everything leather.

"Wow," I whispered. The smell of embers, leather, and iron filled my senses. It was magnificent in its orderly chaos.

A short, plump woman with black hair tied in a top-knot, and a leather apron, stepped out of a doorway.

"Reid!" She exclaimed happily and enveloped him in a hug.

I was startled, having never seen anyone touch Reid so openly. The others spoke with him with so much familiarity, but to touch him? This intrigued me.

"I made a fresh batch of cookies! I'll get some."

He nodded and turned back to me when she left. I lifted a brow. "Etta is... my aunt."

I cocked my head. I never even thought that Reid may have family here. I always assumed they got cut off in the south with the wall. "I—"

"Oatmeal raisin. Your favorite!" The happy woman exclaimed as she bustled back into the room, and I found myself grinning as Reid rolled his eyes.

"Auntie Etta, this is Kaidyn Flynn. Kaidyn, Etta."

I instantly extended my right hand, but she just set the tray of cookies down on a bench, gave me a soft once over, and then encircled me in a hug. She smelled of cookies, leather, and herbs, which I found comforting along with her gentle hands around me. I met Reid's eyes over her shoulder, and he wore a small grin. This was unexpected, but I found it hard not to squeeze her back.

"Cookies first, then to your wares."

I lifted a brow, but when she shoved three cookies at me, I thought of nothing else but their warm, oat texture, the sweetness of the raisin deliciousness. I moaned in ecstasy and noticed Reid holding back the same reaction. I grinned at him, and he at me, as his aunt bustled around us.

"How are things in the castle, my sweet boy?"

I choked on a cookie but tried to hide it with a cough.

Sweet boy? Laughable.

Reid glared at me, but when his face turned to his aunt it was full of love and adoration. "Same as always."

"Kavall hasn't found a nice girl to settle down with?"

I tried to hide my snicker, but I just couldn't.

"No, Auntie, not that I'm aware. Although I don't poke into his love life."

"Shame. He's a wonderful boy." Then her blue eyes whipped over him and narrowed. "Well, let's not even get started with *you!*"

She looked insufferably annoyed. It was adorable.

He began to choke on a cookie, and I stepped over to thump him on the back with the biggest grin I have ever worn on my face. He glared, his midnight eyes dancing with exasperation.

This was *delightful!*

"Can we not talk about *anyone's* love life, Auntie?"

"Well, you are well beyond marrying age."

He was only about four or five years older than me. This world was different, that's for sure.

"Mmhmm," Reid answered, exasperated.

My grin was so plastered on I couldn't wipe it off.

"What about that blonde girl, the tall—"

A choked laugh bubbled out of me, and Reid glared harder. I tried covering my face with my hand and shoved another cookie in my mouth to shut up.

"Okay, Auntie, we have to go. Right now. So—"

"Oh, right! Okay." She ruffled his hair, affectionately, and he grabbed her hand and kissed it. A prickle started at the back of my throat at the familial bond, and I started to miss my family all over again. It must have shown in my eyes because Reid gave me a questioning look before turning to his aunt.

"Is it finished?" Reid asked, and I noted there was a soft uncertainty to his voice. It made me sit up just a little straighter.

Etta looked me over. Her eyes snagged on my hand. "Oh, yes. This... I see. Yes. My finest work yet." The woman was a bluster of bubbly words.

Reid smiled at her, but his eyes were on me. He mouthed *are you okay*, and I nodded quickly, glancing away.

I needed to get home. Soon.

Etta returned with something wrapped in a thin brown blanket and handed it to Reid. He flicked the blanket open, but not enough so that I could see what it was.

"Might as well let you see now, instead of making you sit in suspense. You'll only pester me the whole ride back."

My eyes flicked to his. "What?"

He handed me the parcel, and I took a steadying breath. My eyes went from his to Etta's, to the parcel. He had already given me the sheath and strap he couldn't possibly have commissioned something else for me.

I slowly unwrapped the package, but I wasn't completely sure what I was looking at. They were deep red leather and had hooks and straps. My eyes swept up to Reid's and he nodded to the things. I ran my fingers down the engraved and threaded swirls, roses, filigree, and stars. I noted finger holes, and my heart stuttered.

I tried to grasp the word, and my mouth tried to work past a lump. "Bracers?"

His eyes flickered in approval. "Yes," his voice was soft, and I noted it was just he and I. Etta had left.

"I... I don't—"

"Want to make sure they fit?"

"I..." My eyes glanced from the thick leather to his face, and I swallowed. "Yes."

He nodded and stepped in front of me, tentatively taking them from the blanket and setting one aside. "Let's try this one first and see if my measurements were right."

I swallowed again, finding it harder to do. When his eyes met mine, and he stepped closer, I found my foot shuffling. It wasn't from discomfort, or distrust, just Reid and I usually were not this close unless we were sparring, training or he was showing me moves. I brushed my eyes up his leather-bound, muscled chest to the column of his tanned throat, to the scruff at his chin and above his lip, and then to his eyes. They were on mine, and there was heat in them, and something...I couldn't place.

He held the bracer between us and tipped his head down. I chewed on my lip but extended my right arm for him. He began strapping with clinical precision. The bracer went from my elbow to my first knuckle, but there were two layers. The hard leather layer went from elbow to wrist, and then a softer leather that went from wrist to knuckle. It made it more moveable but still protected from sword blade, string, or whatever else.

I flexed my hand, knuckles, and wrist once it was fully strapped. It felt lightweight, but it was armor. I felt like a warrior. It was such a simple thing, like my thigh strap, but I felt empowered, bolstered wearing it.

"Wow," I whispered, and his eyes went from the bracer to my face.

"Does it fit okay?"

"Like a glove," I said breathlessly.

His grin spread rapidly, and I realized my joke. It wasn't my intention, but my lips kicked up in response. "It's beautiful, Reid, and light and... perfect."

"Let's try the other one. I had... Well, it is more custom, of course." He slowly brought the bracer to my left arm, and his eyes met mine. "I have to..."

"I know. It's okay."

He inched closer and began strapping the bracer. This close, his heat licked at my body. His scent caused a ricochet of butterfly wings to flutter inside my rib cage. I had never experienced a feeling even remotely close to this, even with boy crushes in school. Reid was so... male. Imposing, tall, and strong. His muscles bunched and shifted on his forearms. I had noticed, from a distance, that when he fought with his guards he lost his shirt, but never did with me. Not that I would have minded. Heat crept up my neck with the thought. From what I had seen, he was sculpted and magnificent beneath his clothes. An intriguing tattoo went around his bicep to crawl up his shoulder. I had no idea what it was, or what it meant.

I needed to stop my sinful thoughts, but he dominated my space so thoroughly I forgot to breathe. When I finally did, it whooshed out and I felt his gaze on my face. I peeked at him from beneath my lashes and he was staring at me with an expression I had never seen before. It was intense and... that tightening in my belly matched his eyes.

He swallowed hard and stepped back. "Ah... All done." He exclaimed, his voice low. He cleared his throat, and it took me a solid minute to move my gaze from his face to my arm, but when I did, I almost forgot about Reid. *Almost.*

This bracer had little curved spikes on it. The leather went all the way around my missing fingers, but the thumb and forefinger, that I did have, had the half-knuckle fabric on them. My hand was thoroughly encased in soft leather, although more flexible than the arm part, it was more protected than my fingers. So, there were three different types of leather for this one. I flexed my fingers and rotated my wrist. It was incredible.

I felt the prickle run from my heart to my throat, to my eyes, and I sniffled. "Reid... I can't even begin—"

My eyes reached his and I knew moisture had collected in mine.

His eyes shuttered and he took a step closer, our bodies nearly touching. "The spikes are for catching sword strikes. You can catch the blade with them and push it away."

Wow. I swallowed. "Reid... Tha—"

"It's no—"

"If you say *it's nothing,* I will punch you." But I sniffled again—the threat lost in my tears.

"Love to see you try," he said with a soft chuckle, but his eyes were gentle. The blue was so purple it melted me where I stood, rooted me, and I felt the moisture in my eyes fall, but heat curled in my belly. I watched his hand slowly come up, and his fingers grazed my cheek. He caught a tear on the pad of his finger. I watched him, my eyes wide. His face was close, his eyes still shuttered, but there was no coldness to them, no annoyance, instead, there were things I couldn't comprehend, but I wanted to.

I had to thank him. I swallowed twice before I began again. "Reid, I don't know what to say. This is exce—"

"Do they fit?" Etta bustled through the door but stopped in her tracks when she caught how close we were, the tears in my eyes, and the softness in Reid's.

He dropped his hand. I took a step back and quickly wiped my eyes. "Yes. They are perfect," I said a little too loudly.

"I...I—" She stuttered, but Reid went over and wrapped an arm around her shoulders.

"They are incredible Auntie."

"Yes," I said with a smile. "I love them."

"Reid said," she glanced up at him with a twinkle in her soft blue eyes, "that you were prickly like the thorn of a rose, but just as beautiful. Stunning strength to be admi—"

Reid coughed loudly interrupting her. I stared wide-eyed between them. That was the sweetest thing anyone had ever said, and true—as far as the prickly part. I had never considered myself beautiful. My face had appealing qualities, but beautiful? He had told his aunt... that?

My eyes snapped to him, but he was looking anywhere but at me, and Etta was grinning massively.

"*Firedrake,*" Reid said under his breath, and Etta smacked him on the back of the head. How she reached his head I will *never* know, but he looked at her completely chastised. "Sorry, Auntie. At least I didn't say *fuck.*"

"Goddess! Don't speak that way in front of a lady."

"Bah! Neither of you are ladies. You should hear the mouth on that one." He pointed at me. "It's *abysmal.*"

Playing along, I pointed to myself innocently and implored Etta. "Me? Oh, never! I didn't even know a cuss word until I met him!"

Etta howled with laughter, and Reid grinned at me.

Something had shifted during this encounter. Reid showed me he was a man that also happened to be the guard captain. But he wasn't *just* a guard captain. Granted, his life was to serve the king, to protect the Celestria family, but it wasn't *all* he was. He was so much more, and I felt my heart stutter in response.

After hugs and kisses from Etta to both of us and a massive batch of cookies, we rode back to the castle. Reid's uncle and cousin had been at the coast selling wares, which was why Reid had chosen to visit this day. He said he didn't like his aunt alone at the shop and planned on coming there for dinner as well since the men wouldn't be home until after nightfall. I found that incredibly sweet, but at this point, I was not surprised at this side of Reid. I had learned much about him today, and all of it made me like him so much more.

I kept stealing glances at him and I know he caught me on numerous occasions. I wore the bracers so that we could see how well I could ride and hold the reins with them, and they were very comfortable. By the time we reached the stables of Hawksedge I barely even noticed them.

When we dismounted and a stable hand took our horses, Reid bid me a quick goodbye claiming he had things to attend to. I stared after him a long enough moment, that he looked back at me. That softness in his eyes was there, albeit a little more shadowed.

Finally, with a sigh, I headed to the castle.

CHAPTER 13

I am the storm

The bracers made sword fighting easier, and Reid taught me how to block and parry with them. Aven was envious, as was everyone else, of the beauty of the armor. I was embarrassed, yet thrilled Reid had given me such a fine gift.

I'd been training hard with Aven, Reid, and Bronwen, too. Reid dragged her into sparring with me, and she was like a dancer, all fluid grace and birdlike floating. She showed me no animosity and we had a budding friendship. She praised how I was still training; despite how many times I could have given up. I told her how much I admired her strength and beauty. She was a warrior just as much as Reid, and I liked that about her. I tried my best to ignore it when she sent Reid appreciative glances. They were lovers or had been or...

Did I want Reid? Was the outlandish feeling I felt around him... desire? I was afraid of the answer. I had been for a while.

I waited at the castle gates at dawn, but Reid was nowhere in sight. Had I gotten the time wrong? It *was* overcast. Did I read the light of the sun wrong? My body had been waking at dawn on its own for weeks now and I didn't think it would betray me so thoroughly.

The guards at the door heard it the same time I did. Horse's hooves outside the castle door.

"My lady," one of them said as I approached.

"I need to find the captain."

"He's in the stables."

"Thank you."

Dawn painted the dusky gray cobblestones in lavender hues and my eyes went to the pastureland to my left and the mountains beyond. It was still the most beautiful thing I had ever seen. I heard a whinny. Fain stood at the pasture gate. He let out another high whinny, and I ran over to him. It sounded off, that sound—as if he sensed something was afoot, and my skin prickled.

We had been training with Leiri every day and I had gotten on his back the first time a few days ago, but she didn't think we were quite ready to just ride off into the sunset yet. He needed more *groundwork* to get used to me asking him to do things. He was a free spirit, and she thought he might have a challenging time taking cues from a rider. Not that he had shown me any resistance yet.

Fain calmed as soon as I touched him. I looked around the pasture but didn't see Javarr.

"Kaidyn."

My head whipped to Reid. He stood at the open stable doors. I could see men in motion behind him. The set of his body was tense, his men's movements concise and rushed.

"What's wrong?" I took two steps toward him.

"There's been a disturbance in the highlands to the southeast. I must check it. You can train—"

"Take me with you." I took another step.

"No," his voice and eyes were stern.

I finally reached him and tipped my head up. "A magic disturbance. That's what you mean, isn't it?"

His eyes scanned my face, my body—assessing my attire, my worth—I don't know. If I pushed, he'd cave. I could see it. I was dressed in my usual fighting attire, with my dagger strapped to my thigh and my bracers on.

"Reid, I'm ready. I want to help." I touched his arm, pleading. He dipped his head to stare at my fingers, his eyes then lingered over the bracers before he met my eyes. "Let me help," I said, with strength.

"I don't want you to get hurt," he whispered.

My heart contracted with that small statement. It sent a shiver of awareness through me. Reid... cared about me. He cared about my well-being. My throat tightened, but I would think about his feelings, and my own, later.

"I'm ready, Reid. Let me do this. I am the Keeper, aren't I?"

Something flashed in his eyes. Not anger, but something else. Satisfaction?

"Fine," he said, finally. He turned to Nic, the lead stableboy. "Ready Miss Flynn's horse."

I snapped my eyes to him, but he already turned away. He grabbed a bow and quiver of arrows from the side of the stable and handed them to me. Without hesitation, I strapped the leather quiver to my back and slung the bow over my shoulder.

"I guess it's time to see what you and the pony are made of." His voice did not waver, it was not gentle. He was speaking to a soldier now. I straightened my spine and I licked my dry lips. He would expect me to uphold his orders, no matter what.

Fain sidestepped under Nic's hands, and I went to him. I smiled at Nic before I ran a hand down my horse's nose.

Nic grinned. "He's a fine horse, Miss Flynn. He has the heart of a warrior. Like you."

I jerked in surprise. Nic's chin dipped before he went to help with the other horses. I patted Fain's neck and whispered words of encouragement in his ear, and before anyone could help me, I swung myself into the saddle and reined my horse to Javarr before Reid had even mounted.

He sent me a long look then turned to the other guards and fisted a hand over his heart. The men chanted, "Death before dishonor."

I didn't know what that meant exactly, but the men rode with Reid unquestionably, and Fain trotted along with them without hesitation.

We skirted the city along a jagged pass far to the right; a narrow trail that took quite some time to traverse. Fain was sure-footed and easily followed Javarr. It was me that had far more reservations. I didn't mind heights, but the pass was enough room for a horse and that was it. It seemed perilous. One misstep... I jerked a breath and didn't look down. I didn't take a full breath until the trail widened and we rode out onto a rocky cliff, then navigated onto a grassy outcrop.

Mountains greeted us on the right. Ahead was pastureland, dotted by shaggy cattle, and beyond that was a dark forest. As we navigated across the highlands towards the forest something clenched in my belly. The back of my neck prickled, and I felt queasy. I would die of mortification if I passed out or threw up, so I fought the feeling. We descended further and spires of boulders met other boulders, creating land bridges of moss and stone. I noticed the ruins of an ancient watchtower, and then I saw standing stones and my heart stuttered. Like Druidic standing stones from Scotland.

"Druids used to use those stones to speak with the gods." One guard said when he noticed my stare. I believe his name was Evril. I had sparred with him once. He had taken it way too easy on me and had checked me out far more than necessary. Reid didn't let me work with him again.

I glanced back at the standing stones at his use of words. "Used to... Are there no more druids?"

"Evirness' magic can only handle so many magic users before it... kills them off."

"Evril." Reid's warning caused Evril to snap to attention, and he reined his horse a little away from me. I glanced at Reid. Marida had told me about Evirness' magic but the gravity of it hadn't sunk in. Was this more dangerous for me than people were letting on? Was I a lamb to be led to slaughter?

Reid urged Javarr toward a lake. Fields of wild, yellow flowers sprouted from the rocky outcroppings. We walked through a massive stone land bridge covered in moss and purple flowers. This place was beautiful, but a shiver up my spine had me wondering if I underestimated Evirness's unpredictable magic.

A lazy stream cut to the right, but we hooked left towards the forest. My eyes hung on an outcropping that looked like a cave mouth. I swallowed some spit that accumulated in my mouth at the thought of what may live in such a massive cave. Drake? Servine?

I had felt so safe at the castle, the grounds, in the city—I had felt completely at ease, but I realized that the rest of Evirness may not be so safe. I wasn't sure if it was the magic, or the land itself, but it felt massive. The highlands cut in every direction, each curving boulder opened to another spot of land, each mountain showed a pass to somewhere new, and every ridge opened to a cascading waterfall or a tranquil lake. The land was far vaster than I had thought. All the roads Reid had taken me on previously had cut directly through the heart of civilization, but this was... wild. Untamed.

As we edged into the dark wood, that shiver of trepidation erupted into an almost panic.

Had I bitten off more than I could chew asking Reid to let me come? Did I need this as a wake-up call to get the hell home? I wasn't a coward, despite what it seemed sometimes, but this was formidable in a frightening way.

Reid must have caught my look because he sent me a knowing smirk. "Scared, Keeper?"

"No," I said a little too quickly and scowled. He rolled his eyes and slowed Javarr so that we could ride abreast. I wasn't sure if he did it for comfort, but I appreciated it, regardless.

As we plodded through the forest I felt the prickling at my neck increase, and my left hand started to vibrate. "Reid," I breathed because the suffocating presence of something amidst us was bothering me.

He glanced over and stopped. "What is it?"

My panicked eyes searched his. "I think magic." It felt the same as it had the day I had ridden with Reid to Hawksedge.

He nodded calmly and tipped his head to his men. He rattled off names and sent them in different directions. It was me, Reid, and Holt who rode where the sensation grew, and then we left our horses. I felt a buzzing along my skin, and I followed it. They followed me without question.

Soon I heard humming and stopped. Reid put his hand on my back, and I glanced back at him. "Do you hear that?"

He shook his head.

The magic sounds were just for me. Wonderful.

I followed the humming. We rounded a clearing and I stopped in my tracks. Reid bumped into me. His solid warmth pressing against me was the only thing that stopped me from turning and running in the other direction. Up ahead, was an arched gateway. Made of stone and branches, it looked like it had been there for ages, with vines crawling up it and strange symbols etched into the wood. My left hand vibrated uncontrollably, and I glanced down, just as the surrounding earth trembled, and something scurried from the doorway. I watched in horror as six massive spiders—I mean the size of a Saint Bernard—crawled out of the doorway.

I squeaked in terror, and Reid pushed me behind him.

Holt was in a fighting stance, sword at the ready.

"Holt, get the others."

Holt's brow furrowed. "But Captain—"

"Do it! I have a feeling there's more in there, and before we're overrun, we need the others."

"Yes, sir." Without further hesitation, Holt ran back to his horse. I gulped, watching his retreating form, and then glanced back at Reid. I didn't have my sword on me. My dagger and borrowed bow were it.

His eyes flickered as if he knew my thoughts. "Stay back. Use your bow if you're compelled to."

Of course, I was compelled! The idiot. What did he think, I'd let him just fight these spider monsters on his own? I may not be daring or strong, but I wouldn't let him fight while I watched from the sidelines.

The spiders skittered toward us, and Reid swung his sword. It was a marvel watching him, and for a second, I could do nothing but stare before I snapped out of it. I pulled my bow from my shoulder and nocked an arrow. I loosed the bowstring, and the arrow flew wide.

I quickly nocked another, finally hitting one of the slower spiders. It barely even squeaked.

"The head and eyes!" Reid bellowed, as he neatly decapitated one spider right in front of me. He whirled and pivoted in a deadly dance. He was epic in his ferocity. The intensity of it shivered across me. I had known from watching him spar with his men that he was impressive, but seeing him out here fighting spiders in the middle of the wood? He looked like the devastatingly handsome, valiant warrior from every single heroic story I'd ever read.

Reid yanked his sword from one spider to twist it against another. I shook my head. Instead of gaping at him like an idiot, I fired another arrow. It missed the spider by inches as the furry-bodied monster advanced on Reid. Without missing a beat, he hacked one of its legs off and then ran it through with his sword. I looked around and all the spiders were dead. He had killed them all.

He looked as though he could have killed a hundred more. He wasn't even out of breath.

"God," I whispered. It was all I could think of. He was no prince, no king, there was no shining armor, but he looked like a hero. A warrior. Like a storm.

A quote from an unknown source popped into my head.

Fate whispered to the warrior; you cannot withstand the storm. The warrior whispered back; I am the storm.

Reid was the storm.

Then the world trembled. The gateway shimmered, creaked, and vibrated against the earth at our feet.

Our eyes met. I must have had panic written across my features because he stepped toward me, but before he made it, the earth's trembling increased. A strange squelching noise echoed through the glen and then a strange clicking sound. Like a dog's claws on stone. The noise raised the hairs on the back of my neck and arms, and Reid's face tightened.

A leg of a spider, the length of a birch tree, encased at the end in something that glinted like steel, made an appearance through the open doorway. My breath hitched in terror. What the—

Another leg stretched from the opening. Reid cursed and looked around wildly. For his comrades or a place to hide, I wasn't sure, but I hoped it was the latter. He slung himself towards me and looked back as another leg poked through. He grabbed my hand and dragged me into the woods. We ran a few steps, and I heard a squeal as if the creature saw us. When we looked back, the massive beast was through the portal. I heard the telltale clicking and noticed massive pincers four feet long at its mouth. Eight beady eyes, bulbous and glistening, trained right on us. My mouth went dry. Reid dragged me backward and ran. As the creature moved, it shook the earth. We ran another few feet, but its massive size and huge legs brought it closer and closer. Reid stopped and sized up a tree, then slung me behind it. He pressed against me and peeked out.

My chest moved up and down in a panic.

"Calm down," he whispered in my ear. His warm breath caused an uncontrollable shiver. "It can feel the vibrations of us running, I think."

"There's a huge ass scary spider and you want me—"

He hissed. I felt myself spiraling in fear, but I tried to remain rooted, to not give in to the coursing of my blood and the tremor that wanted to knock my knees together. I rested my forehead against his shoulder. He stiffened but didn't move away. It calmed me, being this close to him, and I felt him shudder a breath. I had wanted to touch Reid before, but I had always resisted the urge. Now I needed his strength, his courage. He softened, and I felt his hand come up and rest on my waist. He shifted, brushing deeper against me. Giving me comfort.

Reid cursed softly, as we heard the spider scuttle further towards the path. "It could decimate a village." His eyes scanned; assessing, calculating—all very *Reid* things.

"You're going to fight it?"

"I must," he said with vehemence, already planning his moves. He stepped back, his body no longer against mine.

"Okay. I just need a minute." I took two steadied breaths, shook out my shoulders, and licked my dry lips. "Let's do this," I said.

He cocked his head. "You want to fight the big scary spider?"

"Well, duh. Can't let you have all the fun, can I?"

He gave me a withering grin, then sighed. "Kaid…"

"I can help, Reid." My eyes narrowed when he turned and started to stalk off. When I reached him, I said, "I can—"

"Distract it if you feel the need to help." He gestured to the bow. "But stay back, Kaidyn. I mean it. You're too important to get yourself killed."

Too important? To the realm. Right. I didn't feel very important right now. I was a Keeper, yet I had no idea what to do. I think we both knew I wouldn't stay back. Even though I was petrified of the massive monster spider, I knew my heart and soul would never allow me to watch him fight alone. The small spiders had been a cakewalk in comparison to this one, but I wouldn't sit on the sidelines. If I could help, I would.

He gave me one more glance—but before I could decipher what was in those blue-purple eyes of his, a crashing of the brush was heard, and the earth shivered.

Reid trotted off, and I gave him a full thirty seconds before I rolled my eyes skyward and followed.

Where the hell were the other guards? I thought with annoyance, as Reid sidled up to the spider. I stayed back in the tree line, as he had declared I should do, and watched him. He crept up behind it before it noticed him and then hacked at its legs. It whirled, long legs clattering against grass and stone. My heart raced, but I tried to root myself from running away. I could get away now that Reid had its attention, but I wouldn't. I knew I wouldn't. Not only did I respect Reid in every capacity, but I wanted to fight this thing. Some innate strength and resolve had slithered up my spine and tangled with my soul. I wanted to rid this world of evil. Perhaps it was the magic in my blood, my connection to this land due to my Keeper senses, or simply bred into me from the centuries of women who also fought to rid this land of wicked magic. It certainly wasn't just me as a person, because I was terrified.

My body tensed as the spider's pincers came down to pierce Reid. He rolled out of the way just in time. I sucked in a breath as the back of my neck tingled. The brand called to the magic in my blood, and I had to move. Staying hidden in the shadows of the trees with my bow was my best chance at helping Reid. If the thing came after me, I knew he would forget all else to save me, even if it meant getting himself killed in the process.

I darted closer, close enough—I hoped—and pulled my bow from my back. It wasn't Aven's, nor the one I used during training, so it was set for someone with more arm strength than me—meaning I would tire quickly. I took a deep breath and loosed. My arrow flew wide. Grumbling, I stepped closer. I followed the same steps, and my arrow flew again, arching gracefully... and bouncing off the spider's thick face. Its bulbous eyes darted around Reid to me, but I smoothly dodged its glance. I stepped closer and nocked another arrow. When the creature bellowed as Reid's sword bit into one of its legs, I let loose. It sailed too far to the right. I quickly nocked another arrow and stepped closer. This time my aim was true... but it bounced off the hide. The creature's furry body was too thick. Its eyes were too small of a target for me to capably wound.

I exhaled deeply; assessed and calculated as Reid did. In all my readings of fantasy, there was always a weakness in monsters. With spiders, it was usually... the underbelly!

I watched the creature dart this way and that, nearly trampling Reid as he fought to swipe at it with his sword. The iron-tipped legs chased after him, trying to impale. Its pincers clicked together in anticipation of sinking into his flesh. I took a deep breath and lunged closer.

Reid's eyes darted back to me, and he growled, "Stay back!"

"This is getting us nowhere!" I yelled, but he just growled again, twisted his sword, regripped, and lunged at the spider.

I groaned. I needed to stop this. I needed to close that gateway. That's what they wanted me to do, wasn't it? Close gateways with my Keeper magic.

"Don't you even fucking dare, Kaidyn!" It was as if he could sense the wheels spinning in my head, but I was already there. I'd already clicked my brain off to everything but the fact that Reid killed at least six of those pony-sized spiders, and he was willing to fight this massive creature alone to ensure it didn't hurt innocents. I couldn't let him do that alone. His heroism inspired something in my heart. Every cell in my being was crying out for me to help.

Some innate bravery took hold of my limbs and I darted past him. I narrowly avoided one spider leg and adjusted my bow back over my shoulder. I careened into another leg and nearly fell on my face. I sidestepped at the last minute when another leg skittered toward me and I landed on my side. The creature pivoted and I stumbled to my feet and raced ahead again. I stopped, skidded, and slid across the forest floor. I watched Reid a second, as he sliced at the thing with all his might, all the while watching me with an impressively pissed-off expression.

He wanted to wallop me back to my realm. It was clear on his face and blazing blue eyes. "What the fuck are you doing?"

I have no idea what came over me, but my face plastered into a shit-eating grin. No clue why my mouth betrayed my true feelings, which were insane panic and nightmarish terror.

What the hell was wrong with me?

But I felt exhilarated at my plan too. I had played enough video games, and read enough books about slaying monsters, I could do this.

I threw myself between two legs, and finally, I looked up. The underside of this spider was black with white spots, softer in appearance than the rest of it. I quickly tipped myself back up and kneeled. I hastily grabbed an arrow from my quiver, watched a leg come dangerously close to me, blew out a deep breath, and adjusted the bow. I was glad I had tossed my bracers on that morning and quickly nocked the arrow. Blowing out a breath, my eyes darted again to ensure I was all good, and then I fired. My arrow sailed and hit just a little to the right of the center of the belly, but it struck and embedded. I quickly nocked again. The creature wrenched a horrible shriek and began spinning, but it didn't trample me—not yet anyway. I fired again, this hit was more direct. My arrow embedded, blood dribbling against the white.

I pulled another arrow, but the spider monster darted to the right, and I had to scramble up to avoid iron-tipped legs. Its pincers snapped at Reid, which he avoided. I tried to keep up and remain beneath it, but just as I pulled my bow into position and nocked an arrow, the spider pivoted again and caught me in the arm with her sharp leg. Most of it snagged on the bracer, but it did slice into my bicep. I ignored the burning pain and fired the arrow. It landed just a bit left of the center, but it was still firmly embedded, and blood poured from the wound. The creature shrieked so loudly that the earth shuddered and my ears rang. The spider crashed and stumbled through the woods.

Rough hands gripped my arms and hauled me to my feet from where I was still kneeling on the grass. Reid's body vibrated from adrenaline... Or was that mine?

I swallowed, and my eyes drifted up to his face. His look was one of anger, shock, and awe. "What in the stars were you thinking!?"

"I wasn't," I breathed, for lack of a better response, and the coursing of adrenaline strained against my skin.

I had just helped take down a monster! *What!?*

Kaidyn Flynn Monster Hunter had a nice ring to it. I had played this video game with Kial—

"You could have gotten yourself killed!"

"But I didn't!"

"That's beside—That's not—"

A vibration shook the ground below our feet, and the humming of the gateway thrummed across the dark wood in a throaty resonation.

"You... Kaidyn, do you think you can close it?" His round eyes met mine and I breathed in deeply.

I had no idea how to close the gateway but the way his violet eyes looked at me as if I were their Goddess Henna herself.... Whoo. I could live a thousand lives and still revel in that look. Not that such was warranted. The man fought ten or more Great Dane-sized spiders and was willing to kill the big one or die trying. He deserved that awestruck look, not the other way around.

We didn't have enough time to dwell on any of this as the humming of the gateway yawned and I had a feeling something else was going to make its way through if we didn't hurry our asses up.

Reid stepped toward it, and I knew he thought so too.

I had to close the doorway. Something I had said I wouldn't do. But here I was battling spiders and magical doorways with a sexy warrior at my side. I no longer felt fear. The fear had seeped away, in its place were anticipation and pride.

Together we walked to the doorway. It was massive; as large as a two-story house. The brand on my neck stung, my left hand vibrated, and I knew, without looking, that my hand's form was already blurring. My Keeper powers were surfacing from the nearness of the doorway. My body knew what to do, even if my mind didn't.

It flashed across me. I was the Keeper of the Keys. I could feel it as I neared the doorway, deep in my bones, in my blood, in my being. I just needed to accept it.

"What... What do I do?"

Reid's eyes were round and hesitant. "I'm caught," he whispered, "between pulling you as far away from here as possible and letting you do whatever your magic needs to do to close it."

He looked at me, and I could see the torment. I gripped his hand in mine. He didn't hesitate but held it firmly, and we walked to the stones and branches of the gateway. It was majestic, otherworldly. I seemed so out of place smack in the middle of the woods yet looked like it had been there for a millennium at the same time. Magic shimmered against the stones and my body vibrated with it.

"I'm... going to just try to touch the stones and see..."

He nodded solemnly but didn't let go of my right hand. I took a deep breath. The tug of the doorway pulled at my core. My left hand was vibrating uncontrollably, and I pulled it from my side. Reid sucked in a breath.

Slowly, I stepped up to the stones and placed my left hand against them. In an instant, the doorway shivered, and slowly stone by stone it sunk back into the earth. Reid made an indecipherable noise behind me, but his hand still gripped mine. I stepped back once my hand stopped vibrating and just tingled.

We watched side by side, as the doorway sunk into the earth as if it had never been there. We were silent for a long moment.

"I need to make sure the spider has met its end."

I nodded. A bellow rumbled in the air, followed by male yells. The cavalry had finally arrived. About damn time, I thought with a shadow of anger. Where the hell had they been?

"Captain?"

"Here!" Reid yelled, his eyes held mine, then with my hand still in his, he tugged me towards Holt's voice.

"Huge spider... We finished it. Did you..."

"Yes. Kaidyn and I... You ended it?"

"Yes, sir." Three more guards trotted over to them. Out of breath, with gashes and scratches.

"What in the skies happened?"

"Small spiders, *everywhere*."

"Firedrake." Reid scrubbed a hand down his face. The doorway had been open for a while.

"Do you think you killed them all?"

Holt shrugged. "No idea, sir, but we haven't met anymore. Seems they could sense us moving. I would imagine they'd come scuttling over to us if there were more."

True. I was glad they had ended that huge spider. Despite its terrifying presence, I knew the wounds I had inflicted would lead to an excruciatingly long, sufferable death. I was glad Reid's men had ended it swiftly.

Reid sent me a look, and I shrugged. He sucked in a deep breath. "Let's round up our horses and get back on the path. See if we can discover anything. I'll send another team out when we get back to Hawksedge. I think we all deserve a little rest after all this."

I slept the rest of the day. The physical exertion and the use of my magic drained me. But I had definitely earned the captain and his guard's respect, and my own for that matter.

CHAPTER 14

Dragonstooth Bay

"Put on some decent undergarments."

I whipped my head to Marida. "*What?*"

Her laugh settled over me, and I took a breath. I should feel envious of her incredible beauty, but I was thankful for our friendship. She often looked at me like I was the beautiful one. I had never considered myself attracted to women, but if I was...

"Just do it. Wear something concealing... *or not.*"

I narrowed my eyes, and she laughed harder. "That's vague, Mar."

She rolled her eyes. "Just trust me."

I did.

It had been two days since the spider. The castle was abuzz with what had transpired. Everyone stared at me with awe. Rhone, Reid, and I had a meeting where what happened in the forest was explained. Reid kept his assessment of the situation professional, but I noted the draw of his words. He admired me, and he made sure Rhone knew it. It was an interesting turn of events, considering when I'd arrived in the north, he couldn't contain his dislike for me.

Rhone didn't pressure me to close any more doorways.

Reid insisted I'd learned plenty from my training since I'd been the one to discover the spider's weakness and exploit it, so he gave me more freedom. I felt his respect for me, deep in my soul. It felt good to play the hero. Too good. Addictive. This feeling of elation, the high of killing a monster, of gaining everyone's respect and adoration—I could get used to it.

I pulled my thoughts from hero worship to my traitor cat. I ran my fingers over Silas' shoulder, and he leaned into me as he lay stretched out on my bed. My fingers lingered in his fur. I noticed him coming out of Reid's room again that morning.

I snapped my mind back to the present. Wear concealing undergarments. What the hell?

I heeded her advice and wore a black camisole with panties that came up to my belly button and ended in lace at my thighs. They resembled shapewear in my world.

When I stepped from my bathing chamber, she nodded her approval. "Perfect."

Marida wore similarly, but her midriff was bare, and she showcased more thigh than I. She tossed me a sheer gold overdress and put on a black one of her own. I felt exposed but stamped down the embarrassment and self-consciousness. The muscle I had gained over the past few months made me feel powerful, strong, and beautiful in a way I had never thought possible.

I strapped the dagger to my thigh and braided my hair over one shoulder. I was excited but nervous about whatever was happening.

"I feel ridiculous, Marida. What's going on? Just tell me."

Marida laughed. Her lush pink lips spread into a perfect smile. "You just wait and see!" Her eyes scanned me from head to toe, and heat bloomed at my cheeks from her scrutiny. "Let's go."

I had done simple drills that morning with Reid, Aven, and Bronwen, that consisted more of us just talking about the spiders than any real training. When Reid had let me go, he'd done so with a smile, which made me nervous. He had suggested I spend some time with Marida, and he'd see me *soon*. No clue what he meant, but now with Marida making me wear this getup... Whatever was going on was connected, and it made my stomach flop.

"We need to hurry if we're going to have any fun at all!"

Marida dragged me down the hall.

Fun? My whole body seized at the word. I was terrified to think what that meant.

Aven sauntered out of the dining hall looking smug but stopped in his tracks when he spotted us. He whistled loudly, and Marida posed for him.

I closed my eyes and grinned. *These people.* "Do you know what's going on?" I asked Aven.

He smirked. "Aye."

"Care to divulge to me?"

"Oh, I'd like to divulge your ass in that gol—"

"Aven Bergren Estrada, don't you dare finish that *horrid* sentence! You talk to Kaidyn with respect!"

We all whipped our heads to Eranora, who stood in a magnificent deep blue gown that slithered on the stones as she walked and accentuated her slim waist. Her straight black hair was unadorned aside from a simple silver star circlet as a crown.

"Yes, my queen. I'm sorry."

"Do not apologize to *me*!" Her lips pursed; her brows drew together. She was a vision of a queen. Someone cold and indifferent on one hand yet tied to this land by duty and respect. I knew the people loved her and were intimidated by her in the same breath. She was the voice of reason and logic when Rhone led completely with his heart. They made a perfectly balanced pair, and although it had grated on me at first because of my aunt, I couldn't deny my respect for their union and them as a couple.

"Sorry, Kaidyn," Aven said with a grin. His sly voice pulled me from my study of the queen.

Eranora made an irritated sound in her throat and stepped closer. "Goddess of the stars, save us," she cried and put her hand to her heart in exasperation and appalment.

I tried my best to stop a grin from spreading.

"Kaidyn, next time he says *anything* like that to you, please—" She gestured to my thigh. "Cut his balls off!"

My eyes widened in shock, and I gurgled with laughter. Marida laughed heartily, doubling over, hands on her knees. Aven looked stricken and impulsively put a hand over his crotch.

Eranora chuckled and fluttered her hands. "Off with you, imbeciles." She gave me a wry grin, and her eyes twinkled. "But I will not be upset if he comes home *castrated*." She dipped her chin to me, and I snorted with laughter. Unable to contain it any longer.

"*Fuck,*" Aven said.

"Language, Aven!"

"Shit," he whispered and looked like he might vomit.

Damn. I didn't know Eranora had a playful side, or a sinister side for that matter because that was brutal and hilarious. She looked like teasing Aven was one of her favorite things, as she sent him a motherly glimpse of exasperation that didn't include an apology for what she'd said. And then, in a swirl of skirts, she turned on her heel and left.

"That's evil," Aven said with a hand still at his crotch and a sickly expression mottling his handsome face.

I chuckled. "She's different from what I thought she'd be."

"She's wonderful," Marida said with a small smile. "It took her ages to come out of her shell, but she surprises everyone with her humor."

"*Dark* humor," Aven said as the guards opened the doors.

I agreed with him, as I noticed a carriage in the courtyard. It was dusky gray, with dark trimmings. Two large dapple-gray horses were pulling the carriage, and I realized one of them was Javarr.

My eyes scanned the courtyard and fell on Reid, who was speaking to a few guardsmen. His eyes lifted when we walked across the archway and down the stairs. His eyes scanned mine, then traveled down my body and up again. I tried telling myself, as my entire body heated from his examination, that he was assessing my attire. And going to give me a boatload of shit for it, but it still thrilled me.

Heat swirled low in my belly as he ignored the guard completely, who floundered a second before skulking away, and prowled towards us. There was dark heat in his eyes.

Oh shit. I was about to get my ass handed to me. I thought he had given me the afternoon off...

"Ladies." He gestured to all three of us, and Aven snickered.

"Honestly, after what Eranora just told Kaidyn to do to me—that assessment is fair."

Marida snorted, then giggled uncontrollably, and a grin plastered my face in response.

Reid stared at us blankly, but Marida put her arm around his shoulder. "Eranora told Kaidyn to chop off his balls because he told her that ass looked delicious in what she's wearing."

Reid's eyes snapped to Aven, a scalding glance causing Aven to look up at the sky. Then Reid's eyes swept over my body again, landing on my rear end. I squeaked from the attention and looked away.

Reid didn't find any humor in what Aven had said and sent Aven another glare. Aven held up his hands in mock surrender. I resisted the urge to laugh or fling myself off a cliff in embarrassment.

My eyes swept over the carriage and Javarr again, and I still didn't quite understand what was going on.

"Ready?" Reid's voice was soft at my side. I scanned his profile against the late morning sunlight. His face was rugged with stubble dark against his skin. I think he shaved once a week, always at night, because in the morning there would be a shadow of growth. I liked it. Most men were either well shaven or had a beard. It was as if Reid couldn't decide what he wanted to do but got sick of the growth after a week, then shaved it. It suited him. He seemed so controlled about everything that the stubble gave him a wild, sexy look.

When his eyes caught mine from the corner, I quickly looked away with my heart racing. Thinking about Reid being sexy lately was *bad*. Bad, Kaidyn. Ugh.

Aven gestured to the carriage, and I lifted a brow. We were riding by carriage but to where? He gave me a grin and put his hand on the small of my back to guide me closer. Reid gave Marida his hand, and he assisted her into the carriage. Aven let me go and went to speak to the driver. My eyes lifted to Reid's and my heart raced. His eyes rose from my feet, over my body, and finally met mine. He wore a small smile, but his eyes had darkened, and the look he sent me was something I had never witnessed before... and I didn't know what it meant.

"You loo—"

"Say nothing about the outfit, Captain, or I'll cut out your tongue."

He chuckled. "So violent, Keeper. However, I think I'd like to see you *try*."

My eyes widened, and he sent me a smoldering smirk. I had nothing to say, my mouth had gone dry. He offered his hand, and I took it. He guided me into the carriage, and I looked back over my shoulder, and he was—staring at my ass!

Holy crap, the Captain of the Guard, *who hated me*, was ogling my butt! Hell hath frozen over.

Marida lifted a brow as she noted his look.

I sat next to her and Reid, to my surprise, sat across from us. A second later, Aven entered as well. Reid's leg bumped into mine as he adjusted to give Aven more room.

"Wouldn't it make sense for one of you to sit over here?" Aven said as he extended a hand over the back of Reid's shoulder. Reid elbowed his arm away. Aven grumbled and rubbed the spot gingerly, then lifted a brow to ensure his meaning was clear. With a chuckle, Marida stood up, and Reid switched places with her. His solid warmth settled against my side. His bare arm brushed mine. I peeked at him from beneath my lashes and there was a tiny kick at the edge of his lips as he looked at me from the corner of his eyes. With a shaky breath, I rooted my face to the window. The musical lilt of Marida's laugh fluttered across the carriage. She and Aven bantering back and forth lulled me.

The carriage jolted down the road. I noticed we went straight past the barracks instead of swooping right to the city. We followed the pasture, and I saw Fain from the window and grinned as my horse lifted his head and trotted next to the fence as if he knew I was inside.

"Smart boy," Reid's deep voice vibrated against my body. His chest pressed against my arm as he shifted. I had been ignoring his warmth, the friction of his arm and thigh against mine, but his voice vibrating against me had me glancing at him.

It wasn't long that we moved well beyond the castle pastures, across fields of hay and wheat, beyond Eagleridge, and past watchtowers.

Where were we going?

I peeked out the other window and noticed a massive lake. Around it were large homes, a waterwheel, and gardens. Massive slate rocks jutted in outcroppings and waterfalls crashed. It looked... magical.

"The village of the healers."

I met Reid's eyes for a second before glancing back. "Healers?"

It was Marida who answered, "They have raw magic and prefer to stay in solitude instead of living in the city. Healers are empaths and can take away a person's pain, but in a city that can become overwhelming."

I nodded and noticed standing stones. "Are those druid stones too?"

"The healers can draw magic from the land with the stones. Once there were druids, witches, and others, but... even before the wall, Evirness' magic was unpredictable. Times changed, progression transpired, and they had begun to peter out. Once the divide happened some were pulled from their ancestral lands, and each other. Without the stones or their brethren—the druids, like the witches—slowly vanished."

"That's terrible." Evril had tried telling me this the day of the open gateway.

"It happened far later than it had in your world, yes?" There was a not-so-subtle hint of accusation in her voice.

I swallowed. She wasn't wrong. "Man exterminates what they don't understand," I whispered, echoing something Rhone had said to me once when we had talked about the magic of Evirness and the lack thereof in my world.

Marida nodded and sighed. "It is a travesty, but the magic of Evirness isn't something to understand, or control—not completely. Keepers are the only ones that can balance it. I'm surprised so many of our healers, and a few sorceresses have been allowed to live. Rhone thinks it's because somewhere down the line they have the blood of the Keepers in them, and that protects them from the magic of Evirness, but as I told you before there is much we don't understand, and the magic is ever-changing, keeping us guessing."

Was Marida spared because she had Keeper magic somewhere? It was an interesting theory. The only thing I had ever seen her do was to start a fire with a flick of a finger and I knew she did a lot with alchemy.

"I hear Fain was the perfect boy for you on your voyage," Aven prompted me. Never one for a too serious conversation, I was all too happy for the change of subject. Speaking of the magic in the land was a somber topic.

We came upon a stunning stone bridge. Two rivers diverged into a lake, and the massive structure fanned across. It was arched and impressive. The man-hours it must have taken to erect such a marvel. I smelled the salty tell of the ocean, and my eyes stuttered. We were near the coast. I noticed the walls of a city as we crossed the bridge.

My face whipped to Reid and he smiled gently at me.

At the gates, Reid hopped out and spoke to the guards. The city of Dragonstooth Bay sprawled out around us. Aven disclosed it was called such because not only did the spires of cliffs that lined the back of the cove appear like dragon's teeth but also legend stated that the white sandy shore was made up of the bones of dragons. And there was a large dragon skull on the beach. It sounded more of a tall tale, but who knew. Considering Saul's scars were from a frost dragon and I had read about Servine's, it didn't surprise me.

The cobblestones were pale in color, the shops a lovely dusky sandstone, the roofs russet. It was a pristine coastal town. There was a watchtower to the right, and I noticed a small castle up on a cliff, and... I could see *the* wall. The divide. It cut clear across the ocean. Probably where a cliff once sat to make the port a cove, there was just the ominous giant wall. I gulped at its ferocity, even from miles away.

We came upon another low wall; the gates were slung open but there was another large watchtower.

"The towers signal when a ship has been seen on the horizon. A signal tower is lit up the cliff to the city gates. Whether it's friend or foe. There used to be a light tower that projected light onto the water for ships to navigate safely at night and in storms, but the divide settled right over the top of it. Ruining it." Reid's breath fanned my ear as he leaned over to see what I was looking at. It sent a shiver down my spine. I refused to look at him, that close it would bring my lips far too close to his, and I had thought too much lately of how temptingly soft they might be.

Our carriage stopped at the gates. "The path down onto the dunes to the beach is too dangerous for a carriage. So, out we go," Reid stated, as the carriage attendant opened the door.

He and Aven hopped down and offered us a hand. Aven took mine, and Reid Marida's and I realized what this leisure trip was all about. Marida must have mentioned to them that I missed the beach, and swimming. I had told her a few nights ago that I loved to swim. We had chatted about it at length. I had explained the swim team and the competitions I'd been in. I told her about my home in North Carolina, the mountains, and the coast.

In my melancholy thoughts, I had expressed missing the ocean.

My eyes fell on Marida after taking in my surroundings, and she sent me a temptress smile. I returned it.

I wasn't sure how she'd roped Reid in, but he sucked in a deep breath, inhaling the ocean air and I saw him close his eyes. He liked the coast. I could see it in the relaxed set of his shoulders, the second deep inhale through his nose. He looked so casual when he was officially off duty, which happened so rarely with this man. Something around his eyes and lips softened, making him less stoic, less like *the captain*.

I was watching him so intently, that Aven elbowed me.

"Enjoying the... *view*, Keeper?" He glanced between me and the captain who was now riveted on our conversation and I felt heat rosy my cheeks.

I glanced around to hide it. "Yeah," I breathed hastily, but I grinned at being caught staring. I peeked at Reid, and he glanced at me with a smile, before turning to the driver.

Marida produced two large-brimmed, floppy leather hats from the back of the carriage, and a large picnic basket. I'd no idea she had even packed for this. This was well-planned, and the sweetness of the gesture, from all of them, swept a warmth through my heart.

"Thanks for this," I said as I helped Marida remove her pack and she set a hat on my head.

She grinned. "I mentioned it in passing and Reid ran with it. The picnic was his idea. He said you deserved a break." Her eyes brightened, and a mischievous grin played on her lips. "He admires and *likes* you. *Likes you.*"

"Psh. No way," I said quickly at her repeated use of the words, but my eyes traveled back to Reid's muscled form. He cared about me, I knew that from the things he'd said in the woods while dealing with spiders and the gateway. But *liked* me?

She sent me a knowing look. "I think you'd be surprised."

Aven and Reid approached, and I tried to hide my pleasure at the idea that Reid liked me. There was a mutual respect that we'd come to, and I felt as though we had reached a tenuous friendship. We'd fought spiders together which certainly bred allegiance and friendship. If it didn't, I don't know what did. But she was insinuating that he liked me *more* than that.

You are looking way too far into this, Kaidyn. Stop.

Reid took the basket, Aven took the bag and they gestured to the dunes. There was a switchback trail down the side of a short cliff, dunes, and then miles of open coast. Rocky and sandy beach. Massive boulders broke up some of it, but it was coastal oceanic gorgeousness. We quickly made our descent.

I stared, slack-jawed when we reached the white sand. I always felt so small when I looked out at the ocean. I always felt like my problems were so trivial when the expanse of the sea stretched at my feet, the lap of waves at my toes.

The crash of the surf on the cliffs was awe-inspiring. "Wow," I stated, breathlessly.

Aven elbowed me in the arm. "Pretty spectacular, isn't it?"

I nodded.

"Dragon skull?" He asked with a grin.

"Bring it on!"

He whooped in laughter and kicked off his boots. I watched him with a lifted brow.

"What, you think you can be so scantily clad, and Reid and I are going to soak up the sun and surf in our fighting leathers and boots?"

"I guess..." I glanced at Reid who was also kicking off his boots and rolling up the cuffs of his pants. "Kind of, yeah."

Aven barked a laugh and wrapped his arms around my shoulders. "I *adore* you. Even in that ridiculous hat."

I grinned and let him lead me across the beach.

So, there *was* a dragon's skull. It was old, weathered and some of the teeth had decayed to dust, but it was unquestionably a dragon skull. It was massive, easily the size of a house. How had Saul fought something this huge?

"This is... Wow."

"Aye," he said with a grin.

"There are still dragons around?" I'd already asked but I felt the need for yet another stint of validation.

"Oh, aye. They are well hidden, and in dwindling numbers, but they're out there. Drakes are most common."

"Smaller dragons?"

"Well, they don't have wings. There are fire drakes and frost drakes, same as dragons. We've not seen a dragon in a hundred years in Evirness. Drakes, on the other hand, wreak havoc sometimes."

I squeaked. "Wingless dragons?"

He laughed. "Aye. They're about the size of... Javarr."

So, a massive war horse-sized dragon. Holy moly. Still terrifying.

"Did you know that Kaidyn does swimming competitions in her world?" Marida interrupted us.

I was partially thankful; this conversation was making me find Evirness even more terrifying than I already had.

"Really?"

I explained to him about the time trials.

"We used to do stuff like that as kids," Aven gestured to himself and Reid. "With Kavall. We'd swim from the docks of Sky Harbor to the first island of Sierce and race each other back."

I found I could envision the three boys playing together and it tugged a smile from me. I wanted to hear more stories about them as youngsters.

Marida shook out a blanket and settled down on it. We followed suit. For an hour we ate, chatted, and laughed. It felt so good and normal. The camaraderie that was so easily extended to me was remarkable. I didn't feel like an outsider as I had in the beginning. I felt like I was a part of them. They treated me like they'd known me their whole lives. As if I had always been here. It sent warmth to my soul, but it also scared me. I was becoming too complacent, too familiar with this. I was forgetting my home, where I came from, and where I needed to get back to.

Kial's face swam into my mind, and I fought back tears. My mind went to the fact that my brother's birthday would have come and gone if I was in my world. I prayed that everyone was alright, and my world's time truly stopped, otherwise my parents would be in a panic. I felt guilty that I was going on with my life, and they weren't. I was guilty about how right being here felt. None of it shocked me. I didn't miss a single commodity from home. I missed my family, but that was all. I didn't miss how I felt constantly out of place. How I always felt like people stayed away from me once they saw all of me. How I had to hide my hand from people before they looked at me with pity or disgust. I had always felt out of place, and I had always wondered if it wasn't just because of my hand, but something *else*. It was not like that here. I regretted that I had to go home and that made me despondent.

This place was beginning to feel more like home than mine ever had. I loved this place. These people. My mind went to Fain, to the training, the time that Reid enlisted not only himself but his people to train me, with no payment. Nothing. I thought of the bracers, the cookies from his aunt he had divvied up and shared with me and told me not to tell a soul, otherwise, he'd beat my ass.

My lips turned up at the thought. I thought of fighting alongside Reid, the heated expressions he sent my way.

I was beginning to not want to go home.

I was startled when Reid sat down next to me, his knee brushing mine. I glanced at him, and his hand came gingerly to my face. He gently brushed a wayward lock of hair from my temple, and my eyes locked on him. I sucked in a breath and forgot to let it out. I held it there as his midnight blue eyes burned into mine. His fingers lingered on the shell of my ear. I shivered at the contact.

Who knew your ears were sensitive?

A heat shot to my belly and curled there. I swallowed. He gave me a rueful smile and dropped his hand. I let go of my breath and bit my lip. His eyes followed the movement. That heat in my belly unfolded and crept so low I pushed my thighs together at the intensity.

"What's wrong?" He whispered.

I had to shake myself to remember the time, place, and everything else, aside from the brush of his fingers and his eyes on mine. I sucked in another breath and glanced away. "Nothing."

He lifted a finger to my cheek but didn't touch me. "It is *not* nothing."

I wiped my cheeks quickly. "I miss home."

He looked away, over the crashing surf. "I'm sorry about that."

I opened my mouth to thank him for bringing me to the ocean—

"*Fuck.* How do you two handle all the sexual tension?"

Reid sputtered, and I stared at Aven open-mouthed. *What? The sexual what?*

"Aven, it's not—That's not—" Reid growled, stood up, and stalked away.

Marida let out a chuckle and I cut her a glare. She stopped, at least a little, and put her hand over her mouth.

"It is not sexual—" I fluttered my hand, my cheeks rosy. "Sexual whatever."

Aven grinned massively and wiggled a brow. "Say it again, so we might believe you."

"Aven, leave her be," Marida said, but she still held a smile.

I took a deep breath. There wasn't sexual tension between us, was there? Hell. I *was* attracted to him. I mean anyone would be, the man was gorgeous, but I legitimately desired him. I was attracted to not just his looks, but all of him. I had been for a while, and just ignored my body's reaction to him, telling myself he was an asshole, and he didn't like me like that...

"Let's go swimming," I said, trying to ease the tension. Everyone agreed, although Reid had stalked off, he sauntered back to us when we stood.

Marida was the first to shred her overdress and stand in the sunlight in her linen and lace strapped camisole. It would be like a bralette in the human world. It came down to her first rib and left her stomach bare. It displayed her perfect, creamy white breasts and flat stomach. The panties rode high on her waist, but ended at the bottom of her butt, like high-waisted bathing bottoms. My attire was less revealing, but with her next to me no one would look at me anyway. I shed mine and she and I walked to the water. We toed the cool spray. Then holding hands, we plunged into the gentle surf.

When we both surfaced, grinning, we glanced back at the shore. Both men shed their clothes and were left standing on the shore in nothing but what I would consider boxers back home. Simple linen shorts that came to mid-thigh and slung low on their hips. I took a shaky breath as my eyes roved over them. Well, mostly Reid. His stomach was ridged, chest and arms muscled. That tattoo curled across his shoulder to his heart and held the Celestria insignia of the crescent moon and stars, and it wrapped his bicep in lines and stars. His waist was lean, and I noticed—and wished I hadn't—a tiny trail of dark hair from beneath his belly button to be lost in the waist of his shorts. I sucked in another breath, but never released the first, and choked.

Marida chuckled beside me. I glared at her, but she just lifted a slender shoulder. "It *is* a magnificent view," she said conspiratorially as both men entered the water, and quickly plunged beneath the waves.

For hours we splashed, swam, and laughed together. Until our skin was dried from the salt, we were burnt from the sun and utterly exhausted.

We watched a dark cloud descend against the ebbing night over the water, as a coastal storm rolled in. The storm and the darkness would chase us home.

After we returned to the castle, Marida asleep against Aven's side, Reid turned to me. He opened his mouth twice before something came out. "Do you feel refreshed?"

"Yes, thank you for…" I fluttered my hands. "Everything."

He smiled. "Of course. Meet me at dawn?"

I nodded. "Of course." And that was all that was said between us. His touching me in front of Marida and Aven seemed to snap him out of…whatever he had been doing, the words Aven spoke resonating. It did for me too. I wasn't here for romance. I didn't want to fall for the captain and then leave, and my heart to break. I knew if I let him keep touching me and being nice to me that's what would happen.

Marida had shown me some maps of mines and caves where we could find the gemstone that could make me a portal to get home. It was far past time to start checking them out. I would tell Reid tomorrow that I wanted to take a break from training to begin my search for the gemstone in earnest. He would help me, or he would laugh in my face and tell me that he wouldn't waste his resources or people on me. I could respect that if it came to it. I would ride to those spots myself if need be.

Yes, I thought as I tucked myself in bed with Silas curled against me, I was going to begin my trek home.

CHAPTER 15

My Pegasus

"Remember, defeat is inevitable, discouragement is optional. Your failures are only what you make them be. *You* decide if you learn from them or let them defeat you."

I groaned as I threw the dagger. I had told Reid about the gemstones, and that I wanted to search for one. He'd sent Aven to look. It had been five days since I fought the spiders with Reid and closed the gateway. I think everyone was still surprised at my bravery and, despite the glowing awe and praise I received, I tried to continue with my days as if nothing had happened.

Reid acted differently with me—or it was my imagination playing tricks on me since Aven's words. We sparred, bantered, pushed each other, and the tension grew between us. Something intense and heated. If it was sexual tension, as Aven suggested, I was hyper-alert to it now. When Reid touched me, even in the most chaste way, I went aflame; my face, my core, and places I felt embarrassed just thinking about. It was intoxicating. I found excuses to touch him in return.

Feeling those hard muscles under my hand was something I couldn't explain. Reid and I were dancing around something deep and exciting yet frightening. I didn't know how to move forward from here. I tried to tell myself—again—that romance wasn't in the cards for me, and I needed to get home. But each day, each time I tried to say something, my resolve slipped.

Reid smacked me in the arm, pulling me from my filthy thoughts, and a blush crept over me. He had turned his back, thank goodness, and didn't see. His next words, however, pulled me from the image of him kissing me.

"You are even stronger than they were, Kaid—the women before you. Your hand is the key! The other Keepers had magic that could call keys, but you *are* the key. It's incredible. You are the most impressive Keeper this world has seen."

I scoffed, but the words resonated in my heart. The passion in his voice curled my toes. It shouldn't. It—he—should not have this effect on me, but it did. He did. Damn him. No one had ever believed in me like this. Save my brother, but not to this extent. Not with the look Reid gave me like I was a precious gift from the gods.

"Reid, I'm not... that. I'm not—"

"People aren't typically born a hero. It's not always in their blood. They begin unimpressive and unassuming. That is what sets them apart. It is what sets *you* apart. The blood of legendary women is in your veins. You were born a hero for our people, for our realm, but you are so unassuming, so incredibly humble. The strength of your courage, your bravery, the fire in your veins, and your compassion are to be admired. Rallied behind."

"I'm not strong or brave."

"You are! You fought a giant spider and closed a gateway!"

When I pursed my lips, he gripped my arms and forced my eyes to meet his. His were lit up with a passion that burned my soul. "Kaidyn, I beg you to stop overthinking, stop feeding self-doubt and start feeling and *knowing* you *are* enough. You are enough for this world. You *are* what we need. What you did with the spider, the doorway... Most people would have run like Lamphiere himself was chasing them, but not you."

"Lam—who?"

He chuckled. "The lord of the underworld."

"Oh." His words spread a warm thrill through me. His midnight blue eyes shined in the sunlight and never wavered. He was just solid, unyielding, but it no longer intimidated me. I trusted him beyond all others for his candor and unwavering, ferocious bravery.

I wanted to be everything he said I was. I wanted it as deeply as my next breath. So, I inhaled a deep breath, focused, and lifted the dagger. Holding the blade, I released my breath. I closed my eyes and felt in my soul that I was enough. If I was enough for this man, I was enough for me, for them, for this. I flicked my wrist, and the dagger flew. It flipped twice in the air before it burrowed into the hay bale target. Directly. In. The. Middle. The smallest circle.

Reid's eyes were bright when they met mine. I had done it!

They had taught me so much—these people—and not just about weaponry and defending myself. They had taught me about love, lust, strength, courage, and what it was to have genuine friendships. The kind that would span realms, time, magic, and laws. The type of friendship I had read about, I had yearned for my entire life.

That afternoon, in the beautiful ebbing sunlight, Marida and I ate dinner in the gardens. I spent as much time with Marida as I could, and felt a soul-deep connection to her. I loved her with a piece of my heart that was reserved only for Kial. Marida was a sister to me. Yes, I felt a tiny thread of attraction to her— but it was nothing I would act on, and it was nothing like what I felt for Reid.

Shoot. I had promised myself I would not think of the captain tonight. Epic fail.

Marida was talking about the gateways, and I only half-listened. Silas trotted along beside us. He enjoyed our jaunts outside and was far more comfortable than I expected him to be here. He moved freely from room to room, and I often caught him with Eranora. They'd formed a sweet friendship. He liked to sit in her lap as she painted. Even Vern had taken to making my cat special meals. Spoiled rotten feline.

Reid had given me the next day off, and Marida and I had plans to binge read a bunch of smutty novels, but the last part of our night involved Vern, and so we made our way to the kitchens.

We caught Vern and Saul in the middle of a very heated kiss when we entered. Marida let out a choked giggle, and they broke apart. I couldn't say they were a cute couple because Saul was massive, dark, and deadly but the way he looked at Vern was one of the most beautiful things I had ever seen. Saul, to his credit, ducked his head and removed his body from the vicinity in speed that no one that large should possess, and Vern's cheeks were heated with a blush. Marida fanned herself with her hands.

"I want my very own Saul."

Vern laughed, a little higher than usual, and turned back to his work. Bread that smelled of rosemary and paradise.

"I know he's one of a kind and all, but I want my own." Marida grinned and pulled Vern into a goofy dance. They twirled and dipped around the kitchen, both giggling. I couldn't help the grin plastered on my face as I watched them. My heart felt bright with love and light.

Marida and I secured cookies, cakes, and snacks for our girl's night and ventured to my room to sit on the balcony.

"Tell me about your brother."

I bit my lip to stop myself from the tears I felt prickle up my throat. "Kial is... Kial is my biggest fan. My confidant, my best friend. He's my older brother by two years, but he's my only real friend in my world"

She cocked her head at me. "That can't be true. You've made friends so easily here."

I scoffed. "It may come as a shock, but I'm quiet and withdrawn at home. I just hike, read and stick to home. I don't really go out or try to make friends. Most people are too..." I lifted my left hand.

Marida's eyes narrowed at my insinuation, then she took a breath. "I'm a bit of the same. I feel like most of my life, I've been waiting for something to happen to me, instead of going out and *doing* something. Even small adventures with Aven. He asks—I always say no. I have no idea why, honestly. I know I'd have fun. He'd keep me safe, but I find myself in my gilded room. Alone." She exhaled again, sharply. "I envy you."

"Me?" She sounded like me with Bronwen.

"Your riding, your training, your spiders." She looked away, biting her lip. "I learned to use a sword with the boys at an early age before I became a woman. It was easy then. Whenever Reid, Aven, and Kavall came here, or I went to Silvercrest, they treated me like one of them. They included me in their training, their banter, and their games, but once I hit puberty and grew breasts, they stopped. I was no longer included in their boyish fun. I was expected to uphold a certain decorum. It was no longer ladylike to go off gallivanting. Instead, I was stuck with my mother, Eranora, and the ladies of the court to sew, knit and gossip, and all the other boring things they do. I had a duty to uphold, and soon Kavall fell into that pattern, too. He couldn't go off with Reid and Aven as much because his life was too valuable to mess with. Then Reid became the Guard Captain, and... Well, everyone became so serious. Aside from Aven, who never changed who he was, and I envy him for that too."

"But why envy *me*?"

"Because you can be anything you want. A warrior, a Keeper, a spider hunter. You have the freedom of your own destiny."

Did I? "You do too."

She gave me a solemn smile. "To a degree, but not nearly as much as I lead on. I have to marry to continue the line of succession for Hawksedge. I am to be its lady and so I must be a good girl. Especially because I have a small bit of magic. I'm afraid that Evirness will only handle so much of me, before..."

I dreaded her next words. They terrified me to levels I hadn't known existed. I felt my mouth go dry. "What, Marida?" I needed to hear her say it, to know that harsh truth.

Her gold eyes met mine. "Before it kills me off."

"No. I won't let that happen. I will balance the magic in any way I can to ensure that *does not happen*." My voice held conviction and she smiled and put her arms around my shoulder. Her hug was warm and welcomed. I threw myself into her, my nose against her neck. She smelled like cinnamon. I wouldn't let anything happen to Marida.

We fell asleep together with Silas curled up between us. I don't think I had slept so soundly in my life as I did with her scent in my nose, and my cat's warmth. Marida's breath feathered across my arm where it was drawn up between us.

The next morning, we had breakfast sent up and ate it on the balcony. We weren't ready to deal with the day. We were sharing something intimate. Immersing ourselves in each other's lives deeper than we had before. We both looked up from our berry pastry when a shriek cut through the morning. We both looked up at a gorgeous red-tailed hawk.

Marida sat up straighter. Her knuckles went white as they gripped the side of her chair.

"What is it?"

"The hawk…"

It swooped down and landed on the balcony rail in front of Marida. I jerked and glanced between the two. Marida's eyes became unfocused, and she teetered in her chair. I shooed Silas back, so the hawk wouldn't make a meal of him. I knelt at Marida's side and put my hand on her shoulder.

"He… He's showing me…"

"What?"

After another few minutes, the hawk sent a shrill cry into the air and took off. The waft of his take-off shivered against my skin.

Marida's eyes slowly focused on me, and her face went taut and bleak. "Reid and Aven… gateway at the coast."

My eyes swept across the balcony as if I could see past the barracks and stables to the coast. My heart stuttered. "I must…"

"Yes, yes." She waved.

I hesitated. "Come with me," I blurted as I got up. "We could use a sorceress."

Her smile was quick and bright. "I'll ride with the guards. We'll be right behind you. I'll follow you down as soon as I change."

She wore a long gown. I dressed, like always, ready for training. Breeches, tunic, vest, dagger. She knew I wouldn't wait for guards, an army, or whoever else would be sent to assist Reid. One rider on a fast horse would move far quicker, not hindered by a large troop. Honestly, I was glad she hadn't agreed to come with me, waiting for her to get ready and ride out would have ruined my already racing heart.

After I squeezed Marida's shoulder, I strode to my room. I petted Silas and kissed his nose before strapping on my bracers and grabbing the bow that Reid had given me, fully adjusted to my draw strength. I wouldn't take the time to find a sword, and I wasn't all that good with one, anyway.

After I exited my room, my steps quickened to a near run. As I made it down the stairs and across the atrium, I hollered to the guards to get men down to the beach. They looked at me questioningly for a split second before they opened the door and yelled. I barreled through the doors, raced to the pasture, and let out a shrill whistle without stopping.

His golden hide glistened in the sun as Fain galloped towards me, full tilt. I opened the gate and had enough time to grab the brown leather halter and lead rope hanging next to the gate before Fain was through and skidded to a stop. There was no time to saddle him or search for a bridle, so this would have to do.

Fain lowered his head to me, and I fastened the buckle with shaky fingers. After I finally secured it, he sidestepped against the fence. I jumped onto the rail and slung onto his back. I lowered my body against his neck. I was going to be asking a lot from him and myself. I'd never ridden bareback, although I had dreamt of it. There was no bridle either. One lead rope and a halter were all I had time for. I didn't know how this would go but I needed to get there. The back of my neck burned, and I felt panic rising.

I rubbed Fain's neck and leaned against him. "Run, my friend, as fast as you can to the coast. We must save them."

He needed no more words as he took off. I adjusted on the fly, wrapping the rope around my right hand, my two left fingers tangled in his mane. He flew through the castle gates, already slung open for whatever reason, but I didn't think of my luck as the horse careened over cobblestones, past the watchtowers, and down into the city. The rough cobblestones sounded loud against Fain's hooves, but he didn't slow as people bustled and jumped back as we galloped through. He barely slowed for corners, beelining for the coast. A small child ran out after a dog, and my horse leaped over them as if he did this daily. I swung my head back as the child gasped and yelled in excitement. I bet Fain had looked like a mighty unicorn leaping over the child. The mother yelled after me in terror, but Fain did not slow. He threw himself down into the center of the city. I did little to guide him, giving him his head. It was the most direct route through the city, to the northern gate to the coast. Fain did not falter.

In what felt like moments, we burst through the city gates and down a worn dirt path. Shrubby grasslands spread out on each side. Soon we came to farmland stretching for miles. Fain gained speed, his hooves colliding with the packed dirt. His speed on the cobblestones was impressive, but on the dirt, his hooves flew, gaining better purchase. The path led through a crop of dense trees; the sunlight blotted out and a chill settled over us, cooling my horse. As we galloped, I saw the standing stones to the right. Their tall arches, fingers to the sky, worshiping ancient gods and people long since gone. I shivered as their slumbering magic washed over me. I felt it in my bones.

Eagle Ridge came into view, through hills and mountain peaks. Four watchtowers stood as sentinels against the rugged terrain. Instead of taking the left path heading toward the ridge, Fain veered right at the crossroads, heading into another small forest. We burst through it, and I saw the windmills and farmlands that lay just before Dragonstooth Bay.

Finally, we came to the bridge. My eyes blurred as Fain once again gained speed. He was a marvel, never breaking stride, never slowing. Sweat slathered, and white foam slung back on my legs from his mouth. I was asking a lot of him. He was young for the endurance this voyage required, and I tried to slow him. I tried to yank his lead, but he was having none of it. I had given him his orders, my request, and my stubborn horse would do everything in his power to do what I asked of him.

My eyes stung with tears. I rubbed his neck, whispering encouragement to him. His devotion to me never faltered.

The castle was to the right, but it was the straight path into the port that my horse took. I could see the sprawling city, the temple in its center. Once we burst through, Fain veered down a narrow alley, away from the city center. A few people jumped out of our way. Then I noticed a crossroads with a small cart in the way.

Oh. no! We were going to career right into it! But my incredible horse leaped over it like it was nothing.

This horse... had to be part Pegasus. I looked down at his sides to ensure he hadn't sprouted wings.

The buildings passed in a gray blur. Fain's hooves pounded on the brined cobblestone. I shimmied lower on his neck. I had no idea how he knew where we were going. It was like he was linked inside my head, or he was following a scent. Of course! Alida's. She was down there on the beach with Aven.

Fain charged through the city like his tail was on fire. Salty air settled over me and the scent of the ocean filled my nose. We were so close. A gull called overhead. We were going to make it. I would know if my friends had fallen, wouldn't I? In answer, my left hand vibrated against the horse's mane, and the brand tingled at the back of my neck. We were close to a gateway; I could feel the pulsing of magic being released. After the last doorway, my body understood the magic and it trembled against my skin; in my pores.

Finally, we came to the high walls of the city's end; the gates were slung open. Luck again. The route down to the beach was a perilous switch-back path. Fain slowed as he took the winding pathway, with dunes high on each side. My surefooted horse did not stumble as he thrust himself down, down, down.

My eyes lifted to the sea. A massive ship—straight out of a pirate movie—swayed on the horizon. The coast spread out, spanning miles. The waves crashed, unforgiving and violent, against the slate and stone. To the right, the coast stretched to a calm bay. The ship must have tried docking there but couldn't swing with the wall.

I thought of nothing else though as my eyes swept the gateway. It was massive, three stories high. Bigger than the one in the forest had been. As my horse flung himself down the twisting path, spider creatures scuttled out of it. There were about two dozen of them that Reid's men were fighting. I noticed a few men dressed in long, flowing black clothing, and wondered if they were from the ship because they weren't Hawksedge guards.

My horse's hooves meet sand as my eyes trained on a familiar tall figure that battled two spiders at once. He was a vision. Chop, dip, arch, pivot, dodge, well-placed strike, the spray of black blood. I sent a prayer to Henna for Reid's safety, as my horse galloped to him. I saw a blond head and watched as his arrow struck a spider that had launched itself at Reid. Gods, they were impressive. Both, for such different, yet the same reasons.

Fain must have felt my urgency because once again he impressed me with his surge of speed. I was at Reid's side in an instant, arrow nocked and flying. I hadn't even realized I had pulled the bow from my back, nor steadied my horse. I didn't think of anything but assisting my friends. My arrow landed straight and true, embedding in one of the spider's eyes. Reid's head whipped to mine and he took me in. The sweat-slathered, tackless horse, my tattered braid, the bow naked in my hands. I could see from the flash of his eyes that he wanted to scream for me to get out of here, but he must have seen something savage in my eyes because he returned it with a lethal smile that made my stomach knot with something that should have no place at this moment.

"Just in time, Keeper!" Reid yelled and pivoted, swinging his sword impressively, severing the head of a spider.

He was incredible. A warrior in every inch of his powerful frame, in every beat of his strong and courageous heart. I understood why the Celestria's had appointed him the captain of their guard, despite his youth.

My eyes swept back across the beach. There were so many wounded that the spiders were relentlessly going after. Fain pivoted his back hooves, his front raising, as a spider launched at us. An arrow was nocked and flying as if I were just a puppet to its strings. The arrow flew into the body of the spider, and Reid finished it with his sword. I swallowed, and my eyes ran across the beach again, where a guard was scrambling back from a spider, his leg bleeding into the sand, another guard coming to his rescue.

"We need to get the wounded off the beach," I stated, more to myself than anyone else. "The blood is making them more interested. They will wind up dead if we don't get them out of here."

Reid looked at me decisively, then bellowed a command to a guard, but I was already hopping off Fain. I looked my horse over. He'd given his all to get me here. I also knew he had plenty left in him. His soulful brown eyes met mine. I felt tears prick my eyes at his bravery, his incredible strength, and unwavering loyalty. He'd done this because I asked him to. My wild, spirited boy was at my command, and I didn't know if I was worthy of such dedication, but I would try to be. He was a marvelous horse.

"Take my horse," I said. "He will stand calmly while you put the wounded on his back. All you need to do is tell him to go back up to the harbor, and he will do so without guidance. Use Alida, Aven's golden mare as well. She will see her colt and follow."

The guard glanced at Aven, then stared at me, then the horse disbelieving. "Your pony—"

Pony?! Rage washed over me. Reid had called him that fondly, but he was no pony. This horse had gotten me here at record-breaking speed, and this guard wanted to call him a pony?

I stepped up to him, ready to go toe to toe, but Reid touched my arm. The guard glanced between us.

"Don't question her," Reid growled, his eyes alight. "Do as she says now, or the stock's with you!"

"She's *the Keeper*," Aven stated proudly. "Her magnificent steed is the only reason she made it here before all our sorry asses were dead! I'd advise not questioning anything she says."

Reid gave a nod, and the man looked at me with renewed vigor. "Yes, my lady. I'm deeply sorry."

"Don't apologize to *me*," I said between clenched teeth, but ignored all of them to turn to my horse.

I kissed his nose despite the foam that splattered it. "You're a good boy. The *best,* the fastest, bravest boy in the world." I rubbed his neck. He deserved a week of rest, considering he had gotten me here in what I could only guess to be about twenty minutes versus the two and a half hours it had taken our carriage that day. *He flew.*

Aven gave the blonde horse an affectionate pat on the rump before he nocked an arrow and let it fly through the head of an oncoming spider that had gotten too close. Goodness.

Reid patted Fain and whispered something to him. I couldn't hear, but the horse's ears flicked, and I knew he listened to Reid.

"Don't push him," he said to the guard, sternly. "If he needs to rest, let him. He's done his job, gotten his rider here safely, and with unfathomable speed."

I nodded my chin to Reid in thanks and handed the lead to the guard who noticed the lack of tack for the first time and gave me an appreciative glance that I think had less to do with me being the Keeper and more to do with... just me and my horse.

"Firedrake," Aven exclaimed, excitedly, as he touched my shoulder, a massive grin flashing his dimples. "It's damn good to see you, Kaid!"

I grinned back and tried not to allow fear to creep against my skin, as the magic bristled there. Fighting with them was familiar. I tried to think of this as just another training exercise. Aven handed me a short sword. I twisted the small, light sword in my right hand and bounced on my legs. Shaking out the stiffness from the hard ride.

"The hawk was just here... less than an hour ago," Reid said.

"Yeah," I said dismissively and looked around again. Assessing the gateway, our distance to it, the spiders, the pirate-looking men fighting with the Hawksedge guards.

"You got here—"

"Yeah, my horse fucking flew." My eyes skirted back to his, impatience grating on me. "Let's not talk about this right now, Reid. Don't we have spiders to kill?"

He cocked his head, then grinned crookedly. It sent heat spiraling through my insides. He arched an incredulous brow. "Not scared, Keeper?"

Well, didn't that line sound familiar? I felt ready. Fear was there, but I *wanted* to be here. I wanted to be at their backs as they fought these things. There's nowhere I'd rather be. That revelation shivered against my being and made courage trounce the fear.

I let a dark grin spread. "In your dreams, Captain."

He let out a husky laugh. It should not have sounded that sexy. I had thought only... what, less than two months ago, of him as insufferable? Now I thought he was magnetic.

"Oh, no, Keeper." His voice dipped and became huskier. "In *my* dreams, you are *far* from being scared."

Wait, what? I whipped my eyes to him, all laughter gone. His blue eyes were scorching. He dreamt of me... Is that what he was insinuating?

Aven's bow made a *ting* sound as it was loosed next to my ear and his arrow embedded into a spider that had gotten too close.

"This is really great and all, but can we flirt, undress with our eyes and talk about sex dreams *later*?" He grinned hugely and his words sent heat rushing across me.

I glanced at Reid, who was grinning too, as his sword cleaved a spider in half.

Spiders the size of ponies, gateways, sex dreams... My life couldn't get any stranger.

"To the gateway," Reid said. His eyes scanned my body, then settled on my face, silently pleading with me to not take any unnecessary chances.

Bah. As if he didn't know me. If anyone were in immediate danger, I would step in, regardless of the repercussions for myself. He knew it. His nostrils flared as he saw it in my eyes. He'd never make me stay behind, he wasn't that type, but I saw fear for me in his eyes and it matched how I had felt as my horse had raced to the coast. Fear for *him.*

Something was between us, both incredible and devastating. I wasn't sure if I could handle it, either way. But it was something that would need to wait until after we dealt with this gateway.

Reid and I advanced on the doorway, Aven at our right shooting arrows as he walked. About ten feet from the gateway, it shook and trembled, and the sand kicked up a few inches. We stopped in our tracks.

"Fuck," Reid exclaimed, and I agreed as I watched an iron-tipped leg jut out of the doorway.

"No!" I could close it before the thing fully manifested through, but Reid was already shaking his head.

"Don't. We need to make sure it's safe—"

"Nothing is safe, Reid. Let me—"

But before I could finish, the spider scuttled through, the doorway shimmering against its furry obsidian body. A twin to the one we had fought, popped from the gateway.

A shout bellowed behind us, and my eyes darted there. A man with dark hair and a billowing cape stood with a cutlass in his hand, his eyes wide. Around his neck swung a dragon-head medallion, and his fingers winked with rubies and other polished gemstones.

Reid began, "Captain Markks, I suggest you—"

The sea captain's eyes darted from Reid to me, then Aven, and back to the spider. As if he knew we weren't enough. He stood his ground, assessing. He was exactly what I pictured a pirate to be. His dark looks left no room for questioning, he planned to help and that was that.

Reid noted it too. "Captain Markks and I will try to get as close as we can, Aven shoot—"

"Reid, we both know the thing will not go down unless it's hit under its belly."

Captain Markks' eyes snapped to mine, as he stepped closer. "You've fought one of these terrors before?"

"We have," Reid said as his eyes followed the scuttle of the spider.

"You killed it by..."

"Kaidyn got beneath it and shot arrows into its belly."

The captain's eyes snapped to me, and he gestured with his thumb. "This little girl—" Reid's growl and Aven's annoyed grumble stopped the captain cold before he could finish that degrading thought. "Apologies, but can't we—"

Reid's eyes swung to Aven, and a few seconds of silent communication was all it took before Aven gave a nod and sent me a blistering grin. Only he would get a twisted kick out of whatever he was asked to do.

A small spider scurried over to us, and Captain Markks showed us his skills by slicing its head clean off. I noticed his cutlass had an engraving of a compass and dragon on it. I was unaware of the anatomy of the cutlass, aside from having seen that type of sword in a pirate movie. I knew it was a cutlass because the tip end was wider, and it tapered smaller to the hilt. Looking like a mix between a machete and a short sword. His was ornate, and from the nicks and scratches on the thick blade, it was well used.

Reid gave him a discerning nod and advanced on the gigantic spider, who was bumbling at the water's edge. It seemed slightly disoriented, but its beady black eyes were searching. When they finally fell on us, I swallowed hard before dropping my sword and picking up my bow again. I felt like I would be better suited to help them with that as my weapon.

I glanced behind me and watched as two golden horses carried wounded guardsmen to the safety of the city gates and exhaled a shaky breath. We needed to end this spider before it wreaked havoc on the city or our wounded men.

Our. I shook my head, mentally pushing that thought from my head. Reid's men, not mine. None of this was mine.

Aven was letting arrows fly with no break, and I was standing there stupidly debating trivial things in my head. Moron. After taking a deep breath that calmed my frayed nerves, I gathered my bow and nocked an arrow. I stepped closer to Reid and fired. The arrow soared and lodged in one of the spider's eyes. It let out a tumultuous shriek and skittered closer. Reid and Markks shifted from foot to foot and moved their swords hand to hand, mirror images of the other, as they readied their attacks. They went at the creature together and then spread out as it scurried back and forth. They hacked at its legs as I loosed another arrow. This one flying high. Aven was dancing around the spider, trying to get a chance at its underbelly.

I fired another arrow, but the arrow bounced off uselessly. Eyes or underbelly were the only chance we were going to get at this thing. Although it could still feel us even if it were blinded. I stepped closer and fired another arrow. This one caught the creature's face, just below an eye. The spider clacked its horrible pincers and advanced on Reid. Its sharply tipped leg trounced down on him, but Reid dodged at the last second. Markks hacked at one leg, and nearly had the damn thing off, which was no easy feat considering the legs were as thick as a birch tree. But the spider lifted another leg, spun a little, and shot it down on Markks. He gave a painful cry and landed on the wet sand holding his thigh. I could see blood from here and knew if we didn't get him out of here, the massive spider, and her little rabid spider babies were going to have their way with him. I yelled and waved my bow, trying to gain the spider's attention from the pirate captain. But at her interest in Markks, Aven was able to get under her belly. I watched as he knelt and expertly fired two arrows together. Something I had never seen another individual do, neither in a movie or in real life.

The spider let out an ear-piercing shriek, and I swung my eyes to Reid as he fought the spider, keeping it from Markks. I loosed another arrow. It lodged in the spider's eye just before she began spinning from the pain of her underbelly. Aven shot another arrow at her before dodging her flailing limbs. Reid hacked at her legs whenever they got close enough, but the spider stumbled into the water and let out another shriek. Aven loosed a few more arrows, as did I until she finally succumbed to her wounds—black blood draining into the surf.

I ran to Markks, yanked my tunic from my pants, and ripped off a strip. I fell to my knees next to him and saw the gaping wound in his thigh. It looked bad and already had green goo coming out of it.

"Poison," he hissed between clenched teeth.

I sucked in a breath. The one in the woods had not had poison-tipped legs. Otherwise, I would have been poisoned, as its leg had gotten me in the arm, but I had to agree with Markks. The wound didn't look right, and it smelled like... sulfur. I swallowed past the vomit that wanted to come up my throat and quickly tied the strip of fabric off and wound it tightly around his thigh to stop the bleeding.

"We need to get you out of here," I said breathlessly, and glanced around. I whistled as Reid and Aven finished the spider.

A blond body came galloping toward us. I could see no falter in his sure hooves as he skidded to a stop at my side.

"Good boy, Fain."

The ship's captain sent me a long, appreciative look. "Please dismiss anything I said or tho—"

"Not the time!" I scolded as I helped him stand. The ship's captain gave me a roguish smile, and I returned it. Battling spiders together gives you an unexplainable camaraderie I'd learned.

Aven rushed over to help move Markks. We heard hoofbeats and glanced up. A regiment of men galloped toward us. Finally, reinforcements had come. A little late to the damn party, but I noticed a streak of auburn hair at the front. Marida got her adventure. A few spiders scuttled to them, and the guards hopped off their horses to attack.

"You must close the gateway, Kaid," Aven said gently, his hand on my back.

"Yeah, yeah," I waved at him. "Got it covered, but please get Markks up on Fain."

"Of course, my lady." Aven brushed a hand over my face and pulled me to him. He quickly kissed my brow before rubbing my horse's sweat-slicked neck. Then he took the ship's captain from my grip. I stared at him for a second, taking in the sweet gesture, before I turned to my horse. Fain nudged me with his nose, and I kissed it.

"You are a hero, Fain." I rubbed his neck and kissed his cheek before I turned to the ship's captain. "He'll get you to safety."

"I have no doubt, Miss. You and this horse..." He swallowed, and his tanned skin paled before my eyes. I knew the poison was taking hold. "Tales will be told of your heroics across the seven seas."

I snorted. "Oh, please," I said with a grin before I watched Aven heave the ship captain up on Fain's back. "Make sure my horse is taken care of, Captain Markks."

"On my life, my lady." He tipped his head and slouched on Fain's neck.

I patted the horse one last time, and Fain slowly made his way up the beach and towards the path, not jostling the captain.

"You think he'll be, okay?" I asked Aven, but it was Reid that answered as he came up to my back. I felt his warmth.

"I'm sure he'll be fine. Ship crew are a disturbingly resilient lot."

I turned to him. He had a spattering of black blood on his arms, and across his face.

"Poison," I mumbled. "I hadn't been—"

Reid shook his head. "Let's thank the gods for that later. Shall we close a doorway?"

I smiled thinly and nodded. I didn't want to thank the gods for my fortune. I was just curious why that one hadn't had poison and this one had. But Reid was right, I could dwell on it after the gateway was closed.

Well over an hour later, I stumbled into the stable to check on my horse. He had a belligerent amount of hay, grain, carrots, apples, and a huge bucket filled with fresh water. Next to him was Alida, with the same treatment, and I noted Javarr and the other guardsmen's horses were all housed and resting. I exhaled shakily and went into Fain's stall. He must be tired to allow them to stable him at all, but I didn't question it as I laid my tired head against his neck. It had taken a little more magic to close this doorway than the one in the wood. This one was thicker, sturdier and I felt a darkness slick against me as I pushed my magic into it to close it and push it down into the beach sand. I felt it, my magic, the doors magic, the lands magic, even Marida's gentle magic as she had come over to us. It shimmered, swayed, and swelled. I felt mine reach up to match the darkness of the doorway. Light to dark. I hadn't believed I had any magic, but after speaking with Marida about hers, I knew I did. I felt the well, as she had explained it to me.

Mine was not vast or deep, and I could only feel it when my neck prickled, or my hand vibrated. I didn't carry the magic all the time. It was something that only popped into place when it was necessary to close a gateway or whatever other Keeper things I would ever need to do. Honestly, for that, I was grateful. I couldn't handle dealing with magic all the time. Now I could understand my own and the land's magic. With that knowledge, I noted this doorway felt... sinister. Dark. My teeth had chattered in fear the entire time, and I think I would have run away had it not been for Reid's hand in mine. Just like last time, he had twined his fingers with mine. His steady warmth filled the coldness that leached into me, as my left hand had touched the stones. Aven, Marida, Saul, and even Prince Kavall had stood at my back. Their solidity and light gave me the courage to do what had to be done.

But now, against my horse, a tear dripped down my cheek, and I felt exhaustion pour into my limbs. Fain let out a shrill whinny when I fell against him and passed out.

CHAPTER 16

A man in my bed

Sometime later, I drifted back into consciousness in a strange room illuminated with the dancing embers of a fire and pillars of candlelight. My body felt a little achy, but I seemed well enough. The room was decorated with sea glass, shells, and paintings of ships and surf. I must still be in the coastal city because none of the rooms in the castle looked like this.

"You're awake," said a familiar, husky voice.

I was startled and swung my eyes to the other side of the bed. Reid sat in a chair. His hair was tousled, his eyes had dark circles beneath them. "I... What happened?"

"I heard Fain panic and rushed to his stall to find you in a heap at his feet. You're lucky he didn't trample you."

I shook my head. "He'd never."

Reid sighed. The sound came from deep in his soul. My eyes roamed him again. He was still in leathers and dirty clothes, although his arms and face were clean of the spider's blood.

"Markks?"

Reid gave me a long look and then threw his head back on the chair with another sigh. "Fine. Fain got him here in time, and the healers got out the poison. It'll be a while before it's completely out of his system and he's well again, but it's a good start. You..." His eyes met mine. "You saved his life by

Fain getting him straight here. The poison was fast-moving. The healers... It took a lot."

I let out a deep breath. Thank goodness. I glanced around the room. "Where are we?"

"The Sea Glass Inn."

I squinted at him for a second, and then glanced around again. It was dark, but I could see the flickering of city lights out the large windows. It had been just after lunch when I'd gotten to the coast. Probably close to dusk by the time I had gotten to Fain's stall, after closing the gateway and speaking with Marida and Prince Kavall.

"How long was I asleep?"

"Probably," he cocked his head, "nine hours, I'd say."

"Nine hours!" I nearly shot out of the bed until I realized I was naked beneath the sheets. Well, I had on panties, but still. I yelped and pulled the sheet up to my chin. Reid watched my reaction with a grin.

"Why... Ho—" I began, but honestly, I didn't know where to start.

"Savina and Bronwen cleaned you up."

"Sav—Bronwen?"

He arched a brow. "I figured they were better than me doing it myself, no?"

"Well, yes... Ah. Yeah." Had he... carried me inside from the stables? Most likely. *Embarrassing!*

He chuckled as if he knew where my thoughts had gone. "Savina is the innkeeper's daughter."

Oh. That made sense. I glanced at him as he scrubbed a hand down his face. He looked exhausted. "Have *you* slept?"

"A little."

I made a shooing gesture. "Go. I'm alive. Get some sleep."

"This bed looks quite cozy."

"I... What?"

"I'll just—"

"Ah, no. Nope." I shook my head. He did not need to be so close to me in such a state of... undress.

He grinned brightly and sat up. I put up my hands to ward him off. "Reid..."

"What?" He stood in front of the mattress and pushed his hands down on it. "Comfy."

"I—I..."

His grin turned soft. "I'll turn my back so you can use the bathing chamber."

"Ah... Oh. Okay." I swallowed and watched as he did just that. I quickly glanced around but didn't see any clothing. What the hell.

"I think Savina left some clothes for you in there," he said with a chuckle.

He *had* known I was naked. My face flamed with mortification, and I hopped up as fast as I could and ran for the bathing room in nothing but my underwear. I slammed the door shut and heard a masculine chuckle.

Damn him. But I smiled. He had waited at my bedside, in a chair, while I slept. He hadn't waited the whole time in that chair, had he? For nine hours?

The bathing room was aglow with candlelight, and I found several articles of clothing laid out for me. Clean panties, a shift, and a long pale green dress with a braided gold wrap. *Seriously?* I thought in annoyance. With a disgruntled sigh, I washed my face. The room smelled like lavender, as did my skin. I put on fresh underwear and the shift dress. I felt fatigued to my bones. A little more sleep would do me some good. It was still completely dark outside, so it wasn't like I'd be able to go anywhere. So, back to that comfy bed, it was.

After relieving myself, I walked out of the bathing chamber and stopped halfway across the room as my eyes befell my bed. Reid was asleep above the covers. One arm slung above his head, the other on his stomach. A light snore drifted to my ears.

I couldn't help the smile, as I crept to the bed. With a small sigh, I looked him over. It was an enormous bed, easily made for one huge guard captain and a girl my size. I could lay comfortably and not touch him in my sleep. Plus, he was atop the covers, fully dressed. He'd taken off his vest; it was slung over the chair, his weapons tossed haphazardly. In his dusky gray tunic and black pants, he looked soft. More like... just a man. Not a man whose job was to command dozens of guards and protect the royal family with his life. He looked serene in sleep and devastatingly beautiful. His dark hair flopped over his brow; his bicep muscles bulged over his head, dark ink peeking out of his tunic. My mouth went dry. A heat stirred low in my belly as my eyes devoured him. In any world Reid was breathtaking. He looked younger in sleep, and my smile remained as I wrenched my eyes from the stubble on his chin and crawled gently into the bed, trying not to jostle him awake. His snoring ceased for a minute as I snuggled in, then it picked up again after I settled. His warmth seeped through the blankets, and I let my body push against his side. After only a few moments, the contented warmth ushered me to sleep.

A dusky light slanted across the bed when I woke. A noise on the other side of me had me whipping my head. Reid was stretching. I watched his muscles shift in his back at the movements, and my uncontrollable yawn had him glancing at me over his shoulder.

"The Keeper awakes."

I smiled softly and pushed my hair from my face. "The captain awakes."

He grinned at me, then scratched the back of his neck. "Yes, well..." He glanced at the bed, then at me, then out the window. His attention went back to his vest and he fiddled with it in his hands.

"You want to get out of here before someone gets the wrong idea," I whispered.

He scoffed but bit his lip. I know it had run through his mind. It had mine too, but I found I didn't care. Let them think whatever.

Did he fear what Bronwen would think?

"That's not—I—"

I held up a hand. "It's okay. I get it."

"Kaidyn, I don't give a Drake what people think, I just don't want you to—"

"Get the wrong idea?" I offered.

He ran a hand through his hair. "No, not that... I just—"

"Just go. I understand," I said with a laugh, trying to cover up the hurt. "I need to get dressed, and check on Markks and Fain."

His gaze swept over me, then the bed again. "I... We'll head back to the castle after breakfast."

"Okay," I whispered and combed my hair with my fingers.

His eyes swept over me one more time, watching me run my fingers through my hair. His brows pinched together for a second before he turned and left.

I heaved a sigh and threw myself back on the bed.

Reid had slept in a bed with me. *What!* I almost shrieked with the heated giddiness I felt. We didn't even touch, he hadn't even been inside the blankets, yet it felt so intimate. It felt... right. Goodness, it would scandalize my parents. Even though I was nineteen—almost twenty, everyone back home would be surprised. I imagined telling Bree about Reid. She'd never believe someone like Reid laid in bed with me. She'd be so jealous. I laughed at myself but sobered. I couldn't tell *anyone* about this world, let alone Bree. The people and this world could only live in my heart, my soul, and my memories once I returned home.

I heaved a deep, soul-wrenching sigh.

I donned the green dress; the golden braided belt was a delicate touch and showed off my curves. The scoop neck was a little revealing, but it was pretty. I would need pants before I could ride back to the castle, so I needed to beg for mine back.

The smells that wafted up from the first floor were amazing. Fried eggs, bacon, ham, bread. I descended the stairs. At the landing, I could see the first floor below me. A driftwood chandelier graced the ceiling, and beautiful gray wood floors gleamed. Straight ahead was a small bar with various alcohols on display, well-made barstools with blue cushions. Many windows were open to let in the coastal breeze and the scents of salt and sand. There were tall tables scattered throughout the room and a few lower, longer ones against the wall had church pew-like benches. To the left was a massive stone fireplace with a roaring fire, a few pots suspended above it.

My eyes found Marida, who was speaking in hushed tones to Aven. They both snapped their heads up to me. Aven shot me a charming grin and waggled his brows. He met me on the last stair with his hand out. I took it and sent him a small smile.

"You look beautiful, Keeper."

"How are you feeling?" Marida asked, concern lacing her words.

I turned to Aven. "Thank you." I patted his hand, then kissed his cheek. He gave me a dimple-flashing grin.

I turned to Marida. "I'm fine, thanks. How are you?"

"I did little."

"You got Saul and the guards here. You lent me strength and your magic."

She nodded and gave me a soft smile.

"Silas?" I had worried about him after I woke up this morning, and hoped he wasn't freaking out because I hadn't gone back to him last night.

"Kavall went back to Hawksedge last night, and I sent him with stern orders to make sure Eranora saw to Silas."

I rolled my eyes. "Just what Silas needs, the queen doting on him even more."

Marida grinned. The cat would not want to go home after all the love he received here. Neither would I.

"Breakfast will be out in minutes," Aven said, nearly salivating. They must have remained here last night as well.

"Why didn't you guys return too?"

"We wanted to make sure you were well. You fainted!"

"Oh." *Embarrassing*. But they'd stayed for me... "Thank you."

"Reid told us you were doing fine. Just tired. Using your magic is draining, especially how you have to take the magic of the gateway into yourself to balance it."

I had discovered that the gateways' excess magic transfers to me. It absorbs into my power. What exactly happened to it from there, I had no idea. It drained me, that I knew.

My thoughts drifted to my sleeping arrangements this morning. Marida was staring at me with a lift of her lips. My cheeks heated. "Yes," I squeaked.

She cocked her head at me, then glanced at Aven, who was drumming his fingers against the table. When he noticed her looking at him, he snapped to attention. "What?"

I bit my lip and arched my brow at Marida. Her smirk turned positively mischievous. She knew something had gone on, but didn't know what, and from the look she gave me, she'd want every tiny shred of detail.

I opened my mouth to downplay what she was thinking, but the door in the hall to our right opened, a bell ringing in its wake. In walked Bronwen, Reid, and Holt.

Marida glanced between me and Reid and smirked even more. I elbowed her in the arm, and she hid a cackle against her hand.

I felt my cheeks heat as my eyes met Reid's, and he gave me a small knowing smile.

"Finally. Can we eat, already? I'm starving." Aven grumbled, oblivious to anything but his stomach.

"What's new," Bronwen exclaimed with an eye roll. Then she met my eyes and gave me a nod. I mouthed *thank you* and gestured to myself. Bronwen sent me a wide smile and pushed her braid over her shoulder. I owed her. No guard should have to clean someone, yet she'd done it to help me. I returned her smile, and she sat next to Aven. He put his arm around the back of the bench and played with the end of her pale braid. I expected her to brush him off, but she didn't, and I smiled at their familiarity.

Holt was speaking to Reid, but I could see half of his attention was on Holt's words, and the other half was on... me. Something intimate snapped between us after last night and I had no idea how to act with him now.

"Breakfast and home?" He asked me gently when Holt sat down.

"Yes," I said, then jolted. *Home.* Hawksedge was not home, despite how much it felt like it. I needed to remember that. My home was a portal trip away, not a few hours west. I shook my head but took up a seat next to Marida and devoured a hearty breakfast, probably enough food for three people, but the others did too, so I didn't look like a glutton.

CHAPTER 17

Keystone

I sat on my bed in Hawksedge, staring at Marida's hands. She held a stunning grey dress. Rhone had insisted on a celebration dinner tonight for what had transpired at the coast. Not just for me, thank goodness, but for everyone involved. Rhone had thanked me repeatedly for closing the gateway. Even Eranora had kissed my brow, startling the crap out of me. I tried passing it off, but everyone was thrilled that me closing the gate in the wood wasn't a fluke. Me included. Plenty of people, including the Prince of Evirness, had seen me with this one, so it was no use denying it.

Roarke Markks, the ship's captain, was still at the inn but was expected to make a full recovery. He was the only one hurt by the enormous spider. The smaller spiders had injured several, but the large one was the only one with poison.

Rhone was beside himself with my horse's role and promised Fain would get everything he could ever want. Not that I knew what else one could give a horse that lived in the stables of a king, but what do I know. It pleased me he would get extra attention, regardless. It was he, more than me, who saved the day. If not for him, I wouldn't have made it there at all—or at least not in time. Markks and many others may have died had my horse not been there.

This fancy-ass dinner, though... Ugh. I was not one for fancy dinners, as Ainon's little dinner in my honor had left a sour taste in my mouth, but I knew

Rhone and these people were a far cry from Ainon Barthol. Never once had Rhone paraded me or even made me speak to the people about my role as Keeper. My actions spoke louder than any words Rhone could have told the people anyway.

I glanced at the lovely dress again. It was gray and silver cinched at the waist with a wide belt and fell to my knees in a skirt with silver leaves embroidered along the hem. Silver strings attached the bodice to my neck, and I had strappy sandals to complete the ensemble. Marida's gold dress was the same cut.

"Is this really necessary?" I asked Marida for the tenth time.

She rolled her eyes. "For what this time? The dress, the praise, the celebration?"

I fluttered my hands. "All of it."

She grinned. "Same answer as last time, K. Finding things to celebrate in these times is hard. So, this is a *massive* reason for celebration."

I groaned, then sent her a sly grin. "Your engagement would be a good thing to celebrate."

"My... what? Oh, please." She shook her head with a smile, which turned devious. "*You* are far closer to that than I."

She sent me a wink. I pursed my lips; the laughter was gone. I had told her about Reid sleeping in my bed but reassured her nothing happened.

"I haven't even kissed a man in three years," Marida said with a wistful sigh.

"I've... never kissed a man."

She lifted a brow. I had told her I was inexperienced, but I had never voiced *how* inexperienced. "Never?"

I shook my head.

"Goddess Henna and the stars, why ever not?"

"I... No one has ever shown any interest in kissing me."

"That's impossible. You're beautiful."

I lifted my left hand.

"Your realm is really that ridiculous?"

"As a kid, yes. Now that I'm older, I think it will get better. College *will* be a better experience, I keep telling myself."

"Explain what college is to me later?"

I chuckled. "Of course."

She sighed. "Well, from the way Reid looks at you... You should not have a problem getting the first kiss."

I looked away and stroked Silas' back as he lay in my lap. Silas had been very excited about my return. Eranora had admitted he had slept with her last night, and the thought made me smile. My cat had a way of making even the most stoic people smile. It was his gift. Not that I saw Eranora as stoic anymore. Honestly, she was growing on me. A lot. Her love for Silas and his love for her helped.

"Maybe." I wanted Reid to be my first kiss. I could admit it. The fantasy had taken hold, and it was getting harder to look at him without desire and sensations I couldn't describe. Being around him was becoming difficult even before we had shared a bed.

"Tonight is a full moon. When Henna is at her strongest and she bestows her favor. This is the night for wishing on stars and for them to be answered. For dreams to come true. For our wildest yearnings to—"

I held up a hand with a grin. "What will *you* wish for?"

"For a handsome stranger to come to sweep me off my feet."

I lifted a brow. "Strong women like you don't need a shining knight."

She laughed, that tinkling, musical lilt I had grown to love and need in my life. "It wouldn't hurt," she said softly.

"What about the ship's captain, Roarke Markks?"

"Oh, my... He is rather roguishly handsome, isn't he?"

"Yes, most definitely," I sniggered. We laughed and prepared for the dinner celebration.

Dinner wasn't extravagant or fancy. It was fun. Way more fun than I ever expected. Every one of the guards that had been at the coast, which were not too badly injured, were in plainclothes and high spirits. Those injured were given special meals for themselves and their families. Rhone made sure of it. He, Kavall, Reid, and Aven had gone into the city a few hours before dinner to ensure those guards were well taken care of and given plates of everything that was being served, and loaves of fresh-baked bread that Vern had made especially.

Rhone was the type of king men gladly served, and willingly died for. I'm not going to lie and say that a lump of emotion did not settle in my throat as I watched them leave, because it did.

Eranora stood beside me with a smile. "He's the best man."

I smiled back at her and nodded. "Yes, he is."

He was. I still wished my aunt was here with him, but then *I* wouldn't be here, would I? She would still be the Keeper and I would still be home. Stuck in my life. In the rut that I had set for myself. Remained stagnant with my dreams, always feeling out of place and never knowing there was somewhere else I belonged. I knew now that the feeling I had always had—the one where I felt out of place constantly—was because of Evirness, and the magic that lay dormant in me. A missing part of my soul had been *here.*

Evirness and the people here had given me a new lease on life. They had made me strong, independent, and revered. My self-esteem was higher, and my outlook on life and myself was far different than what it had been when I'd arrived. Everything about me had grown. I'd risen from ashes I hadn't even known a fire had set and burnt to a crisp. I was grateful. I would never forget this time, this place. And I would return. Unlike my aunt, I would come back. I would help them after I went home and checked on things there. Aven's trip to the mines had yielded no gemstones, but another mine had been found and he was planning on venturing to that one in the next few days. Things were looking hopeful for me to get back home. Once I returned home, spent time with my family, and recuperated, I would return and dive into learning everything I could about the Keepers and their magic, and then I would take down the wall, so Rhone and the Celestria's could take back Evirness.

Rhone's speech at the beginning of the evening had said it all. I don't think there was a dry eye in the place, and everyone's heart was bigger from his appreciation of them. No one was left out. Even the guards and the crew of the Salty Siren were in attendance, aside from their captain. And everyone injured had their name spoken as part of the dinner. Not a single person perished on the coast. Each guardsman and soldier made it off the beach in time with help from their comrades and the horses. Rhone spoke of my involvement and my horse's, and although embarrassed by the attention, I was thankful for the recognition. Everyone had fisted their hands over their heart to me. A shiver of heat had erupted in my soul, a warmth in my heart. This felt... unexplainably right.

What I did, anyone would have done. It was not heroic, but I had felt that way while doing it. It was the right thing to do, coupled with the fact that I was the only one that could close the gate. I contributed my newfound bravery to Reid. It was *his* doing.

My eyes settled on him now where he danced with Marida. A silly twisting dance that left them both breathless and giggling.

"I don't think I've ever seen him so happy."

I glanced at Bronwen, who had stepped up beside me. "Who?"

She nodded to Reid.

"Oh," was all I could muster in answer.

Bronwen looked stunning in a long purple gown. A slit up the side made it easy to maneuver or fight if need be. She had daggers in several places, not that you could see them. Her eyes were rimmed in plum, which brought out her blue eyes and complimented that lovely pale hair of hers. She was beautiful in a warrior-goddess way.

"*You're* to blame for this new Reid," Bronwen stated.

Huh? "I... What?" I'd just been thinking that I was acting in part from Reid's influence. Now *I* was at fault for how *he* was acting?

"I see the way he looks at you."

"I..." He didn't look at me... in any certain way, did he? Was she jealous? There was no way. She showed me no animosity. At least none that I had noticed.

"It's okay. I can see you reaching for an apology, but there's no need, Keeper." She sent me a soft smile. "Nothing was promised between him and I. Granted, I will miss his... *skills* in bed, but he was never for me. Not permanently."

I choked on some spit, and she thumped me on the back with a chuckle. "Don't be a prude, Keeper. He is a glorious man, in bed and out of it. He's very well endow—"

I held up my hand caught between terrified embarrassment and heated amusement. "Don't you dare finish that sentence, Bronwen!"

"Oh, you want to find out on your own. Noted. Having the surprise taken from you is rude of me. I—"

"It's not that—I—"

"You don't think you will end up in his bed?" She side-eyed me with a grin. "Keep telling yourself that, sweetheart. You want him as much as he does you."

"I..." I couldn't deny it; I wanted Reid. I wanted him more each day, to the point where being near him was unbearable. It was terrifying, exhilarating, and completely foreign.

Aven sidled up to us. "Ladies." He looked between the two of us. "I couldn't help but notice that some perverse things were going on over here."

"I was just telling Kaidyn how large Reid's co—"

"Holy shit, Bronwen. Shut up!" I squeaked, and she mirthlessly laughed— the kind that sent her head back and erupted from her belly. She looked and sounded like just a woman, albeit a bad-ass one. I had been as intimidated by her as I had been by Reid, but now... Bronwen was someone I wanted at my back—always.

"Oh, stars!" Aven trembled with anticipation. "I must know more!"

"No. No way." I said, but Bronwen took his wrist, and they began speaking in quiet undertones. Embarrassment heated my cheeks as my thoughts went to Reid and his... endowments.

My eyes searched for him as Aven and Bronwen chatted beside me, and Marida danced with Kavall. I had already danced with the prince twice and found him an incredible dance partner. He could waltz a zombi and make them look and feel like a princess. The man was magnetic and charismatic in ways you wouldn't notice if you weren't close to him. He may seem quiet and reserved, but he had a powerful mind and a bold and beautiful heart.

Reid and Saul were deep in conversation. This dinner party I had been freaking out about attending was quite spectacular. I was enjoying myself immensely aside from Bronwen embarrassing me. But even that was incredible in a twisted, carnal way. I had never talked about a man's... dick size with anyone. Bronwen was someone that such a conversation would always run towards the embarrassing end, and it didn't bother me. I felt oddly excited to have that with someone.

My eyes roamed over Reid. He wore a gray tunic, his weapon vest, and black pants. None of us could break the habit of wearing our weaponry—even for the night. My thigh sheath was strapped, as always. Not that it would be very easy to grab, having to lift my dress for it, but still. Reid's dark hair looked freshly cut, his face cleanly shaved. I preferred his few days of stubble, but the clean-shaven Reid looked younger, more carefree, less... dangerous. Standing next to Saul—guard commander and war commander—Reid looked like a boy. He looked twenty-four years of age. Next to the giant of a man, Reid looked small, but there was a light in his eyes, respect that was well written on every inch of him as they conversed. I knew Saul had worked with him when they got stuck here in the north, and they had trained together ever since. Reid thanked him for his being the warrior he was today, and Saul loved Reid. You could see it.

Goodness, these people, the dynamics... it was all... They were mine, and it felt so right.

Reid's eyes flicked to mine at my scrutiny, and he arched a brow. My cheeks heated at being caught checking him out and he sent me a grin before returning his attention to Saul.

"May I have this dance, Keeper?" Aven grabbed my waist, and I giggled. It surprised me it had taken him so long, although several court ladies vied for his attention all evening. The village Lord's and high-standing nobles were in attendance, and many of their daughters were competing for eligible bachelors. I'd noticed many of them asking Reid to dance, and he had dismissed all of them.

I had yet to grow the gumption to ask him myself and I probably wouldn't dare. Would Reid dismiss me as he had them? I had a feeling after sharing a bed, dancing would be nothing. I tried not to let that thought dominate my mind, as I watched a stunning blond girl of about seventeen ask for a dance. Reid declined with a smile and shake of his head. He gestured with his hand to Aven but came up short when he noted Aven pulling me onto the dance floor.

I lost sight of Reid as Aven pulled me close and we swayed to a gentle beat. I let myself forget Reid and enjoy being snuggled in the man's arms. Aven was sunshine on a cloudless day—a brightness never dimmed by anything—even fighting spiders.

"I love you," I whispered, as I laid my head on his shoulder.

He jerked with my heartfelt admission. I felt his smile against my hair. "And I love you, dear Kaidyn. Keeper of the Keys, warrior-goddess on her golden horse."

I chuckled. "None of that."

He stroked a hand down my back, and I took in the comfort. Familial love flooded my heart.

"You were just as brave as I, Aven. You're the one that took down that bitch on the water."

"Perhaps, but without your shining golden light to guide the way—I'm not so sure it would have been done."

I exhaled a slow breath. I'm not sure he's wrong. I had felt in my core, as the hawk had made its presence known, that something wicked had come. If I hadn't made it there in time, peril would have befallen my friends—the people I had begun to love. I had felt it against my skin as I rushed to my horse. I may not be a hero, but my magic was still what had saved them.

When Rhone pulled me into a dance, I felt a tether, a pull to him. He was the reigning monarch, and if the stories about Keepers were true then my fealty was to him. My magic recognized him. I had never noticed it before, but

I had finally succumbed to my Keeper's magic and allowed it to take shape, and take hold of my soul. I could feel the magic of the land against me. Despite the magic being dormant unless it was needed, I felt the comfort of it there, felt the power of it. *I was powerful.* It was exhilarating. The power in my core recognized Rhone.

"The magic of the Keepers is telling me that you are the rightful king to Evirness."

I felt him startle and he looked down at me with those beautiful bronze eyes. "Is that so?"

My lips curled into a smile. "Which you already knew, of course. I did too, but with Ainon... Well, I refused to allow my judgment to persuade the truth. But my magic—it knows. I just had to listen."

"That's very astute of you."

I grinned. "You're trying not to say *I told you so*."

"A little," he said with a chuckle. "About a few things."

I rolled my eyes. He was right about me wanting more out of my time here too—and we both knew that's what he meant. He had always known I'd want more. That I would feel the magic and the need to balance it. He'd known but had allowed me freedom anyway, and for that, I couldn't express my gratitude enough.

"Thank you for not pushing me."

He smiled and squeezed my shoulder. "You don't need to be pushed, Kaidyn. You have the heart of a warrior, the blood of legendary women. You were destined for greatness, and even as a king, I would never sway that. Follow your own path, dearest. I'll never control you. Your beautiful heart and free spirit cannot be tamed, and no one here will try. Of that, I can promise you."

My heart lightened and soared at his words. As a Keeper, my powers were tied to the land's magic but also to the sovereign of Evirness.

"Like your majestic horse. Free spirits, both of you. Never lose that, Kaidyn. Even if you return to your world, never lose that wild heart of yours."

I swallowed hard. I had never considered my heart to be wild, but I guess I could see it. I needed to be free, to be just a little wild with my bravery, my thoughts. It was interesting to have another person—someone who barely knew me, recognize my heart so well.

Rhone was a truly incredibly monarch, one I wished to return to his rightful seat. But I didn't know how, or if I even could. The thought of failure terrified me.

"What do I do now Rhone? I want to go home, I need to go home, but I feel..."

"Like this is your home too?"

I squeezed my eyes shut. "Yes."

"You're not disregarding your family or loved ones, Kaidyn. I assure you that your home and time are unchanged. However, if you remain here for a long time, eventually the magic will allow time to shift."

"What do you mean?"

"I only know a little, but the magic of Evirness and the Keepers concocts some sort of history as to your disappearance or erase your existence from your world entirely. Keepers have remained here indefinitely and only went through the portal to ensure the rift remained opened and balanced. It is said—now this is a legend, mind you—that there is a gateway that will bring you to a land that is for the Keepers, a world parallel to this one and yours. One that only allows the Keepers through. It's where the Keepers can go to ensure the balance, but not return to your realm or this one. Legend says there's a keep there called Keystone, where many Keepers live out their days. Lyria—the Keeper before your aunt—is said to live in that realm. Choosing to not live in either your world or here. She had passed her knowledge and power to your aunt and then... *retired* if you will."

"Wow." That was a lot to take in.

"Yes, but it's also a... comfort, is it not?"

It was—to a degree. Keystone intrigued me. "Could I go there to see Lyria? Since I had no one to teach me how to be a Keeper..."

He cocked his head. "Hmm. If legend is true, then yes, that's not a bad idea."

I smiled, and for the first time since coming here, I felt like I may have direction as a Keeper. Like I had a purpose aside from closing gateways and keeping spider monsters out. I wanted to find Lyria and get some answers, some Keeper magic training, history, and even some insight into who my aunt was because it was clear Aunt Millie had been far different from the woman I had known, and I wanted to hear her story.

CHAPTER 18

Moondust and starlight

I rubbed my hand down Fain's neck. What he did yesterday would go down in history. They would sing ballads of him.

My little Pegasus.

The pasture was quiet, a nice reprieve from the warmth and rowdiness of the castle. The moon beamed on the swaying grass, and a chill breeze fluttered my hair. I was glad I'd changed before coming outside. I wanted to check on my horse before retiring for the night, but I remembered what Marida had said about the moon and was compelled to worship its splendor.

Javarr lifted his head, and I realized why, as my whole body tightened. Reid came to stand at my side. Fain nickered as Javarr trotted over to his master. Reid ran a hand gently down the stallion's nose. Reid patted Fain's neck when my horse arched his head over to him. Fain lipped at my shirt once more before he nipped Javarr's hind flank.

"Be nice," I scolded under my breath, as Javarr retaliated and they bucked, playing together.

Reid chuckled. I peeked at him and caught him staring at me. I swallowed. As the night had wound down after my dance with Rhone, I had tucked into myself the information he'd provided me. Reid had seemed to want to speak to me, but I'd avoided him. The feelings he drudged up terrified me. They were so foreign, and I was scared of rejection, yet I wasn't sure how long I could resist. That much *need* horrified me.

"What you did yesterday... Stars above, Kaidyn." His eyes were full of pride and emotion I couldn't place. "The people at the bay worship you. Our people worship you."

I shook my head. There he went with *our people*, but I couldn't even be annoyed, as I too, considered them mine. "I don't want to be worshiped."

He gave me a crooked grin. "They worship your horse too."

I smiled at that. He deserved it. I would never see myself as a hero. Reid, yes. Fain, and Aven, yes. I was just a deformed stranger from another realm that strange magic had passed to.

I shook my head. I didn't want to talk about what had transpired yesterday, how it made me feel, the things I had done. I didn't want to think of it tonight. Because this night, this beautiful bright moon-filled night, was not meant for those kinds of talks. I wanted to worship the starlight and have a wish granted.

"What does the expression *stars above* mean?"

He gave me a strange look, then smiled gently. "It's an exclamation, I suppose. Our people turn into the stars when they pass on. So, stars above is a kind of oath..."

Their people become the stars. "Like heaven?"

"What?" He looked at me quizzically. "Your people do not believe that their dead are stars shining down on them?"

"Actually, some people *do* believe in something like that. It's called Heaven. Good people, those that have not committed dark crimes, go there."

"Then yes, it's exactly like it."

I smiled. It was faith and gave people hope. A beacon to know their loved ones shone down on them. Beautiful. I wasn't deeply religious, but I could appreciate the need to believe in *something*, the faith in a religion. I respected it. I had things I needed to believe in, some I chose to, and some I refused to. Some things I didn't believe could happen to me, yet I still believed *in* them.

But even this was too deep for such a night.

We were silent for a moment—both soaking up the moondust and starlight. Reid was a companionable presence—he always had been, but I was more tolerable of him as of late. Again, far too deep of thoughts.

The stars in Evirness were like nothing I had seen before. Maybe their loved ones did smile down on them and that was why the stars in this world seemed so much brighter and bolder than in mine.

"Do you see constellations?" I had been trying to find the ones I knew. Before he could answer, I plunked my ass down on the cold grass. My feet and my back hurt.

Reid stared at me for a second. Something twinkled in his eyes before he pulled his tall frame down next to me.

"Of course." He sent me a grin, and his eyes scanned the skies. "There's the stag of the north." He pointed to an outcropping he described, shaped like a deer head with antlers and a crown. It was a constellation that sat just above the highest of the mountains in the Sardarkan range. "He is a figurehead here in the North. Even more so for the villages at the base and passes of the mountains."

I had seen the stag and the crown in paintings and tapestries alongside the hawk insignia in the castle. I then remembered the stag doorway drawing on the journal with the keys above his antlers. I'd have to ask about it because unlike the crests I knew to be Hawksedge and Vanstarr, I hadn't seen the stag insignia anywhere. Was it something to do with the stag of the north?

"There's the big dipper," I stated, pointing it out.

"The *what*?" He choked a laugh.

"The big dipper." My eyes drifted to his, and I found him looking at me openly with a smile. "You don't have that here?"

Reid grinned and scooted closer to me. Butterflies fluttered in my belly. I tried to ignore the way his dark hair still slanted over his brow, and how his eyes glittered in the moonlight. It was harder to ignore that masculine scent he carried, though.

"That's Aumnu's ladle. She's the Goddess of the harvest and grants bountiful crops to our fields and gardens. And there's Boren's bow." He pointed to a perfect bow-shaped constellation with an arrow. "He is the God of the hunt. We pray to him for good hunting and game. Aven is a direct descendent of him."

My eyes found the constellation at his urging, but his words made me grin. "No way! Aven—descendent of a *God*?"

"Oh, yes." Reid's grin widened.

"But he's a scout. As the descendant of a God couldn't he be like a king or something?"

Reid chuckled. "Have you met Aven? Nothing about him is kingly."

"True." I grinned, and he met my eyes. Something shimmered in the air between us. Desire bloomed as we continued to stare at each other. I sucked in a breath and saw his eyes dip to my mouth. I felt... sultry. The way he looked at me made me feel too many things, I was going to explode.

I laid back on the soft grass, trying to hide my flaming face and ignore the intensity. "Everything about this night is breathtaking."

"Indeed." His voice was husky, and I spared a glance at him. His eyes shimmered in the starlight with what appeared to be affection.

He made me feel things I'd only read about in a few of the novels I had found in Aunt Millie's stash. Smut novels. I felt emblazoned. Unabashed. It was enlightening, but also a little disconcerting. Timid Kaidyn had a backbone, a sultry side, a badass side, a sparky side. Who would've thought? Certainly no one back home.

The way the moon cast a silvery glow, the cool tickle of the breeze as autumn shivered its way into the world—tonight was not for worries, it was for sweet kisses and romance.

It was the sort of night the look Reid gave me was for. I glanced at him, and in my throat was all I wanted to say to him, but never would. I tried to pass it off, but I found myself touching his arm. The muscles taut under my hand. His eyes shifted from me to my fingertips and back to my face. I looked at him from beneath my lashes and tugged. Forced him to lie down with me. I think we were both surprised by my boldness, but he said nothing, just settled down next to me. And lying next to him, our heads nearly touching, our arms brushing, I realized I wanted to give myself to Reid. I wanted to kiss him, and I wanted to do more than that.

Heat crept through my core at his nearness, and my mind wandered to watching him fight the spiders, his fingers touching my temple to brush the hair from my face at the coast, him touching my deformed hand and my hips to move me into better positions when he taught me to hold the weapons. My heart contracted when I thought of the magnificent gifts he had commissioned for me and the way he had ogled my butt when we'd gone to the beach. I thought of the last few training sessions when he had spoken to me with that soft voice, I swear he reserved for me. The way our fingers brushed every chance we got. Lately, we had been looking for excuses to touch. I remembered brushing my body against him unnecessarily when he had trained me a few days ago, savoring the charged heat it fissured through me. I couldn't pinpoint exactly when things had changed, but they had.

My heart raced as he looked at me and tension vibrated against us, electrifying the spots where our bodies touched. My head was turned as I stared at him, and I couldn't help it, my eyes dipped to his mouth. Sinful— that's how it would describe in a smut novel. Made for the bedroom. I wanted to kiss him so badly it heated my blood.

I felt overheated and sat up quickly. "I..." I wanted to tell him how he made me feel, that I had never felt like this before. That I'd never been kissed.

He sat up with me, and his fingers touched my arm. Then they moved to my temple and brushed a lock of hair from my neck to behind my shoulder. I sucked in a breath, and my eyes held his.

I shut off everything in my brain but him. I don't know if it was me, or this place, or the strange confidence I had developed, but I leaned into him. His eyes sparkled as he mirrored my movements. We both stopped a hair's breadth from our lips touching. His eyes were hooded with an intense heat that I had never seen before. I lifted my deformed hand to the back of his neck, to the silky texture of his hair. I'd touched nothing so soft with that hand before and the sensation was exquisite.

Reid grinned, and I swear the stars twinkled brighter and my heart stuttered. Goodness, this man was beautiful. I shivered as his fingers caressed my jaw. Then I kissed him.

His lips were warm and soft, yet firm and yielding. Kissing Reid was a perfect contradiction. His hand came up to my hair and his fingers caressed my nape. My hand went to his shoulder, and we pulled each other closer. His lips went from gentle to heated as I slanted my head in experimentation.

Could he tell this was my first kiss? I tried to recall everything I had ever read about kissing, but when his tongue pushed gently, coaxing its way into my mouth, I couldn't recall a damn thing. I forgot to think at all.

He pulled away from my lips with a ragged moan, but his lips trailed kisses over my jaw to my ear, and I shivered at the glorious sensations he sent across my body. How could a kiss on the jaw intensify an ache... far lower?

His tongue snaked out at the shell of my ear, and a moan escaped me. Damn. That was awkward, but it urged Reid to kiss down the side of my neck and his hands roamed down my back and my spine arched into his touch. My hand slid down from his shoulder, across his chest. He had on his vest, but I could still feel his muscles beneath it. This man was all hard muscle and sculpted perfection... How the hell was he interested in me? Sure, I had gotten strong and muscled—a little—in my time here, but I was so... curvy. Not slim and tall like Bronwen, or desirably hourglass-shaped like Marida.

Reid had always had a way of making me feel beautiful. Like I was enough for him. It was unexpected and wonderful.

His lips found mine again, and our kisses became more heated and urgent, and my body heated with desire and passion.

Goodness, I wanted him. All of him, and it startled me. I had never really considered what my first time would be like. My first kiss, sure, but after that... I had no idea what to do, or how to do it, but I never wanted Reid to stop touching me. His hands were gentle but gloriously intense as if he couldn't get enough.

With deft fingers, Reid pulled at the straps of his vest, and it fell into his lap. I broke away from his kiss and stared at it a full second before my eyes met his again.

"I..." He stuttered, his eyes glazed with desire.

I never thought anyone would look at me that way. Ever.

I smiled tentatively and trailed my hand across his chest again. I felt him tremble, and his heartbeat jumped. I trailed my hand across his collarbone, and then down to his ribs. He shivered at my caress.

"Gods, Kaid," he said with a moan.

He fisted his hand in my hair and devoured me. His kisses were intoxicating, and I didn't protest as he pushed me back into the grass and melded his body to mine. Reid didn't demand I remove any clothing. He demanded nothing. My fingers roamed his ribs, and his hand went from my neck to my collarbone then traveled down my side to my hip. His thumb caressed where the tunic had ridden up to expose a minuscule amount of flesh. His touch ignited a heat I already thought had crested its peak, but I was so very wrong. I let out a moan at his ministrations. Just his thumb against my hip had me arching into him. I felt wanton, brazen, and that was so not me. I was not that girl. So, how the hell did he elicit such a reaction from me?

But he wasn't mine. He couldn't be. I had a home to return to in a different realm. I didn't want to end up like Aunt Millie. That thought stilled my blood. That worry crashed into me. I didn't want to fall in love with Reid. I knew it would end in tragedy, and if I gave him all of me, I would fall for him. What little was left not to fall, but I hadn't taken that final plunge. I hadn't given him the most intimate part of me—but I wanted to. My heated body and foggy mind wanted to give him more, and that terrified me. It was the thought of Rhone and Millie, their infinite love lost because she had stayed in the human realm, that stopped me.

What happened if I got stuck in the human realm, as I had here, and couldn't return to Evirness? How would I handle being away from the man I loved?

No. I couldn't—

Reid must have felt my hesitation because he slowed his kisses and rolled onto his side. He pulled me against him, my head on his shoulder, as our breaths slowed.

I didn't *want* to stop. I had wanted him to be my first, right here in the grass under the stars with the mountain backdrop. That scared me. I still wanted him, even with my fears. I still wanted every part of him.

I swallowed hard. "I..."

"It's okay," he whispered. "I didn't mean for it to go so far."

I wanted to ask why, but I just took another long pull of the sweet mountain air. "I just... I'm not... I need—"

"Hey." His eyes scanned my face, and he ran a gentle hand down my arm. "I know."

I swallowed, and a tear shivered at the edge of my eye. I wanted him more than I had ever wanted anything in my life. I wanted to give myself to him, and I knew if I remained here any longer it would come to that, and a thrill—so intense and bright—skated up my body.

I was only nineteen, so it wasn't like he would be the love of my life, right? Not like Rhone and Aunt Millie. I had plenty of time to find Mr. Right for me. It couldn't be Reid. So, what if I gave him that part of me? It's not like we were going to get married or anything. But my heart stuttered at the thought of being with anyone else.

I was in deep for someone who hadn't even seen the man naked. That thought heated my cheeks, but I ran my hand up his arm, across his collarbone, and down his chest. Muscles bunched beneath my hand, and as my ministrations descended to his ridged stomach, a moan escaped him.

"You keep that up and I wo—"

I leaned up, kissed his jaw, and continued my roaming. He had nothing left to say as I straddled him and kissed him deeper. I wasn't ready for this to end, especially on a melancholy note. I wasn't ready to go... all the way with him, but I also wanted to enjoy myself. I felt so desirable, and that feeling was too heady to stop just yet.

We kissed, touched, and laid together under the stars, until the darkness waned and gave way to dusky light. Then Reid walked me to my chambers. We kissed so thoroughly before he opened the door for me, I nearly asked him to come inside but had I asked, we both knew there would be no stopping.

I leaned back against the door for a long while, and as Silas wound his body against my legs, I slithered down the door. I stroked Silas a while longer before I could crawl into bed. My body was still overheated, my thoughts still lustful, my body yearning for something I knew little about, but I wanted to learn. Damn the consequences.

"Kaidyn, what in the stars are you still doing in bed?"

Marida's beautiful face came into view, and I sighed, blissfully. "You're so fucking beautiful it hurts, you know. Like physically hurts sometimes."

She reared her head back, then barked out a laugh that was less ladylike than her usual melodious tinkle. "What in the... What?"

"I don't know," I said groggily and looked around. Sunlight streamed in beams across my floor. Marida had opened my balcony doors wide letting in a gentle breeze.

"Long night?" Marida arched a brow at my rumpled appearance.

"Yeah." I couldn't help but grin as what had transpired between Reid and me flooded back into my mind.

Marida's eyes widened. "What happened?"

"I... Reid..."

Marida threw herself onto the bed next to me, her face close to mine. "Tell me everything! Reid. You. Spill, right now, before I die!"

I laughed. "Water firs—"

She threw herself off the bed, grabbed a pitcher hastily, and spilled most of it as she dumped it into a glass, and in a flash thrust it into my hand.

"Christ, Marida."

"No clue what that means, but drink and then tell me *everything*."

I giggled, but then I told her *everything*. She knew I was a virgin. That I had never even been kissed. She knew everything about me. I had spilled every innermost secret to her over the past few months. There was little that Marida didn't know.

Did she know I had been attracted to her at one point, and may still be, a little? I don't know, but that was the only thing I kept to myself.

"Wow," she said after I finished, her hand to her heart. "I knew he was in love with you."

Wait, what? "I don't think... No."

"Oh, yes. He has never looked at anyone the way he looks at you. I swear."

"Bronw—"

"Bronwen was a distraction. There was no love."

I swallowed. Bronwen had said as much.

"Reid's always been so duty-bound and busy that everyone was thrilled that he and Bronwen were... letting loose together, but Reid isn't the..."

"Booty call type?"

"Ah..." Marida bit her lip as she tried to understand my realm's slang. "If you mean the type to casually have sex with a woman whenever he wants without marrying her, then yes."

I laughed. "Pretty much. Yeah."

"But you..."

"Oh, no." I threw up my hands. "I'm not even twenty yet. I have no interest in marriage."

"So, you want to be a... *booty call?*"

"No. Not... I just don't want that..." I hesitated. "Yet?"

I sat up abruptly and hopped off the bed. Cold reality crashed into me. I didn't want to just have sex with Reid, but what other possibility was there? I wasn't from this realm. I couldn't stay here. It's not like we could date. Talk about long-distance. No, thanks.

"I can't stay here. I can't marry Reid. I can't—"

"Can't, or won't?" Marida said under her breath. She petted Silas another moment before standing.

"I…" I threw up my hands. "I just don't know, okay?"

Marida bit her lip and glanced away. "I don't want to see either of you hurt. I—"

"Don't, okay? I'm hungry. Let's grab breakfast."

"As you wish," she said delicately, but I could see hurt in her eyes at my dismissal, but my emotions were running high. I knew it wasn't fair to her. She didn't deserve my annoyance. But having Marida voice things—*booty call* things—had me reassessing exactly what my plans were. There was a lot to fear with giving myself to Reid, in my world and this one, for varied reasons. I needed to think with my head, not my heart, or my treacherous body that remembered every touch, every tingle, every kiss that we had shared last night. I needed to tread lightly so my heart didn't shatter into a million pieces when this was all said and done.

Rhone glanced up at us from his stack of papers as we made our way into the dining hall. Eranora was picking at some of her fruit, but it was clear breakfast was over.

Rhone gave us a bright smile. "You ladies seem to get on well."

Marida smiled back and took a seat to his left. We *had* until I had to be a complete ass. He must have assumed we were late to breakfast because we'd spent time together after dinner, not suspecting his own Guard Captain was my reason for a late night.

I pursed my lips and took the seat next to Marida. I pulled a basket of rolls to me, and they still felt warm. I slathered butter on one. I would miss freshly baked rolls each morning, with butter churned right here in the castle, once I returned home.

"Reid, Aven, and a small brigade of men have headed to the wall this morning," Rhone said, conversationally, not looking up from his papers. "There was a disturbance there; our watchtower guards sent a message this morning."

Marida and I looked at one another but continued our meal. Marida had waited for me before she even came down and ate, and that fact brought a wave of guilt. She excused herself a few moments later, and I went to go after her when Nic, the head stableboy, came in and glanced around the hall. He bowed quickly.

"Apologies, your highnesses." Nic's eyes found mine. "Miss Kaidyn, can you come to the stables once you've finished?"

"Ah…" I glanced from him to Rhone, who tried to hide a smirk. I narrowed my eyes, and Rhone glanced away.

He was up to something!

"Finish eating," Rhone said and nodded to Nic. "I will send her as soon as she has finished breakfast, Niclas."

"Of course, sire. Thank you." Nic flashed me a killer smile before he trotted out the doorway.

That Rhone knew the stableboy's full name was a testament to the exceptional king that he was. I was beyond curious about what was going on when I noticed Marida saunter back in.

"You'll come with me to whatever this is, won't you?"

Her eyes widened a fraction before they met mine. "If you'd like."

"Yes, please," I swung my narrowed eyes to Rhone. "I feel like I'm going to need backup."

Rhone chuckled and flipped another page. Even Eranora wore a smile.

When we trounced down to the stables, Holt saluted us.

"What's going on, Holt? Be straight with me!"

"Goddess! I know nothing." He said in mock surrender.

I blew out a breath. Then I noticed a carriage. It was pale sandalwood, with dusky grey trimmings. The colors I associated with the coast. I glanced from Holt to Marida, and then back to the stable, confusion masking my thoughts entirely.

"Markks?"

"He's fine. Recovering," Holt explained at my concerned glance.

Nic glanced up when we entered and smiled encouragingly. Another man stood at his side. He was older, tall, thin, and had dark hair tied at the nape of his neck.

"Lord Errant." Marida curtsied, but I just stared. The Lord of Dragonstooth Bay. He lived in the castle against the divide.

Why was he here, and what did it have to do with me?

"Miss Gieron," Errant said with an appreciative smile. Then his eyes swept over me. "Miss Flynn, Keeper of the Keys."

I nodded. "What's going on?" I asked, snappier than I intended, but I was confused. My emotions were in heightened chaos today.

"I have commissioned a sculptor and we wish to get some drawings of you and your horse."

Ah. *No freaking way.* "I am not interested—"

"We were told by the Guard Captain that you did not wish to be entombed in such an art piece."

Thank you, Reid. I scratched the back of my neck. "He's right, I do not."

The tall man sighed. "I will not force such a thing, of course. Although it's a pity."

I shrugged. Not happening, buddy. Sorry, not sorry.

"Your horse...?"

I cocked my head. "Fain."

"Yes, Fain."

"I'm not sure if he'll stand for drawings but he's a vain creature, so I wouldn't be surprised."

Lord Errant grinned.

"He likes carrots and apples. Bribery works wonders."

Everyone laughed at this, and the tension and confusion evaporated. So, Rhone really had a sculpture commissioned. The crazy king.

CHAPTER 19

Sacrifice

A few hours later, after the drafter had sketched my horse in a dozen poses—I had several sketches of my own, and some that the drafter had given me—I returned to my room. I apologized to Marida, and we seemed less at odds. She had tried to understand what I wanted, but I didn't understand it myself. I tried explaining that to her. I wanted Reid, but I had to leave at some point, and growing attached to him would be a terrible idea.

She looked at me with sorrow and said. "And what of us, who have grown attached to *you*?"

I hadn't a clue what to say to that. I had only ever thought about myself. I was selfish. I had never considered how these people would feel when *I* left. How the friendships I had made would be impacted. I was leaving *them,* not the other way around. It was a predicament I hated being a part of.

Marida said I should explain to Reid about leaving and being fearful of giving him more of myself for that reason. I didn't want a *booty call*. I didn't want to have sex with the man just to leave. It wasn't me, and I knew it wasn't him either. I didn't plan on staying here, living here—so giving myself to Reid would do nothing but cause us both heartache, and after speaking with Marida I assured myself that Reid deserved to hear that from me.

I was at the pasture fence giving Fain carrots when I saw the gates open, and Reid, Aven, and a half a dozen guards enter. I watched them with a keen eye and noted that something was *off*. Reid's body was tense, there was a rigid, coldness to him that I had not seen since I had first arrived in the north.

What had happened at the wall?

Even Aven skirted around Reid, staying out of his way, and looking forlorn. Fear and concern wormed into my belly.

I waited for them to walk to the castle before I trotted over. Aven gave me a somber smile, and my steps faltered.

"What happened?" My eyes went to Reid who had stopped, his back to us. His body was hard as stone and strung tightly.

I reached out to touch his shoulder, and he shrugged me off.

"What the hell is going on?" I barked.

"You tell us, Keeper," Reid spat, and I jerked back from him. That tone, I had not heard in a long time.

My eyes swung to Aven. "What's going on, Aven?"

He swallowed and gave me a tortured look. *What the* hell*?*

"I think it best we speak with Rhone," Aven said gently.

"Reid, please, tell me what's going on? Are you okay?" I wanted to reach for him again, I needed to know he was alright.

"Since none of this was real anyway, Keeper, let's just end this charade now, shall we? You don't belong here, and Aven and I have places to be—duties to attend to," Reid growled.

My entire body trembled with confusion, and tears pricked my eyes. I stumbled back a step, away from them.

Aven ran a hand down my arm, but I whirled away as tears spilled. I felt rejected, and confused. *What was he talking about?*

What wasn't real? Last night—was he talking about last night? How had he already... No. Marida couldn't have said anything.

My heart ached. This was why I didn't want to get close to anyone here. I had no idea what was going on, but I felt smothered by my emotion.

You don't belong here. Those words trounced all others and attacked my heart and soul. I felt like I belonged here, but his words twisted confusion and hurt in me.

I needed to go home. I didn't belong here.

I would take this place, these people, and tuck them into a special place in my heart. I would return someday to Evirness. To this place that made me strong, made me whole, made me *me.*

I'm not sure who I would be when I returned home, but I needed to go. I'd been putting it off too long. I didn't want to admit, even to myself, that it was mostly because of how Reid rejected me after our shared passion. I had never acted so boldly. I had taken a chance, and he had acted *so* interested, so heated, as *desperate* as me. I couldn't fathom how he could then act cold, and distant.

How could he say it wasn't real? It had felt *very* real.

I didn't understand, but it snapped me from the spell I had been under. I had spent enough time here, and it was time to go. Now.

"I want to go home."

Marida was sitting at her desk writing something when I burst into her room. "What?"

"I need to go home. Now."

"We don't have the gem, K." She said it with a hint of exasperation, and I wanted to cry.

I swallowed down the rise of tears. "I..."

"We'll go check that mine I read about. I'm sure Reid and A—"

"No!" I balled my right hand into a fist at my hip. "No, I want to go home *now*."

Her eyes widened at my anger, at the frustrated tears in my eyes. "What has happened, my friend?"

You don't belong here.

"Don't call me that. I want to go home."

Hurt flashed across her eyes. Damn it. I didn't want to hurt her any more than I already had today, but I wanted to go home. I was upset by how Reid treated me, and I was *mad*. I had spent far too much time here. The lines had blurred. I had begun thinking of these people as family. I loved them. This world was not *mine*.

"Get me a portal, Marida. Please. I beg you."

You don't belong here.

"You know I don't know—"

"You said there may be another way... before." Before I had agreed to wait to find a gem. Before I had agreed to train. Before I had begun to love this place, these people.

She shook her head.

"You *know how*!" I screamed.

Her eyes were hard and pained, as she wrung her hands. The emotion that flashed across those beautiful golden eyes of hers made my heartache. I hurt her, and there was little I could say now to take it back, to fix it. I just needed to go home now. Better she hates me now. It would make it easier to leave.

"Kaidyn, I advise—"

"Please Marida, I beg you. I need to go home."

I don't belong here.

She looked away quickly. She could never deny me anything. I had never used that love, trust, and friendship before, but now—

"I believe to do that you must sacrifice something."

What? "Like a freaking sheep or something? Or like my first-born child?"

A wisp of a smile appeared on her face. "Goddess, I love you, Kaidyn. Stay. We can figure this out. *Together.*"

My heart constricted, it physically pained my chest to hear those words. I wasn't sure if she said it to break the tension or what, but my heart ached at the open sincerity in her eyes. I wanted to spout my love for her, how much she meant to me, how a piece of my heart and soul was hers to keep and do as she pleased. I wanted to tell her she was my sister by soul.

You don't belong here. A gaping black hole sunk into my belly.

"What has happened, Kaid?"

"Nothing," I said immediately. Spilling any of it to Marida was too much. I couldn't comprehend it myself, and my heart would shatter into a million pieces if I relived it.

"Something must have—"

"Marida... Please. I need to. I need my brother, my family."

When she looked at me, her eyes were lined with a sliver of moisture, and I wanted to hug her. To tell her I cherished our friendship above everything else that had transpired here.

"I am unsure what kind of sacrifice is needed, K. I am simply reading from the pages of this book. I wish I knew more. I truly do. This... I've never dealt with this before."

Had the Keepers always had the gemstones? The book stated there were other ways, but they were still unclear. And Marida had less time to unravel those secrets because we spent so much time together—just to be together. To be friends. Doing things that had nothing to do with getting me home. I didn't regret it.

Right now, though, panic, and confusion had settled as a burning need to return to my world and be away from this. Him. The image of his rigid back, and the snarl he sent me as he shrugged my hand from his body. After all the caresses we had shared last night, for him to do that... I couldn't understand. His words were burned into me. How could Reid—the same Reid that had slept in my bed, that had told me he admired my strength even as I doubted myself, the same Reid that had kissed me with so much heat and passion—turn so cold; so mean? How could he say those things to me? Was there something I was missing?

I needed to get the hell out of here.

"How did they do it without the gemstones then?"

"You know I am unsure. I need more time. The portal had been opened by an elder, I have inscriptions, but..." She wrung her hands and looked around quickly.

Reid wasn't wrong. My leaving was for the best.

Silas let out a low meow drawing my attention to him. I bent down and rubbed his neck quickly.

"I need to go, Marida. I don't care about the sacrifice."

How could the book not say what kind of sacrifice it needed?

Frustrated tears threatened my eyes.

She stared at me with confusion. "What in the Goddess has happened?"

A tear slithered down my cheek. "I need t-to g-go." My words wobbled. If she didn't do something soon I was going to break down.

"Kaidyn, stay. Please, my friend. You know—"

"I don't belong here. This is not my home. Not my battle. Find another Keeper to figure out the divide."

"I... Where is this coming from?"

"Get me the fuck home, Marida!"

Her eyes went wide at my outburst, but a seriousness flashed in her beautiful golden eyes. "It just doesn't work like that."

I shrugged. I didn't care how it worked. Reid had made me feel useless. I didn't deserve how he had treated me, no matter what kind of epiphany he had, or whatever it was. Clearly, he regretted last night.

I missed my family, which was no lie. I wanted to return to my world where I was just a girl, deformed but loved. I was nothing there, and... I liked that, didn't I? Far less expectation. Far fewer duties. I had a few months of high school to finish, and college to attend. I missed my brother, my parents, and Zena. I missed being just a girl in the world and not a warrior Keeper. I was such an important entity here. Worshiped. I didn't want any of this.

My heart thrummed. I was torn. I was part of something here. Something huge and important. I felt needed, looked upon with honor and respect but also with responsibility. Was that something I really wanted? In truth, I was frayed. I missed my family terribly, but there was a calling in my spirit. I felt purposeful here. It was an exhilarating feeling that I would never experience in my world.

I knew I was giving up something massive, but my heart was aching. I was a torrent of hurt, confusion, and rejection.

"K, you haven't given me enough time. I need to search those books. If you just give me—"

She was grasping for things to placate me. I threw up my hands. I wasn't angry with her, not really, but I was just so... mad. Mainly at myself for feeling *everything* for this world.

"I just need to go, okay?"

"I know but the broken gemstone is—"

"I don't care!" I knew I was being a childish asshole, but I didn't care. The pressure to be their hero, along with the sensations I felt being here, the precarious situations, and the training. Not to mention Reid last night and this morning... I needed out.

"But Kaid something like this... the kind of magic needed for this will want something. It will need—"

"I don't *care*," I screamed. "I want to go *home*." Tears pooled in my eyes, and I angrily swiped them away.

My ancestors, the females of my line, may have been brave, strong women, but I was not. I was weak. I didn't belong here.

Silas stood at my feet, those huge, luminescent turquoise eyes so uncannily intelligent. He looked at me as if he knew some secret. I bent to pick him up but stopped as Marida spoke.

"I—Kaid, you must understand—"

"Do *something*, M."

Her eyes turned sorrowful, and she exhaled deeply. I watched her shake out her arms, her eyes on me. Begging me to stop her, to stay. I didn't. I couldn't.

She waved her hands and began to chant, her eyes filled with resolve and remorse. The book lay open, she had found the passage she needed. Her eyes still begged me to stop her. To not to do this. I ignored it as my heart raced and the back of my neck tingled from the onslaught of magic.

Her chanting continued.

Eventually, the broken stone began to hum. Orange and amber swirling vortex spiraled out of the gemstone. But then it stuttered.

"It needs something—"

My eyes went back to Silas, and I bent to pick him up again. Wanting him in my hands. I abruptly had a terrifying feeling. A large pit in my stomach yawned open. The back of my neck and my left hand tingled uncontrollably. I suddenly felt like this was not a good idea at all. My childish hurt seemed ridiculous. The shift of something bad shivered in the air, and my heart raced.

My fingers brushed Silas' fur, but he stepped out of my reach. "Silas," I called frantically. He began to walk to me but stopped and looked at the swirling vortex of colors.

Then, before my eyes, he began to be pulled away. I scrambled to snatch him up, but he was pulled out of my reach. I needed to stop this. I glanced at Marida, but she was deep in the throes of the magic that was piecing the stone together enough to make a portal.

I yelled. Marida had known it needed something; she had warned me. My need to get away from here had outweighed the risk and now...

When I turned back Silas was being sucked up. I screamed his name and lunged forward, but he was no more. He had turned into the swirling gray of twilight and storm clouds. The swirling smoky substance moved towards the gemstone and wrapped around the fiery colors, they churned around each other until a brilliant pewter gray portal blurred, stuttered into existence, and then solidified.

I had no time to think as it pulled me through. I met Marida's eyes. Tears were streaming in hers—and mine.

And then there was nothing.

CHAPTER 20

You don't belong here

I was lying face down on the floor in my bedroom. *In my house.* My mind was fogged, and I felt an ache in my throat. My knees hurt from the impact of the portal tossing me out. Then the loss of Silas seeped into my heart.

I laid there for what felt like forever before I pulled myself up. The rawness in my throat was from screaming, the ache in my eyes and head from crying. The hurt in my heart was a gaping wound of heartache and grief.

Marida had warned me and I'd ignored her. The only thing I could sacrifice in that place was my cat, and I hadn't foreseen it. I hated myself. I'd wanted to go home so badly, I hadn't listened to reason. I got what I wanted—and would suffer the consequences.

They had been right about the time in my world. It had stopped while I'd been in Evirness. For that, I was grateful. It was a burden that lifted when I came out of my bedroom to discover my family unfazed by my absence. I was home, but I felt empty. I became a shell of myself. I made up a story that I had left the door open, and Silas got out. For two weeks I left cans of food out for him, and my family believed it because of how desolate I was.

After four weeks, my parents openly, loudly worried. I was barely eating, barely doing anything. I had missed my family and Zena, but I was so empty. I felt hollowed out.

Zena became my constant shadow, and I know she felt the loss of her new friend, too. I couldn't tell them Silas had been... killed. Let them believe he had simply gotten out and had walked into another loving family. I tried to believe that too—but I knew the truth. I had killed him. My selfish actions had killed my cat. My sweet Silas, who had been an innocent party in all of this.

I quit the swim team. Swimming reminded me of the coastal trip we'd taken. I stopped reading all fantasy-related books because they reminded me of their world.

My parents stared at me when I ventured down to eat with them, but the food always felt too heavy, tasteless, and I excused myself after two bites. I felt their weighted looks, their fear over my state of despair.

After nine weeks, they made me seek a counselor for depression. I had been down the counselor's road before. I had battled depression *this* was nothing like that. What I felt was deeper than depression. It was a rift in my heart and soul. I felt the loss everywhere. Not just the loss of Silas, but all of them. It felt like a yawning pit of misery and sorrow.

Kial's twenty-third birthday came and I tried to rally my spirit for him. I had missed my brother and just being around him made everything slightly better. I got him hiking equipment for his birthday, and we went hiking the following weekend together. Just him and I, and I enjoyed myself. I had only thought of the mountains of Hawksedge briefly, which was progress.

School—I barely remember going to school. I spent every class sketching cats, spiders, castle parapets, mountain ranges, and the scrollwork from the windows in my room in Hawksedge. I sketched faces after a while. Marida's, Aven's, Reid's—not that I liked to admit to the last one. I sketched Fain and Alida.

I moved the cloak, dagger, and everything that came with it back into the trunk and asked my dad to put the trunk in the attic. I couldn't even have it in my room. Tears clogged my throat every time I saw it.

You don't belong here. His words still echoed in my mind. It was still a jagged pain in my heart, even months later.

The only thing that gave me any kind of feeling was the bow I had commissioned from the old mountain man. Kial had led boy scouts there for camp-outs and helped around the man's homestead. I had asked Kial about a bow—a proper bow. Like the wooden longbow, I had used in Evirness. Kial had looked surprised, but ever the good brother he was, he provided the information and asked no questions. Once it came in, he'd asked to see me shoot. I thought he might fall over as he watched me use the bow. He'd never expected my prowess. Evirness' finest scout had taught me well. Not that I could tell Kial that. Instead, I told him we had learned in school, and I had loved it. He bought that. I practiced two or three hours a day in my backyard. It kept me sane.

June came swiftly, and I graduated—not that I know how I managed it. My parents gave me my mother's hand-me-down Honda as a graduation present. It was a great car, and I was happy to have transportation.

I thought of Evirness and the people I had left there a little less each day. I trudged on, and the loss of Silas dulled. The ache of missing Aven and Marida and...the others shadowed a quiet ache in my heart.

I started a job, one I had applied for long before I had entered Evirness, as a kennel attendant at the local veterinarian hospital. It was supposed to look excellent on my resume after college, but I no longer wanted to be a vet tech. I still loved animals but after Silas... I just couldn't bring myself to feel passionate about that any longer.

I'd been naïve and foolish. I could admit it. After all that had transpired, I saw myself for what I was—a coward. I had left because I'd been hurt by an action and a few words from a man, and I had run back to my realm with my proverbial tail between my legs.

I loved my family, but I missed *my* life in Evirness.

September came, and with it, college. I didn't have the energy to apply anywhere, so I ended up going to the community college, much to my parents' chagrin. I entered an art program, but after two months of school, my art professors said my assignments lacked heart and passion. And they weren't wrong.

The sketches I did of silver tabbies and castles were just for me. I couldn't share them, but every feeling I felt was in *those* sketches. I didn't have any room for emotion when I sketched for school. They came out technical and bland.

I tried reaching out to Bree, my only friend—loose term, I might add—in this world, but she was too busy for me, and we had little in common to talk about anyway. I bonded with my roommate in college a little, but we were also very different and she was more of a party girl, unlike myself.

I started dating. Well, a date, I guess I should say. I didn't go on many dates, just one really. Garrit. He was a sweet, nerdy guy my roommate had introduced me to. He was in a computer technology program and played a *lot* of video games. But it was okay because he liked me and being with him made me feel *something*. Alive. Less of a shell. He was sweet. Kissing him was... nice.

My first kiss had been intense, incredible, and passionate. It had been because it was my first kiss and not necessarily who I had kissed. At least, I tried to tell myself that.

Kissing Garrit was pleasant. Pleasurable, in a safe way. I couldn't be consumed with need and I was glad of it. I wanted it to be good; wanted desperately to be content with Garrit and our kissing. He was companionable and I enjoyed spending time with him.

He had been a little squeamish around my hand, and I honestly think he blocked it out most of the time. I tried to use it less in his company, and not touch him with it. He never stared or made me feel like it disturbed him, but it did. He just hid it better than most.

I lost my virginity three weeks after we started dating. Honestly, I did it more just... to do it, to get it over with, as messed up as that was. I had pictured my first time with Reid after we had kissed beneath the stars, and it had been so overwhelmingly passionate and earth-shattering, that the real thing... Well. I felt let down. I had expected so much more. So, I tried it again and again— enticing Garrit, seducing him... waiting for the magic. It felt good, don't get me wrong, that is after the awkwardness and scattered appeal of the first time.

After that, it became less embarrassing and more pleasant, but it still lacked something. Some build-up that I didn't even know, having never done it before.

I *tried* to keep our coupling a focus, but it was difficult with our schedules, and we did less intimate things than we should have. Most of the time, we merely spent time in the same room, not even speaking. It was a mutual thing, though. Part of me was just dating Garrit to not feel alone. To prove to myself that I didn't need Reid when another man could make me feel the same way... Except it wasn't true. Not really. But I tried with Garrit. I tried to be normal. I *wanted* to be normal. I didn't want to live my life in the third person, looking down from a black cloud. I *wanted* to live; I just didn't know how, but I was doing the best I could.

My twentieth birthday came and went with little fanfare. I went hiking with Kial. It seemed to have become a birthday ritual, and I loved it. I soaked in his familiar presence. I had missed him the most while in Evirness. Kial was, and always would be, my hero.

He wasn't impressed with my choice of men and didn't like Garrit, but maybe that was just an older brother thing. I still enjoyed our time together, and despite our separate lives, we still made time for each other. Kial had been, and always would be, my first and best friend. We talked via text or Skype nearly every day, even if it was one-word greetings. Kial was my tether to the life I wanted here. He was the anchor that kept me sane and gave me a small glimmer of light.

Holidays rolled around. Garrit asked if I wanted him to come home and meet my family. Holy cow, *did I?*

I guess I did because I agreed. My parents were thrilled, Kial not so much.

CHAPTER 21

Thanksgiving

"What are you going to wear?" My mom asked, gently.

We always dressed up for Thanksgiving, but I knew from the glint in her eyes she didn't mean for the holidays as much as she meant for the guy.

I had always seemed older than I was, and Mom had been treating me like an adult for a while. "I don't. I haven't thought about it..."

"Well, let's find something."

So, we bonded over clothes. It was nice. We hadn't done this since Aunt Millie's death, and it was a turning point into normalcy for me.

My fingers grazed a green sweater dress I had bought trying to impress Bree. She'd said the dress would bring out my green eyes. I thought it was a little...racy. It was clingy and came to mid-thigh. But now I was a woman, and I couldn't deny it was lovely.

"Ooh, that's the one," Mom said, and I had to agree.

I went to the bathroom and put it on. It didn't fit as snugly considering I had lost an immense amount of weight over the months I had been back. The dress looked wonderful though.

When I stepped out, my mom came over and kissed my head. "It's perfect." She curled and pinned my hair.

I looked good. I hadn't felt this way since I had a dagger strapped to my thigh in Evirness. For some reason, that ensemble had made me feel femininely empowered. Even more so when I caught Reid looking at me. I'd never had a man look at me like that.

But I was not in Evirness, and I had no dagger strapped on, nor a guard captain looking at me with lust. I needed to get him and his parting words out of my damn head.

I sighed as my mom smiled at me and said, "Dinner is in a half-hour." She was oblivious to my inner turmoil. I'd gotten better at hiding it over the past nine months.

I stood in the middle of my room and felt a tingle in the back of my neck. I quickly stamped down all thoughts of Reid. I needed to think of nothing but my family and Garrit tonight. I didn't belong in that world, and I needed to get over it. Over *him*.

Brown boots. I had brown knee-high boots in my closet that would look great with this dress. I may feel like crap inside, but outside I would look fantastic.

My eyes scanned my closet, finally landing on the top shelf. Why in the stars... I needed to stop saying that. No one understood it here. All this—being home and thinking of Reid, brought it all back, even the mannerisms and speech. I needed to be *normal* tonight.

I stood on my tiptoes and grabbed the boots, but something hit me in the head on the way down. Grumbling, I looked down at the offending item. It was a book, a burgundy leather—Oh, *no*. It was Aunt Millie's diary. Not today. Nope. I refused to even pick it up.

I put the boots on while staring at the diary. Finally, with a moan, I grabbed it. A zing went through my left hand, which was odd, as it never had before with the diary. I tossed it on my nightstand. I just needed to forget I had uncovered it, so I went to the mirror and did a twirl. The boots complimented the outfit spectacularly. Since Evirness I had higher self-esteem and confidence—which had stuck with me when I'd come back home.

I turned to the door to exit, but my treacherous eyes and curious nature went back to the diary. My neck tingled again. I *should* ignore the diary. I needed to go back downstairs and spend time with my family. My Keeper senses were pulsing. I should ignore them, but—

Screw it. For Aunt Millie, for her memory, I would read *one* page. Get this crazy feeling out of my system. Torture myself with some semblance of Evirness, with a familiar name or place. What the hell. Why not?

It was Aunt Millie's passing that had put me there. She was the reason for my time there. While I had been there, after a while, I had forgotten her involvement in my purpose there. I had begun to think of that place as mine, those people as mine. If I read something maybe the restlessness and tingling would quiet for the night.

It was wishful thinking.

I sat on my bed and opened a page at random, somewhere in the middle.

I met a man today, while I was out looking for truffles for Nyla. He said I looked like his daughter Mina. He was looking for truffles for his granddaughter Aoife.

Wait, what? Aoife? Wasn't that fake King Ainon's wife's name? Yes. It was an uncommon name in my world, but in Evirness was it common?

I skipped ahead a few pages and discovered the name again.

I saw Uther, again. This time with his little granddaughter. Aoife is about six, I think, and she's a magic vessel. She can harness Evirness' magic. She turned a flower into a butterfly, a blade of grass into a grasshopper. It was incredible. But Uther warned her to stop before she was knocked unconscious. He didn't go into a lot of detail but said that if she used the magic too much it knocked her unconscious and her body became a vessel for the magic to do as it pleased. And sometimes Evirness' magic wasn't always beautiful and pleasant. Sometimes it was hostile and twisted, and it could make the vessel hostile and twisted as well.

A what? Holy moly. That was—Whoa. Was that the same Aoife, all grown up now? Could she still use Evirness' magic? Was she... *Stars above*, could she harness the magic to create... portals? Gateways—like the spider ones? Or the walls that cut people from resources?

As a false royal family, would they want the wall to come down? Likely not. The Barthol's had seized an opening when the wall materialized to divide the kingdom. They had snatched the opportunity to rule through some far descended lineage. It would be legitimate if the Celestia's were dead. Rhone's ancestor's last name was Celestia—which translated to Stars Devine. They were the Goddess Henna blessed rulers of Evirness and I had concluded that part of the reason the magic wreaked havoc even more after the wall went up, was that their ancient lineage no longer ruled the province entirely. Yes, the untamed magic ran rampant because there was no Keeper to hold it in check, but I also think the magic was wilder because of the Goddess blessed rulers being unable to... Well, rule, all of it.

I had been charmed by the Barthol's upon my arrival to Evirness, but they had explained little of what I was there for, what I was supposed to do. They housed me for a few days, showed me the city and village, made me a beacon of hope for the people, put me with their son who flirted with me awkwardly, and then they dropped me at the wall and told me nothing.

Did they want to decimate the Celestia's and legitimately take over Evirness, then somehow bring down the walls themselves?

I had no idea what to think, but I couldn't afford to think now. I snapped the journal shut, my left hand tingled, but I ignored it. Then a whisper of parchment caught my eye in the folds of the journal. I don't remember ever putting a note inside, and I had touched the book a hundred times and never noticed one.

It landed on my lap, and I swallowed. My blood hummed and my left hand tingled uncontrollably.

No. Nope! It was folded into the shape of a star.

Not even going to look! I couldn't look. This could be nothing good. I had to resist.

I shoved the folded note back in the journal and stood, hellbent on putting the journal back up on the shelf, but as I reached up—I stopped. I was curious by nature. It was a horrible trait. I hated surprises. I liked knowing. Curiosity killed the—*Stop.*

I swallowed and took the folded paper out. A star, seriously?

My left hand itched and prickled with anticipation. This was bad. Slowly, carefully, I unfolded the note.

It was... blank? That was strange. I flipped it over and over, but it was still blank. My left hand trembled, and finally, I let my Keeper senses out to play, and they shivered at the freedom. My left pointer finger trembled as it scrolled over the page. A shiver whispered up my arm as a blinding gold light erupted on the page. I closed my eyes to the onslaught. Once it was done, I stared at a loopy script in a hand I recognized and my heart shuttered.

Kaidyn,

I hope this letter finds you well. Things are so much worse here. The magic is volatile, as if enraged. It is barring people in their homes. Causing them to die of starvation and dehydration.

Walls and gateways are popping up all over Evirness.

I found a cave with a mine that I think holds another Di'himira crystal, but when I went back, a wall was blocking my path.

Assassinations have been monumental. Reid was nearly killed in the last one. We need help, Kaid. I'm afraid if it's left unchecked much longer, the magic will overtake us. It will block us from all resources. I'm sorry to put this on you, I know you don't want this responsibility and you know I would not ask anything of you unless it was dire.

Please, my friend.

With my love,

M

I wanted to rip up the parchment, burn out my eyes, and pretend I had never read it. My heart throbbed, and a swell in my throat threatened tears. Damn it for making me feel an ache in my heart for my friends there, for that land, those people. A tear spilled, and a stone of dread settled into the pit of my stomach. Fear speared across my limbs.

The ringing of our doorbell made me jump.

Shit. Garrit.

I wiped quickly at my eyes and smoothed a hand down my dress. With a shaky exhale, I tossed the note back in the book and threw it unceremoniously onto the top shelf. There was no time to think about it now. I needed to try to be normal. I would dwell on the note later.

"Wow, Kaid, you look incredible."

I gave him what I hoped was a smile. Garrit looked... nice. He had dressed nicely and brought flowers for my mother. He was so nice. Damn it! Was I really going to keep describing him that way? He was a *great* guy. Super cute, in that sexy nerdy way. Yes, that's right. I loved his dark-framed glasses, his sandy brown hair, and his brown eyes. I liked him. A lot.

After being in Evirness around warrior princes, and guard captains who looked like chiseled gym-loving models it was hard to compare a normal man to any of that. I tried not to. I also had to stop swearing. That was another thing I had picked up in Evirness. Those men had potty mouths and I had just picked it up like nothing. Fudge.

After a chaste kiss, I invited him inside.

Dinner was nice. Shoot. *I had to stop with the* nice. It was great. Normal. Garrit said all the right things.

Kial was seeing someone as well and seemed a bit more disconnected than usual. My brother had a hard time relating to Garrit since he was so outdoorsy, and Garrit was so *not*. My interest in someone that wasn't outdoorsy surprised Kial, and he didn't try to hide it. I tried to convey to him to be nice with my eyes, but he had always been bad about reading signs like that. If I was distressed, or if someone teased me, then he was good at reading me. When I was trying to get him to knock it off—not so much. I think it was intentional. A brotherly thing, surely, because Aven had... *Stop thinking about them, Kaidyn!*

I tried not to think of Evirness or the note. I freaking *tried*, but I couldn't. Every moment a conversation wasn't directed to me my head spun.

Could Aoife have something to do with the walls? Could she be a vessel for the magic intensifying, the volatility of it? Her witchy, bitchiness could certainly make me see her as this same Aoife magic vessel. Did the magic make her all bitchy?

Stars. Ugh! I was trying, but my mind kept going back to the note. Marida seemed so distressed. Was her life in danger? Would Everiness' magic attack her?

And Reid had *nearly been killed.* I had been trying not to let my mind wander to that part of the note.

Could I help them? No. *No.* I did not belong there.

My mom's voice finally broke through my torrid thoughts.

"Did you hear me, honey?"

"What?" I shook myself back into the present.

My brother looked at me with open contemplation.

"Do you not like the turkey? I did it exactly as you like."

"Oh, yes, sorry. It's delicious."

"You've barely touched it," my brother chimed and I glared at him. He shrugged and looked pointedly at my plate. My stomach was in such turmoil I didn't dare eat anything. I swallowed past the lump in my throat and pushed food around again. Kial gestured, annoyed.

Since it would be far too childish to stick my tongue out at him, I finally stabbed a piece of turkey and put it into my mouth. I made a point to slowly chew and gulp. It felt like a paper towel, dry and huge and I had to try to swallow twice before getting it down.

As soon as it hit my stomach, I bolted up. "Excuse me."

I tried to remain calm, to not arouse suspicion, but I bolted up the stairs, to the second-floor bathroom. Away from prying ears.

Once in the bathroom, I barely made it to the toilet before I threw up the turkey and water. I was a mess. I needed to get over this. I wish I had never opened the closet, had never opened the journal. My mind was a jumble of indecision. I had been a shell of myself since I had come back. Evirness called to my heart and soul. To think that darkness was descending on it, that the royal family could be extinguished—Well, it made my heart race and my blood boil. But I could do nothing for them. I hadn't even tried while I was there, not really. I had gained strength I never knew I could possess, and they had requested nothing from me. Even after closing gateways, I still never helped them with the final piece. Instead, I had run home, in a move that had taken everything from me.

I had done this to them; to myself; to Silas. I was to blame. All the strength and self-love I had developed were because of them. And I had returned and simpered right back into that quiet girl—not the cheeky bantering, dagger-wielding warrior I had been. I was no longer sure which Kaidyn I was. Was this the real me—quiet, sullen, boring, and in a relationship for the sake of it? Or was that person me—the one from Evirness—that wielded a bow, rode a stunning gold horse, and closed gateways with a sexy captain?

I just didn't know. I was lost. I could say I was content with the way my life was going until I had found that note—but that would be a lie.

I washed my mouth out from the acrid taste and brushed my teeth. I washed my face and looked at myself in the mirror. I looked gaunt, pale. I may have once been pretty, but right now I looked... half dead. I was pale from not enjoying the outdoors and I had lost so much weight that my body barely had any curves, my face had lost all roundness, and was at narrow angles that made me look older. I had tried makeup, but it made me look worse. My emerald eyes had no shine, my long wavy brown hair had no luster. I tried to tell myself it was the pressure of college, the losses, and the tribulations I had faced, but I knew that was not true. The reason I was such a mess was because of how I left Evirness—the way I left. I hadn't said a single goodbye, not even to my friend who helped me open the portal. I had screamed at her, begged her to do something she didn't want to do and hadn't even thanked her. I had been so childish and selfish, but I'd had ten months to grow the hell up. To realize my mistakes, and dwell on making them right and now I had a chance. A real reason to return.

I didn't know if I could be what they needed, but *I* needed closure. I needed to tell them why I left, that I was sorry for walking away from everything the way I did. I owed Marida an apology for putting her in an impossible position.

I don't know if I could fix Evirness, but I—at least—wanted to explain and thank them for all the time and energy they had put into me.

I didn't belong there, per the captain, but Marida deserved an apology. I could never move on if I didn't give her one. I was a wraith of the person I had been, and it wasn't fair to my family, friends, myself

I gripped the counter, enough to turn my knuckles white. I knew what I needed to do.

Without thinking about it, I went to the attic. My body tingled with anticipation. Damn it. Damn it all to hell for that—that exhilaration. The key that was branded on the back of my neck, the reason I always wore my hair down, burned and tingled. My left hand vibrated with the need to unlock and it was all too pleased to unlock the trunk, all too pleased to finger the thick material of the red cloak I knew would magically come through the portal with me. My senses were all too pleased as I slowly, gingerly took the amber crystal from the fabric. My body, my heart, and everything inside me vibrated with anticipation as I let my left pointer finger glide down the length of the crystal. A swirling vortex of orange glimmered in my finger's wake. It swirled and danced until it erupted from the crystal and spiraled into the air.

I stepped back and took a breath. My whole body hummed, and I nearly dove into the arched doorway as it glimmered to life in all its golden-orange splendor.

As I stepped into it—

"Kaidyn!"

I looked back to see my brother's stricken face, filled with wonder and confusion.

Then *nothing*. Blackness.

I was returning to Evirness.

ʌCKNOWLEDGMENTS

This book would be nothing without the work of my incredible beta readers. You are all wonderful, beautiful, incredible human beings and I cannot express my gratitude enough.

Mel Wright: Lady, you have been so incredibly helpful, I can't even begin to express how much your insight has helped me. Look her up at getproofreader.co.uk

Tianna Twyman and Vickie Still: Thank you for your interest and feedback.

Reader:

I hope you enjoyed Kaidyn and her growth.

Please be kind and leave a review. Reviews not only help the authors but also other readers looking for feedback on a book before purchase. I would appreciate any kind of review.

If you enjoyed this book, you may also enjoy my other books!

Trisha Lynn Books (YA Fantasy)

T.L. Thorne Books (Adult Fantasy books)